Naughty 2:
My Way or the Highway

Naughty 2:

My Way or the Highway

Brenda Hampton

www.urbanbooks.net

Urban Books, LLC
78 East Industry Court
Deer Park, NY 11729

Naughty 2: My Way or the Highway copyright © 2009
Brenda Hampton

ISBN-13: 978-1-60162-220-4
ISBN-10: 1-60162-220-1

First Trade Paperback Printing May 2009
First Mass Paperback Printing July 2010
Printed in the United States of America

10 9 8 7 6 5 4 3 2 1

Distributed by Kensington Publishing Corp.
Submit Wholesale Orders to:
Kensington Publishing Corp.
C/O Penguin Group (USA) Inc.
Attention: Order Processing
405 Murray Hill Parkway
East Rutherford, NJ 07073-2316
Phone: 1-800-526-0275
Fax: 1-800-227-9604

ACKNOWLEDGMENTS

Always, a special thanks to my family, readers, book clubs, bookstores and friends. To Carl and Martha Weber, and the Urban Books family, your dedication to my literary career is truly a blessing. I can't think of any other team of people in this industry who I enjoy working with more. I owe all of you a heartfelt thanks.

An extended thanks to my Heavenly Father for not being with me only when times are great, but for looking over me when times are hard. I give all praises to You and look forward to the future that You have waiting for me . . . whatever it may be.

Chapter 1

Jaylin

It was almost midnight and I crashed into a lawn chair on the balcony outside my bedroom. No doubt there was no place like home, but the mansion that I lived in, or my extreme wealth, was not enough to kick the loneliness I felt inside. To me, this day had delivered hell, and I wished like hell that my pain from Nokea's rejection would go away. I hadn't felt like this is a long time. The hurt brought back my anguish from being placed in that orphanage at nine years old, after Mama was killed. I was in that place until I was sixteen. During those years, I looked forward to Nokea and her mother visiting me. Their faces always brought me true joy. I could rarely recall a time that Nokea's presence didn't make me feel good. I never thought the day would come when I didn't want to see or hear from her again.

The roaring thunder kept interrupting my sleep,

but I was finally awakened by my ex-girlfriend, Scorpio, kissing my lips. She rubbed her fingers through my naturally curly hair, and straightened my thick eyebrows. I slowly opened my eyes and just stared. I was in no mood for fucking. All I wanted to know was why? Why wouldn't Nokea give me what I wanted? She said that she loved me and for damn sure knew how much I loved her, so why? Why did she walk away from the altar earlier that day?

I was humiliated. Downright pissed off and seriously ready to kick somebody's ass. After she left me standing there like a fool, I didn't know what else to do but walk away too.

I sat with no emotions as Scorpio stared deeply into my grey eyes. She leaned in for a kiss, but I turned my head to avoid it. All I could think about was how the "Atomic Dog" in me was getting ready to come out. Whoever crossed me this time was going to pay. My cousin Stephon was at the top of my list and Nokea, the woman that I still loved, was closely behind.

Scorpio demanded my attention by rubbing her fingers along the sides of my neatly trimmed beard. "Say, I know you're hurting, but can I at least get a smile out of you? If you didn't want to be bothered, then why did you call me to come over?"

I moved Scorpio away from me and went into my spacious bedroom. While loosening my tie and unbuttoning my shirt, my throat began to ache. I didn't want Scorpio to see the obvious pain I was in, so I went into my walk-in closet. She followed. "You haven't said anything to me since I walked through that door. Whenever you want to talk, just let me know. I'm not going to pressure you," she said.

She helped me out of my shirt and laid it across her arm. Then she removed my belt and unzipped my pants. When she squatted down to help me out of them, a pleasant thought came to mind.

"Give me some head," I asked softly.

"What?" She looked up.

"You heard me."

"Jaylin, you know better coming to me like that. You haven't said anything all night, but you have the nerve to ask for some head."

I looked down at her still squatted in front of me. "Listen!" I yelled. "Are you going to do it or not? If not, then get the hell out of my closet! I'm not in the mood for any bullshit!"

Scorpio stood up, laid my shirt on my shoulder, and left the closet without saying a word. I grabbed her arm. "Where do you think you're going?" I asked.

"I'm going home." She snapped, snatching her arm away. "You are one crazy high-yellow Negro. I don't have the time or energy to curse you the hell out because I'm trying to be patient and understand what you're going through. Mackenzie told me about what happened at the wedding, and I didn't want you being alone. That's why I came, but I'm not going to let you dump on me because some other bitch fucked up your day."

"She's not a bitch, so watch your damn mouth, okay?"

"Defend the B-I-T-C-H if you want—that's your choice. But I call it as I see fit. In the meantime,

I'm getting the hell out of here. Call me when you're willing to get your act together."

Scorpio grabbed her purse off the chaise and headed toward the bedroom double glass doors. I dashed out of the closet and blocked her path. "Hey, I'm sorry. Don't go. It's been a messed-up day, and I really need you to stay." I gave her a quick peck on the lips, but when I tried to get some tongue action, she wouldn't open her mouth.

"Jaylin, kissing me doesn't make up for how you've treated me. I'm sorry too, but I'm going home tonight. So, please move out of my way."

She pulled on my arm that was in her way. I didn't budge.

"I said stay. Please," I begged.

"And I said I'm leaving. Now, move your arm so I can go."

I let her pass by. When she reached the stairs, I ran up behind her and begged again. "Don't go, Scorpio. Make love to me, on the stairs, like you did when we first met. Please . . . I need you to relax my mind and put me at ease for the night."

She ignored me and kept on moving down the T-staircase. I hurried in front of her and carried her back up the steps, but she kicked her legs, trying to make me lose my balance.

"Put me down, Jaylin," she yelled. "I said I'm going home!"

When we reached the top step, I dropped her to the floor and kneeled between her legs. I eased my boxers low enough to expose my dick and massaged it to make it hard.

Scorpio sat up on her elbows and moved her head from side to side. "Not tonight, Jaylin. I'm not letting you do this to me, not after how you've treated me."

"I'm sorry! Damn! How many times do I have to say it?"

She backed away from me, crawling to my bedroom doors. I grabbed her ankles and lifted her skirt. She rested on her stomach and I laid my body on top of hers.

"I told you I didn't want this," she said. "Why are you forcing yourself on me?"

I squeezed her hands together with mine and placed my lips on her ear. "Because I need you, baby. Can't you see how much I'm hurting? You said you'd be here for me, didn't you?" I lowered my hand to rub her ass, then moved her panties slightly to the side.

I rotated my fingers inside of her and the juices started to flow. "Can I have you now?" I whispered in her ear. "I'm dying to feel the inside of you."

Scorpio's eyelids fluttered, and when she nodded, I went for it. I inched my way into her wetness and took deep strokes, my eyes closed. The feeling of her juicy, warm pussy always had a way of relaxing me. I moved her long hair away from her back and pecked it with my lips. "Damn, you're good," I said. "Too, too good."

She backed me up and got on her hands and knees. That was even better. As I slammed my hardness into her from behind, we started to sweat. Scorpio took deep breaths and dropped her head in defeat. "Le—Let's go to the bed Jaylin. You're hurting me on the floor and I really need to get comfortable."

I removed my nine and made my way to the

California king-sized bed. I sat with one leg on the floor, and patted my lap so she'd know I was ready for a ride. She stood at the door and worked her skirt over her curvaceous hips.

"I told you not tonight, but why do you always insist on having your way?"

I winked. "Because my way is the only way."

"Not always, Jaylin. Goodnight and I love you." She blew me a kiss and flew down the stairs so I couldn't catch her. By the time I got out of bed and made it to the stairs, she had closed the front door behind her. I was left holding a hard dick in my hand, and had to resort to the *Black Tail* magazine in my closet. I couldn't believe Scorpio had played me. I'd for damn sure make her pay for it later.

After lying across my bed for hours, sulking about Nokea, I finally got up to take a shower. The water sprayed my body as I pressed my hands against the marble wall, thinking about my dramatic day. Nokea had looked so beautiful. All she'd had to do was say yes. We could be celebrating our honeymoon right now, if she hadn't shown how much a coward she was by running out the door.

Stephon, my own damn flesh and blood, seemed devastated that Nokea had walked out on him too. He knew better than to try and marry the woman I loved, but was foolish enough to run after her. I had already made a complete idiot of myself by interrupting their wedding and walking up to the altar. Every eye was on me. When Nokea's father yelled for me to, "get the fuck out," that was enough. My baby girl, Mackenzie, took my hand

and we walked out together. I saw Nokea drive off, leaving Stephon with his hands in his pockets and shaking his head. I wanted to run his ass over. If Mackenzie hadn't been in the car, I probably would have. She really helped me keep it together, but I was glad to drop her off at home. She had too many questions and I wasn't in the mood to answer them. When Scorpio had come over, I thought it was to comfort me. But at a time when I needed her most, she had the nerve to play games and walk out on me.

Nokea, though, had always been there for me. In the past, she seemed to be willing to give me what I wanted. I guess my relationships with other women had her singing a new tune. I was so sure that she'd forgiven my past mistakes, but apparently I was wrong. Her being there for me was one of the many reasons I loved her so much. Even though that hoochie ex-girlfriend of mine, Felicia, also gave me what I wanted, I could never love her because of her whorish ways. She wasn't nothing but a freak, and I couldn't believe she had the nerve to have sex with Stephon after all that good-ass loving I kicked down. I chuckled and realized that I had taught her well.

Saturday night was working on Sunday night by the time I moseyed out of bed. The phone had woken me several times, and at one point, I sat up to check the weather in St. Louis. I lived close by in Chesterfield, an upscale neighborhood. When the weatherman announced more rain heading our way to cool the one-hundred-degree temperature, I turned off the television and pulled the covers over my head.

My stomach growled, so I went into the kitchen to look for something to eat. It was pathetic—couldn't find much of nothing in the fridge. There was a small container of strawberry ice cream in the freezer; it would have to do. In the dark, I straddled a stool in front of the kitchen island and started to eat licking the ice cream from the spoon, wishing it were Nokea. The last time we made love felt so right. All I could think about was her bright smile, her scent, and her silky smooth, petite body that I caressed in my arms that day. We were both filled with emotions. I just knew she'd do right by me and our son, LJ, short for Little Jaylin. I wasn't sure how I was going to approach my situation with him, but some serious changes had to be made soon. Simone had already taken our daughter, Jasmine. I'd be damned if I let another child slip away. LJ wasn't even a year old yet, and he needed me. I might not have been prepared to talk to Nokea or Stephon after how they betrayed me, but I'd make them regret ever stabbing me in my damn back.

I finished my ice cream and reached for the phone to check my messages. There were seven; I listened to them one by one. Scorpio had called explaining why she left me hanging last night, and then she'd called again and reminded me about picking up Mackenzie today. I had so much shit on my mind that I forgot. My secretary, Angela, had called to tell me she wasn't going to make it for work tomorrow because she was ill. Brashaney, one of my lovers, had called to tell me how badly she wanted me to fuck her, and Stephon had called, insisting that we needed to talk. Calls seven and eight were Nokea. She felt like she owed me an explanation and wanted to come by. I deleted each message. The only person I wanted to talk to was Mackenzie, so I called Scorpio's place and asked for her.

"I was wondering when you were going to call," Scorpio said with a bit of snap in her voice. "Mackenzie has been asking for you all day long."

"Then cut with the attitude and give her the phone."

"I will. Before I do, though, I want to talk to you about last night."

"There's nothing for us to discuss. Now, put Mackenzie on the phone."

"Jaylin, you know you were wrong for—"

"Woman! Didn't you hear what I said? I don't want to hear your mouth! Put Mackenzie on the phone, so I can apologize for not picking her up today. After we left the church yesterday, I told her I'd pick her up."

Scorpio hung up and I called right back. "Helloooo," she said in a sarcastic tone. I didn't find any humor in her games.

"Don't make me disrespect you, all right? Now, I'm asking you nicely to give the phone to Mackenzie."

"She's asleep right now. I hope you didn't expect her to stay up all night waiting for you."

I hung up on her. She called back as I was getting

ready to go over to her place, but I didn't answer because I figured Mackenzie was probably already upset with me.

Scorpio refused to open the door. When I reminded her I had a key to let myself in, she opened it. I walked by her to Mackenzie's room, and climbed into bed with her, rubbing my nose against hers until she slowly opened her eyes. I turned on the lamp so she could see me. Trails of tears had dried on her face.

"Why were you crying?" I asked, tickling her to cheer her up. She gave me a hard time like Scorpio and wouldn't even crack a smile. "Okay, then I won't tell you what I have planned for us next weekend." She folded her arms and pouted. "I guess I'll just have to take Barbie to the circus with me, since you don't want to go."

She revealed her pearly whites and gave me a hug. "Are we really going to the circus, Daddy?"

"Yes, and after the circus we're going to stop at McDonalds for hamburgers." She pouted again. "Jack-in-the-Box?" I said. She rolled her eyes. "How about Burger King?" Her eyes looked like they disappeared to the back of her head. "Okay, what about one of my favorites? Outback Steakhouse." She smiled. No doubt about it, I was teaching her to have the best. At five years old, I was lucky to get a hamburger from White Castle.

Mackenzie took her arms from around me. "Daddy, why didn't you pick me up today? Did you go make up with your wife that left you at the church yesterday? You were so mad and it looked like you wanted to cry."

Damn, I thought. *Now, why did she have to go there?* "No, Mackenzie, I didn't spend the day with her and she's not my wife. Daddy was just tired today. I kind of . . . got my feelings hurt and wanted to be alone. I know I should have called you, but I slept most of the day."

"Did you cry when you got your feelings hurt?"

"A little bit, but, uh . . . Let's talk about something else, okay?"

"Okay, but your wife looked really pretty yesterday. Will you buy me a dress like hers?"

"Mackenzie, I told you that she's not my wife. And yes, she did look pretty. I promise you I'll buy you a dress prettier than hers when you get married."

She hugged me again and scooted underneath the covers so she could get back to sleep. Bottom line, she kicked me out after I told her I would buy her a dress. But I didn't care; she was definitely one person who could get anything she wanted from me.

After I closed Mackenzie's door, I went into Scorpio's bedroom. She was lying naked across the bed, flipping through a cookbook. Her sexiness always gave me a rise. The shapely mountain of her backside couldn't be ignored. I gazed at her perfect moisturized body, but played down my desire for her. "Hey, I'll let myself out. I just wanted to say thanks for not making a big deal about me coming here to see Mackenzie."

She pulled her long hair over to one side and

teased it with her fingers. "You're welcome. I'm glad you came because she was really upset when she didn't hear from you today."

"Well, we worked it out."

Scorpio closed the book and rolled on her back. She bent her knees and rubbed her thighs. I awaited her next move. When she massaged her breasts together, she looked in my direction. "Are you possibly in the mood to work out something else before you go?" she whispered.

I folded my arms, enjoying her performance. "What kind of workout do you have in mind?"

She turned sideways and slid her hand between her tightened legs. "Do you have to ask? I was hoping to get one of those all-nighters that I haven't had in a long, long time."

"Um, I see where you're going with this. But, uh, I don't have all night. I gotta get up early for work because my secretary ain't going to be there. So, I'll take a rain-check."

"You're just saying that because I left you hanging—aren't you?"

"You're damn right I am. And you know what else?"

"What?"

"I'm going home to call this sweet young tender who's been begging me to fuck her. So, that all-nighter you just asked me for, I'm going to have the pleasure of giving it to her."

"Tuh, yeah right. You're crazy but you're not that stupid to rely on somebody else to give you only what I can."

"You're not as good as you think you are, Scorpio, so don't be so sure of yourself. As a substitution for the night, you might want to make sure the batteries in your vibrator are working because my dick has other plans. Goodnight, and I'll see you whenever."

Scorpio turned her back to me and I left. As soon as I got home, I called Brashaney and she was there in a flash. I couldn't give her that all-nighter I'd promised Scorpio I'd give, but I damn sure made Brashaney's visit worth it.

Scorpio rang the phone several times throughout the night, but I was busy fucking and sleeping. It was almost six o'clock in the morning when I asked Brashaney to reach over and answer it. "Hello?" she said in a soft tone. Her eyes widened and she grinned as she gave the phone to me.

"What?" I yelled.

"You are one low-down, dirty, ignorant, stank Negro, Jaylin. I can't believe how trifling you are. If you want to play games, then hey, let the games begin. I guarantee you—"

"Some other time, Scorpio," I said, casually. "I'm sorry that your vibrator didn't do the job you thought it would do, but I'm busy. A trifling man like me doesn't want to disrespect my company so I'll get back with you when I can."

I gave the phone to Brashaney and asked her to hang up. When she did, Scorpio called right back. I snatched the phone and told Scorpio if she wanted to listen to what was about to go down, feel free. I laid the phone on the nightstand and rolled on top of Brashaney.

"Jaylin, why don't you hang up the phone? I don't care to let another woman—"

"In a minute," I said, placing her legs high on

my shoulders. I inserted myself and Brashaney let out a loud moan. She closed her eyes and sucked in her bottom lip.

"I . . . This would be so much better if you'd just hang up on her."

I dug deeply into Brashaney, and, figuring that Scorpio had heard enough action, reached over to slam down the receiver. I quickly wrapped up my business and tried to get some rest before going to work.

Chapter 2

Nokea

I had mega explaining to do. Daddy was so furious with me for not marrying Stephon that he wasn't even speaking to me. Mama, on the other hand, understood what I was going through. She told me to take some time for myself and use the days I had set aside for my honeymoon to relax. Knowing how messed up I was, she told me she'd keep LJ until I got myself together.

No doubt, I was so screwed up. The only person who was really happy about the whole thing was my best friend, Pat. She didn't want me to be with Jaylin or Stephon. Right after I'd escaped from the church, she'd left a message on my voicemail and thanked me for not making the biggest mistake of my life.

Still, I felt terrible for leaving Stephon at the altar. And I'd never forget the look on Jaylin's face. I spent hours trying to make sense of the whole thing, and had gotten a room at the Ritz Carlton in Clayton just to clear my head. I'd been there since Saturday night; my mind was starting to feel at ease. But Jaylin wasn't returning any of my calls. If I talked to Stephon first, I was afraid I'd say something I really didn't mean. My true love, Jaylin, was the one who deserved an explanation of why I couldn't marry him. Knowing him, though, he'd probably never want to speak to me again.

After a long bubble bath at the Ritz, I went downstairs to have breakfast. When I finished, I went back to my room and held the phone in my hands. I called Jaylin at Schmidt's Brokerage Firm, where he works as an investment broker. Expecting his secretary to answer, I was speechless when he did instead. I was silent.

"Jaylin Rogers," he snapped again.

"Hi, it . . . It's me, Nokea." No response. "Jaylin, are you there?"

"I can't talk right now."

"Okay, then can we talk later? I'm at the Ritz in Clayton. Will you stop by after work?"

"Yeah."

"Listen, if you're not going to come just tell me. Please don't have me waiting for you. We really need to talk."

"Damn, I said I'll be there," he snapped. "Gotta go." He hung up. I hated this side of him, but I knew his attitude was because of me.

I picked up the phone again and called my parents' house to check on LJ. When Daddy heard my voice, he gave the phone to Mama. I couldn't believe how he was treating me, like it was his life or something. But I also knew he just wanted the best for me.

"How's LJ?" I asked Mama.

"He's doing fine. Stop worrying so much, you know your baby is in good hands."

"I know, Mama. I just miss him, that's all."

"I understand. Have you spoken to Jaylin yet?"

"No, but I plan to speak to him later."

"Okay. If you need me, I'm here."

There was a knock at the door so I hurried to end my call. "I know, Mama, and thanks. Give LJ a big kiss for me and I'll see you soon."

We said good-bye, and when I opened the door, I was so glad to see Pat. She came in and we held each other tight. I couldn't help crying on her shoulder. "I know, sweetie, I know exactly how you feel," she said, comforting me.

I wiped my tears and we walked over to the couch to take a seat. "Why don't this bad dream just go away, Pat? Why is it just one thing after another?"

"Because, that's just how life is. God never said it was going to be easy."

"I feel like I'm failing Him too. I can't seem to get anything right. Tell me, where did I go so wrong? All I want is to be happy."

"Nokea, I didn't come here to give you one of my lectures. I'm here as your best friend and not a psychiatrist. You didn't sound well when we talked yesterday, but I at least wanted to give you time to think about what you need to do. Have you eaten anything yet?"

"Yeah. I just had breakfast not too long ago."

"Good. 'Cause if you hadn't, I was hoping we could order one of those pizzas we ate when you were pregnant."

We laughed.

"Girl, wasn't that a mess," I said. "We should have been ashamed of ourselves."

"We? No, you should have been ashamed of yourself. I wasn't the one who was pregnant. I worked mine off very well," Pat gloated, holding her waistline.

"And so have I," I bragged.

"Oh, be quiet. You've always had an awesome petite body. I knew that pizza wasn't going to do a darn thing to your figure. Me, I had to work hard to get those pounds off. Chad and I were at it day in and day out trying to work off those pounds."

"I'm sure the two of you had fun." I chuckled, and then went into a daze, thinking about the last time Jaylin and I made love.

Pat snapped her fingers in front of my face. "What grabbed your attention that fast?" she asked. I smiled. My best friend knew me all too well. "Forget it," she said. "I don't even want to know. When are you going to forget about him and move on, Nokea?"

I stood up and walked toward the window with my arms folded. "I can't forget about him, Pat. I've tried so many times to move on, but I can't. I love him so much that it scares me."

"Well, why didn't you just marry his sorry ass? When he stood there making a spectacle of himself, you should have just married him."

"Because the timing wasn't right. That's why."

"And the timing ain't never going to be right, if you ask me. I wish like hell you'd just find someone else."

"I know you do, but I don't want anyone else. As a matter of fact, I've never wanted anyone else, and being with Stephon was a big mistake. I wish everyone would realize that the love Jaylin and I have for each other is deep and it will never go away."

"Your love or his love? Honestly, I can't see Jaylin wasting anymore of his time on this. You'd better wake up and smell the coffee, because I'm sure he's making up for lost time right now."

"No, he's not. Actually, he's coming over to see me after work today."

"For what? Nokea, I know you ain't going to sleep with him."

"No, no. We're just going to talk. Talk about why I did what I did, about our future, and about LJ."

"Girl, I don't know what to say. I'm staying out of it because all Jaylin is going to do is hurt you again. Don't even mention his name to me anymore; I don't want to hear it, okay?"

"Okay, I won't discuss Jaylin with you anymore. But, will you promise to be there for me?"

Pat cut her eyes at me and smiled. "Of course, you know I will."

We chatted for a few more hours, then went downstairs to the lobby. As we shared good-byes, Jaylin came through the revolving doors with his cell phone to his ear. I rushed Pat off and made her promise not to say anything to him. She didn't, but when she walked by him, she rolled her eyes.

"Hello to you too, Pat. Nice to see you." He grinned, closing his phone. Pat kept her promise to ignore him and made her exit.

Nervous, I stepped up to Jaylin, holding my hands behind my back. "Thanks for coming. I know you didn't want to, but I guess you figured we needed to talk."

"Yeah, yeah, but keep it short. I have somewhere I need to be within the hour."

What an attitude, I thought as we headed up the steps. He walked in front of me like he knew where he was going. I didn't mind; it gave me a chance to check him out from behind. He was looking and smelling good, as usual. Leather squared-toed shoes were shining, haircut was fresh, tailored suit was well-fitted. But a smile wasn't there.

When we reached the third floor, Jaylin turned around. "What's your room number?"

"I thought you knew. The elevator would have been quicker, but you seem to know everything, so I'm just following you."

He stepped down and looked at me with a raised eyebrow. "Nokea, I don't have time for the bull-shit. I told you my time is minimal so—"

"So, go up one more flight of stairs and turn to your right." He moved to the side and motioned with his hand for me to go in front of him.

"Thank you." I smiled and led us to my room.

It was obvious when we walked inside that Jaylin wasn't in the mood to waste any time. He didn't even sit, just stood by the doorway with his suit jacket pulled back and his hands in his pockets. I took a seat on the couch, and when I asked him to sit next to me, he declined.

"You're so upset that you can't even sit next to me? That's taking things a bit too far, Jaylin."

"Nokea, cut the act. What do you want from me?"

"I'd like for you to relax and come sit next to me so we can talk."

He removed his jacket and put it on the coat hanger by the door. Then he loosened his tie and headed toward me.

"Now what?" he said, sitting back on the couch with his arms on top of it. "What else do you want me to do, Miss 'I'm calling all the shots around here'?"

"Please stop with the attitude, and this is not about me calling the shots. It's about what's in our best interest, and what the future holds for us."

"Can I answer that question? You know, the one about our future."

"Sure. I'd like to know what you think we should do." I had a feeling he was about to tell me what I really didn't want to hear.

He propped his feet on the table in front of him and rubbed his trimmed goatee. "Nokea, we don't have a future. It's time we go our separate ways for good. I suspect you love me and I for damn sure still love you. But we are a prime example of two people who love each other and just can't be together. I'm hurting. Bad. I've never felt like this in my entire life, even when I was in that jacked-up orphanage. Right about now, you definitely don't need a man like me in your life. It's only going to get worse for us if we try to be together, and I don't see this thing working out any other way."

"Wait a minute, you . . . You lost me. What do

you mean it's only going to get worse? We have a child together and that's going to keep us together forever."

"Right, right, oh, you're so damn right. It's going to keep us together as being loving parents for our son, but that's it. From this moment on, Nokea," he said, pointing his finger at me, "you, your mama, your daddy, my cousin Stephon, Pat, N-O-B-O-D-Y is going to keep me from being with my damn son. I mean that shit and if you want to make plans, start making plans for me to see him. If you don't, I'll get with my attorney to make sure this works out for me."

"Are you threatening me?"

"I'm just telling you like it is! I've been without my son long enough, and it was foolish of me to let you control this situation."

"I have no intentions of keeping LJ from you any longer. He's your child and you have every right to be with him as I do. I just need to know about us. Are we going to work through this or are you making preparations to end this again?"

"Baby, don't you see? You ended it when you left me standing at the altar. Nobody has ever humiliated me like you did. All you had to do was say yes! Simple as that, and we could be married right now. You had a choice and I gave you nothing but time. So, now, fuck it! I don't give a shit what you want right now, and what you want doesn't even matter anymore."

Jaylin stood and removed his tie. He put it in his pocket and reached down to lift my lowered chin. "You really hurt me, Nokea. I know I did a lot of shit to you in the past, but none of it compares to what you did to me."

I stood and hurtfully looked into his eyes. "Jaylin, I wanted to marry you more than you will ever know, but my wedding with Stephon was not the time or place to do it. There was no way to continue the ceremony with you, and you put me in a very uncomfortable position. Stephon would have been crushed, my parents would not have understood, and let's not talk about all of my friends and family who came out to support me. Marrying you that day would have been a complete disaster, and that's not what I wanted for us. Please, let's take this one day at a time before we go making any critical decisions about our future."

"I had plans to marry you Saturday. You shattered my damn dreams, made a fool out of me, and I have to live with that hurt for the rest of my life. I begged you to marry me, Nokea. I stooped to an all-time low and embarrassed the fuck out of myself." His voice got louder and words were stern. "You chose Stephon, your parents, and your friends over me! Don't stand here and tell me what you wanted when you could have damn well had it!"

I followed him to the door. "Please don't leave under these conditions. I understand how you feel, but now is the time for us to heal together. Haven't we hurt each other enough?"

Swinging the door open, he said, "I want to see my son on Sunday, Nokea. Make plans for me to do so, or my attorney will deliver papers to you by noon."

He slammed the door behind him.

I wanted to go after him, but I knew he needed time to cool off. I just wished he wasn't so darn stubborn and would realize we were meant for each other. Couldn't he see that the more time we wasted trying to convince ourselves any differently, the more mess would come between us?

In an effort to clear my thoughts of disappointment, I decided to change clothes and go downstairs to mingle. As soon as I got down to my lime-colored lace bra and v-string panties, there was a knock at the door. Jaylin asked me to open it. When I did, I didn't bother to cover up.

"Yes" I said.

His eyes were glued to my cleavage. When I noticed my hard nipples, I folded my arms across my breasts and rubbed my shoulders.

"I . . . I forgot my jacket," he said.

I reached for his jacket and gave it to him. "Here you go."

"Thanks."

"You're welcome. And if there's anything else you forgot, just let me know."

He stepped up to me, and eased one arm around my waist, pulling me close to his body so I could feel his hardness. We looked into each other's eyes, and he sucked my lips into his. As our tongues intertwined, I anxiously pulled the back of his curly soft hair and felt relieved. My heart raced, but he backed away and wiped his soaked lips.

"My son, Nokea. All I forgot was my son, and I expect to see him soon."

He left again.

Later, I went downstairs to get a drink at the bar. I listened to the pianist play soothing music, and realized how wrong I'd been all these months to keep LJ from Jaylin. Our kiss was on my mind too. That kiss in no way implied that our relationship was over. I also thought about what I would say to Stephon when I made arrangements to see him on Friday.

I called Stephon on Thursday to confirm our meeting the next day. It was at my insistence that we meet at his place; I didn't want him visiting me at the hotel. Afterward, I called to check my messages at work. I was Director of Marketing and Sales for Atlas Computer Company, and even though I was on vacation, the phone calls from my customers were still coming in. I transferred the calls to my assistant and asked her to handle them for me until I returned to work.

On Friday, I arrived at Stephon's house and he anxiously invited me in to take a seat on his couch. "Why did you do it, Shorty?" he asked, using his nickname for me. He sat next to me, shirtless and in pressed, faded jeans. I admired Stephon's chocolate, cut body, but even that didn't seem to faze me anymore. Jaylin had my heart, but how could I simplify that for Stephon?

"I don't know how to tell you how sorry I am for what happened," I said. "It took so long for me to call because I needed time to sort through some things."

"And what have you decided?"

"I've decided to move on, Stephon. I shouldn't

have accepted your proposal and doing so was a big mistake."

Stephon swallowed and I put my hand on his leg. He looked bothered, but seemed to handle my news fairly well.

"Have you talked to Jaylin?" he asked.

"Yes. I spoke to him on Monday. He's really upset, but deep down I know I did the right thing."

"Maybe you did, but what about how you played me, Shorty? You left me hanging too. And then, not to call me until almost a week later? Now, that was foul."

"I know it was, but I just didn't know what to say to you. After having the baby, I thought things would get better between us, but even you knew I never stopped loving Jaylin. I was so wrong for sleeping with you, and by the time I wanted to tell you I couldn't go through with our wedding plans, it was too late. Mama and Daddy were so excited, and so was everybody else. I went with the flow, and ignored everything I was feeling inside."

Stephon put his hand on top of mine. "Shorty, it was a good thing that you didn't call me after you left the church because I probably would've done something I would've regretted. These past few days I've had time to think about the whole fucked-up situation. I understand why you had to walk away. Honestly, neither one of us deserved you, and I'm kind of pleased that things turned out the way they did." Stephon lifted my hand and kissed the back of it. "I do love you, Shorty, but I know there's a man out there who can love you more. Maybe Jaylin. I don't know, but I want to thank you for having the courage to do the right thing."

I put my hand on his cheek and rubbed it. "You don't know how much it means for me to hear you say that. I regret taking our friendship to another level, because I really feel like I'll never be able to get it back."

"Yes, you will. I'll always be there for you, Nokea. Just like I was before. This time, though, I promise you that I won't interfere in your relationship with Jaylin. I'm going to work hard at getting my relationship back with him because he's all I got. I regret what I did to him, but when you love someone it sometimes makes you do stupid things."

"I wouldn't exactly call loving me stupid. Your love means a lot and it always will. I blame myself for not being honest with you from the beginning."

Stephon pulled me close to his bare chest, then kissed my forehead. I placed my head on his shoulder and clinched my hands together with his. "Stay the night with me, Shorty. I'm not asking for us to make love. All I want to do is hold you in my arms one last time."

There was no way I was going to turn Stephon down. After what I did to him, the least I could do was allow him to hold me for one more night. He leaned back on the couch, and I laid my body on top of his. He wrapped his arms around me as if he never wanted to let go.

Chapter 3

Scorpio

I was so upset with Jay-Baby trying to play me like he did. He was out of his mind if he thought, for one minute, I was going to tolerate anymore of his mess. I had much love for the brotha, but what he did the other night was low. First, to try and take something that wasn't even his, then to make me listen to him screw another woman. That was even lower. Lower than I ever thought he would go. But then again, I should have expected this from him, especially since he got his male ego crushed. I wasn't mad at Nokea for playing him like she did, because if anybody had it coming, he did.

I just somehow wish I had the nerve to break this off with him. One day I find myself loving him dearly, and the next day I can't stand to be around him. I know that he's probably going to be eating out of Nokea's hands. If not, he's going to be *eating* everything else in sight.

So, for now, I was chilling. I got myself somewhat of a new friend, Shane Alexander, and I was dying to know how Jaylin was going to react when he found out. Especially since Shane was just as educated, fine, sexy, and qualified as Jaylin. He's hooked-up in all the right places: body tight, about six feet two, carmel as a Caramello bar can get, and gave twisties a whole new name. The only thing I didn't like was the diamond earring in his left ear, but his light brown eyes allowed me to overlook it.

I met Shane at Career Days on Friday, upset, of course, because Jaylin had told me he was going to Nokea's wedding. Something inside of me knew he was planning to stop her wedding, but I didn't want to tell him he would be wrong for doing so. I was the last person he would have listened to, but after the fact, I was sure he wished somebody had stopped him. I loved Jaylin with all my heart, but he needed to be taught many lessons before he would ever think about getting his act together.

I called Jaylin late Friday night to remind him about taking Mackenzie to the circus. She'd been bugging me all week, and since he seemed to be suffering from amnesia lately, I didn't want him forgetting about her.

"What time would you like for me to have her ready?" I asked.

"I'll pick her up around ten o'clock in the morning. I'll have to bring her home afterward, because I have a charity banquet I'm supposed to go to tomorrow night with my boss. I'll pick her back up early Sunday morning so she can spend the whole day with me."

"Charity banquet, huh? So, who's going to accompany you? I'm sure you have a date."

"None of your business. All you need to know is that I'm not going alone."

"That doesn't surprise me. Is it anyone I know?"

"Naw, you don't know her, but I'm sure you heard her the other day."

"If it's that chick who answered your phone, you really should be searching for a new sex partner. Those moans I listened to sounded pretty damn fake to me. Didn't seem like you were giving it your all like you do when we're together."

"Aw . . . I gave it my all. You just happen to listen in when I was just making my entrance."

"Jaylin, that bitch was fake as ever, and she made those noises to insult me. On another note, please be on time picking up Mackenzie."

"Sure will. She's one woman who will never have to wait for Jaylin Rogers, baby."

He hung up, and even though he was working my nerves, I wasn't about to let him know it.

I put Mackenzie to bed, and sat on my bedroom floor trying to get the homework done I'd been neglecting. I knew I couldn't count on Jaylin to pay my bills forever, so I definitely had to get my priorities straight. He'd already done so much for me and Mackenzie, and because he'd purchased my condo and paid for me to pursue a degree in business, I felt a serious need to accept the situation I was in with him. I wasn't sure how long my patience would last, but I knew there was nothing he wouldn't do for me, and vice versa.

Shane was a math professor, and since I seemed to be struggling with algebra, I called him to see if he wouldn't mind coming over to help. When we talked at Career Days he'd offered, but I didn't anticipate taking him up on it so soon. I had a little over one year of school under my belt, and I had to do what was needed to continue my education. It sure in the heck beat taking off my clothes for men any day of the week.

I was so engrossed with my work that when Shane rang the doorbell, I realized I hadn't even taken a moment to get myself together. My hair was in a ponytail lying over my right shoulder, and I still had on a dirty white T-shirt from cleaning earlier. My hipster Levi's had dried paint blotches on them from painting my bathroom today and my face was pale without any makeup. I looked in the mirror and tossed my hands back. I figured this look would just have to do. Jaylin said I looked beautiful without makeup, so maybe, just maybe, Shane would feel the same.

"Hello." I smiled and opened the door for him.

"Hey, Miss Lady. Good to see you again. I hope you're doing well."

His eyes searched the surroundings, and as he stepped into the sunken living room I got a good look at him from behind. Meaty ass, clean-cut, smooth skin, and nice, I thought.

"Yes, I'm doing well, Shane. But I'm getting a slight bit tired of my Algebra class already."

He laughed and followed me into the kitchen. "I think I've heard that statement a million times before. I'd love to help and that's why I'm here."

I realized that my books were in my bedroom, so

I asked him to have a seat. He placed his motor-cycle helmet on the table, turned the kitchen chair around and straddled it. I took a deep breath. His finesse had me in awe. *Lord help me* was all I could think. I looked at him and smiled. "I need to go get my books. Can I get you anything?"

"No, no, I'm fine. But thanks."

I hurried to get my books. Mr. Alexander wasn't looking bad at all. He actually looked a lot better than when I saw him at Career Days in his dark brown suit. And, boy, did I have a thing for a man with bulging muscles and who could ride a motor-cycle. His jeans were gripping his ass in all the right places, and his scent was addictive. *Whew*, I thought. But that earring. The earring had to go.

I gathered my things and went back into the kitchen. "Here, let me help you," he said, standing up to take my books.

"Thank you." I sat across the table from him so I could gaze into his pretty eyes. Besides, I knew the farther away I stayed, the better.

Shane spent nearly two hours explaining alge-bra to me, and I was even more confused. I gave up pretty quick, and just decided to enjoy the sexy man that was now sitting beside me. Halfway through our session, I pretended I couldn't hear and moved closer to him. I gazed at his lips when he spoke. I thought about the woman who was fortunate enough to do his twisty's so neat. His dimples were working me too, and when my pussy had gotten the message, I knew I had to chill.

I took a deep breath. "Shane," I said, moving my ponytail to the other side, then massaging my neck.

"I've taken in enough for one night. I'll never be able to understand all this stuff."

"Yes, you will. It's not as hard as you think it is. You'll master it in no time. I promise, but you can't go giving up on it."

"That's easy for you to say. You've probably done this most of your life. This is really something new to me. I mean, I remember algebra in high school, but that was so long ago."

"Again, that's what I'm here for. Give it some more time, and with me being your tutor, you'll know this stuff in no time at all."

"If you say so," I said, yawning.

He stood and stretched his arms. I couldn't help but notice a nice-sized hump in his pants.

"I won't keep you up any longer, Scorpio." He removed his helmet from the table. "When would you like to get together again?"

"I have a test on Wednesday. Would you be able to pencil me in on Tuesday night?"

"It'll have to be late. I have a class until eight o'clock, but after that I'm free."

"That's fine. I'll call you on Tuesday morning to confirm."

I walked Shane to the door, hating to see him go. He sped off on his motorcycle and waved good-bye. *Really nice*, I thought. Maybe he was just what I needed to get Jay-Baby to straighten up and fly right.

Chapter 4

Jaylin

I got up early Saturday morning because I had a busy-ass day ahead of me. I was already late picking up Mackenzie, and still had to stop by the Plaza to get my tuxedo by five.

I'd decided to take Brashaney to the charity banquet with me. I felt bad about fucking her all the time, and wanted to give her a taste of what it felt like being on the outside of Jaylin's world. She was thrilled when I asked her to go, and since I was already running late, I asked her to meet me at my place by seven o'clock tonight. She agreed.

When I pulled up, Mackenzie was looking out the window. Her hands were pressed against her cheeks; she was already pouting. I knew I was late, but damn. Seemed as if I couldn't please anybody lately.

I thought at least she would smile after she saw me, but she didn't. And I knew she'd really throw a fit after I broke the news about bringing her home after dinner.

Scorpio opened the door and rolled her eyes. I gave her a slight push in her back.

"Don't start, and I'm not in the mood to hear your mouth," I said.

"I haven't said a word. You're going to hear it from Mackenzie, so what the hell?"

Mackenzie walked to the door and took my hand. "Are you ready now?" she asked, looking up at me.

"Yeah, baby, let's go." I licked my tongue out at Scorpio and she smiled.

"You know, you could have asked me to go. I like the circus too," she said, standing in the doorway.

"Damn, I could have, couldn't I? But I think they got enough clowns there already, so maybe next time." She slammed the door, as Mackenzie and I laughed.

We enjoyed the Universoul Circus. I had never been to a circus before, and really felt like I missed out as a kid. Mackenzie for damn sure didn't miss out on anything. She had to have everything she could get her hands on. I was down 300 bucks when we left and she was all smiles. I still had to break the news about taking her back home, but I thought all the things I bought would make it easier. They didn't; she cried and cried. Damn near made me want to cry. So, after we left Outback Steakhouse, I called Nanny B, an elderly woman who did her best to take care of us, to see if she would watch Mackenzie while I went to the charity banquet. She said it was fine, and told me she would be there by the time we got home.

We stopped at Plaza Frontenac and picked up my tuxedo, then drove back to my place. When we got there, as promised, Nanny B was parked in the driveway. I was running tremendously late because it had started raining, and I'd taken my time driving with Mackenzie in the car. So, as soon as I got into the house, I jetted upstairs, took a shower, and changed into my black tuxedo. I trimmed my beard and gazed at the mirror at one confident and fine black man. I rubbed my goatee straight with the tips of my fingers. Didn't no one need to tell me how much I had it going on. Tonight, my boss, Mr. Schmidt, was definitely going to be proud of me. Since I was the one whom he had chosen to represent his company and hand out the check, I had to make sure there were no flaws in my attire.

Just when I started wondering what the hell was taking Brashaney so long, I heard the doorbell ring. Nanny B and Mackenzie came from the kitchen, and I jogged downstairs to open the door. I slightly titled my head and looked Brashaney over. I had a serious problem with the hot pink, long silk dress she wore; it was much too loud for the black-tie occasion. Her accessories were silver, and when I looked down and saw mud caked on the heels of her shoes, I could have died. If that wasn't enough, she hadn't even had the decency to get her nails and toes done; polish was chipped and looked a mess. Her weave looked stiff, and why wear a weave when she didn't even need it? This was not the sexy young lady I'd met several months ago, and her appearance was a no-no for a man like me.

"Hey, baby, wha . . . What's up with the way you're looking? Didn't I explain to you how important tonight was for me?"

She put her hands on her hips. "Excuse me! What do you mean by the way I'm looking?" She looked down at herself. "For your information, I went over and beyond for you tonight. Don't be so darn critical."

Nanny B and Mackenzie looked at me, said hello to Brashaney, and went back into the kitchen.

I stepped into the great room and paced the floor, trying to figure out if I was going to work with her tonight or not. "Okay, if you comb your hair back into a neat ponytail, maybe that'll work. Your round face is very pretty and the dress is too, but couldn't you have at least had your nails and toes done? I could have given you the money for that." She rolled her eyes and walked toward me. The mud on her shoes put dirt marks on my plush carpet and that just about did it for me. "Whoa . . . Wait a minute! Don't go any further. I do not want that shit you got on your shoes all over my carpet. Just stay there for one minute."

Brashaney stood with her arms folded, tapping her foot on the floor. I ran back upstairs to my room, and reached for the phone. Scorpio answered and sounded like she was asleep.

"Wake up," I said. "It's too early for you to be sleeping on a Saturday night."

"Well, you know, this clown needs all the sleep she can get," she mumbled.

"Yeah, you do. But, uh, I need a favor."

"What is it?"

"Do you remember that black dress I bought you when we went to the Bahamas?"

"Yes."

"Put it on, comb your hair, and put on those shoes I bought you too. I'll be there in less than an hour to pick you up."

"Jaylin, are you crazy? I'm tired. Besides, I thought you had a date for this damn charity banquet tonight."

"I do. Well . . . I did. Anyway, I'll explain it to you later. Just do what I asked, okay?"

"No, it's not okay, but I'll do it because you seem desperate. Next time, get your shit together ahead of—"

I cleared my throat. "Desperate? Never. In need? Yes. So, get dressed and I owe you one."

"Oh, you owe me more than one."

"Okay, then two, damn! Hurry up and don't wear your hair down. Pin it up at the top and let the back dangle on your shoulders how I like it. You know . . . Make it sexy."

"Now, that's asking too much. That particular way takes time. If you give me two hours then maybe I can get it together like that, Your Highness."

"One hour, that's all you got. I'll be there in one hour."

I hung up and ran back downstairs to break the news to Brashaney. She just didn't make the cut. Sorry, but she wasn't fit to be in Jaylin Rogers' circle.

"Don't give me any excuses, Jaylin," she said, pointing her finger at me in anger. "I know exactly what you're up to. I swear . . . This is the last time you're going to play me. You don't ever have to worry about me calling your house again. You are a cold, cruel motherfucker and you don't deserve to have a woman like me."

"You're right, I don't," I said, escorting her to the door. "But can we talk about this some other time? I really need to be going." Brashaney reached up and tried to smack me. I let her get away with that shit one time before, but she wasn't going to mess up my handsome face tonight. I grabbed her wrist and squeezed it as tight as I could.

"DO NOT," I yelled, "touch my damn face, Brashaney. You're taking this a bit too far, so please, get in your car and make your way home."

She snatched her wrist away from me. "Ooo . . . I swear this is it! You better not ever call my house for as long as you live!"

As I walked to my car, she followed behind me and continued to rant. I opened the door and gave her confirmation. "I promise you, I will never call you again."

I got in my Mercedes and slammed the door. I heard a clunk when she walked past, so I hopped out to see if she had caused any damage to it. "Don't play, silly-ass," I said, looking to make sure everything was cool. She gave me the finger, and walked abruptly to her car.

As I was backing out of the driveway, I reached for my cell phone to call my baby Mackenzie. I forgot to tell her good-bye, and when Nanny B answered, I asked her to put Mackenzie on the phone. She blew me a kiss, and told me how handsome I looked. I smiled because that was all the approval I needed.

It was ten minutes after eight when I honked the horn outside of Scorpio's condo. Normally, out of respect, I would go to the door. But since I had already called to let her know I was around the corner, I expected her to be outside waiting. I got out, leaned against the 'Cedes, and waited.

Almost five minutes later, she strolled out, taking her time. But when I saw how amazing she looked, I couldn't do nothing but smile. She wore the black satin dress I'd bought her, her hair was just like I had asked: pinned up with a few strands dangling on her shoulders. Her makeup was flawless, and her thick, perfectly arched eyebrows could have put her on the front of *Essence Magazine*. Her scent was like a bed of roses, and it gave me a rise. To complete the look, her finger and toenails were polished to perfection. It made me feel good to have a woman like her by my side and I would never have it any other way. I opened the door for her and puckered for a kiss before she got inside.

She put her hand in front of my face. "Save it. Don't go being all nice to me now."

"Just be quiet. Did anybody ever tell you that you talk too much?"

"No, but did anybody tell you that you're a control freak?"

"All the time, baby." I gave her a peck on the cheek and closed the door. I ran over to the driver's side and got in.

"So, what happened to your date?" I knew she couldn't wait to ask.

"She didn't make the cut," I said.

"Jaylin, please. So, now women got to audition in order to be with you, huh?"

"No, nothing like that, but there are certain things I'm very particular about."

"Certain things like what?"

"Like a woman's hair, her skin, her smell, her clothes, her nails, her makeup, her ass, her pussy." I rubbed my hand on Scorpio's leg near the good stuff. "You know how I am about that, don't you?"

"Okay, I got your point. But who in the hell are you critiquing us like you do?"

"I'm J-A-Y-L-I-N, if you wanna be with me, you got to fit in."

"So, you're a rapper now, huh? You are so full of yourself it's ridiculous. And by the way, please don't quit your day job because *that* was pathetic."

We both laughed.

"Anyway, uh—" I cleared my throat. "Are you gonna shake a brotha down tonight or what? You know it's been awhile since I tapped into that ass, right?"

"So, you're asking now? And if my memory serves me correctly, it's been less than a week since I tapped into that dick, right? Besides, I thought you were the kind of man who just takes what he wants."

"Yep, that would be me. But you know I wanna take it right now since you're looking all pretty and everythang. You are so lucky we're heading to our destination, and I don't want to mess you up."

"Was that a compliment?"

"Yes, it was. I gotta hand it to you, baby, you really out did yourself tonight. You know a brotha appreciate it, don't you?"

"Well, he'd better. 'Cause if he don't, he won't be getting near my good stuff anytime soon."

"Um . . . So, does that mean if I act right, I'm getting some juice tonight?"

"Juice? That depends on how well you arouse me."

Scorpio reached over and placed her hand on my goodness. It gave her some attention and she started to unzip my pants.

"Don't play, Scorpio. I'm already running late, and if you pull that motherfucker out, you gon' be in deep, deep trouble."

"I love trouble. Bring it on."

"I got you later, and you'd better be ready for me to fuck the shit out of you too."

Scorpio laughed and pulled her hand back.

I flew down Highway 40 trying to get to the Adams Mark downtown. By the time we got there we were nearly two hours late. The presentations had already started, but there wasn't anything I could do.

We quietly walked through the elegantly decorated ballroom with dimmed lighting from the hanging chandeliers. Our round table was dressed with a white tablecloth, fine china, and gold silverware. Nearly everyone had on formal attire. I was relieved Brashaney wasn't by my side. Schmidt was so glad to see me; he didn't even seem to care how late I was. He stood and shook my hand as he introduced me to his unattractive wife, like I'd never met her before. In return, I introduced the entire table to Scorpio. The men at the table, who were Angela's husband, Doug, Roy, and Clay, another one of my coworkers, had their mouths wide open.

I pulled back the chair for Scorpio. Flattered by all the attention, she crossed her legs in front of her. Considering my past history with Angela, she cut her eyes and tooted her lips. I ignored her and reached over to shake hands with Roy's and Clay's wives.

The ceremony was too damn long. I found myself getting tired, even though the conversation at the table was flowing. They were all up in Scorpio's and my business. Asking questions about how long we've been dating, and where we met. I hoped like hell that none of them had known she was previously a stripper, and when Roy asked what she did for a living, I quickly intervened.

"She's an entrepreneur. I'm assisting her with her career in fashion merchandising. She's very creative when it comes to designing clothes, and can model any piece remarkably well."

"Really?" Scorpio replied. "That doesn't sound like a bad idea, Jaylin. We should talk more about that later." She picked up her wineglass, took a sip, and shot bullets at me from her eyes.

I was glad when the Mistress of Ceremonies introduced Schmidt's Brokerage as a sponsor and called me to the podium. I stepped up, cracked a few simple-minded jokes, and presented the chosen organization a check for $5,000. As the audience applauded, then listened to the president of the company speak, I looked around the room and wondered, *where in the hell are all the black people?* I always felt out of place and wondered if anyone else felt as I did. I scanned the room for a while, and noticed Felicia at a table with her employer. She was staring so hard; I couldn't do anything but nod and smile at her. When the president was finished, I spoke about the importance of giving. The crowd agreed, and loudly applauded as I made my way back to the table. Schmidt stood, gave me another proud handshake, and pat me on my back. I took a seat and Scorpio leaned in to give me a kiss.

"Good job," she whispered. "I'm so proud of you."

Shortly after my presentation, it was Felicia's turn. She stepped up to the podium wearing a white silk strapless dress with tiny slits on both sides. Her braids were wrapped in a French roll, and two curls dangled on the sides of her face. She wore a four-tier diamond necklace that sparkled, long shimmering diamond earrings, and a bracelet that matched the necklace. Her shoes looked like Cinderella glass slippers and for damn sure didn't have any mud caked on them. Classy, I thought. Sure looked classy for a woman who was truly what I considered an "undercover ho."

After dinner was served, I was ready to go. Scorpio was making conversations with everybody, even Angela. Fucked me up, because when she found out Angela and I used to be banging buddies, I was sure her tune would change.

The night dragged on. The band started playing some old-time, boogie-down funky music that had nearly everybody on their feet looking ridiculous. I really wasn't up for this shit and I was in no mood for dancing. I was ready to go and get my fuck on, but Scorpio kept running her mouth and prolonging the night.

"Come on, Jaylin, let's dance." She stood and reached for my hand.

"Woman, you have got to be out of your mind. I ain't dancing to no bullshit like that."

"Please," she begged. "Trust me, it'll be fun." She tried to pull me out of my seat, but I wouldn't budge. Seeing that I wasn't going to cooperate, she walked off and said something to the musician. He immediately slowed it down and kicked up some jazz.

"Okay, get up now," she insisted. When I still didn't budge, she leaned in and whispered, "You know that sex we talked about—"

I stood up. "Come on, damn. I just knew you were going to go there."

Scorpio escorted me to the dance floor. I put my arms around her waist, pulled her in close, and left no breathing room between us.

"Damn, Jaylin, why don't you just pull me to the floor and fuck me?" she said, trying to scoot back.

"Why don't we just get the hell out of here so I can get you out of this booty gripping dress and then fuck you?"

The couple dancing next to us heard our conversation and moved away. We looked at each other and cracked up.

"You know I can feel your hard thang pressing against me, don't you?"

"Baby, please. You of all people should know how big my thang is. It ain't nowhere near hard. It just can't help itself." Scorpio slid her hand down my back and squeezed my ass. I grinned and slightly moved back. "Quit playing. You don't want to get hurt when we get home do you?"

"I'm really starting to look forward to tonight.

First I'm going to get in trouble, and now you're going to hurt me. By—"

"Excuse me," Felicia interrupted, tapping Scorpio's shoulder. "Do you think I can steal your man for a minute . . . Maybe two?"

"Sure, why not?" Scorpio said, backing away from me. "Take more than two minutes, if you need it." She looked at me. "Baby, I'm going to go mingle for a while. Don't be too long, okay?"

"Hey, you really don't have to—"

"No, no . . . By all means, dance. A dance never hurt anybody." She looked at Felicia. "Right, Felicia?"

"Right, Scorpio. Thanks, sweetie, you're such a charm."

"Jaylin seems to think so too." Scorpio touched my face and gave me a juicy wet kiss before she walked away.

I held Felicia in my arms and left just a little room in between us. "You know that was kind of bold, don't you?" I said.

"Yes, but, oh well, she'll get over it. Your tricks always do, don't they?"

"I'm not so sure about that. You still seem a little bitter and I really can't say that you've gotten over our abrupt separation."

"I was never your trick. I cared deeply for you, Jaylin, and I'm curious to know how have you been doing?"

"Very well, Felicia. I can't complain. And you?"

"Couldn't be better. Missing what we had, but Stephon's definitely doing a great job taking your place."

"I'm glad to hear that," I said, trying to keep my peace because I knew the bitch was trying to piss me off. "You look nice, though, Felicia, I mean really nice."

"So do you, but would you ever expect anything less from me?"

"No, really can't say I would. Just only if you had the personality to go with the look."

"Ouch, that hurt. I could really say the same about you, but I won't. Besides, you were such a good teacher for me. I only learn from the best. And oh, before I forget, how's the wife and kid? I heard about all your drama with Nokea, but I see you still got the Playboy bunny, I mean, stripper or hooker . . . or whatever you want to call her."

I snickered. "You know, Felicia, you haven't changed one bit. I thought that maybe after Scorpio took this nine-plus inches of solid good dick away from you, you'd get some sense. It's really a shame that Playboy bunny, stripper, hooker, or whatever you want to call her these days, got more fucking sense and respect for herself than you ever will have. So, I don't care how spectacular you look tonight, you still the same ol' stank, tramp-ass slut that you were when I was with you." I took my arms from around her waist and walked off the floor. Damn shame she made me show my ass in front of these white people, but I couldn't help myself. I know some of them heard me, so it was definitely time to go. I found Scorpio coming out of the ladies room with Angela, laughing like they were the best of friends. I grabbed her and told her I was ready to go. She waved good-bye to Angela, saying she'd call her tomorrow.

"Call her for what?" I asked as we waited for one of the valets to bring my car.

"Call her because she seems like a nice person. We talked about getting together sometime."

"Well, that ain't going to happen."

"Why? Who are you, trying to pick my friends for me?"

"Scorpio, she's my secretary. She knows more about me than anybody does. I don't want her sharing all my personal business with you."

"And what personal business you got that I don't already know about?"

"It's personal. That means I don't want you to know." I tipped the valet and we got into the 'Cedes. Scorpio kept running her mouth, refusing to let go of the situation with Angela.

"So, tell me. What else is there to know about you, Jaylin, other than that you're a ho."

"Okay, if that's all you see in me, cool. But remember, I'm a good damn ho, baby. One of the best damn ho's you'll ever meet in St. Louis. Now, if you really want to know what I was talking about pertaining to my personal business, I was talking about my finances."

"Oh, I don't care about those. That is your business and she would be wrong for sharing that information with me. I thought you were going to tell me you and her used to mess around."

I kept my eyes on the road and didn't say a word.

"Jaylin Rogers!"

"What? Scorpio Valentino!"

"Don't tell me. Are you fucking your secretary? Okay, you don't even have to answer, I can tell by that smirk on your face. No wonder she was asking me all kinds of questions about our relationship. The nerve of that bitch."

"All right . . . all right. Just let it go. It was a long time ago, and since I'm such a ho, what else would you expect?"

"You're right. I wouldn't expect anything different, but how long ago is a long time ago in your vocabulary?"

"So long ago that I can't remember. I just know it's been awhile. Actually, she's been exchanging juices with Boy Roy lately."

"Roy . . . Roy . . . The tall, skinny, white dude who was sitting at the table?"

"Yep."

"But he's married. And, so is she. What is the matter with people these days? Do you all have some type of free-for-all at work where everybody gets a chance to screw the secretary?"

"Scorpio, just be quiet. Can I get you to shut your mouth for the rest of the way home?"

"I thought you'd never ask," she said, reaching over and unzipping my pants. "Maybe if you put something in it, who knows, it just might shush me."

"You're finally talking what I want to hear."

I was on cloud nine and damn near lost control over the steering wheel trying to stay focused. I held it tightly with one hand and rubbed her soft coal black hair with the other hand. Scorpio's performance was definitely to my satisfaction. Her throat seemed so damn deep. She took all of me in and massaged me with her hands while sucking me. I was about to have a panic attack, and could not concentrate on driving. I got off at the Forest Park exit to find a quiet place to park.

Scorpio worked hard at getting me to come, and when I slightly lifted myself from the seat to pump her mouth, she got what she wanted. I felt drained and dropped the back of my head against the headrest.

"*That* was tasty," she said. "But the park, Jaylin? This is really tacky. All kinds of crazy people be roaming through here at night. You must be out of your mind if you think I'm getting naked up in here."

"Let's just chill for a minute, okay? You don't have to get naked. All I want to do is play around for a lil' bit."

I leaned over and sucked Scorpio's glossy lips into mine. Then I pecked my lips down her neck and sucked it. I reached for the adjust button on her seat and moved it back as far as it could go. I rubbed my hands on the outside of her dress, and searched her private parts. My hand crept between her legs. I could feel the heat coming down. When I moved her silky wet panties to the side, I circled my thick fingers inside her.

She squeezed my hand and tried to halt my rhythm. "Ba—baby, can we please go home?" she moaned.

I was having fun teasing her hard clitoris, so my fingers didn't move. And when I did remove them, I dropped my face into her lap and my tongue replaced them. Scorpio pressed her feet against my dashboard, her legs falling further apart. I tore up her insides with my tongue, and the deeper it went in, the more she trembled and hit her foot against the dash.

"Stop this," she cried out. "If you don't start up this damn car and get to your place in ten minutes, the deal is off!"

I ignored her and had the pleasure of slurping her juices when she came. She took deep breaths and couldn't even move.

"You were so, so wrong for that. Give me a minute to regroup, okay?"

I started the engine and headed home. Scorpio had a smile on her face as she eased down her dress and teased her hair with her fingers to straighten it. We were home in less than fifteen minutes, but when we got out of the car we saw Nanny B sitting in the living room reading a magazine. We crept around to the back of the house.

I removed my bow tie, and was ready to get down to some serious business with Scorpio. She caught me off guard and pushed me into the Olympic-sized swimming pool. I tried to keep my balance, but I couldn't. The loud splash and laughter had Nanny B running outside. She slid the patio door open and stepped into the pool area.

"So, I see you two made it back," she said.

"Yeah, but we're going to chill outside for a while," I said, floating in the water.

"That's fine. Mackenzie's been asleep since ten. I'm going upstairs to soak these old feet and watch a movie, if you don't mind."

"No, not at all. We'll be up in a minute." She went back into the house. I looked at Scorpio. "Uh, Miss Lady, get your butt in this pool with me."

"I don't think so. That water looks icy cold to me. Besides, I don't have nothing to wear." I hopped out, dripping wet in my tuxedo. Scorpio started running because she knew I was coming to get her. I quickly caught up with her and slung her over my shoulder.

"Jaylin, you wouldn't!" she screamed, kicking her feet and laughing. "Please don't throw me in the water with this dress on! It's too expensive and you'll ruin it!" I tossed her in the pool and dove back in.

Scorpio's wet hair covered her entire face; I could barely see her eyes. I made my way over to her and put my arms around her. When I moved her hair away from her face she gave me a blank stare.

"Look what you did. This dress is ruined," she pouted.

"So, I'll buy you another one."

"My body is shivering."

"So? So is mine."

She looked into my eyes without blinking. "I want a commitment, Jaylin."

"So? So does everybody else."

"But, it's time. Don't you think so?"

"Nope, not until I live up to your expectations of being a ho."

Before she could say another word, I placed my lips on hers and removed her dress. It floated off into the water, just as my tux had when I took it off. Since I couldn't hit it like I wanted to while we were in the pool, I straddled Scorpio on the diving board, and as usual, had my way with her. She was exactly what I needed in my life to keep my mind off loving Nokea. Besides, Scorpio's good-ass pussy and dedication to our relationship had me looking at things a little bit differently this time around. However, a commitment to one woman was, without a doubt, out of the question for now.

Chapter 5

Nokea

I was so glad to be home. A week away from every-body really gave me a chance to clear my head. One thing was for sure, I wasn't going to give up on Jaylin. Some day, this all had to come together for us, and this time, I was in it for the long haul. Our nine-year relationship had turned to ten. Ten years of good times and bad times, but the most important thing now was our son. Hopefully, LJ was going to bring Jaylin and me closer together, and eventually Jaylin would come around and see things for what they truly were supposed to be.

Sunday was a day I had longed for. I woke up at five o'clock in the morning just to prepare myself. I'd left a message with Nanny B the night before, and asked her to tell Jaylin we'd be there no later than one o'clock in the afternoon. I knew he'd said by noon, but one extra hour wasn't going to kill him.

I ate breakfast, then went into LJ's room. He was still sound asleep. When I'd checked on him earlier, he'd had a smile on his face like he knew he was going to see his daddy today. He was lying peacefully, and I couldn't resist holding him. All I could think was how Jaylin and I had made such a beautiful child. He was the cutest little baby I'd ever seen and was looking more like his daddy every day.

When Stephon and I had talked, he'd said he'd like to continue to be a part of LJ's life, but I had convinced him that under the circumstances, it wouldn't be the best thing to do. He'd agreed, but made me promise to at least bring LJ by his barbershop sometimes to see him.

Stephon's forgiveness really had me worried, though. For me to walk away from him at the altar, he was handling himself extremely well. Deep down I knew he was hurt, but he was putting up a front like he really didn't care. Maybe he did understand why I couldn't go through with the wedding, or maybe he had somebody else in his life and didn't know how to break the news to me. I wasn't going to stress myself too much about it because I believed my decision worked out for all of us.

Around 12:15 P.M., LJ and I were just about ready to head out. There was no sense in me calling Jaylin to let him know that we were on our way; I was sure he was having a fit already since we were late.

LJ looked darling. He wore a blue-jean outfit with a hat to match. I put on the white Nike tennis shoes I'd found at St. Louis Mills when Mama and I had gone shopping earlier. LJ's soft, curly hair peeked out the sides of his hat, and his grey eyes sparkled when I looked into them.

We pulled in front of Jaylin's house, and I carried LJ on my hip as I walked to the door. I rang the doorbell and patiently waited for someone to answer. After I rang it several more times, Jaylin finally opened the door. His face lit up as he reached for LJ.

"Well, hello to you too," I said, handing LJ over to him.

"Hey, sorry, come in. I actually forgot you were coming," he said, looking like he had just gotten out of bed.

"I left a message with Nanny B last night. She didn't tell you?"

"No, but that's okay. I'm glad you came. 'Cause if you hadn't, you know I was coming for you."

I followed behind Jaylin to his office. I took a seat on the couch, and he sat in his chair while lifting LJ up in the air, looking at him eye-to-eye. "Do you know how happy your daddy is to see you?" he said, talking baby-talk to him. I couldn't do anything but smile after finally seeing them together. At that moment, I knew just how wrong I was for trying to keep them apart.

I watched him sharing precious moments with his son, and after a while heard someone walking down the steps. I'd thought Jaylin was alone. When Scorpio came into his office, I could have died. My smile vanished as she looked over at me. "Hi, Nokea," she said dryly, then turned to look at Jaylin.

"Hello," I replied.

Jaylin sat LJ on his lap, then turned him around so Scorpio could see him. "Look, baby. Ain't he handsome? I bet you didn't think I could pull something off like this, did you?" he asked her.

"Yes, Jaylin. He is gorgeous, and I never said you couldn't, so be quiet." Scorpio turned toward me. "Do you mind if I hold him?"

"No, not at all," I said. Of course, I didn't want her to touch him. I only tolerated her because of Jaylin, and I cringed as she took LJ off his lap to hold him. When she sat down in one of the leather chairs, her silk robe slid open and showed her goods. She quickly crossed her legs, but I had already seen that she didn't have on anything underneath. Of course, with Jaylin having come to the door in his robe, I figured they had probably been in the middle of screwing when I rang the doorbell. If not, I was sure they had been at it all night long.

It really wasn't like me to hate on another woman when it came to Jaylin, but after listening to him call her "baby" my feelings were hurt once again. And if that wasn't enough, Mackenzie came into the room and added to my pain. She hopped in Jaylin's lap, and put her arms around his neck.

"Good morning, Daddy." She kissed his cheek and he kissed hers.

"It's not good morning, Mackenzie, it's good afternoon. And what did I tell you about speaking to guests when you see them in the house?" She laid her head against his chest.

"But I didn't see her," she said, looking at me, then putting her fingers into her mouth. She lifted her head and her eyes got wide. "Hey, that's your wife, Daddy! That's the one who you married the other day."

Jaylin shamefully covered his face and shook his head. I smiled at Mackenzie, and Scorpio stood up and brought LJ over to me.

"You have a beautiful baby, Nokea."

"Thanks," I said, taking him from her.

"Come on, Mackenzie." Scorpio took Mackenzie by the hand. "Let's go make some of your favorite pancakes." Mackenzie pulled her hands back and wrapped them tightly around Jaylin's neck. "Mackenzie, did you hear what I said, honey? Let's go make breakfast."

"But I don't like the way you make your pancakes. I like the way Daddy makes them."

Jaylin chuckled and kissed Mackenzie on the cheek. "Baby, I'll be in there to cook you some pancakes in a minute. In the meantime, eat a big bowl of Captain Crunch, okay?" Mackenzie hopped down off his lap.

"Okay, Daddy, but hurry, all right?" She waved at me. "Bye, Daddy's wife."

Scorpio and Jaylin both yelled, "She's not Daddy's wife, Mackenzie!" Scorpio followed Mackenzie to the kitchen.

Jaylin got out of his chair and sat next to me. He reached for LJ again and leaned back, laying him on his chest. He removed the little denim hat and stroked his curly hair. With a huge smile on his face, he rubbed his hands up and down on his son's back and squeezed him.

"He feels so good in my arms, Nokea, you just don't know. Thing is, I can't figure out if I'm upset with you for keeping him from me, or if I'm happy that we have a damn good future ahead of us."

"Jaylin, all I can say is I'm sorry. I was wrong for keeping him from you, but at the time I thought that I was truly doing what was best for me."

"Right, right, but going forward I don't want no shit from you about him, Nokea. I want to see him a minimum of three or four times a week. I'm willing to adjust my schedule to make sure that happens."

"Now, you know how complicated your schedule can be. Why don't you just call me on the days you're not too busy and I can bring him to you? If you call ahead of time, that will make it easier for me."

"That might work. And whenever you have something to do, let me know and I'll make arrangements as well."

"Sounds like a plan to me," I said, enjoying our pleasant conversation.

"What about his expenses? How have you been handling those?"

"It's been okay. I mean, he's not wanting for much, but having a baby has put a slight hole in my pockets."

"Well, no child of mine is going to be just okay. Once I found out he was mine, I set up several mutual funds for him. There are some other things I wanted to do like investing in his education, but I just haven't gotten around to doing that yet. I've been thinking about child support for him. You have my word that I will take care of him, so I don't want no damn court telling me how much I need to pay. If you don't mind, I'll have my attorney put together a promissory letter that says I'll give you . . . let's say five thousand dollars a month? Will that be enough?"

"Six sounds better," I said jokingly.

"Okay, then six. But you better use this money for him. Your hair, clothes, nails . . . and all that other stuff remains on you, all right?"

"Don't you worry about that because I got me. And six thousand is too much, I was just kidding. Four would most certainly suffice."

"I say five. So, I'll call my attorney tomorrow, and once he puts everything in writing, I don't want you reneging on my offer."

"I won't, but honestly, you really don't have to go through all the trouble. I trust you."

"Naw, thing is, I don't trust you. I've been honest with you about almost everything in my life. You're the one who be telling lies." Jaylin gave LJ back to me and went over to his desk.

"That's not so, Jaylin, and you know it. I allowed Stephon to lie to you about LJ being his because I had to."

He pulled his calculator out and bounced his pen up and down on his desk. Then he opened a square leather burgundy book and started writing. He looked up at me.

"There are certain things that shouldn't be lied about, Nokea, like your love for someone, your credentials, and your loving children. You catch my drift?" He dropped his head and continued to write.

Jaylin ripped the paper from the book and gave it to me. "This should financially make up for my lost time. I don't care what you do with it, but several months ago I had another responsibility. You made sacrifices, so I'd like to repay you." I took the paper out of Jaylin's hand. It was a check for $65,000.

"Jaylin, no. You don't have to do this. I know you would have taken care of LJ had you known, and there is no need for you to give me this much money."

"Nokea, I'm not going to argue with you. There's no reason you should have a hole in your pocket when I don't. This money is petty when it comes to my son. I'll make it up in a few months anyway. So, take it. Fifty-five thousand is for your financial setback, and ten is for the ten years of any pain and suffering I may have caused you. If you have any problems at your bank, let me know."

Now, after breaking it down like that, I wasn't going to argue with him about the money. Every bit helps, and this was more than any court would ever offer me. Besides, I was sure Jaylin had plenty of money hidden away and this wouldn't set him back. The courts would never know his true net worth, and even though he never shared with anyone how much money his grandfather's estate was worth, by Jaylin's lifestyle, and many years of investing, I knew he had inherited millions.

After Jaylin cooked Mackenzie's pancakes, he asked me if LJ could spend the day with him. He told me to pick him up by ten o'clock that night, so he could get some rest before he went to work. I asked him if Scorpio was going to help him, but he said he was kicking her out too to have time with his son and daughter.

This was definitely the Jaylin I'd fallen in love

with. He seemed so different, but my only problem was his relationship with Scorpio. It seemed as if she wasn't going anywhere any time soon. I felt like I had the upper hand because I knew he was still in love with me. I also knew that if I didn't work fast at getting him back, she would eventually replace me. I was willing to do everything in my power to make sure that never happened.

Chapter 6

Jaylin

I was running around the house like a chicken with his head cut off. Trying to man up—pretending that I could handle two kids in the house at once and I was paying for it dearly.

LJ was lying on my bed screaming at the top of his lungs, and Mackenzie was trying to get him to stop crying by giving him her Barbie dolls. When I realized that maybe he was wet, I took off his diaper, only for him to piss right in my face. I sat on the edge of my bed laughing and thanking God these kids had mothers. I for damn sure wasn't cut out for this and the proof was in the pudding.

LJ did number two and it seeped out of his diaper onto my satin Gucci sheets. I threw my hands in the air and did what I did best: called Nanny B. She'd already made plans, but when I pleaded with her, she changed her mind and told me she was on her way.

There was no way I was calling Nokea or Scorpio for their help. After I'd kicked Nokea out, she'd made me promise not to call her until it was time to pick up LJ. Scorpio had said she was leaving anyway, insisting that she had some homework to finish.

The doorbell rang and I rushed to it thinking it was Nanny B. Instead, it was Stephon on the porch with his head hanging low.

"Say, can I come in?" he asked.

I held the door open to let him inside. "Please, make it quick. I'm spending time with my kids today." I felt proud as I was holding LJ in my arms.

"Cool, I won't be long, but, uh, why haven't you returned any of my phone calls?"

"Man, I hope you didn't come all the way over here to sound like one of my women with this phone call bullshit. You know damn well why I haven't returned your phone calls. Been busy and ain't got time for snake-ass niggas in my life."

"Okay, that's fair. But I just wanted to say that I'm sorry. I made a big mistake asking Nokea to marry me, but I can't change what's already happened. If time is what you need, fine, take all the time you need. When you're ready to talk, call me or come holler at me at the shop." He turned toward the door. When I opened it to let him out, he stood with his hands in his pockets.

"What?" I yelled. "Why are you still standing there?"

" 'Cause, Jay," he said as his eyes watered. "I tripped, cuz, and the last thing I wanted was for Nokea to come between you and me."

"Well, too late for that shit. You should have thought about the consequences a long time ago."

Stephon took a hard swallow and walked out. I took my foot and slammed it against the door, closing it. When I looked out of the window, Nanny B was getting out of her car. She was talking to Stephon for a while, then started laughing when she saw me open the door with LJ in my arms.

She took him from me. "Jaylin, he's been crying because he's wet. I can feel how soaked he is just by holding him."

"Damn, I just changed him. How many times does he have to go?"

She shook her head and slowly walked up the steps with him in her arms. I followed. Mackenzie was taking a nap in her room, so Nanny B went into one of the guestrooms. She laid LJ on the bed and started to undo his diaper.

"Aren't you going to put something underneath him? That comforter cost me a fortune," I said.

She gave me a hard stare. "Go get a diaper, please," she said, kissing LJ on his feet. I rushed into my room and grabbed a diaper out of his diaper bag. I went back into the guestroom and gave it to her. "Did you see how you put his diaper on? It wasn't wet. He leaked through the sides because it's not taped up on him. Now, come over here and let me show you how to do this right."

I walked over by Nanny B and looked down at LJ. "But the comforter . . . Can't we put something underneath him so he won't mess it up? I just had to change my other sheets—"

"Jaylin! Go get a towel or something, please!

This anal behavior of yours has got to stop. Especially since you have children around the house." I ignored Nanny B and ran to the closet to get a towel. She snatched it out of my hand and slid it underneath LJ's bottom. Then she showed me the correct way to change his diaper. I guess since I hadn't removed the sticky tabs on the side, that could have been why it wouldn't stay up on him. I'd thought that pulling his pants up would keep his diaper in place, but what did I know?

Nanny B sat in my beige leather rocker and laid LJ on her chest. She rocked back and forth a few times, and in less than five minutes, he was asleep. I sat on the edge of the bed and felt like a proud father with the little progress I'd made today. I didn't really know what I would do without Nanny B around, so I asked if she would move in with me.

"There's plenty of room, Nanny B. Besides, you're here most of the time anyway."

"Jaylin, I don't know. Let me think about it. You really seem like a man who needs his privacy."

"I do, but I need my children in my life even more. I need proper care for them, and that means more to me than anything. So, please," I begged. "Think about it and let me know in a couple of days."

"I will," she whispered. LJ squirmed around in her arms. "Why don't you go get some rest while Mackenzie and LJ are both asleep? You look tired. If you and Scorpio wouldn't have been up all night fooling around, maybe you could have gotten some rest."

I kissed her cheek and left the room. I checked

in on Mackenzie, and since I knew she probably felt neglected because LJ was around, I climbed into bed with her. She woke up just long enough to put her arms around me and went back to sleep.

LJ's loud crying woke up Mackenzie and me. I sluggishly went downstairs to the kitchen to see what all the fussing was about and Mackenzie followed. Nanny B had him all taken care of. He had a bottle in his mouth and was going at it.

"He's fine. Babies do cry, you know?" she said.

"I know, but he cries a little too much, doesn't he?" Mackenzie said.

"I agree," I said, giving her five. We both laughed.

"He doesn't cry any more than you two did when you were babies," said Nanny B. "And, Mackenzie, you still cry, don't you?" Mackenzie's eyes watered, and she wrapped her arms around my legs as if her feelings were hurt.

"Come on, baby," I said, rubbing her back. "Let's go upstairs and see if we can get LJ together."

I took LJ from Nanny B and we all headed upstairs. I put some old sheets on my bed so my good ones wouldn't get messed up, and Mackenzie, LJ, and I sat up watching the Cartoon Network channel.

Mackenzie's Barbies were all over the bed and LJ was staying occupied by putting them into his mouth. He was learning early, I thought, and was definitely going to have his way with the women just like I did.

Nokea came thirty minutes early. Nanny B was downstairs and opened the door for her. When she came into my bedroom and saw me sitting in bed with my kids, she smiled and put her hand on her hip.

"I knew you couldn't handle it. So, don't lie. You called the nanny, didn't you?"

"Woman, please. Nanny B comes over on the weekends anyway. So, don't go talking nonsense."

"Jaylin, stop lying. She already told me you called her crying, begging, and pleading for her to come over here. You should be ashamed of yourself for lying. I thought you said earlier our child is one of the things we shouldn't lie about."

"Okay, busted. But you know I was just playing too, don't you?"

Nokea lifted LJ off the bed. "Yeah, I thought you were playing, but I also knew how much I missed my little baby today." She rubbed noses with LJ and kissed all over his face. I was slightly jealous because he started cracking up as she talked to him. When I talked to him he just looked at me and stared. Shortly after, he'd start crying. I guess he probably wasn't comfortable being around me yet.

"Hello, Mackenzie," Nokea said, noticing Mackenzie's frown.

"Hi. Is LJ going home?" she asked.

I scooted Mackenzie next to me in bed. "Yes, but he'll be back with us next weekend, okay?" I said. She smiled and laid her head against me.

"Jaylin, you know you got that little girl too spoiled. She isn't going to be any good when she gets older."

"Don't go telling me how to raise my kids. If I want to spoil them, I can."

"Well, don't come running to me when they get out of control. You have to start putting your foot down and you can't let them run over you like Mackenzie does."

"Just . . . Be quiet," I said, irritated by Nokea's comments. "Things were going cool between us, until you started running your mouth trying to tell me how to raise my kids. First of all, don't say that shit in front of her. If you got something to say, pull me aside. Have a little respect, all right?"

"And you have respect by cursing like that? I just think—"

"I just think you were leaving." I got off the bed, gathered LJ's things, and escorted Nokea to the door. Before she left, I held LJ and kissed him again. Nanny B and Mackenzie gave their good-byes as well.

After my long nap earlier, I couldn't go back to sleep for nothing. I called Scorpio and told her Mackenzie and I were on our way. It was raining outside, so I covered Mackenzie with my jacket and we ran to the car. Mud covered the bottom of our shoes and messed up my floor mats. I thought about how badly I'd dissed Brashaney for the mud on her shoes, and seriously thought about calling her to apologize, since it had been raining that day as well. But when I thought about her trying to slap me, she was better off left where she was: behind.

I parked in Scorpio's driveway, and there was a nice-ass silver-and-blue Kawasaki motorcycle parked there as well. I wasn't sure who it belonged to, but I covered Mackenzie again and we ran to the door. Scorpio opened with a pencil in her mouth and a grin on her face. She wore a short flimsy flowered sundress that showed her shapely, pretty legs and her cleavage. Mackenzie rushed in, but I stood outside and observed her.

"Are you coming in or what?" she asked while fidgeting and teasing her hair with her fingers.

"Don't you have company?"

"Yes, but he's just—"

"I'll talk to you later, all right?"

I walked off and Scorpio ran up behind me. "Jaylin, why are you tripping? It's not even like that. He's just my tutor, and he came over to help me with my homework."

"Your homework, huh? That's cool, then go do your homework. Why you out here trying to explain something to me that really ain't my business?"

"I just don't want you getting the wrong idea. But seems to me, you're a little jealous."

The rain had slacked up a bit, so I had a moment to set the record straight with her. I stepped face-to-face with her. "Scorpio, let's get something straight, right here and right now. You are free to date any damn body you want to. And, so am I. So, jealous? No. Disappointed? Yes. Disappointed that I fucked you the way I did last night. You really didn't deserve it, and it was a waste of my time."

Her mouth opened in disbelief. "What? If anything, you don't deserve me. I'm trying to be nice and spare your fucking feelings, but you're too much for me. If you really want to know, your dick ain't that damn good, Jaylin, I've been the one wasting my time."

"Okay, if you say so, baby. But the next time I

fuck you, or if I decide to fuck you again, keep all that hollaring, moaning, and groaning, 'Oh, I love you so much' bullshit to yourself."

"I will. And the next time we get up, it'll be my call, not yours."

The rain started to pick up again, and I was in no mood to stand outside continuing this argument with Scorpio. Her gripes about my ill treatment fell on deaf ears, so I got in my car and headed home.

The windshield wipers screeched against the window, as the rain slowed again. My mind wandered back to my amazing day with LJ and Mackenzie. They had turned my whole life around and made me feel like I could breathe again. My only problems were these damn crazy-ass women I had in my life. Nokea, Scorpio, Brashaney, and Felicia, who at least wasn't too far gone. I couldn't figure out which one was stressing me the most. Was it Nokea for declining my proposal and denying me my son all these months? Was it Scorpio for allowing me to support her and thinking she could bring home any Tom, Dick, and Harry she wanted to and I would keep paying the bills? Or Brashaney, who was just flat-out downright stupid, and couldn't look like a true lady no matter how hard she tried? Maybe even Felicia, who really wasn't stressing me at all, but I couldn't stand because we had too much in common.

I snickered about how Scorpio claimed I wasn't *that* good. What nerve? Out of all the women I'd slept with, she knew better than to let something that stupid slip from her mouth. Every time we had sex, she'd be coming four and five times in less than an hour. As a matter of fact, since I'd met her ass, she hadn't been able to go one week without my dick inside her. The only time she'd been without it was when I kicked her out for lying to me about being a stripper. So, she could kiss my ass with that statement. She knew it didn't get any better than this, and whoever it was at her place, he was wasting his time.

I was on Wild Horse Creek Road in Chesterfield when I noticed a silver Jaguar slumped on the side of the road. I pulled over behind it and got out of my car. As I neared the Jag, a young white woman with long, straight blond hair was inside dialing her cell phone. She looked frightened, but when I offered to help she seemed to relax. She opened the car door and got out as the rain started to pour down on both of us. I took my jacket off and put it over her head.

"Thank you," she said, wiping the rain from her eyes.

"What happened?" I asked.

"My car slid. I tried to get out of the mud, but it's getting deeper. When I called for help, my cell phone went dead."

"Come get in my car. You can use my phone, or if you live close by, I can take you home." We hurried to my car and got in. She wiped the rain from her face again and pulled her hair back.

"Thanks again, Mr . . . ?"

"Jaylin, Jaylin Rogers. And yours?"

"Heather McDaniels." We shook hands.

"Nice to meet you, Ms. McDaniels, but, uh . . . Do you live close by?"

"Yes. Less than ten minutes away. Would you

mind taking me home? I'd like to call someone to come get my car."

"No problem."

I turned up the heat to dry us, and Heather rubbed her hands together in front of the vents.. I immediately noticed a blinding platinum diamond ring on her finger. Had to be at least five or six karats, and the baguettes really set it off. Somebody was lucky. I just wasn't sure if it was her husband or her. From what I could see, though, he was the prizewinner. She was an attractive white woman. Had a nice slim body, big, juicy, succulent breasts, and a fairly shapely ass. I had already peeped that when she got out of her car.

Heather directed me to her house, and I pulled my 'Cedes into the curvy, stoned driveway. The house was built like a castle, with a beautiful waterfall in front of it. It had to be least a two- or three-million-dollar home, and here I'd thought my million-dollar home had it going on. If I would stop all the splurging and cut back on the material bullshit, a home like this would be no problem for me.

"Jaylin," she said, reaching out her hand. "Thank you so much. You are definitely a life-saver. I don't know what I would have done if you hadn't shown up."

"Glad to be of assistance," I said, shaking her hand back. She reached into her purse and tried to give me a hundred-dollar bill.

"No, no, please, I can't take it. Like I said, glad to be of assistance to you in your time of trouble."

She put the money back into her purse. "Okay, well at least come inside for a drink. Besides, my husband is out of town on business, I could use some company."

"A drink, huh?"

"Yes, whatever your heart desires. I'll show you around the place, too." I tapped my fingertips on the steering wheel and hesitated. "Come on, Jaylin. If my husband knew what you did for me, he'd insist. He'd actually kill me if he found out I didn't repay you."

With that being said, we headed to the tall glass double doors that opened to the entrance of the house. Nothing but beauty hit me as I walked in. In the foyer sat two baby grand pianos: a white piano on one side and a black one on the other. Above them was a T-staircase that went from the great room to the dining room. Every piece of drapery that covered the windows was satin white with black embroidery, and thick, black tassels pulled them aside to reveal the sheer curtains in the middle. The floors were covered with black, gray, and white swirling, so shiny I could see a clear image of myself.

As I followed her into the bonus room, I just shook my head. It was located in a sunken area next to the breakfast room, and had a floor made of glass to show off the lower level. Designed like a sports bar, a cherry-wood bar stretched from one end to the other, with everlasting bottles of alcohol behind it. A humongous television was built into the wall, and cherry-wood cocktail tables circled the floor. Above the tables were crystal lights that hung from the cathedral ceiling. I had never seen anything quite like it. Now this was what I called straight-up living right. I stood, mesmerized, and Heather gave me a towel.

"Jaylin?" she said, trying to get my attention.

"I think your place got it going on, that's what I think."

"Yeah, we've put an extreme amount of money into our home to get it like this." She walked behind the bar. "So, what are you drinking?"

"Some Remy would be nice." I sat at the bar and she poured me a glass of Remy. She poured herself a glass aside of mine.

"Jaylin, while you're drinking up, I'm going upstairs to get out of these wet clothes and make a phone call. Make yourself at home. If you would like another drink, feel free to pour yourself one."

"Okay, but one will be fine. I don't want to over do it, you know what I mean?" She nodded and left the room.

Thirty minutes must have gone by when Heather returned. She came in the room with a little of nothing on. She wore a soft pink lace top with skimpy lace boy shorts to match. I could clearly see the hardness in her nipples, and the nicely trimmed brown hairs covering her pussy. She definitely wasn't a true blonde. When she walked behind the bar, her bronzed ass was begging me to fuck her. I dropped my head and smiled. I knew I was moments away from going where I had never dreamed of going before. White women had never been in my vocabulary, but maybe it was time for a change.

I had finished nearly half of the Remy bottle and felt woozy.

"You're quite a drinker, Mr. Rogers," she said, holding the bottle in her hand.

"No, I'm really not. I just couldn't help myself. Got kind of lonely waiting on you to return."

"Well, a handsome man such as yourself should never be lonely."

"I'm cool with it sometimes. At least being by yourself gives you a chance to think things out and sort of put shit in perspective."

"I agree, but I get my share of being alone, too." Heather took a few sips from her glass, and by the way her eyes flirted with me, I could tell she was ready to dig into me. I was straight-up feeling digging into her as well.

We chatted for at least another hour, and there was no doubt about it that she was lonely. Husband was a millionaire and couldn't even find the time to make love to his beautiful wife at home. Financially, she had it going on, but physically, she was deprived. So, not trying to rush the pussy, I pretended like I was getting tired and was ready to go. I stood and yawned as I stretched my arms.

"Well, Heather, I really must be going. Got a busy day at work tomorrow and need to get my rest."

She came from behind the bar. "Jaylin, I really enjoyed your company. You're awfully handsome and maybe some day you'll invite me to your place for a drink, since you live close by."

"I just might do that." She walked in front of me and headed toward the door. My head was spinning, but not enough to keep my dick from getting hard while looking at the cheeks of her ass slightly peeking through her shorts.

"Goodnight," she said, opening the door.

I stepped onto the porch. "Goodnight, Heather."

I reached in my pocket and felt for my keys. Wet again from the rain, Heather followed behind me, and grabbed my hand as I pressed the chirper to open my door.

"Stay," she said, tightly holding my hand. "Besides, you shouldn't be drinking and driving anyway. I'd hate for something to happen to you."

I looked at her pretty self as the rain poured down on her body. She moved her hair behind her ears and pressed herself against me. Then, she lifted my shirt and pulled it over my head. She rubbed her hands across the ridges of my six-pack, and placed her lips on my nipple. I was turned on, and wiped my eyes as the rain fell harder. Heather continued to lick my chest and I stood wondering if this was something I really wanted to do.

I quickly came to my senses pulling her hair back and leaning down to kiss her. Her lips were soft like butter melting, and they did just that when I sucked them into my mouth. I squeezed her ass while she rubbed her hands up and down my back. Then I ripped her shorts, and sunk my finger into her wetness.

Her head went back and her voice softened. "Jaylin, I'm getting so wet."

I whispered in her ear, "From the rain, or from how I'm touching you?"

"Definitely from the way you're touching me."

She moved away from me and lay down in the grass. When she opened her legs, the last thing on my mind was how dirty I was about to get by fucking her on the muddy, soggy ground. Too, I was glad that the house sat on several acres of land and no one would see us. With that in mind, I stepped out of my pants and kneeled down in front of her. My knees slightly sunk in the mud, as I leaned forward and slid myself inside of her.

Trying to keep her body free from the rain, I lay over her. She was tight as ever and I was only able to slide about six inches of my nine inside of her.

"Why are you doing this to me?" she said, painfully.

"So, what are you saying, Heather? Would you like for me to stop?"

"No, and I want you to give it all to me."

All she had to do was ask, so I prepared myself to do just that. She turned around and kneeled in front of me, while pressing her ass against my thang. I lifted her shirt over her head and massaged her breasts together. When I felt she was ready, I had my way with her. I gripped her tiny waistline from behind and slammed my nine-plus inches of goodness against her tight walls.

Mud covered our bodies, and we continued rolling around on the ground fucking each other. After a few more minutes of intense screwing, we worked our way into the house and finished up in the foyer. She looked over at me and laughed, as we lay with dry mud covering nearly our entire bodies.

"This is fucking crazy, Jaylin. I can't believe I let a complete stranger screw me the way you just did."

"Yeah, this was some wild shit, wasn't it? But look at it this way—just pretend that I met you at a party tonight and we're having a one-night stand. I mean, what's the difference from what we just did? People do it all the time."

"But not like this, Jaylin. I mean, you are really a satisfying man. I don't think I've ever had sex to that extreme before."

And you probably never will again, I thought. It wasn't that Heather wasn't cool to kick it with, but I already had enough on my plate. The last thing I needed was a married white woman hounding me.

Heather asked me to join her in the shower, but I declined. I told her I needed to be going and she understood. She walked me to my car, kissed me again, and said good-bye.

My car was a complete mess. Mud was everywhere and my clothes were drenched. I was pissed at myself for letting something so expensive get messed up like this. When I got home around four o'clock in the morning, I took a thirty-minute shower and scrubbed off the mud I had on my body and in my hair. I put on some clean clothes, and drove to the nearest car wash. I did the best I could cleaning it considering I wasn't a professional, but most likely, I'd have to take it to a cash wash later to get the inside detailed the right way.

By the time I finished my half-assed job, it was almost six o'clock in the morning. There was no way in hell I was going to work, so I climbed into bed, and sat up for about another hour thinking about Miss Heather. I had broken all the rules and couldn't understand why. One thing just led to another, I'd guessed. If anything, the jealousy I felt about Scorpio being with another man might have been my reasoning, but who knows. Stephon warned me a long time about sticking to my rules, and said if I didn't, I'd for damn sure pay for it. He'd left me several more messages about us discussing what had happened, but I hadn't found it in my heart to forgive him just yet. I expected a bunch of bullshit from my women, but never did I expect him to play me like he did. Soon, though, we'd have to work it out because I missed being around him.

Chapter 7
Scorpio

Icouldn't believe Jay-Baby being upset with me
because I'd had company. If he had come inside
he really would have been upset after he saw how
gorgeous Shane was. Thing was, I really didn't anticipate seeing Shane on Sunday. I asked him to
come back on Tuesday after his class, but when he
called Sunday, and I just happened to be studying,
I invited him over.

On his second visit, I started to understand algebra a little better. The first time he'd come over, I
think I must have been too occupied with how
handsome he was and couldn't stay focused.

I knew how important it was for me to get the
hang of things, so I put my feelings aside and managed to learn something this time around.

Who was I fooling? I thought. Jaylin's spectacular
loving the night before had me thinking about
him all day long. And whether I wanted to face the
truth or not, his loving had me messed up. I

couldn't let him know that, of course, but nobody could lay it down like he could. He was keeping me so satisfied that I really had no desire to go anywhere else.

Shane, however, was looking awfully spiffy last night. And something about the way he lifted his thick, muscular legs on and off his motorcycle just did something to me. Feeling foolish about not even trying to pursue a relationship with him, I decided to call him. He answered with a deep, masculine voice.

"Shane?"

"Yes."

"Hi, it's Scorpio."

"I know. I mean, I recognize your voice."

"Listen, I was just calling to thank you for coming over last night. Also, I wanted to be sure you made it home safely in the rain. My intentions were to call last night, but it was kind of late when you left."

"Yeah, I did all right. My bike slid a few times, but I made it."

"Well . . . that's pretty much all I wanted." I tried to get my thoughts together. "Oh, by the way, Shane, you don't have to come by tomorrow since you stopped by last night. I think I'm starting to get the hang of algebra."

"Are you sure? It gets a tad bit harder, you know."

"Yes, I'm sure it does. Unless . . . you'd like to have dinner tomorrow night."

"Dinner? I thought you'd never ask. Remember, I'll be a little late, though."

"That's fine. Would you like to eat in, or eat out?

I mean, dine in, or dine out," I said, correcting my-self.

He laughed. "I'd really like to eat out, but din-ing out will be better, for now anyway."

Now, this fine Negro just might have started something. "Let's say we meet at Houlihan's in the Union Station around nine?"

"Sounds perfect. I'll see you tomorrow, Scor-pio."

Shane hung up, and I got dressed to leave. If any-thing, tomorrow would shed some light on what direction I wanted to go with him. For the first time, no business between us, strictly personal.

Mackenzie was now in some type of uppity pre-school that Jaylin put her in. I was totally against her going there because there were no black chil-dren around for her to play with. I wanted her in a school that had a diverse student body. Not in a school where she'd be accustomed to only one par-ticular race. For now, she seemed to enjoy school, so I wasn't going to make too much fuss about it.

I dropped her off, and was heading to school myself when I picked up my cell phone to call Jaylin at his office. First, I wanted to see if he was still soaking about my company last night, then I wanted to talk to him about Mackenzie's school.

Angela answered, so I pretended to be someone else. I had no intention of befriending any woman who slept with the man I was in love with. When she said he was out of the office today, I called him at home. I didn't get an answer, so I turned around and drove to his house. His car was in the driveway, and I parked mine next to it.

I knocked on the door and could hear Jaylin's

shoes sliding on the floor. He opened the door and gave me a blank stare.

"What?" he yelled with attitude. "Can a brotha get some peace around here!"

I pushed him aside and walked in. "Why didn't you take your lazy butt to work?" I looked around the room. "And where is she? I know somebody's over here."

"Scorpio, I was on the phone in my office when you knocked on the door. And if I do have company, that ain't your business."

"Yes, it is, so stop fooling yourself thinking that it ain't. I'm sorry for interrupting your business calls, but I just stopped by to talk to you about last night. Also, about this pre-school you enrolled Mackenzie in."

"I'm not in the mood to talk about last night," he said, still standing by the door. "Come back some other time. Besides, I'm tired—getting ready to go back to bed."

"Now that's an interesting thought. Can I join you?"

"Nope. Ain't in the mood for that either. Anyway, didn't I just give you enough of my horrible-ass loving the other night? Besides, I'm sure your mystery man can pick up where I left off."

"I'm sure he can too," I said, walking toward him. "But, I see how you wanna play this. We only get down when you want to get down, right?"

Jaylin nodded. "You got that right. And since I'm kicking it down like I know I do, I say when, where, and how it happens. Thing is, if you say it's as bad as you claim it is, don't be over here begging for it."

"Beg? Never. Just remember, though, I'm not on your time, Jaylin."

"Yes, you are, Scorpio. So stop standing here wasting your time going through the drama. You're on my time just like everybody else is." He opened the door for me to leave. "Now, goodbye. I gotta get some rest and I'll call you later."

"Oooo . . . Listen to you. You really think you have me under your wings, don't you? And even if you do, people and situations change all the time."

"And I expect them to change. But remember, they also change back. So, you go ahead and let your little mystery man tag that ass, and when he don't fuck you like I do, don't come running back to me. I don't work too well with leftovers anyway."

"Come on, now. All you've been dishing out is leftovers. Leftovers that should have been bagged up and thrown out like a week-old piece of bread. Don't fool yourself thinking I'm some doormat you can step on whenever you want to. Lately, I've been feeling up to a challenge anyway."

"Look, well, challenge your ass out of this door." He swung the door open even wider. "I'm not in the mood for this shit, damn, I'm tired. You know how groggy I get when I tired, Scorpio, so call me later, all right? I promise you we'll talk then."

I rolled my eyes and walked out of the door. Jaylin smacked me hard on my ass. "Do me a favor and tell the brotha, whoever he is, not to straddle you from behind. That's my work place." He winked, laughed, and slammed the door behind me.

Jaylin knew he had me wrapped around his finger. Our half-assed relationship and respect for one another was slowly, but surely, dissolving.

Thing was, I couldn't tell if he was jealous about me seeing somebody else, or if he really didn't give a shit. The more I thought about it, I knew I had to put him to the test. I had to know for myself what his true feelings were for me. And even though I hated to play games with him, Shane was going to help me figure Jaylin out.

Tuesday rolled around with the quickness. Jaylin and I never had that conversation we were supposed to have. When I called him Monday night, he said that he was busy and he'd have to call me back. When he did call, he asked for Mackenzie, stayed on the phone with her for about fifteen minutes, then hung up. I wasn't going to make him talk to me, but eventually he'd want to. And whenever that time came, I was not going to make myself available.

I sat at a table in Houlihan's waiting for Shane. I remembered him saying he was going to be a little late, but I had a serious problem waiting on people, especially men. I went to the ladies room for the third time to make sure I was looking delightful. The mirror didn't lie. I couldn't complain about anything. My tan, linen, spaghetti-strapped mini-dress was working every curve of my body. My hair hung down on my shoulders, and was full of bouncing behaving curls. The three-inch brown leather heels I wore gave me just enough height to swish my ass from side to side as I walked. And after getting approval from the men that were staring, I went back to the table and continued to wait for Shane.

When I looked up and saw Felicia heading my

way, I let out a deep sigh. She grinned and sat at the table with me.

"Girrrrl . . . you know we really should stop meeting like this," she said, picking up a piece of bread from the table, and biting into it.

"Yes, we really should, especially since we don't even like each other."

"Now, I never said I didn't like you, Scorpio. All I ever said is that Jaylin can do a hellava lot better, that's all."

"You think? Do you really think he can do better than me? And if so, with who? You?"

"Of course with me," she said, sitting up straight, and clinching her hands together in front of her. "You see, Scorpio, you didn't check out the way he looked at me the other night, and you sure don't know what type of history we have together. So, if I were you, I'd be counting the days down I have left with him. And in case you haven't noticed yet, we're like two peas in a pod, they always stick together."

I placed my elbow on the table and put my hand on the side of my face. "Felicia, I feel so sorry for you. You have one hell of an imagination. You know what," I said, sitting back and reaching into my purse. I fumbled through my wallet and pulled out a business card. "I previously dated a psychiatrist. Here's his card. Feel free to call him any time, he could really help." I slid the card over to her.

She picked it up and tapped it on the table. "Funny, bitch, but after I call him, and screw him, that'll make two men we've shared. And when I find out how—"

"Felicia Davenport?" Shane interrupted, walking up to the table. She stood up and wrapped her arms tightly around him.

"Shayneeeee Alexander. Long time, no see. What are you doing here tonight?"

"I'm here to have dinner with Ms. Valentino." Shane looked down at me sitting at the table.

"Hello, Shane," I said, closing my eyes because I knew Felicia was about to eat this up. And after he leaned down and gave me a quick peck on the cheek, she went at it.

"So, you two know each other?" she asked.

"Yeah, we do. Scorpio's one of my students. And I take it that you two know each other as well."

"Of course. Scorpio and I go way back. We were just catching up on old times before you came."

"Well, don't let me interrupt. I'll go grab another chair, and Felicia, you can join us for dinner." Shane walked away to get a chair.

Felicia leaned down and whispered in my ear. "If you fuck him, ho, that'll be three men we've shared. He likes a woman with a deep throat so, uh, treat him well, okay? Being the experienced tramp that you are, I'm sure you won't bite." She quickly rose up, as Shane came back to the table. It took everything I had not to get up and kick her ass. Instead, I just smiled as if I wasn't even tripping.

"Shane, I'm sorry," she said. "I really must be getting back to dinner with my bosses. I'm sure they're wondering where the heck I went." She gave Shane a pat on the back, and another squeezing hug. "Shane, call me sometime. It'll be good to catch up on old times." She looked at me, but I turned my head to look away. "Scorpio, tell Jaylin I said hello. Shane, you remember Jaylin don't you? Jaylin Rogers?"

"Yeah, you know I remember Jay Rogers. How can I forget? Anyway, I haven't seen him since I've been back from Atlanta."

"Well, I'm sure Scorpio can find him for you. She's got a way of sniffing him out." Felicia walked away from the table. I couldn't believe how ignorant she was. That was one bitch whose eyes I wouldn't mind scratching out.

"Did I come at a bad time?" Shane asked and then took a seat.

"No, actually, you came at the right time. As you can see, Felicia and I really don't get along. I used to date Jaylin and so did she. She's got a problem with letting go of the past."

"The past, huh. So, does that mean you're not seeing him anymore?"

"No, I'm not seeing him anymore. He adopted my daughter, Mackenzie, and takes very good care of her. Other than that, our relationship has been on the down-low for a long time." I felt bad lying to Shane, but I wasn't really sure how well he knew Jaylin. "So what about you and Felicia? How well do you know her?"

Shane smiled. "I'd say I know her very well. We used to kick it, but, actually, she started seeing Jaylin and things got a bit complicated. Jaylin and I used to be very good friends, boys. We hung out together and everything."

"Really?" I wanted to know more. "So, did the two of you fall out over her?"

"Somewhat, but I really didn't trip. Besides, Felicia wasn't worth the fight. She was dating one of my other boys when I met her, so we just passed her on down. I don't know what Jaylin said or did to her, but she kicked it with him for a long time. From my understanding, he was the only brotha tapping that for a while. And as promiscuous as Felicia is, that's a miracle."

Now, I for damn sure knew why, I thought. When a woman did step Jaylin's way, it was so hard to let go. I was a prime example of that. Since I wasn't really sure how to handle the news about Shane being an old friend of Jaylin's, I quickly changed the subject.

"Are you ready to order?"

"Yes, I'm starving." Shane glanced at the menu, then put it down. "Hey, tell me something," he said.

"What?"

"You don't have to answer this unless you want to, but are you in love with Jaylin?"

I tapped my fingernails on the table and thought about being dishonest. I didn't want to talk about Jaylin the entire night, so I answered and tried to move on. "Yes, but I'm working on getting him out of my system. You know what I mean?"

"Scorpio, I know what you mean, but somebody could get hurt. And this time, it's not going to be me."

"Let's hope not," I said, and looked down at my menu.

Shane and I had a marvelous dinner. Jaylin's name didn't come up again for the rest of the night, but Felicia's did. We couldn't help but talk about her. And even though Shane dogged her out, part of me knew when he got home, he was going to be making a phone call to her. So, with that in mind, I was going to hold off on giving myself to him a tad bit longer.

Chapter 8

Nokea

LJ's and Jaylin's birthdays were less than two weeks away. Our setback with the wedding incident was almost a month ago and it seemed as if he'd put his bitterness behind him. I called Jaylin because I wasn't sure if he'd already made birthday plans. He suggested that we go through our normal routine and have lunch at Café Lapadero, in Clayton, then take LJ to Chuck E. Cheese. A birthday party was out of the question. I told Jaylin I wasn't up for it, but the truth was that Daddy was still upset with Jaylin and didn't want him around. I figured it was best to keep them as far away from each other as possible. And since Daddy was still barely speaking to me, I kept my distance.

Pat, LJ, and I went to Plaza Frontenac to shop. I put LJ in his stroller and rushed through the door to spend my portion of the money Jaylin had given me.

We spent hours and hours at the mall, and when it was all said and done, we had a security guard help us back to the car with our packages. I bought so many outfits for LJ, and found some exquisite clothes at Neiman's for myself. Pat bought shoes from nearly every shoe store she could find, insisting that, since she and Chad were on a budget, shoeboxes would be easier to hide.

We laughed as we got out of the car and sneaked into Pat's house to hide the boxes. Chad was in the living room watching TV, so we went in the back way, hoping he wouldn't see us. But as soon as we came through the back door, he stood before us with his arms folded. Pat shoved all the bags at me.

"Girl, now you know you shouldn't have bought all those shoes. I told you I don't have any outfits to match them," she said, trying to play it off like the shoes were mine. Chad put a piece of chicken in his mouth and smacked.

"I don't see how or why she would bring all those shoes in here if you two don't even wear the same size. It doesn't make no sense to me. What do you think, Nokea? Does it make sense to you?"

I placed my hand over my mouth and laughed. Pat was caught up. "All right, all right," she said. "I'm busted. But baby, sorry, I couldn't resist. They had some good sales at the mall. You should go out there yourself."

Chad ignored Pat and left the kitchen. She told me to have a seat, while she went upstairs to put away her shoes. LJ was sound asleep in his baby seat, and I didn't want to wake him. I would have asked Jaylin to watch him, but LJ was already spending too much time with him. I was feeling kind of neglected. Since Nanny B had moved in with Jaylin, he was coming over to pick up LJ every chance he got. I didn't mind, but LJ running back and forth from both of our houses was driving me crazy. When I tried to complain, Jaylin said I wanted to deny him time with his son, which was something I definitely didn't want to do, so I kept quiet.

Pat was taking forever, so I went to the refrigerator and pulled out a pitcher of lemonade. As I reached for a glass on the shelf, Chad came in and stood behind me.

"Let me get that for you, Nokea." He reached up and took a glass from the shelf.

"Thanks, Chad. So, how's the cleaning business going? Pat said it's been booming."

"Yeah, it's doing okay. She's just spending money as fast as we can make it."

"Well, you know how she is. Hasn't changed a bit since you married her."

"No, she hasn't. So, uh, how are things going with you? She told me about what happened between you and Jaylin. Sorry that it didn't work out."

"Yeah, I'm sorry too, but at least we got that little precious child over there to share."

"He's adorable. I wish Pat and I could have some children. We talked about adopting, but she keeps putting it off."

"Don't go giving up just yet, Chad. It might happen one day. Seems like she's seeking all options from what she's telling me."

"That might be what she's telling you, but Pat really don't want any children, Nokea. Every time I

talk about having a baby she just blows me off."
Chad frowned and took a seat at the kitchen table.
I walked over behind him, and placed my hand on
his back.

"It'll be fine, Chad. If she can't have any children, there are plenty of them waiting to be
adopted." He dropped his head, and with true
concern, I softly rubbed his back. "Don't be so
hard on yourself. You and Pat have a wonderful
marriage. What's meant to be will be."

I poured him a glass of lemonade and wondered what was really going on. He seemed like he
was going through something. I wasn't sure what,
though, especially since Pat made everything seem
all good between them.

As I stood with the glass in my hand, gazing out
the window, Chad came up from behind me again.
This time, he put his arms around my waist, and
touched his lips to my neck. I immediately turned
and pushed him back.

"What are you doing?" I yelled.

"You are so beautiful, Nokea. The way you
touched me, I knew—"

"Wait a minute," I said sharply. "What do you
mean by the way I touched you?"

Just then, Pat came back into the kitchen.
"What's all the fussing about? I hope y'all ain't in
here arguing over those shoes. Listen, Chad, if it's
that big a deal, I'll take them back."

"Naw, baby, you don't have to. Nokea and I were
just arguing over who LJ looks like." He waited for
a response, but I didn't say a word. I was so
stunned that he would step to me like that, I didn't
quite know what to do.

He kissed Pat on the cheek, and went back into the living room. I gathered LJ's things and hurried to go. Pat noticed my demeanor.

"Are you okay?" she asked.

"I'm fine, Pat. I just got a severe headache all of a sudden. I'd better get home and lie down."

"Okay, you do look a little flushed." She felt my head. "Seems like you're running a fever, too."

Pat helped me gather my things and walked me to my car. I strapped LJ in his car seat and took off. I was sick to my stomach on the drive home. How was I going to tell Pat? She'd been like a sister to me. But there was no way in hell I could keep something like this from her.

The phone was ringing off the hook as I made my way through the door. I tried to put LJ down before I answered it, but couldn't get to it in time. Whoever it was called right back, though. When I answered, it was Chad.

"Nokea?" I remained silent. "Listen, I'm sorry about tonight, but I just couldn't help myself. You're really looking good these days and I was just hoping—"

"Chad, if you ever, and I mean ever, put your hands on me again, I'll tell Pat everything." I hung up. The phone rang again. "Hello," I yelled.

"You won't tell because you want me just as much as I want—"

I hung up again and rubbed my temples. This was too much, and I knew it meant nothing but trouble. When the phone rang again I snatched it up and gave it to Chad.

"Listen!" I screamed. "You sorry motherfucker! Stop calling here!"

"Damn, what in the hell did I do?" It was Jaylin. I was relieved, but still upset. I couldn't help but cry. "Nokea? Are you okay?" he asked. "Where's LJ?"

"I'm fine." I sniffled and tried to get myself together.

"Well, you don't sound fine. I'm on my way."

"Please, don't. I said everything is fine."

He hung up.

I took the phone off the hook because I didn't want Chad calling back. I gave LJ a bath, sang him a lullaby, and he was out like a light.

When Jaylin knocked at the door, I was getting ready to take my bath. I slid into my robe and house shoes, and went to the door.

"You really didn't have to come," I said. "I told you everything was fine."

"I came by to make sure everything was cool with my son, that's all. So, where is he?"

"I just put him to bed, Jaylin. You can go check on him if you'd like, but please don't wake him."

Jaylin went into LJ's room and I went back into mine. Moments later, he came in with LJ on his shoulder.

"What did I tell you, Jaylin? You just don't listen, do you?"

He sat down on the sofa. "No, I don't listen, especially when it comes to my son. If he wakes up, I'll take him home with me."

"Do whatever. I don't even care anymore."

"I know you too well, Nokea, what's ailing you?"

"Everything."

"Everything like what?"

"Everything like you, the baby, my job, Pat."

"Okay, so what about me?"

"You just seem like a different person, that's all. I really thought you would have worked things out with me but you seem to be moving in another direction." I continued to express my concerns about us being together, but Jaylin ignored me. He wouldn't even look at me, just kept kissing LJ's cheeks. "Jaylin, did you hear what I said?"

"I heard you. But, I told you what was up with us. I need more time. Still hurting from what you did. Give me time to heal, all right?"

"How much time do you need? I'm feeling really lonely these days. The only thing I do is work and come home to be with LJ. On the weekends I at least had Pat to chill with, but I'm not sure how much longer that's going to last."

"Why? Did y'all fall out or something?"

"No, nothing like that, but Chad made a pass at me today and it upset me. When you called, I thought you were him. I don't know what to do, and if I tell Pat, I'm not sure how she's going to react."

"I knew that motherfucker was up to no good. You always bragging on how he's such a good man, but I knew something wasn't right. Honestly, though, you do need to tell her. Don't keep anything like that from her. If she's a true friend, she'll understand."

"Yeah, I guess you're right. I'll tell her. I don't know when, but I will."

"I suggest you not wait like you did in telling me about LJ. You see how much damage that's done, right?"

"Yeah, I know, but it's not going to be easy telling my best friend that her husband came on to me either."

"No, it's not, but you just got to deal with it and do the right thing."

After hearing Jaylin's deep voice, LJ lifted his head off Jaylin's shoulder. Jaylin stood up and started to leave the room. "I'll take him home with me tonight. Get some rest and I'll bring him back tomorrow."

"Jaylin?" I said, softly.

"Yeah."

"Please don't go. Stay with me tonight. I don't want to be alone." My eyes watered as I waited for him to respond. I just knew he was going to say no, but when he sat back down on the sofa, I smiled.

An hour later, Jaylin put LJ back to sleep. When he came back into my room, I had already taken my bath and was standing naked while drying myself.

His eyes stayed glued to me. "Hey, sorry, I didn't know you were—"

"It's okay. It's not like you haven't seen me naked before." He walked further into the room. "Here," I said, handing him some peaches-and-cream lotion. "Would you mind rubbing this on me?"

He took the lotion bottle from me. I lay on my stomach and rested my head on my hands. Jaylin stood motionless for a few seconds, then sat on the bed next to me. He squeezed some lotion in his hands and rubbed them on my back. I just knew he was going for my butt first, but he didn't. I closed my eyes, and his hands felt like they were melting into my body.

When he did get to my ass, I was on fire. He massaged it in a circular motion, and not being able to handle his touch anymore, I rolled over and sat up. His eyes lowered to my breast.

"What's wrong?" he asked.

"Nothing, nothing at all. I just—" I paused, and before I said anything else, I leaned him back and straddled him. I placed my lips on his and he went with the flow kissing me back. He bent his left leg, lifting me a bit so I could feel his hard dick poking me through his pants.

Our intense kissing came to a halt and we stared into each other's eyes. "I love you, Jaylin. Only God knows how much I love you."

I reached for his shirt to take it off, but he stopped me. He pecked me a few more times on the lips and held my face in his hands.

"I love you too, Nokea, but I can't do this."

"Yes, you can. Just let go of your anger and make love to me, please," I begged.

He pecked my lips again and rose up. "Trust me, you don't want to be with me right about now. All I'm going to do is hurt you even more. I'm no good, baby. And making love to you is only going to complicate things. I won't be able to live with myself if I keep on hurting you."

A tear rolled down my face and I rested my head on his chest. "How can you lay here and not want to make love to me? Don't you want me anymore? Don't I even appeal to you?"

Jaylin wiped my tears. "Of course I want to make

love to you. And yes, you do turn me on. But I'm saving the best for last. I'm not going to put you in this mess I'm in right now. So please, don't make me do this to you, okay?"

His words didn't ease my pain, so I got off him and lay sideways. Jaylin turned on his side too and placed his hand on my hip. "Nokea, you don't ever have to be lonely. Just call me, and you know I'll always be here for you. I need you to be strong for our son. Don't let anybody stop you from being there for him, not even me."

"I'm trying, but I don't understand why we just can't be together. If you love me, then why do you continue to fight this so much? Don't you see what this is doing to us?"

"Yeah, I do. It's making our love stronger and stronger every day. It's making me feel as if I'm missing out on something. Like right now, our being apart is making us want each other even more. I'm not playing a game with you, Nokea, I'm just making sure when marriage presents itself again, we're both going to be ready."

Even though I disagreed with Jaylin, he wasn't giving in. It seemed as if he was going to take all the time he needed, but I felt as if time was on neither of our sides. I fell asleep in his arms, and when I woke up, he was lying on the living room couch with LJ on his chest. They were knocked out, so I gave them a kiss and went back into my room for the rest of the night. I was hurt that Jaylin wouldn't make love to me; I wanted him to so badly. Deep inside, I truly felt that he was making promises he wouldn't be able to keep. How could he promise what he did with life being so darn unpredictable? I knew his feelings for Scorpio were getting strong, and I also knew he was still making love to her. *So why?* I thought. *Why not give me what I wanted for a change?* Truly hurt, I laid my head on my pillow and cried throughout the night.

Chapter 9

Jaylin

There wasn't enough time on the weekends to handle my business, so I called Angela and made myself another three-day weekend. Mr. Schmidt knew that I really didn't need a job, but working at the office got me out of the house. Awhile back, he'd agreed to let me create my own schedule, so going to work on Mondays was eventually going to become a thing of the past. Taking Mondays off would give me an extra day with LJ and Mackenzie. Nanny B was living with me now, so everything was running pretty smoothly.

I got up around seven o'clock in the morning and headed for the gym to work out my thirty-two-year-old body. I had a workout room in my basement, but I loved conversing with people at the gym. I hadn't gone for a while, though, because I was trying to avoid Stephon. Since Nokea had confirmed her love for me, that gave me a little more assurance that she really never loved Stephon to begin with. So there wasn't no sense in me putting off talking to him any longer.

When I got to the gym, I didn't see Stephon anywhere in sight. He was always there before I was, but I figured he'd been slacking too. I took a seat on a weight bench, and laid back to lift the weights somebody had left on the bar. I strained to push the weights up for the tenth time, and looked up at Stephon. He held the bar tight to my chest, so I couldn't lift it.

"Nigga, why haven't you been returning my calls," he said. I pressed back and strained to lift the weights off my chest.

"Because, I don't like your motherfucking ass, that's why."

"Good. And I don't like your ass either."

We continued forcing the bar in opposite directions, and after a few more minutes of intense work, I gave up and let the bar rest on my chest. Stephon lifted it and put it back on the bench.

"See, that's what your ass get for not working out. I've been here every day, and thought I would see your high-yellow ass. I guess you've giving up on working out too, huh?"

I sat up on the bench and stretched my back. "Naw . . . I've been working out. Just not at the gym. Besides, I didn't want to see your punk-ass anyway."

"So, what you want, Jay? Do you wanna fight and get this shit over with or what? You might be a year older than me, but you know I'll kick your ass right about now, don't you?"

"Hell, yeah, I wanna fight. Meet me outside so I

can finally get this shit off my chest." I stood up, and we headed toward the door.

"Come on you little Mighty-Mouse-looking motherfucker. And when I kick your ass, don't go running home to your bitches crying like a little punk," he said jokingly.

"And don't you go running home to that bitch, Felicia, telling her my damn business either."

When we got outside, we continued to rant back and forth. We stared each other down with balled fists. "Jay, I'm gonna say this one more time and one more time only. I'm not going to kiss your ass like your women do, so this is it, man. I regret what happened and I'm sorry. I over stepped my boundaries and I know it. I got straight-up love for ya, cuz, and if you can ever find it in your heart to forgive me, I'd be grateful." He put up his fists. I did the same, then slammed him in the face with a left hook. He fell backward, and sat up on his elbows.

"Next time," he said, "bring out some blood, nigga, all right?" I reached out my hand and helped him get off the ground.

"Naw, next time, don't let this shit happen again. When I tell you a woman that I love is off limits, I mean it. And Nokea, she's off limits. Anybody else is fair game."

"Scorpio too? You know I've been waiting for her to shake a brotha down."

I grinned. "Hmm . . . talk to me about it before you do, and I'll let you know my status then."

We laughed, gave each other a long hug, and went back into the gym to continue our workout.

I was sweating and panting like it wasn't funny. Neglecting my workout really set me back and I had gotten out of shape fast. Stephon laughed the whole time, walking around flexing his muscles, trying to make me jealous because he had kept up with his workout. He said that he wasn't going to let me or anybody else stop him from keeping his body in shape, and admitted that working out took his mind off his frustrations.

We went to the men's locker room and showered. I hated washing up at the gym, but there was no way I was getting my sweaty ass into the 'Cedes. Stephon felt the same way about his BMW, so we hung around in the locker room catching up on women talk.

"So, you still fucking Felicia, huh?" I asked.

"Yeah, man. Just hit that last night. Actually, be hitting that about three, fo', five times a week. She is wild."

"Trust me, I know. That freak is something else. Puzzles the hell out of me why you still fucking with her though."

"Negro, please. You kicked it with her for damn near four years and you don't know why."

I tapped my finger against my temple as if I were in deep thought. "Okay, you got me. She is good at swallowing a brotha correctly, ain't she?" We gave each other five and laughed.

"So, uh, enough about me," Stephon said. "Any new ladies on the agenda, or are you sticking it to anybody I know?"

"Naw, man, I ain't been screwing Nokea, if that's what you're asking. However, the opportunity has presented itself. Other than that, you know the usual . . . Brashaney, Scorpio, and Heather. A lil'

dick sucking here and there. Condoms on and off
. . . you know how I do it."

"Heather, huh. Heather who?"

"This, uh . . . chick I met several weeks ago," I
said, trying not to reveal her identity.

"Where did you meet her?"

"She was a damsel in distress and her car was
stuck on the side of the road. I pulled over to help
her."

"So you pulling them from the streets now,
huh?"

"Naw, nothing like that. Woman needed some
help, so I helped."

"Get it right, fool. Woman wanted to get fucked
and you fucked her."

"Yep, and that I did. Very well, I might say. So
well, that she sent two dozen red roses to my house
the next day, thanking me for my good dick. I
threw them in the trash, but the thought was nice."

"Heather . . . and she sent roses the next day?
This ain't no sista we're talking about, is it?"

I laughed. "Naw man, she's Caucasian. Bad-ass
white gal too," I said, licking my lips.

"No, no, no! Haven't I taught you anything? You
know we don't go there, man. Besides, you're the
one who made that rule up. If I remember correctly, rule number two, right?"

"I know, man, but shit just happened so fast, I
couldn't believe it myself. Got a little oil in my system and one thing led to another."

"So?"

"So, what?"

"How was it?"

"It was wild, dog. Straight-up wild. Fucked her outside in the rain. We rolled around in the mud, and I laid that pussy out. Her stuff was so tight, it had a serious choke on my dick."

Stephon and I cracked up. "You know, for a wanna-be clean Negro like yourself, that does sound pretty wild. So, what's up with it? You still working with it or what?"

"Nope. The experience was cool, but I like the sistas man. Something about the way they be shaking a brotha down just make me wanna holla."

"Well, Scorpio ain't no full-blown sista. And seems like she's been shaking a brotha down pretty damn good."

"Scorpio's got African American blood running through her veins. She might not be all black, but she got sista genes flowing through her body."

"You are crazy, man. But you know what we need to do? Let's go out this weekend. I seriously think it'll be good for the both of us. Some of the fellas at the shop been hyping up The Loft, so let's go check it out. "

"We'll see. You know I have my kids on the weekend. If I feel up to it I'll let Nanny B see about them and I'll make arrangements to go. Call me ahead of time, though, 'cause I might be making plans to get into something else, you know what I mean?"

"There will be plenty to get into at the club. You'll see."

"Yeah, there always is. I could probably use a new collection of women in my life any damn way."

"Cool. Just let me know and it's on."

I told Stephon I'd holla at him before the weekend, and we left the gym on a good note. I'd figured we wouldn't be mad at each other for long, but I'd also had to let him know it wasn't cool for him to have sex with Nokea, lie to me about LJ being his baby, and asking Nokea to marry him.

When I got home, there was a card stuck in the front door. It read:

> Can't stop thinking about the other night. Hubby's out of town on business again, and it sure would be nice to see you.

First, it fucked me up that Heather even knew where I lived. I didn't tell her, so it was obvious she'd done her homework. Second, I had no intention on going there with her again. The card and flowers were cool, but there just wasn't enough of me to go around with all these lonely-ass women in my life. Everybody wanted to get fucked. I was flattered, but damn, dick could use a little down time. I tore up Heather's card and threw it in the trashcan just like I'd done the roses.

Later that day, I changed clothes and drove to the Galleria to find LJ something for his birthday. Chesterfield Mall and Plaza Frontenac were closer, but sometimes I just felt like going where I could fit in.

I roamed the mall, and stopped at a bookstore to buy a cookbook for Scorpio. She seriously needed all the help she could get with her cooking, so I was sure she would appreciate it.

I always stopped in at Victoria's Secret to buy

the ladies in my life something sexy to wear. I bought four pieces of lingerie and two thongs that I envisioned Scorpio's naked ass in. There wasn't no telling when I was coming back to the mall again, so I picked up an extra pair to give to Nokea on her birthday. The sales associate wrapped everything neatly for me and joked about the different sizes. She gave me extra boxes for the gifts and invited me to come back soon.

Nanny B had fired up some juicy and succulent baby-back ribs, so we sat at the kitchen table and grubbed. It was very convenient having her around. I was happier than ever, now that I had her to help out with the kids. I think she was glad too, because she had gotten just as attached to LJ and Mackenzie as I was.

After dinner, I went to my room to relax. I called Scorpio to tell her about the cookbook and thongs, but she wasn't at home. She was probably somewhere with her new mystery man I admit, I was a little jealous.

I lay across the chaise and thought about him fucking her, possibly doing a better job than me. What if they were somewhere at dinner and he was making her smile? The thoughts bothered me, so I showered and changed clothes. I told Nanny B I'd be back later, and jetted.

I found myself parked in Heather's driveway. I went to the door with one of the Victoria's Secret bags in my hand. I stuffed some pink tissue paper inside, so she wouldn't see what I had for her. After I rang the doorbell, I leaned beside the door and held up the bag with one finger.

Heather opened the door and displayed her

pearly whites. "I'm so glad to see you, and thank you so much for thinking about me," she said, taking the bag from my hand.

"Anytime." I stepped into her house. "I want you to go slide into it, right now."

She removed the tissue paper and looked inside. "Darling, there's nothing inside the bag."

"I know. That's what I want you to slide on for me. Nothing."

"Duh, stupid me. Awesome thought, though, really it is."

She walked upstairs and I followed behind her. We went into her room and wasted no time having sex again. It wasn't like the pussy was all that, but it was the new experience that sent me back to her again. Heather, actually, was a slow rider—too slow, but I was a good teacher. I thought that maybe I should stick with it and see if she'd be able to shake a brotha down just how I wanted her to. Besides, she swallowed me a little differently from the others, so I didn't trip.

I got home around one o'clock in the morning and was careful not to wake Nanny B. But when I looked in her room, she was awake watching *The Jamie Foxx Show*. I let her know I was back, then called Scorpio to see if she had made it home yet. When her answering machine came on, I left a message for her to call me.

Scorpio didn't return my call until early Friday morning while I was at work. I wanted to curse her out, but I kept my cool.

"Sorry, but I've been busy, Jaylin. I was at home when you called the other night, but I was studying," she exclaimed.

"Alone?" I asked.

"Yes, alone. And why are you asking me if I was alone? What if I wasn't?"

"No biggie, I just asked. Ain't like I care. I just don't want no naked brotha flaunting his ass around in front of Mackenzie."

"Well, don't worry because that's not going to happen. He has a nice studio apartment I can go to if I decide to get down like that."

"Ah . . . So, you've been to his place?"

"As a matter of fact, I haven't. I've seen some lovely pictures, though. So, is there anything else you'd like to know?"

"Nope. And like I said before, it really ain't my business. Anytime you don't feel like answering my questions, don't. The reason for my call the other night was to tell you that I bought you a cookbook. Thought it might help you out, since you be whipping up those messed-up dishes all the time."

"For your information, Mr. Criticizer, I can cook."

"Shiiit. Woman, don't go lying to yourself like that, please."

She laughed. "Whatever, but thanks. Thanks for at least thinking about me."

"I always think about you, baby. And right before you called, I was sitting here thinking about how scrumptious you're going to look tonight in one of the thongs I bought for you too."

"Damn, baby, you're being awfully nice to me. It wouldn't have anything to do with us not having sex for almost a week now, would it?"

"Six days, Scorpio, seven hours, thirty-seven minutes, and fifteen . . . sixteen seconds, and I'm still counting. It's been that long since I've been sexually satisfied. Tonight, you got yourself a date with the Ding-Dong man."

"Uh-uh. I got plans tonight, Mr. Ding-Dong man."

"Plans with who?"

"Plans with this oh, so fine, sexy, aggressive, juicy-lipped, long fat dick, thick-headed, muscular tight-ass Investment Broker that be sliding that thang deep into a sista's pussy and having it dripping we—"

"Okay, baby, that's enough. I'm at work now. You gon' have me running out of the motherfucker trying to get to your ass. So, don't talk like that no more."

Scorpio laughed. "I won't. As long as you remember our routine, no matter what happens between us. Three times minimum, per week. No ifs, ands, or buts about it."

"Bet, Ms. Porn Star. You know you should get yourself a 900-number talking shit like that. And because you had my ass over here about to explode, that's going to cost you big time tonight."

"Damn, I can't wait . . . but, uh, getting our minds out of the gutter, and back to the real reason for my call . . . I need you to meet me at Mackenzie's pre-school around one o'clock today. Her teacher called earlier and said that she wanted to talk to us."

"Why didn't you tell me earlier? I have a lunch meeting with one of my clients today."

"Well, cancel it."

"I guess I'll just have to. Did her teacher say what she wanted?"

"No, she just said she'll talk to us when we get there."

"Okay, I'll meet you there at one."

When I got off the phone with Scorpio, I called my client to reschedule. I chowed down on the Chinese food Angela ordered for lunch, then left the office to go to Mackenzie's pre-school.

Scorpio's Corvette was parked outside already, and I pulled up next to it. I went inside and saw Mackenzie reading some flashcards. She ran up to give me a squeezing tight hug.

"Hi, Daddy. What are you doing here? Am I going home with you today?"

"I'm here to talk to your teacher. And yes, if you want to, I'll pick you up when I get off work." She gave me a kiss and ran back to the other kids.

I interrupted Scorpio talking to Mackenzie's teacher in her office. "Hello, Mr. Rogers," Ms. Franklin said, standing up, and shaking my hand. "Have a seat, please." I sat next to Scorpio and looked at her. She turned her head away like she was mad about something.

"So, what's this all about?"

"Mr. Rogers, don't be alarmed. I just wanted to talk to you and Mrs. Rogers about Mackenzie's behavior."

"Let me correct you," I said, feeling the bullshit getting ready to go down. I pointed to Scorpio. "This is Ms. Valentino. We are not married, and what in the hell do you mean by Mackenzie's behavior?"

"Well, she has a problem getting along with the other children. She's very bossy and quite controlling—"

"What do you mean by bossy and controlling?"

She let out a deep sigh and clinched her hands together. "I mean, she doesn't share with the other children, she tells them what to do, and when they don't, she gets angry."

Scorpio looked over at me again and rolled her eyes.

"So," I said, shrugging my shoulders. "She's supposed to have her way. And she doesn't have to share shit with anybody unless she wants to. As for telling them what to do, that's all about leadership. She's a leader, not a follower."

"Mr. Rogers, I don't think you understand—"

"No, Ma'am, I don't think you understand. I pay this school fifteen hundred dollars a month, and if you have to put up with a little attitude from my daughter, so damn what. Do it! Personally, I think you got a problem with the color of her skin. I'm sure you're not calling any of these white parents in here with this bullshit."

"Oh, Mr. Rogers, I'm not like that. I really like Mackenzie. I'm just—"

I quickly stood up and looked at Scorpio. "Come on, baby. Let's get the fuck out of here before I snatch her ass from behind that desk."

Scorpio shook her head in disgust. "Jaylin, look, calm down. Ms. Franklin is just trying to tell us about Mackenzie. You act like you—"

"I don't need nobody telling me shit! And I can't believe you're sitting here listening to this nonsense." I gave Scorpio and Ms. Franklin a hard stare, then pushed the chair out of my way and walked out. I grabbed Mackenzie and left. Scorpio stayed behind to continue talking to Ms. Franklin.

By the time I got home, I was furious from thinking about the whole damn ordeal. I couldn't even go back to work, or return any of my clients' phone calls because I was raging mad. When I slammed my keys on the kitchen counter, Nanny B came in.

"What's the problem, Jaylin? Tell me, what's going on?"

I sat at the table and folded my leg across my knee. "Mackenzie, go upstairs to your room and let your Daddy and Nanny B have some privacy." She left and didn't say a word. I took a deep breath, "Ms. Franklin, her pre-school teacher, had a talk with Scorpio and me today. She started talking all this bullshit about Mackenzie being bossy, controlling, and even selfish. She pissed me off and I cursed her ass out."

Nanny B pulled a chair next to me and held my hands together with hers. "Jaylin, I know you don't want to hear this, but Mackenzie is the spitting image of you. I've noticed it myself, but it's not my place to tell anyone how to raise their children."

"But—"

"But nothing. Just listen, please. You need to call that woman and apologize to her. It's not that she's trying to tell you how to raise your child, but it is her job to let you know when something isn't right. Mackenzie is spoiled, rotten to the core, and she has you to thank for that. You're not a bad father, but material things just don't get it all the time. She needs for you to tell her when she's wrong, tell her when she can't have her way, and not let her run over you like she does. If she believes that she can have her way with you, then she's going to feel the same way about others. I know you want to give her everything because you had a rough upbringing. But giving her what you didn't have isn't the answer, okay?" She let go of my hands and folded her arms.

"Have you been talking to my deceased mother or something? That just sounded like something she would say to me. I know you're right, but some things are hard for me to swallow."

"No, I haven't been talking to your mother, but God puts people in your life for a reason. Good people, bad people, and ugly people. I just hope I can be of some good."

"And that you are." I kissed Nanny B on the cheek and thanked her. I told her I would call Ms. Franklin to apologize, and then make it perfectly clear to her that Mackenzie wasn't coming back any time soon.

I was taking a shower when Scorpio came into the bathroom screaming and hollering about how I embarrassed her.

"I can't believe you reacted that way, Jaylin. You were way out of line."

"And I can't believe you didn't have the decency or courage to stand up for your own damn daughter." I turned off the water, and covered myself with a towel as I stepped into my bedroom.

As I sat on the bed, she stood in front of me and folded her arms. "What in the hell has gotten into you? Your attitude is horrible. And now your little fucked-up ways have rubbed off on my daughter. I'm not having this shit, Jaylin, I mean it. "

I felt myself about to go off on her, but instead, I reached for the bag with her cookbook in it and calmly asked her to leave.

"Fine, I'll leave. But please call Ms. Franklin and apologize to her."

"I am, and not because you're asking me to, but because I know it's the right thing to do." I removed the towel from around me and pulled the covers back to get in bed.

"Either way, thank you. And now that we've cleared that up," Scorpio said, getting under the covers with me. "I thought we had plans tonight, Mr. Ding-Dong man?"

"We did, however, I just canceled them until you learn how to stand up for the ones you love. Until then, Ms. Porn Star, get the fuck off my bed so I can go to sleep—alone."

Realizing that I wasn't joking, Scorpio grabbed her cookbook and left. Her disrespect fucked her right out of this good dick tonight.

The Loft wasn't no joke. Women were down to wearing a little bit of nothing. Legs, back, breasts, ass, you name it, I saw it. There were some sexy-ass women in the club, but there was also some sistas who knew damn well they shouldn't have tried to squeeze into those skimpy-ass outfits they wore. I felt like if your back was out, and your rolls were showing, then that wasn't the outfit for you.

This one gal had so many rolls showing that I asked Stephon if he had some butter. We damn near fell to the floor laughing so hard. And Ray Ray had the nerve to ask her to dance.

When I asked Ray Ray about his wife, he said they were already separated and he couldn't be with just one woman. I definitely knew the feeling and was glad I hadn't wasted that kind of money or time on getting married.

Stephon and me kicked down our game all night. We grabbed two light-skinned sistas who were showing all skin, and asked them to dance.

I dropped low and rubbed my dance partner on her soft, pretty legs. I worked my way up from the floor and held her waist. She placed her arms on my shoulders and worked her sexy body to my rhythm. "So, what's your name?" I asked.

"Beaches."

"What?" I said, as I couldn't quite hear over the loud music.

"Beaches," she yelled a little louder.

"Say, Beaches, what do you think about us hooking up tonight?"

She smiled and removed her arms from my shoulders. "You are awfully confident and sexy, but I'll have to pass. I'm engaged and—"

I immediately stopped dancing with her because there wasn't no sense in me going any further. If she was engaged, then what in the fuck was she doing in here? I walked off the dance floor and went over to the bar. Stephon was still on the floor dancing with her sister. I'd hoped he was having better luck with her.

While at the bar, several women approached me about dancing. Since none of them offered to pay for my drink, I declined. But when this thick, mocha-chocolate sista with long wavy hair slammed some money on the bar to pay for my Remy, she got my attention.

"I got your back, and then some, handsome. Question is, are you ready for some serious action tonight?"

"That depends on what type of action you have in mind."

"How about I'll show you when we get to my place."

Damn, do I look that easy? I thought. She was aggressive, but she was my kind of woman. "Baby, what would give you the idea that I want to go to your place tonight?"

She took my hand and eased it in between her legs. Wearing no panties, I felt the goods. And after scoping the thickness of her shiny lips, I quickly downed my drink and whispered in her ear, "I need somewhere to lay my *head*. It would be quite nice if I could lay it in you."

She took my hand, and before we left, I stopped to let Stephon know I was outtie.

"Say, man, call me tomorrow," I said.

"You gon' dog? I thought we were going to the Waffle House tonight?"

"Sorry, bro, waffles don't come like this," I said, looking next to me. "And please understand that plans do change, my brotha, plans most certainly do change."

Stephon checked out the loveliness I had next to me and gave me five. "Do your thang, cuz, and call me later."

"Will do."

I rode to the club with Stephon, so the chick whose name I still hadn't gotten agreed to drive. We searched for her car in the parking lot, and when she had the nerve to step to this gray, raggedy-ass Lincoln, I could have died. But then I thought about when Scorpio first came over to see me in her raggedy Cadillac, and decided not to judge.

No sooner had we gotten inside the car, she was all over me. She unzipped my pants and gagged as she tried to swallow all of my nine. I somewhat enjoyed the feeling, and tried to show her a little satisfaction by rubbing her ass.

I felt very little passion for what was going on, so it took forever for me to come. I even closed my eyes and pretended she was Scorpio, but when I felt the edges of her sharp teeth, I knew something wasn't right. She wrapped up the blowjob, then started the car so we could leave. The damn thing sounded like a garbage truck, shaking our bodies. I was so embarrassed when she sped from the parking lot, my ass flying out of my seat from her abrupt departure.

"Whoa . . . whoa . . . Slow down, damn!" I yelled, holding onto the dashboard. "This car could really use a tune-up, you know."

She took her eyes off the road and grinned. "It's an old car. I'm getting a new one next week."

Sure you are, I thought. *A Lexus, right?*

"You know, you haven't even asked me my name yet."

"That's because I don't want to know your name. Not really important to me." I was infuriated by the way she drove. She had my damn life in her hands and she was swerving in and out of traffic with it. Of course she was anxious to feel my dick, but damn!

When she hit Highway 70 going one hundred

miles per hour then got off near the projects, I'd had enough.

"Pull this raggedy-ass piece of shit over, please!" I yelled.

"What?" she yelled back.

"I said, pull this son of a bitch over!"

"Why? What's wrong with you?" She slowed down and pulled over to the curb. I hopped out and slammed the door.

She tried to lower the window but it got stuck. "You're a silly-ass fool, you know that?" she said.

"And you're a non-dick-sucking, low-down, nasty-looking, trifling freak! Do you know that?"

I started down the street, and as she drove by, she honked the horn and gave me the finger. I pulled out my cell phone and called Stephon. He could barely hear what I was saying because of the loud music in the background. He said that he was on his way to the restroom so he could hear me.

"Man, come get me," I said, laughing.

"Where are you? And what happened to that fine piece of tender you left here with?"

"Man, never ever judge a book by its cover. That fine piece of tender turned out to be a melting snowflake. That bitch was crazy." Stephon laughed. I told him where I was and he came for me.

We sat at the Waffle House and cracked up about what had happened. And after my experience with whatever-the-hell-her-name-was, I was done messing around with women. At least for the night.

Chapter 10

Jaylin

I woke up around eleven o'clock in the morning and almost forgot that I told Nokea I would meet her and LJ at Café Lapadero by one o'clock in the afternoon. My little man was finally one year old today, and I for damn sure wasn't getting any younger myself.

I climbed out of bed and went into the bathroom to freshen up a bit. I looked in the mirror and sung a quick Happy Birthday to myself and thanked God for another year. I didn't look a day over twenty-one, and definitely wasn't feeling like the average thirty-three-year-old man. I thought it was quite odd that Mackenzie hadn't come in my bedroom yet, so I quickly brushed my teeth and splashed some water on my face. I hurried to see what was keeping her from wishing the love of her life, me, a Happy Birthday.

I noticed that she wasn't in her room, so I gathered

my silk robe and jogged down the steps to find her. By the time I reached the bottom, I could see people in the living room.

"SURPRISE!" Everybody yelled. I widened my eyes and smiled because they'd caught me completely off guard. Nanny B walked up to me and placed her hands on my face.

"Happy Birthday," she said, kissing my cheek. I looked into the great room where Mackenzie, Scorpio, LJ, Nokea, Stephon, and his girlfriend Mona, were standing.

"What's up?" I said, walking toward them. "Is everybody trying to get their party on this early?" They laughed and I took LJ from Nokea. I wished him a Happy Birthday too and Nokea wished me one as well.

Nanny B took a deep breath, "Well, I just put together a little something nice for you this morning. I know you probably have a busy day planned, but I wanted to do something special to show you how much we all appreciate you."

"Yeah, man," Stephon interrupted. "I almost slipped and told you about this last night, but I wanted it to be a surprise." He came over and gave me a hug. "I love you, cuz, and appreciate ya."

I embraced Stephon, then turned and looked at everyone else. My throat ached from all the love. "I really don't know what to say, but thanks for thinking about me. I can't ever remember having nobody go all out like this for me on my birthday."

Feeling a bit emotional, I sat back on the leather chaise and put LJ on my lap. When Mackenzie saw me blink, she walked over and put her arms around my neck.

"Daddy, we got you a present," she said.

"Say you did?"

"Yes. Can I give it to you now?" she asked.

Scorpio came over by us and leaned down to kiss me. "Happy Birthday, knucklehead. And Mackenzie, we'll give him his present after we eat some cake, okay?"

"Cake? I get cake too," I grinned.

"Yes, Daddy. And it's your favorite."

Just then, Nanny B came into the living room with a two-tier Black Forest cake in her hands. There seemed to be enough candles on top to burn the damn house down. She said the top layer was for LJ and the bottom layer was for me. I stood up with him in my arms and everybody sang "Happy Birthday" to both of us.

I blew out the candles, and Nanny B went back into the kitchen to cut slices for everyone. It messed me up that we were all actually in the same room talking to each other and everybody seemed to be getting along just fine. How Nanny B ever managed to get Scorpio and Nokea over here without a fuss puzzled the hell out of me. And Stephon, to bring Mona when he and Nokea were engaged before . . . This was, without a doubt, some crazy shit. Stephon had been seeing Mona behind Nokea's back and I figured she had to be wondering what the hell was up. Since nobody else seemed to be tripping, we ate cake and I went with the flow. The only thing I couldn't seem to get with was how jacked-up my great room was from all the cake crumbs and shoe prints on my carpet. Not being able to stand the sight, I got up and collected everybody's plates to throw in the trash.

"Jaylin!" Nanny B yelled.

"What?"

"Sit down, chile, I'll get that stuff in a minute."

"I was just trying to help, that's all."

"No, sit down and enjoy your company. Don't worry about this mess. I'll clean it up when we get finished."

I went back over to the chaise and laid back. Stephon stared at me for a few seconds, then turned to Nanny B. "Nanny B, what are you doing to this man to keep him in check like that?" He stood with his mouth wide open. "I ain't never, and I mean never—did I say never? Never seen a woman have control over him like that."

Scorpio and Nokea looked at me and smiled. I picked up my black velvet pillow and threw it at him. "Nigga, please. Ain't nobody got control over me, fool. Nanny B said she had everything under control so, hey. No need for me to help when she's gotten everything taken care of, right?"

Stephon shrugged. "Hey, I'm just saying I've never seen you listen to anybody without putting up a fuss." He walked over by Scorpio and nudged her on the shoulder. "How about you, Scorpio? Have you ever seen him move like that when you've demanded something from him?"

"No, can't say that I have." Scorpio folded her arms and leaned back on the couch. "Nanny B must got something I don't have." She turned to Nokea, "What about you, Nokea? Does he ever listen to you, or do anything you ask?"

"You know, I really can't say that he has either. Every time I ask him to do something, he causes an uproar. So, Nanny B, tell us. How did you ever get this man to start listening to you?" Nokea asked.

Nanny B scooted her wide hips to the edge of the chair, and rubbed her wrinkly hands together. All eyes were on her. I quickly rose up because I had a feeling she was about to embarrass me. "Nanny B, you don't have to answer any questions. I just, uh—"

"You just what?" she said, smiling.

"Nothing." I leaned back and folded my hands behind my head. There wasn't no sense in me trying to stop her because she was so ready to run her mouth.

"You know," she said as if she was getting ready to tell a story to a crowd of listeners. "I observe men well. And what I've noticed is that Jaylin likes to have control. In addition to having control, he loves confrontation. Wouldn't you all agree?" Everybody nodded and I smiled. "With that in mind, the only way to prevent yourself from arguing with him is to play his game and let him think he's having his way. For instance, when he got his anal butt up a minute ago, in the middle of us having a good time, and tried to clean up, I kindly— and the key is being kind and not stooping to his level—but I kindly told him I would clean up later. Then, I politely asked him to have a seat. Now, he didn't get his way because this room is still a mess. Because my words were not on his level, he chilled and didn't say a word. You see how I got what I wanted and I didn't even have to fuss with him about it."

Everybody cracked up because they knew Nanny B had scammed me. What they didn't know is I had more respect for her than anybody in the whole room. Since I'd known her, she had my back and never put up a fuss about anything I asked her to do.

They all sat around talking and laughing about the situation. The doorbell rang and Nanny B stood to go answer it. I stopped her.

"I got it. Keep on entertaining my guests, I don't mind doing your job."

As I made my way to the door, she rushed past me. "Go sit your behind down, Jaylin. I'm going to answer it because, knowing you, I might not have a job tomorrow."

"You got that right." I laughed and went back to the great room.

When everybody stared at the front door, I turned to see who it was. It was Heather. Nanny B let her in and she stood in the foyer with a short, maroon Chinese dress on and tall black heels. Her long blond hair was pulled over to one side and laid on her shoulders. I noticed a small package in her hand. My eyes were about to pop out of my head. There was no way Nanny B would have invited Heather, because they'd never met before. Trying to get my thoughts together, I cleared my throat and turned back to my guests.

"Sorry, I forgot. This is Mr. Schmidt's daughter, Heather. He told me she was stopping by to bring over some important papers for me to sign. I didn't know he had a gift for me, too."

Scorpio and Nokea took deep breaths and appeared to be relaxed. Stephon was the only one who knew about Heather, and all he did was grin.. I introduced everyone to Heather, and then she followed me into my office. I closed the door behind us, locked it, and took a seat behind my desk.

"Damn, Heather, what's up?"

"I'm sorry, and I didn't mean to interrupt, but I wanted to give you your birthday present. I've called you several times, and since you didn't return my calls, I thought you misplaced my number. Honestly, I really didn't think my coming to see you was going to be a problem." She laid the bag on my desk.

"Well, it is. You just can't be showing up when you get good and ready to. What we have going on is my business. I don't want anybody questioning me, so please, next time call first, okay? If I don't call you back, just wait until I do."

"I don't understand why our relationship has to be such a secret. I would love to meet your friends. I really hope this has nothing to do with me being a white woman."

"No . . . No, I could care less about that. The biggest problem I have with you is that you're a married woman, Heather. I can't go flaunting you around like you're mine. That's ridiculous."

"What do you want me to do, get a divorce? Would that make it easier for you?"

"No, Heather. The last thing I want you to do is get a divorce, trust me. I'm just saying let's keep this on the down-low. I'll return your calls, only if you promise not to show up again unexpected like this."

She shrugged. "I guess, Jaylin. Whatever works for you." She picked up the bag and gave it to me. "Here. I special ordered this for you. Open it."

I reached in the bag and pulled out a box. It was

a Rolex case. I laid it down on my desk and slid it over to her.

"Thanks, but I already have three. And before this goes any further, I don't need you buying me expensive gifts like this."

"Now, that's not fair. How can you refuse it if you haven't even seen it?" She walked around my desk and placed the box in my hand. "Please, open it."

I opened the box and gazed at the watch. It had a face filled with diamonds, was stainless steel, and trimmed in eighteen-karat yellow gold. An Oyster bracelet linked it together. Taking a guess, I'd say she spent a minimum of $25,000. "You have got to be out of your mind giving me something like this. There is no way in hell I'm going to accept this from you."

"But—

"But my ass, Heather. Sorry, I'm not that kind of man. Now, I might play the fuck-me game every once in a while, but this expensive-gift-giving bull-shit is not my style."

I closed the box and placed it in her hand. She moved her head from side to side. "I don't know what else to do. I thought if I bought you something nice, you'd know how much I care."

"You don't have to be spending that kind of money to show me how much you care. Trust me, I know how you feel. Just understand our relationship has limitations. Limitations because you're married, and honestly, I'm a playa. A playa who has no desire to be with one woman, or to take from them either."

Heather swallowed hard and tucked her purse

underneath her arm. She made her way to the door. My eyes were glued to her curvy ass squeezed in her dress. When she turned, she noticed how mesmerized I was by her. She tilted her head and smiled to get my attention.

"Sorry . . . What did you say?" I asked and cleared my throat.

"I didn't say anything."

She kept her eyes connected with mine, and slowly eased up her dress. She raised it above her hips and removed her maroon panties. She had my full attention, so I rested my face in my hand and watched. Her thin, model-shaped tanned legs gave me a rise, and when she sat back on the sofa, I knew her insides were ready to be fulfilled.

She motioned her finger for me to come to her, but I was already moving in her direction. "Five minutes, Jaylin. That's all I need. I know you have guests but I—"

I placed my hand over her mouth and loosened my robe. She looked down at my goods and didn't say a word. "I need you to be extremely quiet, Heather. I know how loud you can get when we're having sex, but please, not this time."

She nodded and I removed my hand from her mouth.

I kneeled in front of the sofa and held Heather's legs apart. She reached for my thang and put it inside of her. Seeing how difficult it was for her to keep quiet, I leaned forward and placed my lips on hers. She held my neck tightly, and rubbed the back of my hair. I soaked her lips with mine, and pounded her insides fast to make her come. And when I leaned her over the sofa, and tagged her from behind, she was just about ready to explode.

"Damn you!" she yelled. I hurried and placed my hand over her mouth. Finally, after fifteen long minutes we released our energy together.

Rushing to get back to my company, I gathered my robe and tied it. Heather eased her dress down, then wiped her lipstick from my lips. I reached for her hand and stopped her. "I don't mean to be rude, and I hate to rush you out, but you know that five minutes you asked for turned into fifteen minutes. I'd hate to keep my guests waiting."

"Oh, I understand," she said, flattening the wrinkles in her dress. "I'll call you tomorrow—is that okay?"

"That's fine. And put a smile on your face. After that, you should be on cloud nine."

I unlocked the door and Heather laughed. She followed behind me, and as we made our exit, all eyes turned to us.

"Heather," I said, shaking her hand. "Tell your father I said thanks." I ran back into my office and grabbed the gift bag off my desk. "Here you go. I must decline his gift at this time, but please, don't forget to thank him for me."

She took the bag from me. "Sure, Jaylin. I'm sorry I took up so much of your time. My father always teases me about rambling on and on."

I opened the door for Heather, and after she waved good-bye to everyone, she left.

I stood by the staircase and tightened my robe. Everybody was still looking at me, so I had so say something.

"I . . . I'm going to go upstairs and change into

something else. It's not appropriate for my guests to see me like this, and if I had changed earlier, my boss's daughter wouldn't have seen me almost half-naked."

"Well, go put on some clothes," Scorpio said. "Why are you standing there trying to explain?"

A sigh of relief came over me, and I hurried upstairs to my bedroom. I grabbed a pair of jeans and a black wife-beater from my closet, then took a quick shower. As I was looking in the mirror brushing my hair, Stephon stood in the doorway to my bathroom.

"Now *that* was risky," he said, folding his arms.

"What?"

"Negro, you know what. Don't play me like a fool."

I snickered, "Was it that obvious?"

"Nope, but if she would have taken her panties with her, I probably wouldn't have ever known." Stephon tossed Heather's panties to me. "I went into your office to use the phone and those were on the floor."

"Damn, man. Did anybody else see them?"

"Uh-uh. And before you ask, they don't suspect anything either. They actually down there talking about what a great boss you have, and how nice of him to send his daughter over here with a gift."

"Whew, I'm so relieved. I know it was risky, but I like doing shit like that. Besides, it's my day, and I intend on going all out."

"Nothing wrong with that," Stephon said, sitting down on my bed. He gripped his hands together and dropped his head. I came out of the bathroom and sat next to him.

"Are you all right? I mean, you look as if you have something heavy on your mind."

"I'm cool. I just wonder when one of us is going to settle down and chill, man. I see how happy you are with LJ and Mackenzie, and I really would like to have that type of love for somebody one day. You know what I mean?"

"Yeah. I definitely know what you mean. My kids mean everything to me. And I do mean everything. A woman will never mean more to me than they do."

"Yeah, but I wouldn't mind having some crumbsnatchers around like you do. It's something about them that be having your ass glowing like a motherfucker. Hopefully, I might have something in the making right now."

"Straight up? So, you got a baby on the way?"

"I think. That's if she ain't lying about it."

"She . . . she," I said rubbing my goatee in deep thought. "Aw, Mona thinks she's pregnant?"

"Nope."

"Rachelle?"

"Nope."

"Fool, I'm not gon' sit here and go through all of your women. Who?" My forehead wrinkled and I gave Stephon a hard stare. "No! No! No!" I yelled. "Don't tell me it's Felicia!" I hopped up and grabbed my money clip off the nightstand. I counted out $500 and threw it on the bed. "Man, please. Whatever you do, make her have an abortion. Take the money, please!"

"Jay, it ain't even like that. You know I don't need your money. Felicia and me talked about it, and I really want her to have the baby."

I plopped back down on the bed and shook my head in disgust. "Why, man? She ain't gon' do nothing but cause you some serious grief. And how do you know it's yours anyway? We both know she be sleeping around like a motherfucker. I know how badly you want a child, but plan this shit out with somebody else."

"Hey, I ain't too thrilled about her being the mother of my child either, but if she's pregnant, then I'm for it. Just like you were when Simone got pregnant. Remember? She was a piece of work her damn self."

"Okay, and don't go bringing up that bitch. I could kill her for taking my daughter away from me, and whenever I see her, I plan to do just that. Anyway, whatever you decide, you know I got your back."

"I know." He reached over and slammed his fist against mine.

"Now, in the meantime . . . I got a question for you," I said.

"Shoot."

"Why do you keep looking at Scorpio, man? I've noticed all day how you can't keep your eyes off my woman."

Stephon laughed. "Cause man, I'm not gon' lie to you no' mo'. But, uh, she's one woman I wouldn't mind getting down and dirty with. Just looking at that ass sends me in la-la land. I sure in the hell be glad when you figure out what you're going to do with her because I am one brotha anxiously waiting."

"Damn, it's like that, huh? But do you straight

up think she'll get down with you, when she got all this to look forward to?"

"I know she would. While she's still kicking it with you, too."

"Negro, please. I thought I was one confident-ass brotha, but you got me beat. I say let's put some money on it. I got five thousand dollars that says she wouldn't give you the time of day."

"And I'll match your five and say that she would."

"Bet. And since you've been wanting to fuck her so badly, I'm giving you the go ahead. I'm not even going to interfere. You got one month to come back here with some evidence. I'm giving you some extra time, but if you are as confident as you seem to be, I don't think it will take you that long. And thirty-one days after today, I'm coming to collect my money. So, you'd better have it. If you don't, I'll send my hit man out to get you."

"Fool, the only thing I'm going to be hitting is that fat ass and pussy on your woman. And when I come to you next week and show you some evidence, don't go drinking your life away trying to soak up the pain."

I grabbed Stephon's hand and pulled him off the bed. Since I had a lot of faith in Scorpio, this was quite easy for me. Stephon and I laughed about the bet and we headed back downstairs.

Nanny B had already cleaned up everything, but the ladies were still sitting around chatting.

Scorpio looked at Stephon and me coming toward the great room. "Just abandon your company. We don't care." She went into the kitchen. Stephon watched her walk away, then he looked at me and winked. Trying to show him who had the upper hand, I followed her.

"You don't feel abandoned, baby, do you?" I asked, wrapping my arms around her.

"Sometimes, yes I do." She removed my arms and had a blank expression on her face. "Do you have plans with Nokea tonight? She's been talking about this café you meet her at every year and said that you were having dinner with her tonight."

I kissed the back of her hand. "It's just dinner, Scorpio. We were supposed to meet there for lunch, but since Nanny B planned this surprise for me, I guess Nokea wants to go there for dinner."

"What about what I had planned for you? I guess I have to put my plans on hold until some other time, huh?"

"No, I didn't say that. I didn't know you had plans for us. Now that I know, let me get rid of everybody, and I'll meet you at your place. I'll schedule a late dinner with Nokea so we can spend some time together before I go. Okay?"

"No, it's not okay and I don't feel right knowing that you're going to be with her tonight. I was anticipating on you spending the night with me."

"Scorpio, look. I'm doing the best I can under the circumstances. I've been dining with Nokea at Café Lapadero on my birthday for years. Don't ask me to change something I've been doing for a long time. Work with me this time, and don't ruin my day."

She rolled her eyes and left the kitchen with an attitude. I followed and kindly asked everybody to clear out after LJ and I opened our gifts. And when I unwrapped a beautifully framed black and white picture of Mackenzie and LJ, my heart melted. They were sitting back to back and were grinning hard like they were looking at me. Excited, I placed the picture next to Mama's on the fireplace mantle. It was perfect. Other than the teddy bear Nokea had given me the previous year, this was the most touching gift I'd ever gotten.

Nokea was the last one to leave. We walked to her car and I told her I'd see her no later than nine. She complained about the time, but it was the best I could do. We decided that LJ and Mackenzie would stay at my place with Nanny B that night.

By five o'clock, I was looking spectacular and was ready to go. I peeked into Nanny B's room, where she was napping with Mackenzie and LJ. I tapped her shoulder and told her I wouldn't be back until later. She told me to have a good time, reminding me to lock the door on my way out. I didn't see any lights on when I arrived at Scorpio's condo, but her car was parked outside, so she was there. I figured she was probably still upset with me, but at least I had the decency to show.

The door was slightly open, so I pushed it and walked in. Candles were lit all over the living room, and on the floor, rose petals had been dropped into the shape of a heart. In the middle of the room was a chair, and, figuring that was most likely my place, I strutted over to take a seat. I loosened my tie and then called for her.

"Patience my dear," she said. "Good things come to brothas who wait."

Scorpio came in, moving her desirable body to

the rhythm of Miles Davis. She knew how crazy I was about his jazz. She wore a short black negligee trimmed with fur. It accented her high-yellow skin, which was oiled all over. Her breasts showed through the sheer material. A black silk thong with tiny diamonds on the string line led to her ass. Much of her curly hair dangled on her shoulders and the rest was clipped on top, just how I like it. As her beautiful eyes stared me down in the candlelit room, I couldn't help but sit there and think how lucky I was. She was by far the most gorgeous woman I'd ever been with. Pussy couldn't get no better than hers, and I was out of my mind for even making such a bet with Stephon. Just the thoughts of another man touching her devastated me.

The music stopped and Scorpio placed her foot between my legs. I put my hands on her hips and started to remove her thong. She stopped me and straddled my lap.

"Do you love me?" she asked, looking into my eyes. I nodded. "Then, I need to hear you tell me. So, again, do you love me?"

"Yes," I said softly. I reached for her thong again, but she held my hands still.

"Why haven't you told me this before?" I shrugged. She put her arms on my shoulders. "What took you so long to tell me?" I shrugged again, then looked away. "Jaylin, if you don't talk to me, I'm going to blow out these candles and call it a night. So, for the last time, what took you so long to tell me that you love me?"

I shrugged again, "Afraid . . . I guess."

"Why?"

"Because."

"Because, why Jaylin? Stop beating around the bush and tell—"

"Because you talk too damn much." I held her waist and moved her off my lap. "Take off your thong."

"No, that's for you to do."

"I've been trying to, but you won't stop running your mouth. Besides, you do it. It arouses me when I watch. Do you mind?"

"No, I don't mind, but I'll need your help." She placed her foot between my legs again, then dropped her negligee to the floor. I reached up to rub her breasts, closing my eyes. In deep thought, I lay my head against her stomach and wrapped my arms around her. No doubt, I was falling for Scorpio. She had definitely made a way out of no way for me. She lightly rubbed her fingers through my hair, and once our peaceful moment was over, I backed away from her. "Would you please take those off for me like I asked you to?"

Scorpio turned in front of me, bent over and removed her thong. "JAYLIN'S" in black cursive letters was tattooed on her ass right above the rose that was already there. She turned her head and smiled, "So, do you like?" she asked.

I placed my finger on the side of my face and pretended not to see it. "Back up a bit so I can clearly see what it says." She backed up and I held her ass cheeks in my hands. "Jaylin's, huh? I guess that means this is my ass, right?"

"Nobody else but yours, baby. So, Happy Birthday, and again, do you like it?"

"It's nice, but you don't have to tattoo my name on your ass when I already know it's mine."

"I just wanted to give you a little assurance. Just in case you think I might be slipping."

"Assurance, huh?" I grabbed Scorpio's waist and circled my tongue across my name. Then I rubbed it hard with my thumb to make sure it was permanent. When it didn't smear, I turned her body around so she could look at me. "Now, that is assurance. I just hope you don't expect me to do no shit like that."

"No, I don't. All I expect from you is for you to treat me like a lady, to respect me, love me, and to fuck me every chance you get. Everything else is totally irrelevant."

Now she was speaking my language. I squeezed my legs tightly together, and could already feel how good this night was going to be. She reached for my tie to draw me closer. After she pulled it over my head, she removed my jacket and started unbuttoning my shirt. Trying to speed things along, I took off my belt and pants. We stood naked, and held each other.

"Why do you love me so much?" I asked.

"Because."

"Because why? And don't play games with me, Scorpio. I'm serious."

She laughed. "Because you are the motherfucking man, Jaylin. You keep it real like no other brotha I've ever known, and you don't have no shame in your game. Most of all, you are a man of your words. When you say something, you do it and not only that, you mean it. There's not too many brothas I can give credit to for doing that." She squeezed my ass. "Plus, let's not forget about how good you are to me. So good, that I don't want to be with anyone else. But, of course, you already know that. Now, your turn, why do you love me?"

I laughed, not wanting to answer Scorpio's question. She backed away from me, folded her arms, and waited. I pulled her back into my arms and continued to laugh.

"If you must know," I said, "and you might not like my answer . . . But since you love me so much for keeping it real, I'm gon' be honest with you."

"Never mind. Don't even tell me. If you plan on keeping it real, I'm sure I already know."

"Okay, if you think you know then fine, I won't tell you."

"So, maybe I don't know. Just tell me. I can take it. I'm a big girl."

I smiled, "I love you because . . . you be fucking the shit out of me. Insides be all juicy and warm, and you be on overtime working that ass like—"

She put her hand over my mouth. "Jaylin, that's okay. I told you I didn't want to know. I was hoping you would find—"

"Find another reason to love you. I just told you that because it's what you expected from me. With that being said, your good loving is part of it, but the ultimate reason is because—Let's make love and then I'll tell you."

Scorpio backed away from me. "Would you stop messing around with me and just tell me?"

"I'll tell you when I'm making love to you, okay?"

I picked her up and carried her into the bedroom. I lay her on the bed and eased in between her soft legs. Our lovemaking went on for hours, before she straddled herself on top and questioned me.

"So," she said, massaging my chest. "I'm waiting. We've been at this for a while and you still haven't told me why you love me."

I tickled her, and when she got into my favorite position on her stomach, I laid on top of her. I slid myself inside, squeezing her hands tightly together. She closed her eyes and turned her head to the side. I kissed her cheek, and placed the tip of my tongue into her ear. As I licked it, I whispered, "I love you because you've never betrayed me. And when I thought you did, you were doing what was best for you, not for me. You stood by me when I needed you the most, and never left my side. Not only that, but. . . ." I closed my eyes, trying not to come, as she tightened her insides, grinding on my thang. "But I . . . I know you're the only woman who will do just about anything for me, and no matter what happens, you'll never let me bring you down. I admire a strong woman. And," I moaned, "along with all this good pussy, I gotta hand it to you baby, you have definitely captured my heart."

"Hmm," she said, stopping the motion. "I got it going on that much and you still don't want a committed relationship with me?"

"Now isn't the time to talk about that. Who knows what the future holds for us? If we're meant to be together, trust me, we will."

"You're starting to sound like a broken record, Jaylin. And you'd better hurry this up if you anticipate on meeting Nokea for dinner by nine."

"Don't rush me," I said, moving inside her again. "I'm not quite finished with you."

Within the hour, Scorpio and I finished up. The time was the last thing on my mind, but I knew Nokea was probably at home, furious with me. After I put on my clothes, I went into the other room and called her. She must have seen Scorpio's number on the caller ID, because when I told her I was on my way, she just hung up.

I went back into Scorpio's bedroom, and sat in bed next to her. She took my hands and rubbed them together.

"Baby, don't leave tonight. Stay. Stay not because I'm asking you to, but because you want to."

"I would love to stay, Scorpio, but remember, one thing you said you love about me is that I'm a man of my words. I told Nokea I was coming, so it would be wrong of me not to show."

She looked away and swallowed hard. "I, uh, almost hate to ask you this, but . . . are you planning on making love to her tonight? I mean, I'd hope you wouldn't after what we just shared but—"

I leaned forward and kissed her. "No, I don't plan on having sex with Nokea tonight. If you'd really like to know, we don't even get down like that anymore."

"Come on now, Jaylin, I know you're still attracted to her. And I know you still love her."

"Woman, please, stop stressing yourself. After that spectacular loving you just gave me, I don't have juices left for anybody."

Scorpio grinned, and before I could change my mind, I kissed her forehead and jetted.

Nokea's house was a thirty-minute drive from Scorpio's condo, and when I got there, she was standing at the door with her arms folded. Feeling bad, I hurried out of the car and started to explain.

"I'm sorry. Time just got away from me and—"

"Whatever," she said, holding up her hand in front of my face. "Let's just go. Café Lapadero closes in about an hour, so it doesn't even make sense to go there now. Would you like to have a late dinner somewhere else?"

"Hey, it's my birthday. And you're the one paying so surprise me."

She huffed and walked to my car. I opened the door, and noticed a different look about her scrawnier dress and inviting cleavage. I closed the door and rushed to get in the driver's side. I had to find out what the new look was all about.

As I backed out of her driveway, I kicked up a swift conversation. "Are you thinking about where you're taking me?"

"You're the one driving, silly. Where would you like to go?" She crossed her legs. Her sexy brown thigh peeked through the slit in her turquoise dress, the soft material of which crisscrossed over her breasts. It bugged the hell out of me. It was classy, but I was used to Nokea being a bit more conservative.

"You know, wherever you want to go is fine with me," I said, not being able to keep my eyes off her breasts. "But, what's up with that?"

"I'd like to go to the Ritz Carlton for the night, and there's nothing up with my breasts."

"The Ritz Carlton, huh? And what do you think is going to happen at the Ritz Carlton?"

"Dinner, maybe. I really just want to spend some time alone with you, if you don't mind."

"Okay, then, the Ritz Carlton it is."

I pulled over at the Mobil on New Halls Ferry Road to fill my tank before getting on the highway. Nokea went inside to get something to drink. Her short-ass dress irritated me, and when I watched this man inside flirt with her, I felt my pressure rise. He held the door for her, then had the nerve to squint at her ass as she pranced back to my car. He nodded, giving me a thumbs-up.

I ignored him, but when he got into his pearly-white Escalade and pulled next to us, I was two seconds from going off.

He lowered his window. "Say, brotha. I'm not trying to be disrespectful, but is that your lady?"

Nokea lowered her window and answered for me. "No, I'm not."

"Well," he smiled and cleared his throat. "You are stunning. Do you think I can get your number and possibly take you to dinner sometime? It would truly be an honor."

Nokea flirted, "Only if you promise to be on time." She reached into her purse and pulled out her business card. She wrote something on the back, and stuck her hand out of the window to give it to him.

Standing in disbelief, I took my hand off the gas pump and rushed to the other side of the car. I leaned down to her.

"What in the hell is up with you? Don't you have any damn respect for me?" I tore the card into tiny pieces and tossed them inside his car. "If you're that desperate, glue it back together and call her."

"Hey," he said. "I don't want any trouble. I thought she was just a friend." He took one last glance at Nokea, rolled up his window, and drove off.

I finished pumping my gas, and slammed the door when I got inside. Nokea jumped. "What are you so upset about?" she asked. "And how in the world did I just disrespect you?"

I jetted off and didn't say a word to Nokea until we got on Highway 270. "You disrespected me when you walked your butt out of the house with that short-ass dress on. If the wind blows any harder, your ass will be showing. That's probably what that motherfucker back there was looking at."

"For your information, I like my dress. And whether I had it on or not, that man would have asked for my phone number. If you don't like it, that's too bad. I didn't wear it to entertain you."

"Please. And don't get me wrong. It's a beautiful dress, however, I do not," I yelled, "want the mother of my child in the streets with nothing like that on. Again, it's too damn revealing for someone as conservative as you are."

"Conservative or not, I like it. It's not my problem that men like you can't keep your hormones under control."

"Oh, I got control. It's going to take more than a dress like that to turn me on."

She turned away and looked out the window,

"Good. Then I guess you won't have any problems keeping your hands to yourself tonight. Besides, I'm sure Scorpio took good care of you anyway."

"If you say she did, then she did. But, now, I see why Chad came on to you like he did. If this is your new way of dressing, then don't get mad when brothas step to you like that."

"Don't even go there, Jaylin." Nokea's voice rose. "Pat and I are having lunch next week and I'm going to tell her what happened. Don't you go making me feel guilty about the way I look, okay?"

"All right, I won't. Sorry if I hurt your feelings. Truth of the matter is, you look good, baby. I don't like no brothas looking at you like that, but if you want to, keep your little come-fuck-me dress on. You just might get what you're asking for."

Nokea laughed and shook her head. "I swear, you are so crazy. Downright crazy, but I love your crazy butt."

I leaned over to give her a kiss on the cheek, while trying to keep my eyes on the road. "I love you too, but you messed up your loving tonight by trying to give that man your phone number."

"Darn, and just when I didn't think I had anything coming. Sorry, though, I couldn't help myself. He was really handsome."

"What? Is that what you call handsome?"

"Yes. He had that Denzel Washington look about him. You know that sexy, confident, masculine . . ."

"Yeah, yeah, yeah, whatever. But evidentially, you must have left your glasses at home because that brotha wasn't about nothing. Ol' buckethead mother—"

"You can say what you want, or call him what

you'd like but he was unquestionably a sight for sore eyes."

Deep down, my feelings were bruised. I decided not to stop for dinner, and didn't say much else to Nokea until we got inside the hotel room. She knew I was upset and tried to make small talk with me, but I went straight to the bathroom and closed the door. I took off my clothes and turned on the shower. As the water trickled down on me, I thought about my wild-ass day with Heather and Scorpio. Now, Nokea. There was no way I was going to get down with her tonight. And even though that dress was begging me to fuck her, and I'd visualized a slew of positions I wanted to put her in, my intentions were to take my ass back out there, talk, and go to sleep.

While finishing my shower, I closed my eyes and went into deep thoughts about my love session with Scorpio. When I heard the door squeak, I opened my eyes. The lights went out, and Nokea stepped into the shower and stood behind me. She massaged my back and rubbed my ass with her hands. I turned and brought her hands up to my lips, kissing them.

"As much as I would love to, I can't do this tonight," I said.

She pulled her hands away, then took my hands and wrapped them around her. Her dress was dripping with water.

"There are no such words as 'you can't,' Jaylin. Because tonight, I don't want any excuses. I say you will." She placed her hands on my goodness and started to rub it. Worked it so good that it gave her some attention. I backed her against the wall and untied her dress. She wasn't wearing any underclothes, so once the dress was off, there was nothing else to remove.

"Why are you making me do this to you?" I asked, touching her chin. "Are you sure you wouldn't want buckethead in here with you instead of me?"

"No. I think you will work out just fine. And as for making you do this to me, you're not doing anything to me that I don't want you to do."

"Yes, I am. I'm going to hurt you, Nokea. I'm only being honest with—"

"Shh . . . be quiet. Just promise me that you'll hurt me in a good way, Jaylin."

She pushed my head down toward her breasts that I'd already cupped in my hands. I started sucking them, and as I made my exchange from one to the other, she squirmed around and turned her back to me. I pressed my naked body against hers and kissed the back of her neck. Working my lips down her back, I squatted to part her legs. When I dove into her, she was relaxed and calm as ever. Fucked me up, too; there was no doubt in my mind that she had been there and done this before. The thoughts of Stephon fucking her kept flashing before me, but I was trying hard like hell to stay focused.

Once we got out of the shower, we climbed our naked asses into bed and got busy. Nokea confessed her love for me over and over again. As good as she had me feeling, I had no shame in telling her how much I still loved her. She gave me head for the first time and did it like a pro.

"Hold on, baby," I yelled, sitting up. "What in the hell have you been doing?"

She laughed. "What do you mean?"

"I mean, you ain't been practicing with anyone, have you?"

"No, Jaylin. I've planned this day in my mind for months, so enjoy, and please don't interrupt me again." She got back to business and I really couldn't complain. Never in a million years did I think my baby would be able to perform like she was. Stephon must have taught her well. The thought discouraged me, but there was no way that he was ever coming back her way again. I'd make sure of that. And as a matter of fact, no brotha out there was going to tap into Nokea or Scorpio again. I could be considered a selfish son of a bitch, but when it pertained to the two of them, I had no intention of sharing.

Chapter 11

Nokea

When I woke up, Jaylin was still sleeping. I had dozed off between his legs, and he'd held me tightly in his arms all night long. I rose up a bit and glanced at the clock: one-fifteen in the afternoon. Waking up this late hadn't been in the plans, but we couldn't help ourselves. We hadn't been this connected in a very long time. I was so glad to have my man back in my possession.

I lay there for a while staring at Jaylin snoring, one hand resting behind his head, turned and sunken into the plush pillow. His hair had curled up even more from all of the sweating last night. Even resting peacefully, he was one handsome man. I took my fingers and rubbed them through his hair. I gently placed my lips on his to wake him, but he didn't budge. I straightened his thick eyebrows and rolled my fingertips across his long lashes. He still didn't move, but when I rubbed myself against his goods, then backed up like I was getting out of bed, he squeezed me around my waist and smiled.

"Where do you think you're going?" he whispered.

"You can stay here and sleep the day away if you'd like. I'm getting ready to go get our son."

"And how do you think you're going to get there without a car?"

"My dress is dry. I was planning on hitching a ride from someone. I'm sure somebody would be happy to pick me up."

"Well, let me get up. I sure in the hell don't want nobody picking my woman up from the street." He removed his hand from behind his head. "What time is it?"

"Almost one-thirty in the afternoon."

He put his hand back behind his head. "Shit, it's still early. I thought it was at least four or five."

"Jaylin, get up so we can go get LJ. He's been with Nanny B all night and I miss my baby."

"He's all right. I already called to check on him and Mackenzie this morning. Nanny B said she was cooking breakfast and the kids were still asleep. She said when they wake up, she's taking them to the mall, then to see her sister."

"Quit lying. You've been laying your butt in this bed knocked out since last night, snoring."

"Naw, that would be you snoring, not me. I dropped the phone when I finished talking to Nanny B and you still didn't wake up."

"Whatever, Jaylin. I do not snore," I said pointedly.

"Besides, I would have felt you move and heard you talking on the phone. And I've been messing around with you all morning."

"Incorrect. You haven't been messing with me all morning. You just woke up less than thirty minutes ago. You looked at the clock, stared at me for a while, played around with my hair, straightened my eyebrows, poked me in the eyes, kissed me, and now you're hoping that I'll get your juices flowing again."

"That's not fair. Were you pretending to be asleep? You couldn't have been awake because your eyes were closed and you were snoring. As for making love to me, trust me, I've had enough for at least . . . two weeks."

He laughed and wrapped his legs around my body. "So what, I was pretending. But I'm not pretending when I tell you I want some more juicy-juice before we go."

"So, I see you're rejuvenated again, are you?"

He smiled. "Naw, baby. I'm just excited to have my pussy back, that's all."

Jaylin and I made up for lost time, and didn't leave the Ritz Carlton until six o'clock. I stood out front and waited for him to get his car. Like a true gentleman, he opened the door for me and shook his head when he closed it. He smirked when he got in.

"What's on your mind?"

"Nothing."

"Why do you keep smiling then?"

"Because I'm a happy-ass man, Nokea. That's why."

"No, I think it's more to it than that. It's the

dress, isn't it? Please don't start with me today, okay?"

"I haven't said a word about it. However, I do want you to do me a favor when we get to my house."

"And what might that be?"

"Please, take that son of a bitch off and cut it up. I don't ever want to see you in it again. That damn thing had my ass hard as a rock. The last thing I want is another brotha to get the same ideas I have."

"No way. I paid $350 for this dress, and I'm not going home to cut it up because you can't handle it."

At the stoplight, Jaylin pulled his wallet from his pocket. He took four one-hundred-dollar bills out and laid them on my lap. "When we get to my house, I'll give you something to change into, since I just bought that dress from you."

I threw the money at him and rolled my eyes. By the time we pulled into his driveway, we were still debating the dress. Surprisingly, Scorpio was standing outside leaning against her car while talking to Nanny B. Mackenzie was inside the car, and LJ was clinging to Nanny B's leg.

Jaylin looked uncomfortable, and when I leaned over to kiss him, he gave me a quick peck on the lips. He at least opened the door for me, but before I had one foot on the ground, he rushed over to pick up LJ. Mackenzie got out of the car, and Jaylin took her hand. He didn't say one word to Nanny B or Scorpio and went inside. I stayed outside to talk to Nanny B and Scorpio, who looked very upset.

"Was LJ on good behavior last night Nanny B?" I asked.

"Yes, he was Nokea. He wasn't no problem at all. He was tired from all that company yesterday."

"Well, thanks for watching him. I told Jaylin how much I miss him when he's away from me."

"I know how you feel. That's my baby too, you know. I enjoy having him and Mackenzie around. I took them to see my sister today and she fell in love. You two really have some beautiful children. I was just telling Scorpio that before you and Jaylin came."

"Thank you. I don't know what we would do without you." I kissed Nanny B on the cheek and gave her a hug.

The whole time I stood talking to Nanny B, I could see the fury in Scorpio's eyes as she checked me out. She'd never given me a second look before because she'd always felt as if she was more attractive than I. True to the fact or not, I definitely had her attention today.

"Nokea, that's a beautiful dress you're wearing," Scorpio said, staring.

"It is pretty, and sexy too. I noticed it when you got out of the car. And that color really looks good on you," Nanny B added.

"Thanks," I said. "Jaylin hated it, though. He complained about how revealing it is. We argued about it last night and this morning."

"Well, I like it," Nanny B insisted. "Turn around. Let me see how the back is made."

"It's nothing spectacular." I turned around. "The color is what makes it."

"No," Scorpio said. "I think it's your thin waist-line and your petite body that makes it. And since it's one of those dresses you can't wear any panties with, I don't quite understand why Jaylin wouldn't like it. Any woman with that kind of dress on would be right up his alley. Since it was on you, I'm sure he was pleased."

Nanny B pulled out a cigarette from her pocket. "On that note, I'm going to take a smoke break. Don't y'all tell Jaylin I'm out here smoking because he will have a fit." She laughed and walked off.

"Listen," Scorpio said. "I didn't mean to be so bold, but it is a nice dress. If I had it, I would definitely wear it whether Jaylin likes it or not."

I smiled, thanked Scorpio for the so-called compliment, and went inside the house to get LJ. She followed. We walked upstairs to Jaylin's bedroom, and heard him loudly talking on the phone, laughing. He was lying across the bed talking to Stephon with LJ sitting on his stomach, and Mackenzie laying her head on his chest.

"Man, you are a fool," he paused. "Let me hit you back in a lil' bit, though, all right?" He sat up.

"Come on, Mackenzie. Let's go," Scorpio said, holding out her hand for Mackenzie to take it. Mackenzie rolled her eyes and got off the bed.

"Why she gotta go? I'll bring her home later," Jaylin said, pulling Mackenzie toward him.

I picked up LJ because I didn't want him in the middle of an argument I truly felt was about to go down.

"Jaylin, she needs to spend some time at home

too. She's over here more than she is at her own damn house." Scorpio looked at Mackenzie. "Now, go get your things and let's go."

"Just in case you didn't notice, Scorpio, this is her house too. I said I'll bring her home later."

Scorpio gave him a hard stare. "Playboy, don't argue with me right now, okay? I'm bound to say something I might regret, so it's best that you let us leave quietly."

Jaylin laid back on the bed, put his hands behind his head, and looked up. "Well, the Playboy says she stays and if you got a fucking problem with that, too bad." Before Scorpio could say anything, I turned toward the door with LJ. "Nokea!" he yelled. "Put my son back down. I was playing with him, if you don't mind."

"Mackenzie, go downstairs with Nanny B," Scorpio insisted, and pushed Mackenzie toward the door. I moved and let Mackenzie pass.

"Jaylin, look, I'm just taking LJ downstairs out of the way," I said.

"Put him on the damn bed like I told you to!" he yelled. I ignored him and turned back to the door. He hurried off the bed, but Scorpio stood in front of him, stopping him dead in his tracks. Nanny B came up the steps, her forehead lined with wrinkles. She took LJ from me.

"What in the hell is going on up in here?" she asked. "Jaylin, I know I don't hear you yelling at these women like that."

"Hey, I was in here minding my own damn business, and they're the ones strolling in here, taking my kids like I'm not even here. What kind of shit is that? So, now, fuck it! Everybody can get the hell out." He went over to his nightstand and grabbed his keys. He tossed them to Nanny B and she caught them. "Please take Nokea and LJ home for me. I don't want you burning all the gas out of your car."

"Jaylin, I'll take them home, but when I come back we need to talk. This type of behavior doesn't make any sense and you know it," Nanny B said, jiggling his keys.

Scorpio was so frustrated that she grabbed Mackenzie and left. I waited in the hallway with LJ while Nanny B went to get her purse. Jaylin yelled down the hallway from his room, "Nokea!"

"What?" I yelled back and went into his room.

He came out of his closet with a long white Ralph Lauren shirt and some jogging pants in his hand. "Take off that dress and put this on."

I put my hand on my hip and shot him down with fury in my eyes. "I will never understand how you can make love to me like you did today, tell me you love me, and then come home and act like a complete idiot."

Nanny B came into the room and took LJ from me. "We'll be in the car waiting." She walked out.

"Nokea, just take off the damn dress and put this on, would you?" He reached out to give the clothes to me. I snatched them from his hands and threw them on the floor.

"I will do no such thing. I'm one minute from losing my religion on you. Please don't make me go there, okay?"

He bent down and picked up the clothes. He held them out to me again. "You're one minute from losing your religion and I'm five seconds from snatching that motherfucker off you. So, take the damn dress off like I asked you to."

"No!" I screamed. "For the last time, Jaylin, I said no! This is my dress, I like it, and it stays on me. If you don't like it, fuck you!" I turned to walk away. When I reached the top of the stairs, he grabbed me from behind and pulled on the dress, ripping the back of it. He stood holding part of it in his hands. I seethed with anger, and smacked him as hard as I could on his face. He rubbed it and grinned.

"So, you got your lil' smack, and I got what I wanted. Just don't touch me like that again or I'll hurt you."

Standing there half-naked, I snatched the clothes from Jaylin's hand and put them on.

"You are one sexy-ass woman when you're mad," he said, reaching for my waist.

I pulled away from him. "If you want to bring out this *sexy* woman you think I seem to be by cursing at you, and by putting my hands on you, please just leave me alone. My parents didn't raise me to disrespect the ones I love. How about yours?"

"Ouch. Now, you really didn't have to go there. But if you must know, nobody taught me shit. If anything, you should know by now that when I say something, I mean it. Next time I tell you to do something, just do it. Then, all this kind of tedious bullshit can be avoided."

"Thanks but I already have a father, Jaylin. I'm not in the market for a new one. And if I were," I said, walking down the steps, "it wouldn't be you." He stood at the top of the staircase, smiling at me like he truly got a kick out of the entire situation.

* * *

After Nanny B dropped us off, I gave LJ a bath and laid him down for the night. I checked my messages. Everybody had called. Mama and Daddy were upset with me for not bringing LJ over yesterday, Pat was cursing me out for not calling her back, and Jaylin called about ten times apologizing. I called Mama and Daddy back and explained why I didn't come over yesterday, and then I called Pat and apologized to her. When I told her I spent the night with Jaylin, she hung up on me. She called back two minutes later and apologized and we made plans to get together for dinner the following Friday. As for Jaylin, I deleted his messages. His mind needed some serious rest and I was in no mood to argue with him again.

Chapter 12

Scorpio

There was no doubt about it that Jay-Baby had to go. He was getting over and successfully doing so. He called and tried to apologize to me, but I wasn't having it. I let him beg and plead for forgiveness to the answering machine and had no intention of returning his phone calls.

Going forward, all of my time was going to be focused on finishing school and taking care of Mackenzie. I wasn't going to stop him from seeing her, but as far as I was concerned, what we had was over. I knew it would be hard for me to move on, but I had to out of respect for myself. If I ever wanted to be with him again, I had to become some type of challenge for him. At least make him think about what he would be missing if he didn't get his act together. Right now, I was too easy for him to get over on and he knew it. I only hoped Nokea was thinking the same way I was. She was much easier than I was and she seemed to cope better than I did with all the bullshit he put her through. I wanted to ask her if he'd made love to her the night of his birthday, but her dress and his inability to look me in the eyes said it all. I was sure that Jaylin worked her and worked her well. Besides, satisfaction was written all over her face. She had a glow about her, and it was a glow that only a man like Jaylin could give a woman after sex. Thing was, though, he didn't even care if we knew about his little birthday extravaganza. He seemed kind of proud to be with both of us in the same night. And then, to make love to me like he did, tell me he loved me for the first time, and promised me he wouldn't sleep with Nokea . . . Shame on me. Shame on me for letting shit go this far.

I left class on Wednesday night excited about the A I'd gotten on my algebra test, and headed to Shane's studio apartment to thank him. When I arrived, I took the black barred elevator to the fourth floor. When I stepped off the elevator, he was sitting on a stool in the corner of the room, talking on the phone. He waved for me to come on back to where he was. I stepped over paint cans and canvasses on the floor. He had a window open to clear the paint smell, and white sheer curtains blew as the wind came in. Paintings and sketches were all over the place. The hardwood floors had paint blotches everywhere, and the entire room could be summed up as cluttered. In the middle of the floor there was a king-size canopy bed with black steel bars. It was draped with sheer white material. Clean, white cotton sheets covered the mattress. It looked odd in the center of the room like that, but I guessed there was no other place for him to lay his head.

I listened to Shane end his conversation, and couldn't help but hear him say Felicia's name. He hung up and asked me to have a seat on an old metal chair that was also speckled with dry paint.

"No, that's okay," I said. "I'm not going to stay long. I wanted to personally come over and thank you for helping me out like you did." I pulled the test from my purse and flashed it in front of his face. "Bam! Look what I got today."

He took the paper out of my hand and smiled. "I told you that you could do it, didn't I?" He gave me a hug. Issey Miyake wore him well, and his scent reminded me of Jaylin. I quickly separated myself from our embrace and took back my test.

"You know, this calls for a celebration," he said. "Why don't you stay a while?" He sat on the stool again, folding his arms in front of him. His muscles bulged from under his white short-sleeved T-shirt, and I thought freaky things to myself. A Gucci black belt held up his dark blue wide-legged Levi's. Since he still had on his rubber boots, I suspected he'd been for a ride on his motorcycle.

"No, really, Shane, I can't stay. I promised Nanny B I would pick up Mackenzie by ten o'clock tonight."

He looked at his watch. "Hmm . . . it's only eight-thirty. You have time for one glass of champagne, don't you?"

"Just one."

Shane kicked off his boots and walked over to the refrigerator in the other corner of the room.

He pulled out a bottle of wine, then grabbed two wine glasses from a shelf.

Just as he headed toward me, the phone rang. He put the wine and glasses down on a bookshelf and answered it. While talking, he leaned against the bookshelf and folded his arms.

He was looking so worthy of my loving tonight, and by the way things were going with Jaylin, there was no telling what I might do. I knew it was in my best interest to exit fast. Even his freshly done twisties had me gazing at him: his hair was neatly parted with the twisty's flowing in the same direction. His brown skin was smooth; it definitely had a shine about it, and his puppy-dog eyes had already undressed me.

I put the test paper back inside my purse and pulled out my car keys. He heard them jiggle and quickly said good-bye to the caller. He retrieved the wine and glasses from the bookshelf.

"Sorry about that. That was one of my students. I try to make time for them whenever they call."

"Oh, I understand. But . . . I need to get going. Let's make plans to celebrate some other time."

"Okay. But it will only take a few minutes for me to pour us some wine."

"Shane, next time, okay?" I turned to walk away and he grabbed my hand. He slid my purse off my shoulder, pulled me in close, and wrapped his arms around me.

"Why do you keep fighting this when we get together?" He looked eye-to-eye with me and moved my hair away from my face. "I've thought about making love to you over and over in my mind. I know you've thought about it too, so let's just do this, okay?"

"Shane I—"

"Don't reject me, Scorpio. I know about your situation and I'm just here to help."

"What about Felicia? I heard you talking to her when I came in. Are you seeing her?"

"No. She's a friend from the past and I'm searching for a future with a woman who doesn't mind letting me show her what she's been missing."

Now, with that being said, I took a deep breath and followed Shane to his bed. I kicked off my heels and scooted back on his bed. The mattress was soft and the sheets felt like cotton balls as they touched my skin. Shane pulled his T-shirt over his head and removed his belt. He put the belt in his mouth while he unzipped his pants. I leaned back on my elbows and watched him pull them down. My pussy thumped from the nice-sized package that was about to enter it. As he walked to his dresser, I realized I had never set eyes on a more nail-gripping ass than his. He pulled out a condom, then turned to me.

"Must we?" he asked.

"Yes."

"I really don't want to."

"But I'm intimate with someone else right now. We don't always practice safe sex, and you don't want to take the risk, do you?"

He opened the package, and as he put on the condom, I watched his goods expand. He kneeled by the side of the bed and put my feet in his hands. After kissing and rubbing my feet, he eased his hands between my legs. He slid my panties down and rubbed them in his hands.

I smiled, "What are you doing?" He ignored me, laid my panties on the floor beside his bed, and stood in front of me. My legs fell apart, and before he put his body between them, he took a lengthy glance. He pulled my dress over my head and stared at my naked body.

"Turn over and lay on your stomach," he asked politely. He scooted back so I could roll over. I knew he'd see Jaylin's name tattooed on my ass, but he rested his body on top of mine. He whispered in my ear, "I take lovemaking very serious, Scorpio. I'm not going to fuck you because I got a feeling that somebody's already doing so. And, I'm not going to talk to you because I don't talk when I'm concentrating on doing something. I will tell you, though, that Jaylin's ass got it going on. If he fail to get his shit together, just let me know."

He placed his lips on the edge of my shoulder and kissed down my back. I was burning hot from his touch, and when he lowered himself and separated my ass cheeks, I didn't know what to do.

My body trembled when I felt his tongue and fingers searching deep within me. I closed my eyes and squeezed my hair in my hands. When he vibrated my insides with his mouth, I completely lost control. I rolled over and put a high arch in my back as I screamed out loud.

Shane laid next to me and pulled the cover over both of us. He pecked the tip of my nose and propped his head with a pillow, smiling. I rested my head on his bicep and rubbed his admirable chest.

"You had no intention of having sex with me, did you?" I asked.

"Of course I did, until you told me you were intimate with someone else. And something about Jaylin's name tattooed across your ass just changed the mood."

"Shane, everybody has somebody to get down with when need be. I didn't think it was in my best interest to lie to you. As for the tattoo, it was a birthday present. There's not much I can do about that."

"Hmm . . . And I appreciate your honesty. It's just that Jaylin and I got some unresolved issues. The last time we butted heads about a woman, I kind of got my feelings hurt. It wasn't that I was in love with Felicia or anything, but the way things went down kind of hurt me."

"But I'm not Felicia. I wouldn't do anything to purposely hurt you."

"I know you wouldn't but Jaylin has a way with women. I never figured out what it was and I just can't believe it's all about the sex. He once told me it was, but I think it takes more than just a big dick to keep a woman. Maybe I'm wrong, but this time, I refuse to let the big-dick syndrome stand in my way of doing the right thing to begin with."

"So, how do you plan on doing the right thing?"

"There's no doubt about it that I'm digging the hell out of you. The reason I held your panties in my hand is because you have an amazing scent about you. One that almost had me taking the risk of hurting myself again. But this time, I'm going to sit back and watch this one play itself out."

I put my head on Shane's chest, then wrapped

my arms around his body. "Are you sure you don't want to change your mind? I was really feeling what you were doing to me, you know."

He laughed. "I could tell. I got a feeling that our day will come, but for now, let's just chill. And when our time does come, I'm going to be a happy man and you're going to be an overjoyed, completely fulfilled woman. Trust me."

As much as I wanted Shane to fuck me, I was kind of glad that he didn't. I was confused, and having sex with him would only confuse me more. I drove home so impressed by him, thinking about how his touch had turned me on so quickly. My short time with Shane had been an eye-opening experience; Jaylin wasn't the only man who could make me quiver.

In the car, I reached for my cell phone to call Nanny B. She told me Jaylin had already left for my place with Mackenzie since it was almost eleven o'clock. I asked if he was upset about me being late and she said he wasn't. But, when I turned the corner and saw his car parked in the front of my condo, I had a feeling something wasn't right.

I walked slowly to the door and thought about what to say. When I went inside, he was sitting in the living room chair with his legs folded and a blank stare on his face. He glanced at his watch.

"Nice of you to finally show your ass up."

I tossed my keys on the table. "You can leave now. I'm here." I went into the kitchen. The door swung and almost hit him in the face as he followed me.

"Classes taking all damn night now, huh?"

"No. I had something else to do."

"Something to do like what?"

"Look," I said, turning to him, "it's really none of your business." I opened the refrigerator for something to eat, but Jaylin pushed me away, slamming the door.

"Scorpio, whether you like it or not, you are my business. I got all kinds of money tied up fucking with you, so therefore, I'm here checking up on my investment." He pulled the kitchen chair away from the table and sat down. "So, let's try this again: where have you been?"

I pulled a chair from the table and put it right in front of him, then held his hands in mine. My eyes watered as I spoke. "Can we please end this? I'm tired, Jaylin. Truly sick and tired of your disrespect. I can't give you what you're looking for. Take this . . . this condo, the Corvette, the watch, the clothes, the gifts, everything. I'm leaving this relationship with what I had when I came into it, and that's love for myself." I released his hands and wiped my tears. He leaned forward and put his hand on my cheek.

"Yeah, whatever. Now, where have you been? Leave me if you want, I really don't give a damn, but I still want to know where you've been tonight?"

It finally hit me. Jaylin really didn't give a damn about me. All he cared about was if somebody was screwing me better than he was. I wished like hell that Shane and I had made a different move, but for now, I put my face right in front of Jaylin's and yelled with gritted teeth, "I was out getting my pussy sucked by an old friend of yours, Shane Alexander! He sucked it so good that I couldn't help myself from coming in his mouth. It's so funny how time flies when you're having fun, ain't it?"

Jaylin sat like a zombie. His stare felt almost life-threatening, and when he shut his eyes, I knew he was pissed. He leaned back, taking a moment to stroke his goatee. When his eyes opened, his eyebrows rose, and he said calmly, "Shane Alexander? That's been your mystery man all along, huh? I should have known when I saw his motorcycle outside that day." He swallowed. "Tomorrow, Scorpio. I want you to get the fuck out of here. I want the keys to your car and I don't ever want to see or hear from you again. As for everything else, the watch, the gifts, the clothes, the gratifying dick— keep that shit. Eventually you'll wind up selling everything for money anyway. Mackenzie, she's moving in with me. If you want to fight me for her you'll have to take me to court. I'll fight you with one of the best damn lawyers in St. Louis. Personally, I don't think a judge in their right mind would side with a stripper or homeless mother, and let's not give Mackenzie the opportunity to tell them how she really feels." He stood and lifted my chin. "I was really starting to love you. Thinking seriously about asking you to be my wife. It's a damn shame you fucked up, though. In the meantime, if you're looking for a way to reconcile with me, call me tomorrow before midnight. Maybe I'll forgive you, or maybe I won't. If you don't call me, Cinderella, your glass slipper and all the gifts and freebees I've been given you turn back into a raggedy-ass tennis shoe." He leaned down, gave me a peck on the lips, and left.

Chapter 13
Jaylin

That hot-ass coochie! Words couldn't express how upset I was with Scorpio. I was so frustrated, I had to go to Stephon's house to talk to him about the situation. It was almost one o'clock in the morning when I called, but I sounded so grim he told me to come right over. I called Nanny B and thanked her for lying to Scorpio about Mackenzie being with me, when in reality she was still sleeping at my house. I hadn't wanted to bring her home, knowing that Scorpio and I were bound to go at it. Seemed like that's all we'd been doing lately. There used to be a time when she just went with the flow and kept her mouth shut, but I guess Shane Alexander had her looking at things a little differently.

He was one motherfucker who just bugged the hell out of me. Since he acted like such a little bitch when I took Felicia from his ass, I ain't had much respect for him. He claimed he didn't love her, so what was the big damn deal? Women come and go all the time and he knew what kind of woman Felicia was. He also knew that ain't nobody's shit safe these days, especially with a brotha like me around. Whomever I want, I get. No ifs, ands, or buts about it.

When I got to Stephon's house, he already had the door open for me. He yelled my name from in the kitchen and told me to come on back. When I came in, he was sitting on the counter, scraping some ice cream from a container.

"So, what's so important you had to interrupt me in the middle of the night?" He put the spoon in his mouth and licked the ice cream. I got a spoon from the drawer, but when I reached for his container, he snatched it away. "Man, you better get your own. It's some more in the fridge."

I laughed and pulled out a container of Ben & Jerry's Confession Obsession from the fridge. Preparing to let off some steam, I hopped up on the other side of the counter and dove in.

"Have you seen Shane Alexander lately?" I said.

"No, I haven't. I heard he was back in town, though. Why are you asking?"

"Because that punk motherfucker is going to be a thorn in my side, that's why."

"What do you mean by that?"

"I mean, that nigga been sucking my woman's pussy. She's been seeing this mystery man that I haven't questioned her about, and tonight, she told me that it was Shane."

"Which one of your women?"

"You know which one, man, Scorpio."

"Damn! Lucky son of a bitch." Stephon shook his head and laughed.

"Man, don't play. I'm serious. Shit hurt me like hell. I was really starting to trust her and that was the only reason I made that bet with you. Too, I was really starting to feel *something* for her ass."

"Did she tell you she wanted to be with Shane or what?"

"Nope. But I know Shane. He's a persuasive brotha. Personally, I think if he even suspects I'm with Scorpio, he's seeking revenge."

"Why? Because of the Felicia bullshit back in the day?"

"Exactly. So, I need you to set up something for me."

"Something like what?"

"I don't know. That's why I'm here. You're a creative brotha. Throw a party or something. Send the man an invitation . . . Do something. I want to see what's up with him."

Stephon rubbed his chin like he was in deep thought. "I just thought of something. I was at Felicia's house the other day, and when I came in, she was on the phone. When she went to the bathroom, I looked at the caller ID and it showed Alexander, S. I laid it down and didn't think nothing of it."

"Do you think it was Shane?"

"Had to be. I didn't press the issue because I could care less about who Felicia talks to."

"You wouldn't have looked at the caller ID if you didn't care. And what if it's his baby she's having and not yours? Wouldn't you like to know? No doubt, the Black Stallion gon' be a problem for us, I can feel it."

"Yeah, you might be right. Listen, I'll get one of my boys from the shop to set up something. It won't be no party because I think just the three of us need to catch up on old times. You catch my drift?" Stephon got off the counter and so did I. "Now, we've got to wrapped this up. I got not one but two ladies waiting for me downstairs. I'll give you a hollar tomorrow."

"Straight up? You going out like that now, huh?"

"Always. I'm trying to get myself in good shape for when I fuck Scorpio. Bet's still on, right?"

"Hell, naw! Fool, don't play. Bet is off! Don't you go near her, man, and I mean that shit."

"As much as I would love to, I promise you I won't. Seems like you kind of got some deep feelings for her, and I will never let another woman interfere with us again. But, uh, with that being said, do you think I can get my money by tomorrow?"

"You don't give up, do you? Ain't like I believe she'll let you shake her down anyway, but since I broke the bet, and I'm a man of my word, I'll wire the money to your account in the morning."

Stephon patted my back. "Five thou is cool. And if you'd like to come downstairs and join the party, I'm sure the ladies would be more than happy to share."

"Naw, not tonight. Knock yourself out. My shit still trying to recover from my birthday."

"I can't believe Heather and Scorpio were too much for you."

"Let's not forget about Nokea. Worked her all night too."

"You lying. Are you working that again?"

"Fasho. And thanks for loosening up everything for me." I winked. "Makes my job a lot easier now."

"No problem. But you know I'm jealous, don't you?"

"Too bad—get over it. You shouldn't have been up in there to begin with."

We laughed, and after he walked me to the door, I jetted.

When I got back home, Mackenzie was still asleep in her room. I knocked on Nanny B's door and she told me to come in. She was wide-awake, lying on her side and watching TV.

"Jaylin, sit down for a minute. I need to speak with you."

"Nanny B, can't it wait until tomorrow? I'm tired. I've been running around ever since I got off work."

"This won't take long. I promise you."

I took a seat and loosened my tie. "Okay, what's up?"

"Don't you ever ask me to lie for you again. Scorpio called in a panic looking for Mackenzie, and I had to apologize for lying to her. I don't like lying to anyone, and you shouldn't have involved me in your mess."

"You're right, and I'm sorry. I just didn't want Mackenzie being around us arguing, that's all. I promise you I will never ask you to lie for me again."

"Good. Because if you ever put me in a situation like that again, I'm leaving. I'm fifty-seven years old, and I do not want to be caught up in the middle of your games."

"That's fair. And once again, I promise you it will never happen again." I stood and headed for the door. I did have a slight attitude, only because Nanny B always tried to check me and put me in my place. This time, though, she was right, so I couldn't trip too much.

"Jaylin?"

I turned at the door and sighed. "Yes."

"I love you like a son. And before you go to bed tonight, call Scorpio and let her know Mackenzie is okay."

"I'll call her tomorrow. And thanks, I love you too."

The phones were going crazy at work and everybody was running around the office in a panic. The stock market had plummeted; all my clients were losing money. I took one call after the next, trying to calm my clients. The market was bound to turn around, but there seemed to be no end to the brutal setback we'd all endured. I was losing money too, but I couldn't let anyone see or know how much pressure I was really under. I loosened my tie from around my neck and kept my eyes locked onto the monitor in front of me. Angela was doing her best to keep up with my calls, but I had to also be the secretary to make sure everybody got served.

By one o'clock in the afternoon, I had to take a break. I still hadn't heard from Scorpio, and was disappointed she hadn't called yet. Nokea called, though. She told me how scared she was about meeting with Pat on Friday, and needed a little pep talk. I told her to bring LJ by on Friday, and let him spend the weekend with me. Her meeting with Pat didn't sound like it was going to be pretty, and like always, I offered her my support.

The moment I hung up the phone, Angela buzzed in to tell me a man was outside insisting we had an appointment today. My planner had nothing scheduled, but I asked Angela to invite him in.

She opened my door, the man following her. He was Caucasian, about six-two, wore a black suit, and had neatly combed back his salt-and-pepper hair. He took a seat before I could offer, and laid a brown leather briefcase on my desk. When he crossed his legs, I caught a glimpse of his expensive-looking, shiny deep burgundy shoes. Diamonds gleamed in his gold cufflinks. I could smell money on him a mile away, which, I thought, could prove to be beneficial for me. I asked Angela to close the door, and introduced myself.

"I'm Jaylin Rogers," I said, offering my hand. "I'm sorry, but I don't recall making any appointments today."

He stood up and gripped my hand. "Jaylin, I'm Mr. Robert McDaniels. We didn't have an appointment today, but I'm positive that you can find time in your busy schedule for me."

I strutted back to my chair, and thought hard about who in the hell this man could be. When he opened the briefcase, it hit me. He was Heather's husband. He turned the briefcase around and removed a tape from inside. Before he closed it again, I saw that it was full of money. I didn't say a word. He slid the tape across my desk.

"Do you have any idea what's on this tape?" he asked.

"Nope, not a clue."

"I think you do know. But since you insist that you don't, I'm going to enlighten you." He moved my crystal framed picture of LJ and Mackenzie over to the side and sat his ass on the edge of my desk. He picked up the tape, and shook it around in his hands. "On this tape is you having sex with my wife. That includes the mud-slinging bash, the foyer fucking festivities, and even the one that burns me up the most. And that's when you took it up on yourself to screw her in *my* bed." He sat back in the chair and rested his finger along the side of his face. "So, Mr. Rogers, we need to have a serious talk. Talk about how I'm going to make you disappear."

I smiled, picked up the blue crystal globe from my desk, and rolled it around in my hands. I looked at him through it, then set it down again. I thought about pitching it into his face, but there was a better way of dealing with this situation. So, instead, I leaned back and bounced a pen up and down on my desk. "Mr. McDaniels, did you learn anything from watching the tape?"

"Yeah. I can honestly say I did."

"Really? And what might that be?"

"I learned that I have a whore for a wife, and I also learned if I have to kill someone I will do so."

"Damn," I grinned. "Sounds pretty painful. But I was hoping that you learned how to fuck your wife better, so a brotha like me wouldn't be able to step in and dick her down like I did. Or, should I say, like I do because I just tapped into that tight-ass pussy the other day. You didn't get that on tape because it occurred at my house, not yours."

"Ha," he shouted and smiled. "You are a piece of work, aren't you? But little do you know, Mr. Rogers, I know everything there is to know about you. So, let's see . . . As a matter of fact, you did lay my wife at your house. On your thirty-second birthday, if I recall. Then you drove around in your fancy Mercedes Benz and found yourself some more pussy for the day because my wife just wasn't good enough. Now, I can understand why because, whew, the woman whose condo you drove to that night was beautiful." He drew the word out, enunciating each syllable. "And the one with the spiked hair and short turquoise dress, wow! I gotta hand it to you Jaylin, you definitely know how to pick 'em." He stood and opened the briefcase again so I could see the money. "If my sources and calculations are correct, I'd say your net worth is about, let's say, one-and-a-half million dollars. And that's at the most. I'm proposing half of that today, and I'm asking you to disappear as quickly as possible."

I snickered at his offer and clapped my hands. He was really starting to work my nerves. After I stroked my goatee a few times, I stood and turned the briefcase toward me. "I must say, you definitely have done your homework." I closed the briefcase and smiled. "Thirty-three, Mr. McDaniels. I turned thirty-three on my birthday, and not thirty-two. Not only that, but you forgot to do the extra-credit on your homework because you are several million dollars shy of my net worth." I picked up the briefcase and opened the door for him. "Next time you come see me, you need to come correct. I'm a Negro that's not for sale, so go home, fuck your wife, and feel free to watch the tape again. You just might learn how to make that pussy talk to you like it speaks to me."

He stood face-to-face with me and took the briefcase from my hand. "Next time, Jaylin, I'm not going to be as pleasant. I'll pay you another visit in the near future, and when Higgins and Schmidt find out what kind of animal they have running things for them, those assets you have are going to disappear."

I laughed. "Animal, huh? I think of myself as an animal sometimes too. Not a monkey, or any animal like that, but like a panther, a black panther that prowls and creeps into your bed at night and fucks your wife when you're not there. And as for my assets, please. This job is playtime for me. I only come here because I don't have shit else to do. There is nothing that you, Higgins, Schmidt, or any other motherfucker can take from me because my true money comes from my inheritance. Black folks get those too, you know? So, for the last time, get your ass out of here so I can get back to business. My message light is blinking, and I'm sure it's probably your wife on the phone begging me to fuck her."

He winked and chuckled. "Jaylin, it's been a pleasure." He held out his hand to shake mine, but I just looked at it and grinned. "You're really going to wish that you never came in my house for a drink that night. Right about now, I'd hate to be in your shoes."

"Good day, Mr. McDaniels, and the next time you come, show a brotha a lil' appreciation for bringing your wife back to life. You failed at doing so, and it's been a true pleasure for me."

He walked out, and Angela gave me a puzzled look. She couldn't wait to question me, but I was in no mood to talk. She told me Scorpio stopped by to see me, but left after being told I was in an important meeting.

I slammed my office door and checked the messages Angela had transferred to my voicemail while I'd been in with McDaniels. Stephon had called to say that Shane would meet us at Freddy's Bar & Grill that night. We had all been friends in the past, and it had been he and I who fell out over Felicia, not Stephon and Shane. Scorpio had called, too, to say she would be back to see me around three. Nokea had called, thanking me for talking to her about the Pat situation. Two of my clients had called, and Heather had left a message about me coming to see her later. I took a deep breath and hung up the phone. Feeling a bit under pressure, I rested my elbows on my desk and massaged my temples. I hated feeling this way, but there was no way I was going to let anything get to me.

I picked up the phone, and punched in Heather's number to tell her about her stupid-ass husband. There was a knock, then Scorpio cracked the door open. "Angela's not out here, so is it okay to come in?"

I put the receiver back in its cradle. "Sure. I've been waiting for you to come. Shut the door behind you." My eyes were all over Scorpio. She looked magnificent. She'd parted her hair down the middle, and both sides were full of long, fluffy curls that hung on her shoulders. Her rosy pantsuit had a long jacket that buttoned down the middle and squeezed her perfect waistline. The cuffs of her pants slightly flared out over her red three-inch heels. She sat down in front of my desk, and when she removed her dark DKNY glasses, her puffy eyes gave her away.

"I guess you know I'm here to talk about this second alternative you mentioned last night," she said, putting her keys on my desk.

"You know, it's really simple. And don't go trying to make me feel sorry for you by letting me see you've been crying. I have no sympathy for you."

"Good," she said, sharply. "Now, what's the alternative?"

"Are you rushing me?"

"Yes. So what's the other alternative?"

"I'm one minute from throwing you out of here with this bad-ass attitude you got, and when I tell you that today is not the day to fuck with me, you'd better believe it. So, let's start this conversation over . . . Are you rushing me?" I yelled.

"Yes, but that's because I can't stand the sight of you, and you can't stand the sight of me. The faster we get this over with, the better. I'm here to do whatever I have to do to keep a roof over my head, food in my mouth, and clothes on my back, until I can do better. So, for the last time, what's the alternative?"

"I never said I couldn't stand the sight of you.

You actually just made my day when you walked your pretty self through the door. What I don't understand is why do you feel that way about me?"

"Jaylin, look, I don't feel that way. But who cares about how I feel? You don't. Besides, that's not the point. The point is that I need to know what to do to make this better between us?"

"That's simple. Question is, do you love me?"

She dropped her head and looked down at the floor. She swallowed hard, then lifted her head back up as a tear rolled down her face. She swatted at it. "What does that have to—"

"Do you love me!" I spat each word at her. "If you do, then let me hear you say it!"

A few more tears fell and she nodded. "Yes, yes I love you, but what the hell does that have—"

"Good! And I love you too!" I picked up the phone and slammed it down in front of her. "Call this motherfucker Shane and tell him it's over! Tell him who you love and tell him you never want to see his ass again!"

She shook her head. "Jaylin, that is so petty. Shane knows who I love."

"Then he won't have a problem with you telling him again." I picked up the receiver. "What's his number?" I asked, ready to dial it myself. She turned the phone toward her and dialed. I hit the button for speakerphone to make sure she wasn't playing no games with me. And just my luck, the bastard answered.

"Hello?" he said.

"Shane, hi. It's Scorpio."

"I know. Recognize your sexy voice anywhere."

I looked at Scorpio with disgust.

"Hey, I need to talk to you about something," she said.

"I hope about when, where, and how we're going to finish up what we started last night. I've been thinking . . ."

Scorpio hesitated and I whispered for her to get to the point. "Shane," she interrupted. "I've been thinking about last night too, but I'm afraid I'm going to have to say that you were right."

"Right about what? Hopefully about us being together?"

"No. About me possibly hurting you because I'm in love with Jaylin. It was wrong for me to let things go as far as they did last night when I still have strong feelings for him. I was just calling to say I'm sorry about the whole thing, and if you don't hear from me anymore it's because—"

"Because you're afraid to let a real man love you. I felt a connection with you last night. And no matter what you say, I know you felt it too. If you're telling me that you're moving on, fine. I'll accept that and I truly wish you well." He hung up.

I turned off the speakerphone. "Now, that wasn't so bad, was it? And since you really love me, that made it a whole lot easier, didn't it?"

Scorpio stood and removed her keys from my desk. She put her glasses back on and headed to the door. "Sex tonight?" I asked. "I think we got a little something to celebrate."

"And what might that be?" she said dryly. "Never mind, surprise me, Jaylin. You seem to be full of surprises lately, so wait until later to tell me. I'm sure whatever it is, I'll enjoy it."

"You always do, don't you? And put on something

sexy. Red is your color, but black makes me rise a bit faster."

"Black, blue, purple, green, whatever," she said, still with attitude. "Your shit will rise no matter who or what color it is. I don't have anything sexy to put on, so don't count on it."

I reached in my pocket and pulled out a hundred-dollar bill. I balled it up and threw it in her direction. It landed at her feet. "Go buy yourself something sexy. Thanks to me, Saks Fifth Avenue probably knows you by name, don't they? And since you're so good at spending my money, I'm sure it won't take long for you to find something *black* that arouses me. I'll be there by nine, so don't disappoint me." Scorpio looked down at the money, rolled her eyes, and walked out. A little while later, I gathered a few of my belongings and left for the day. I noticed that Mr. McDaniels hadn't taken his tape with him, so I tossed it into my brief-case in case I wanted to watch it later.

As I was driving, I called Heather's cell phone number. She didn't answer, so I left a message for her to call me. Sure her hubby would hear it, I spiced it up a bit and told her I was dying to fuck.

When I got home, Mackenzie and Nanny B were in the bonus room watching *Monsters, Inc.* I showered, changed clothes, and told them I would be back later. Mackenzie put up a fuss, but I promised her we would do something together on the week-end when LJ came over.

I got to Freddy's Bar & Grill around seven o'clock. Stephon was already sitting at a booth, and waved at me when I came through the door. I didn't see Shane yet.

Stephon must have had the same idea as I, because his outfit was banging. We both had on our leather pants and lizard-skin boots. He wore a multi-colored sweater with zigzags on it and a hat to match. I wore a black-ribbed, long-sleeved v-neck sweater that hugged my muscles and matched my black leather boppy hat. My gold diamond Rolex glistened on one wrist; my thick nugget gold bracelet on the other.

"I know you didn't try and go all out for this brotha, did you?" I said, grinning and bumping knuckles with him.

"I didn't try, I did. And looks like you did too." We both laughed and sat the booth.

"So, where this ol' wishy-washy nigga at? Probably at home soaking cause I made Scorpio call him today and diss his ass."

"Whaaat? And she did it?"

"Come on, you don't have to ask, do you?"

Stephon shook his head. "Jay, you know you be playing with fire."

"Who gives a damn? I'm so mad at her ass that I could just kill her. Tonight, though, I'm gonna put a hurting on that ass."

"You need some help?"

I laughed. "Naw, man, I got it all taken care of. I'm gonna set that ass out so good tonight, that when another brotha walk by she'll be afraid to even look at him."

"Well, damn. Just don't make it where she don't want to look at my black ass."

"You silly, man, but, uh, I kind of got a bigger fish to fry."

"Bigger fish like what?"

"Mr. Robert McDaniels. Heather's husband. Son of a bitch came on my job today and disrespected me. He threatened me and offered me seven hundred and fifty thousand dollars to disappear."

"And? What did you tell him? You better not have taken the money, Jay."

"Fool, don't you know anything about me? I told him to get the fuck out of my office and damn near put my foot in his ass. Thing is, he's been watching me. Trying to find out shit about me and I don't like that. I'm a private man, and I'd like to keep it that way."

"So, do you want to do away with this motherfucker or what?"

I looked out the window. "Naw, I ain't trying to go out like that, 'cause I hope after today he realizes I ain't no poot-butt Negro he can order around."

"Well, if I were you, I wouldn't even sweat it. If he dig a little further into our family's history, and find out how many relatives we got locked up for murder, he'll back off. If not, all you have to do is say the word. His ass will be the one disappearing. Just like—"

"Man, I know. Don't be talking that stuff up in here. Ain't no telling who might be listening. Besides, that punk-ass fool Shane is on his way in. I just saw him park his car."

"What's he driving?"

"A Lexus. An older one."

Stephon and I pretended to hold a heavy conversation when Shane came in. When he got to the booth, Stephon stood and displayed a wide grin. I didn't say shit and checked out Shane from head to toe.

"Whaz up, man? Ain't seen yo ass in a long time." Stephon said, then moved aside so Shane could slide into the booth next to him.

"Nothing, nothing much," he said. "Just been chillin', that's all. Teaching, tutoring, designing, and painting my life away."

"You forgot something," I said.

"Excuse me. Forgot what?"

"You forgot to mention that you've been placing your mouth where it doesn't belong."

"Ahh . . . So, that's what this is about. Scorpio? Well, I've been doing that, too, but if that's what you two gentlemen want to talk with me about, I don't have time."

"Jay," Stephon said. "Why don't you hold it down?" He looked at Shane who was getting ready to leave. I knew Stephon was trying to calm things down and remind us that we had been good friends once. But he didn't understand the level of animosity that stirred between us.

Stephon continued. "Shane, listen, we didn't call you here to scold you or anything. We just wanted to find out the down-low on a couple of females. Since we're boys and everythang, I thought we might be able to sit down and talk about this like brothas who got each other's backs. So, hang around for a while. Order yourself a drink and let's talk."

"Yeah, man," I said. "I apologize for coming off like that, but I'm having a bad-ass day today. My lady came home last night, late, and told me that she just got off in your mouth. Now, I don't know how upset you would be if it was your woman, but I ain't too damn thrilled about it."

"Trust me," Shane said. "I understand your pain. But a few years ago, my woman came into my bedroom and told me my dick wasn't big enough. Said she found a brotha with a mega thang who liked to work it from behind, and do it in the shower. And the killer part about it was when she said it was one of my closet friends. Can you even imagine how pissed I was?"

"Of course, but why you be out for revenge? Especially over a bitch like Felicia. If anything, I did you a favor."

"I know, Jay. And believe it or not, I'm not out for revenge. I think you have a beautiful woman, and if she wasn't yours, she'd definitely be mine."

"I'm feeling you on that one," Stephon said, pounding his chest. "I've been saying the same damn thing for months."

"Well, I don't care what neither one of you fellas say. She's my woman, she's going to be with me and only me." I paused and gave both of them a serious look. "And even though I have a funny way of loving her, I do."

"What? Shane, did you just hear what he said?" Stephon asked.

"Naw, I didn't. I must have something clogged in my ears. Did he just say he was in love with someone?"

"Naw, not Jay. This is definitely some new shit to me," Stephon said.

"Shut up. Y'all playas need to be quiet. Stephon, you know I've been in love before," I said, thinking about Nokea. I was still somewhat bitter about what had happened between her and Stephon, but I was doing my best to move on.

"In love? With who?" Shane asked.

"My nanny, nigga, that's who."

We all laughed.

After a few minutes of talking, Shane got up and went to the restroom. Stephon and I checked him out; he looked spiffy his damn self with his red Ralph Lauren shirt and blue jeans. He always was a bit more muscular than Stephon and me, and by the looks of things, his workout plan was not failing him at all. I now knew why Scorpio was interested.

When Shane came back to the table he had three drinks in his hands. He set them on the table. "Let me see if I remember this correctly." He gave me my drink. "Remy is your drink." He handed Stephon his. "Remy is your drink, and Remy is also mine. With that in mind, fellas, what does that say about us?"

I answered. "It says that we like the same drink and the same lovely-ass women." We clinked our glasses together in agreement.

Shane scooted back into the booth. "So, straight up, Jay. I'm out of the picture. Now, that doesn't mean if I see Scorpio a year or two from now and she tells me y'all aren't together. I'm letting you know right now that she's fair game."

"What about Felicia?" Stephon asked.

Shane's forehead wrinkled. "Felicia? What about Felicia?"

"Negro, don't lie. I saw your number on her caller ID."

"Stephon, you might have seen it because I finally called her back after she blew up my damn cell phone. I am not the least bit interested in her and I will never forget how she played me. But, what in the hell are you doing at her place? I thought she was with Jay?"

"Man, it's a long story. I've been trying to tell this knucklehead she's bad business," I said, looking at Stephon.

"Stephon, man, please listen to your cousin. She is nothing but trouble."

"Shane, Jay, mind y'all damn business. Y'all didn't say that shit when she was shaking a nigga down, so I don't want to hear it."

"He got a point now, Jay. I must admit, the brotha's got a point."

Shane and me bumped knuckles and cracked up. We sat at Freddy's drinking and updating him for nearly two hours on what had been happening since he'd moved. Numerous calls from Heather tried to interrupt me, but I didn't answer because I was having too much fun.

By nine-thirty, I was ready to call it a night. I told Scorpio I would be there by nine and didn't want to be *that* late since she was already mad.

"Well, fellas, I'm outtie. I'm getting ready to stop by a flower shop, buy my woman some roses, apologize for being an asshole, and make her pay for opening up her legs to Shane."

Shane laughed. "Man, if I could change what happened last night I would. She bad, though, Jay. Baby-Girl is bad!"

"I know. That's why she's with me." I stood, and tossed two dollars on the table for my four drinks, a huge plate of hot wings, onion rings, and a piece of cherry cheesecake.

Stephon cleared his throat. "We are truly jealous about you leaving us, and going home to put it on Scorpio. But bro, what in the hell is two dollars supposed to pay for?"

"I changed my mind, and now, I think my dick might be in the mood for Nokea. Either way, you did get that money I wired to your account, didn't you?"

"Fasho. And thanks for the extra."

"Good. Then I'm sure it will cover the cost of my food and then some. Shane," I said, grabbing his hand. "It's been a pleasure, and keep in touch, man, all right?" He agreed and I jetted.

Even though I might have been thinking about Nokea for a moment, I was on my way to see Scorpio. I was feeling kind of bad by the way I treated her, thinking about how hurt she looked in my office today.

I swerved down Olive Blvd. feeling the true effects of the alcohol. When I parked in front of Scorpio's condo, her car was outside, but there were no lights on. I placed the roses in my mouth and unlocked the door. I slid my boots off and walked back to her bedroom, but when I turned on the lights, she wasn't there. I looked at the bed and saw a folded letter with a set of keys lying on the top. I sat down and read the letter:

I'm sure the bedroom is the first place you would look for me, so there's no doubt in my mind that you would find this letter. Today was a wake-up call for me. You left me with little respect for myself, and I'm going as far away from you as possible to get it back. Never in my wildest dream did I think I would fall this hard for you. But my problem occurred when I started loving you more than I loved myself. You are a cruel man, Jaylin. Maybe because when your mother was killed you had to live in an orphanage, but nobody's life is perfect. I lost both of my parents at an early age and had to do without, but it never gave me the right to mistreat the people who were replacements in my life for me to love. Your watch is in the dresser drawer, your clothes are in the closet, your keys to the condo and Corvette are on the key ring, and, yes, your pussy is gone.

I closed the letter and reached for the phone to see if Mackenzie was still with Nanny B. When she told me Scorpio had come to get her at eight o'clock, I slammed down the phone. Full of anger, I threw the phone against the wall and fell back on the bed.

"Damn!" I yelled out loud. "I'll be mother-fucking damned!"

Chapter 14

Nokea

My dinner plans with Pat had already been made. She wanted to meet at Applebee's on Lindbergh so we could catch a movie at Jamestown Mall afterward. I wasn't sure if she would still want to go to the movies after I told her about Chad, but I had put off talking to her long enough.

She'd blamed my sudden distance from her on Jaylin coming back into my life. I hoped she wouldn't blame my distance on my inability to converse with her about my relationships with Jaylin and Stephon, but at some point, I started to feel embarrassed by the whole thing. I wanted those days to be behind me, and the less I talked about it, the better. Still, I just couldn't face her after what Chad had done to me. More so, I couldn't face him, and I knew that being at her house would make me uncomfortable.

When I got to Applebee's, Pat was already waiting

for me at a table. She smiled and stood to hug me. As we embraced, I closed my eyes and swallowed. I felt devastated about what I had to do.

"Say, Miss Thang," she said. "Good to see you. Have a seat so we can catch up on things, since Jaylin's been taking all my time away from me."

"Pat, you know it's not even like that. I have never put Jaylin before you."

"Please. Yes, you have and you know it. Don't make me sit here and go there."

"Okay, maybe I have. But you know I love you, don't you?"

"Of course I do. That's why I ain't tripping." She laughed. "Anyway, how's my baby doing? I didn't even get a chance to see him on his birthday and I was crushed."

"Well, you know it was big Jaylin's birthday too. Nanny B had a get-together at his house, and afterward, Jaylin and I spent the night at the Ritz."

"Yeah, I know. I remember you telling me, but how can you still sleep with him, Nokea? He is trifling. I mean downright, straight-up trif—"

"Pat, please don't talk about him like that. Jaylin has many good qualities, too. Besides, I didn't come here to listen to you tear him down. I came here to have a nice dinner with my best friend, and to talk to you about something I've been holding back on telling you."

"Fine. I won't talk about the ho-bitch and please, *please*, don't tell me you're pregnant again. I don't think I'll be as excited for you as I was the first time."

"Pat, what is up with your attitude? No. I'm not

pregnant, but if I were, you'd be the last person I would tell right about now."

"Look, Nokea, I'm sorry." She took a sip of water. "Something has been bugging Chad and he won't tell me what it is. I know my husband better than anybody, and I can sense when something ain't right. When I ask him what's wrong he just blows me off like it's nothing. Anyway, I don't want to spend the day talking about these crazy men in our lives. What's been on your mind, girl?"

I took a few sips of my water to avoid eye contact with her. "Has the waiter come to the table yet?"

"Yes, Nokea. But what is it? I can tell you're starting to beat around the bush."

"Did you order for us?"

"Nokea?"

"Okay. I know . . . but this is so hard for me to say."

"Sweetie, we've been friends for fourteen years. You have never held anything back from me, so don't start now. Whatever it is, I promise you I will not make any negative comments about it."

"You promise."

"Yes, I promise."

"Okay," I said, holding Pat's hands across the table. "The last time I was at your house, Chad came on to me. He called and told me—"

Pat released her hands from mine. "Nokea, you know how Chad is. He's always joking around with my friends, and I'm sure he didn't mean anything by it."

"No, Pat. He actually tried to kiss me. He came up from behind me and put his lips on my neck. When I got home he called and tried to tell me how much I wanted him. I wanted to tell you sooner but I . . . I really didn't know how."

Pat yelled at the waiter who was servicing another table. "Would you please get me another glass of water! We've been waiting forever on you to take our order." The waiter hurried over to the table and asked us what we'd like to have.

"Pat, did you hear anything I said to you? I can't sit here and pretend that I'm not concerned about what happened."

"Nokea, I'm ordering right now because I don't know how to respond to you. When I'm upset, food calms my nerves. The sooner my food gets here, the faster I'll be able to say something to your selfish ass."

"Selfish? What do you mean by selfish?"

The waiter looked at us and said he'd give us another minute.

"I mean, all you ever think about is you. What you want. What you like. Who you've got to have. What you've got to have. The list goes on and on. But this time, you've crossed the line. Chad would never approach a woman like you because you're weak, Nokea. And I think Jaylin's got your mind so twisted that you're looking for anyone who gives you a little attention these days."

I tightened my eyes to fight back my tears. "Pat, you know I would never do or say anything to come between your marriage. As your best friend, I just wanted you to know wha—"

"As my best friend, you have stooped to an all-time low. I thought sleeping with Stephon was low, but this is crazy. I should have known I couldn't trust you then, but stupid me, always taking your side and being there for you when you needed me." Pat stood, and after taking a sip of her water, splashed the rest of it in my face. "Get that son of a bitch Jaylin to clean up your mess. You and him seem to be good at making them, so I'm sure he'll help you clean it up." She walked off.

I grabbed a napkin, and dabbed it on my face and silk fuchsia blouse. The waiter came over and gave me another napkin and asked if I needed help. I refused, thanked him for the offer, and left him twenty dollars for being so kind.

On the drive to Jaylin's house to pick up LJ, I thought about my conversation with Pat. Not in a million years did I think she was going to respond so negatively. I finally knew how she truly felt about me. It hurt so badly inside. I hadn't expected her to embrace me with open arms, but I'd thought she would at least talk to Chad before making any assumptions.

When I pulled into Jaylin's driveway, his car wasn't there. Earlier, we'd discussed LJ spending the weekend with him, but right now, I needed my baby in my arms more than anything.

Nanny B opened the door with him resting on her hip. "Nokea, I didn't think you were coming back until Sunday. Is everything okay?"

"Yes, it's fine." I took LJ from her and kissed his cheek. "Has Jaylin made it home yet?"

"No, but he's on his way. He called not too long ago and asked if LJ was here. I told him yes, so stay until he gets here. He's going to be so disappointed if he doesn't get a chance to see him."

"That's fine. We'll just go upstairs to his room and wait for him."

"Thanks, Nokea. Have you had something to eat yet? I cooked a pot roast, and if you'd like some you're welcome to it."

"No, that's okay," I said, walking up the steps with LJ. "Thanks though."

I turned on the light in Jaylin's room and put LJ on the bed. When I lifted his briefcase to put it on the floor, it flew open and papers spilled everywhere, along with a videotape. I put the papers back, and picked up the tape. The white label read, "Sorry son of a bitch," in big red letters.

Curious, I slid the tape into the VCR and pushed the play button. I watched as Jaylin's car pulled into somebody's driveway, and I immediately noticed Mr. Schmidt's daughter on the passenger side. Thinking nothing of it, I pushed the fast-forward button, but hit play again when I saw her walking around the house with a little of nothing on. Jaylin seemed mesmerized by her. When I hit fast-forward again, I saw her removing his shirt. I took a deep breath, fearing what was about to happen next.

I nervously placed my hand over my mouth and watched them having sex. Rain poured on their bodies, and they seemed to be all into it. Not wanting to put myself through this again, I quickly stopped the tape. I reached for LJ and ran out of Jaylin's room. As I moved down the steps, Jaylin opened the front door. I put LJ in his arms and jetted to my car. He yelled my name, but there was no turning back for me. I sped off and hit Highway 40, swerving in and out of traffic. I realized how important my life was, and how much my son needed me, so I finally slowed down. I pulled over and laid my head on the steering wheel. My tears wouldn't even fall; all I could do was scream. I pounded the steering wheel until the palm of my hands turned red. More than ten years of my life wasted, I thought. Wasted on a man who never wanted anything from me but security. I had been his security blanket when others failed him. I had been his security blanket when sex wasn't well within his reach, and more than anything, I had been a fool. A *serious* damn fool for love. My mind traveled back to the day of his birthday, and his visit from the same woman on the tape. I remembered wondering what was taking them so long. And I thought about Jaylin's look of guilt when they came out of his office. Her dress looked wrinkled and her makeup had suddenly disappeared. Why hadn't I put one and two together? He had been with her, Scorpio, and me all in one day. Pat was so right about him being trifling. How dare I defend him? I had never been so disgusted with him or with myself for allowing this foolishness to continue.

For nearly an hour, I sat in my car and thought about my damaged friendship with Pat, and ongoing relationship with Jaylin. What a mess, I thought, and finally drove to Cardwell's in Clayton to get a bite to eat.

The maitre d' asked if I had reservations, and since I didn't, I had a short wait. I sat, looking out the window at the drizzling rain, and dazed off thinking about my situation.

"I don't mean to bother you," said a man's voice, tearing me from my thoughts, "but haven't I seen you somewhere before?"

I didn't even bother to turn my head at the obvious pick-up line. "No," I said dryly. "I don't think so."

"Yes, I do remember you. From the gas station several weeks back."

I looked up at him. Sure enough, it was buckethead. That's what Jaylin called him anyway. Thinking about it, I smiled. "Hello. How are you?" I stood up.

"I'm fine. I saw you when you came in. Are you waiting for someone?"

"No, I'm dining alone tonight."

"Well, would you like to join my business partners and me? We were just about wrapping it up, but I'd be willing to stay awhile longer."

"No . . . no, please. I'd like to have dinner alone, if you don't mind. But thanks for the offer, Mr.—"

"Oh, I'm sorry. Collins, Collins Jefferson. And yours?"

"Nokea Brooks."

Just then, the maitre d' told me my table was ready. Collins kissed my hand, and I thanked him again for his offer.

As I looked through the menu, I could feel Collins staring at me from across the room. He had a perfect view and used it to his advantage. I crossed my legs to make sure he couldn't see up my short black skirt, and put the menu up high so he couldn't see my face. I felt a bit uncomfortable, but when I peeked behind the menu, Collins was getting ready to leave. He waved and I put the menu down on the table to wave back.

When the waiter came to take my order, he put a bottle of wine on the table and laid a business card next to it. He said it was from the gentleman "over there," and pointed at Collins's now empty table.

I picked up the card, which turned out to be Collins's. On the back he'd asked if we could have dinner soon and invited me to call him. I put it into my purse and waited for my food.

I finished dinner quickly, and afterward, I got a room at the Sheraton for the night. Jaylin had been ringing my cell phone like crazy trying to find out what was wrong, but I didn't return his calls. I hoped that Pat would call, but by the way things went down, I didn't expect to hear from her anytime soon.

Chapter 15

Jaylin

I spent the entire night at Scorpio's place, hoping she would come to her senses, and come home. By Friday morning I was sick to my stomach. If she took Mackenzie from me again, I thought, I would kill her ass. Take the pussy, that's replaceable, but a child I've grown to love is not.

Since I'd told Nokea I wanted to keep LJ for the weekend, I hurried home to see him, and tried to figure out what to do about Mackenzie. This time, I didn't give a shit who got hurt. In my mind, I was willing to go to the extreme to get Mackenzie back.

I pulled in the driveway and saw Nokea's car. We talked about LJ spending the night early on in the week, so I didn't understand why she was there. I opened the door and that's when she came rushing out like she was upset about something. I called her name several times, but she ignored me. Nanny B said that she had no idea what upset her, so I called Nokea's cell phone to make sure everything went cool with her and Pat.

Since she wouldn't answer her phone, I left her at peace and went upstairs to my room. I noticed the TV buzzing, so I turned it off. A tape ejected from the VCR. The tape Mr. McDaniels had left.

Nokea was angry because she saw the fucking tape. *Why in the hell would she go through my things any damn way?* I thought. I threw the tape on the floor and sat on my chaise.

"Jaylin," Nanny B said, coming into my room. "What was that loud noise?"

"Nothing. I just dropped something."

"Well, be careful. I was a little worried when you didn't come home last night."

"Sorry about that, I didn't mean to worry you. I needed some time alone to clear my head."

"I know how that is, and if you're hungry, I cooked a pot roast for you." She picked up LJ. "I'm going to lay him down for the night. He's had a busy day."

"Bring him here and let me hold him." Nanny B put LJ down on the floor and he stepped his way over to me. I smiled and applauded how well he walked. I laid him against my chest and kissed his forehead. "Let him chill with me tonight. I'll put him to bed a little later, okay?"

"That's fine. He's your son, you know? I know sometimes I get too attached, but I can't help myself. I love him like my own."

"I know you do. And trust me, I appreciate everything you do for us. Anyway, who can help themselves from getting so attached to him?"

She smiled, reached into her pocket, and pulled

out a piece of paper. "Here. Scorpio's sister, Leslie, called about an hour ago. I told her you would be here shortly, so call her when you get a chance. She sounded like it was important."

"Has Scorpio called?"

"No, she hasn't."

Nanny B gave me the paper and left the room. Before calling Leslie back, I tried Nokea on her phone again. I left a message and told her I knew she had seen the tape and we needed to talk. Wasn't no telling when she would want to discuss it, but I knew it was time to put closure to our half-assed relationship.

I called Leslie's house, and some silly asshole asked who I was, put the phone down, and left me hanging on for about five minutes. Leslie finally picked up.

"Jaylin?"

"Yeah, it's me."

"Listen, I called you earlier to tell you that Mackenzie is with me. I know you and Scorpio had a dispute, but she asked me to make sure Mackenzie spends some time with you."

"So, Mackenzie's there with you?"

"Yes but—"

"I'm on my way. Tell her I'm on my way to get her."

"Jaylin, wait a minute. I understand how anxious you are about seeing her, but Scorpio said she only—"

"Fuck what Scorpio said! She took off, left her child behind, so fuck her! I'm on my way to get Mackenzie, now!"

"Hey! I'm not going to argue with you about

this. I'm just trying to do what my sister asked me to do. And for your information, she was extremely upset when she left. She needs time to get her life back in order. I offered to watch Mackenzie, and out of her love for you, she asked that I made sure Mackenzie got a chance to see you. So, watch what you say about her. She's a better woman than you think she is."

"Yeah, yeah, yeah . . . whatever. Look, just pack Mackenzie's things and tell her I'm on my way."

"Not right now. I'm on my way to the laundromat and she has chores to do. I'll drop her off when I'm finished."

"Chores? Fuck your chores. She doesn't live there, and you're responsible for cleaning your own house. Can't you drop her off before you go to the laundromat?"

"You'd better watch it, fool, or you won't see her at all. I have seven kids and they're all going to help, including Mackenzie. I'm not making any special trips to your place just because you want me to. And the only reason I'm bringing her over there to stay is because she won't stop bugging me about you. So, be patient and I'll be there when I get there."

I gave Leslie directions to my house and told her in so many words to hurry the hell up with Mackenzie. It wasn't like she didn't know where I lived, because the last time she brought her ass over here, she took Mackenzie from me. Just the thought of Mackenzie helping her with her dirty-ass clothes upset me, but wasn't shit I could do.

LJ and I were lying in bed playing on my laptop, waiting for Mackenzie to come. Finally he'd fallen asleep, and at one-thirty in the morning, Leslie decided to show up. I heard the doorbell and rushed downstairs to answer it. When I opened the door, Leslie stood on the porch with Mackenzie standing next to her. Mackenzie held out her arms for me to pick her up.

"Girl, you're getting too big for me to be picking you up." I tickled her and picked her up anyway. She wrapped her arms around my neck and kissed my cheek. "Thanks for bringing her by, Leslie. And if you talk to Scorpio, tell her to call me."

"I'll tell her, but she won't call. And I'll be back to pick up Mackenzie on Sunday night."

I looked at the station wagon parked in front of my house with her seven kids jumping around in it acting like fools. "Leslie, please just let her stay. It looks like you already got your hands full, so let her stay with me until Scorpio comes back. If Scorpio calls for her, tell her to call me. Tell her I won't question her about her whereabouts; I'll just pass the phone to Mackenzie."

"I don't know, Jaylin. Let me talk to Scorpio first. I'll call you Sunday and let you know then."

She kissed Mackenzie and left.

I didn't care what she or anybody else said; Mackenzie was not going back to Leslie's house to save her soul.

I carried Mackenzie up the steps on my back. She laughed loudly, so I told her LJ was sleeping, and asked her to be quiet. She changed into her nightgown and climbed into bed with us. In less than five minutes, she was out like a light.

I couldn't sleep a wink. I had been downstairs

about fifty times nibbling on the pot roast Nanny B
had cooked earlier, and cutting slices of her pineapple upside-down cake. When I passed her in the
hallway, we laughed. I bent down and picked up
some crumbs I had dropped on the floor.

"You should be ashamed of yourself," she whispered. "Is there any left for me?"

"Yeah, there's plenty. But save some for tomorrow, all right?"

"Please. If it's not enough, I'll make another
one. Now, get your greedy butt back in bed before
the children wake up."

In my room, LJ was lying on his stomach with
his thumb in his mouth and his butt in the air.
Mackenzie was lying on her back, her long, curly
black hair spread out on my pillows, looking beautiful like Scorpio. I kissed both of them and tried
to take LJ's thumb out of his mouth. When he
squirmed, I left him alone.

I grabbed a pillow off my bed and laid it on the
floor. Then I slid Mr. McDaniels' tape into the
VCR. I propped my head with the pillow and
started to watch it.

About five minutes into it, I had a smile on my
face. It was straight-up wild. No wonder her husband wanted me to disappear. And Heather, she
was all into it, and looked as if she was enjoying
every inch of my thang inside of her.

I continued to watch the tape and my dick started
to climb. Having no woman in sight, I paused it
and stared at the ceiling. Nokea had to have been
devastated after seeing something like that. I knew
it wasn't in my best interest to lie to her again, so
I hoped she'd call back tomorrow. If not, I was

determined to see her and make things right between us. As for Scorpio, I wasn't sure how I was
going to deal with her. I was already missing her,
but was fighting every ounce of feeling I had for
her. If time away was what she needed, then that's
what I was going to give her. Eventually, she'd realize what she's missing, and come back begging for
forgiveness.

I slowly cracked my eyes, and saw LJ and Mackenzie hanging off the edge of the bed, staring at
me on the floor. I knew LJ wasn't going to keep his
balance for long, so I hurried to grab him. Morning had come that fast. I made my way to the bathroom with LJ, Mackenzie tagging close behind.

"Mackenzie, can your daddy have some privacy?
Take LJ to Nanny B's room to see if she's awake
yet."

She took LJ by the hand. "Come on, LJ. Let's go
downstairs. I think Nanna's in the kitchen."

"Be careful, baby. He's not good with steps yet,
okay? Ask Nanny B to help you."

"Okay," she said, walking slowly with LJ and
holding his hand. Nanny B must have heard me,
because just then she came down the hallway. I
looked at all of them and realized just how blessed
I was. All my tedious problems on the outside
couldn't overtake the love I had always dreamed of
having in my home.

I was on my way out of the shower when the
phone rang. I wrapped a towel around my waist. It
was Nokea.

"Hey, where are you?" I asked.

"I'm at the Sheraton," she said, dryly. "We need
to talk."

"Yes, we do. How long are you going to be there?"

"I'm on my way home. Meet me there in about an hour. And don't bring LJ with you."

"Okay. An hour it is. But, I wanted to tell you how sorry I am—"

"Jaylin, no need to apologize. Meet me in an hour." She hung up.

I slid into a pair of jeans and a thick brown cashmere sweater. Since I'd planned to spend the entire weekend with my kids, I told Nanny B I'd be right back.

Nokea was already at home when I got there. After I knocked, I rubbed my hands together and tried to keep them warm. She opened the door to let me in, but immediately turned away. I followed her to her bedroom. She was wrapping up a call with her mother.

As I waited, I took a seat in a chair that was caddy-corner to her bed. She told her mother that she loved her, and hung up, sitting across from me.

"Aren't you going to take off your coat and hat?" she said. "I do have heat, you know."

I edged up from the chair and removed my coat. I left my hat on because I didn't plan on staying long. "I know you saw the tape yesterday," I said. "Question is, why must you go through my things all the time, Nokea?"

"Jaylin, I didn't go through your things. Your briefcase fell open and the tape came out. I put it in the VCR, wondering why the words son of a bitch was on it."

"Curiosity killed the cat. So now you know that I screw white women too. What's the big deal?"

"Who said it's a big deal? It doesn't matter to me if the women in your life are African American, Caucasian, Italian, Puerto Rican, Irish . . . who cares? It's not about them anymore; it's about you. For as long as I can remember, it's always been about you. You go through life constantly hurting people, and the thing is, you don't even care. Is it ever going to be about someone else other than just you?"

"It is about other people in my life, Nokea. My children, that's who. You had your chance and you fucked up. What in the hell do you want me to do about it?" I rubbed my hands together and told her how I really felt. "You know, the more and more I think about everything that's happened lately, I blame you for creating this monster in me. I was trying to get myself on the right track, and then you played me with the Stephon bullshit."

"Wait a minute," she yelled. "How dare you sit there and blame me for your obsession with women? You need to man up and 'fess up to this mess you've got all of us in. But, somehow or someway, I knew you'd come here and blame me for your ignorance." She stomped over to her nightstand and pulled out a small black pistol. She aimed it at me and demanded that I get on my knees.

"Woman, you're crazy. I ain't—"

"Damn it, Jaylin!" she yelled. "I'm in control now! Don't argue with me, just do it! And don't think I wouldn't shoot you right now because I'm truly feeling as if I have nothing to lose."

I thought about rushing Nokea and taking the gun from her, but under the circumstances, decided that wasn't the best thing to do. After seeing the tape and meeting with Pat, her mind could be anywhere. I wasn't taking any chances, so I did as she asked and eased down on one knee. "Okay, so now that you have my attention, now what?" I asked.

"How does it feel letting a woman have control? For once in your life, how does it feel?" She moved in closer with the gun and aimed it directly at my face.

"Nokea, look. I'm not going to fuck around with you like this—"

"Shut up and listen! Can you do that for one time in your life?" I nodded and saw her hands shaking. "This bullshit between us is over! I don't need any more apologies, no more of your lies, nor do I need anymore of your hand-me-down-ass dick! We have a son together and that's it. Don't call me unless it concerns him, don't touch me unless I ask you to, and don't even think about grabbing this gun because I will blow your damn brains out!"

"Fine. But can't we talk about this without the gun?" I asked, getting ready to get up.

"Stay there! I didn't tell you to get up yet. And no, we can't talk without the gun because you won't listen to me without it."

"I promise you that if you put the gun down I'll listen. You've made your point, all right?"

The phone rang, startling Nokea. She turned her head, and I dove forward and grabbed her waist. We fell back on the bed and the gun hit the floor. She screamed and kicked, as I pressed my body weight down on her so she couldn't move.

"Calm your ass down!" I yelled. "Do you want to know the truth?" We continued to struggle, and once she realized that she couldn't overpower me, she chilled. I looked her in the eyes and held her hands tightly above her head. "I know you don't want to hear this, but I'm sorry. I understand how upset you must be, but I can't change anything that's happened in the past. I love you, Nokea, but I'm not in love with you anymore. My heart is moving in a different direction. Every time I see you now, I think of you making love to Stephon. Every time I touch you, I think of him touching you. I thought if you and I got married it would take away my hurt, but I now know that our marriage would have been a mistake." I let go of her hands and seemed to have her attention. I stood up and pulled her into my arms. "Aside of that, I can't stop being who I am. I love women too much to settle down, and I'm satisfied with the way things are in my life."

"But what about all these years we've shared together? Don't they account for anything? Why do they feel like such a waste?"

"Our years together weren't a waste. We got a beautiful son, Nokea, and we've always had each other to depend on. I knew making love to you on my birthday was a bad idea, but I just couldn't help myself. You will always be in my heart, but I'm having a difficult time accepting your past relationship with Stephon. I know he had his way with you, and I can't deny the change I saw in the way you made love to me. I have to start looking at you in a different way."

"I can't stress how my being with Stephon was a big mistake, but like you said, I can't change the past. After all the hurt we've caused each other, maybe we should consider just being friends." She laid her head against my chest and cried. "I . . . I don't want to hurt anymore, Jaylin. I'm tired of pointing the finger at each other. Do you think we can get on with our lives in a sensible way without being together?"

"Of course I do. But if you ever put a gun on me again, I'll hurt you, Nokea. I don't take shit like that too lightly. You hear me?" I moved her away from my chest to confirm what I'd said.

"The gun wasn't loaded, silly. I just wanted you to listen to me."

I stepped away from her and retrieved the gun from the floor. Once I removed the clip, I saw that it was empty. "You're a dangerous-ass lil' something. Where did you get this gun from and where are the bullets?"

"Jaylin, LJ and I live in this big house alone. If an intruder comes in here, I'm going to be ready. My father gave it to me and I keep the bullets in the drawer."

I opened the drawer and pretended to place a few bullets in the clip. "If an intruder comes in, you can't do anything with an empty clip."

"I took the bullets out before you came because I didn't know if you would try and take the gun away from me."

"Well, don't mess around like that. One of us could have gotten seriously hurt." I walked over to

Nokea and put my arm around her waist. "I'm sorry things didn't work out between us, but you know everything happens for a reason."

"I know. I'm a true believer in that as well, but I will never understand why they couldn't work out for us."

"But in the meantime," I shoved her back on the bed and placed the gun directly on her temple. "This is not a good feeling, is it?" She shook her head. "I don't care how damn upset you are with me, don't ever think about doing this to me again." I pulled the trigger and she screamed loudly while holding her face in her hands.

She snatched the gun away from me. "Jaylin! There were bullets in there. You could have killed me!"

"I didn't feel like it this time. Maybe next time I will." I snatched the gun and put it at the top of her closet. "Keep this damn thing up here. I would hate for my son to get a hold of it. Then I'd really have to kill you."

"Whatever," she said, still a bit shaken up.

Just so she didn't have to be alone tonight, Nokea packed a few things at her house and drove back to my place with me. While in the car, she told me how things went down with Pat. I really felt sorry for Nokea. Pat was the only true friend she had, and to lose her friendship and our relationship all in one day proved to me that she was a stronger woman than I thought.

When we got back to my house, Nanny B cooked a scrumptious dinner for us all, and made another one of her pineapple upside-down cakes. Since Heather had been calling me all week, I excused myself while they cleaned up the kitchen and went into my office to call her back.

"Yes," I said, moodily. "What's up, Heather?"

"What's up is why haven't you called me? My husband has been making all kinds of threats and I thought—"

"Well, you thought wrong. Your husband doesn't have enough courage to follow through with his threats, Heather. And I find it quite odd that you didn't know there were cameras throughout your house."

"I didn't know. Really, you have to believe me," she whined. "If I had known, I never would have asked you to come inside."

"That's bullshit and you know it. All I can say is if you love him, you'd better warn him. If he pays me another one of his unexpected visits, shit is going to start happening to his ass."

"If he wasn't away all the time, and sleeping around with other women, maybe sex between us wouldn't have happened."

"Good to know that you used me. And I'll be happy to say that I used you too, so the game is over, Heather. Have a nice life and holla at me some other time."

"Jaylin, wait! This was never a game for me. I'm feeling something for you. I haven't been happy for a long time, and being with you just makes me feel so wanted. I was thinking about having another rendezvous in your office again."

"Don't think so, baby. I'll pass this time, but whenever you see your husband, don't forget to tell him what I said. Again, if you love him, you'd better stop him from coming around me. Goodbye,

Heather, and good luck with your situation." I hung up and that was the end of that.

I had hoped to hear from Scorpio before the day was over, but she hadn't called. Leslie was supposed to pick Mackenzie up tomorrow, but she left a message that something had come up, and asked if Mackenzie could stay the week with me. It didn't matter to me because Mackenzie wasn't going anywhere. I did call Leslie back to thank her, and reminded her to tell Scorpio to call me.

By eleven o'clock, I was ready to shut down. Nanny B and Nokea cleaned up the kitchen, and LJ and Mackenzie were knocked out in Mackenzie's room. LJ had his own room but it was truly a waste. Either he was in with Mackenzie, or bundled up with Nanny B or me.

I grabbed some extra blankets and pillows from the linen closet, and led Nokea to one of the guest-rooms.

"Sorry, but this is the only bedroom that doesn't have a TV. If you want to, you can come in my room and watch TV with me. I'll be up for a while."

"Okay. I just might do that. But before I do anything, I would love to take a relaxing bath, if you don't mind."

"Well, there are six bathrooms around here. Feel free to use any of them."

"But yours is the only one with a Jacuzzi. Would it be okay if I relaxed in your tub?"

"Hey, not a problem. I'll go run some water for you now."

I went into the bathroom and started Nokea's

water. I dropped in a few flower-scented fragrance balls that dissolved in the water. They were Scorpio's, but I was sure Nokea wouldn't mind. As I sat on the bed and pulled off my shoes, Nokea stood in the doorway with a towel wrapped around her.

"Is it ready?" she asked.

I looked at her silky-smooth brown legs and thought dirty things. "Yeah, it's ready. Go see if the temperature is cool. I like it hot, but maybe you don't."

She went into the bathroom and closed the door behind her. Then she poked her head out of the door. "I like it hot too, but this is scorching hot. Are you trying to burn me or something?"

"No. It's not that hot," I said, getting off the bed and heading toward the bathroom to turn on the cold water.

"No need. I can handle the water, and thanks. Just find something for me to put on when I get out. And, look through your DVDs for a good movie to watch."

"Yes ma'am," I said, saluting her. "Anything you want."

She laughed and closed the door.

I removed one of my long white shirts from the closet and laid it on the chaise. I still had the negligee I bought from Victoria's Secret, but I thought giving it to her would be inappropriate, since we'd agreed to keep our relationship strictly platonic. The last thing I needed was for her to get the wrong idea, even though I knew getting over Nokea wasn't going to be that easy for me to do.

I had already changed into my pajama pants by the time Nokea came out of the bathroom. I was forty-five minutes into watching *John Q* and wasn't tired at all. Nokea walked past the television with a towel wrapped around her dripping wet body. I pointed to the shirt on my chaise, and when she removed the towel, my eyes focused back to the television.

"So, you couldn't wait until I finished before you started the movie?"

I sucked my teeth and gave her naked body a quick glimpse. "You took too long. I thought you drowned up in there or something."

She looked around the room. "Do you have any body lotion around here? You know, something with a feminine touch? My skin feels awfully dry."

"Yeah, I do. It's in the bathroom closet. It's not mine, it's Scorpio's. I hope you don't mind using it."

She flaunted her naked ass in front of me again and went into the bathroom. She came out squeezing lotion in her hands. "I don't care whose lotion it is. My skin is calling for some moisture. And no wonder you're forever taking baths. Your tub is so relaxing. That was actually my first time being in there. I kind of enjoyed it." She placed her foot on the chaise and rubbed lotion on her leg.

"Yes, my tub is very comfortable. I don't know what I would do without that thing in my life."

I continued taking quick peeks at Nokea, and felt my dick rise underneath the sheets. By the way she rubbed herself, I could tell she was teasing me, so I placed my hand on my hardness to keep it down.

Nokea turned off the lamp and got in bed with

me. My California-style king-sized bed was big enough where it left plenty of room between us. She slid two pillows behind her back, and another one behind her head.

"Are you comfortable?" I asked, looking over at her.

"Yes. Very. How about you?"

"Always." I turned to look at the TV.

Nokea yawned. "I'm tired. I think I'm going to call it a night. Besides, I've seen *John Q* about five times already."

"Five times? Why five times?"

Her eyes nearly popped out of her head. "Duh . . . Denzel Washington. Need I say more?"

"Aw, come on. He ain't that fine where you got to look at the damn movie five times."

"That's your opinion. And you're definitely entitled to it." She pulled the covers back and started out of bed. I quickly reached over and touched her hand.

"Sit back for a minute," I asked politely. She hesitated for a moment, then eased back in bed.

"Jaylin, I don't want any trouble out of you tonight. We said—"

I moved close to her. "I know what we said earlier, but this is going to be difficult. I am turned on by your sexiness, and can't we at least try to do without each other after tonight?"

She stared into my eyes, looking a bit defeated. "But I . . . I thought we said—"

"After tonight, okay?" I whispered and started to unbutton her shirt.

"After tonight, Jaylin?"

"Yes, baby, after tonight."

"No," she said, grabbing my hands. "We can't continue to do this."

"And we won't. After tonight, I promise you we won't."

I sucked her lips into mine and started to un-button her shirt again. It fell open and I leaned down to suck her nipples. Her head went back and she opened her legs wide so I could get between them. I pecked my lips down her stomach and massaged her breasts at the same time. She reached up for the cherry-oak thick pole on my headboard and gripped it. Her thighs went into position on my shoulders and I slurped into her insides.

"After tonight," she moaned.

I licked her wetness from my lips and pecked her thighs. "I promise . . . after tonight."

When I got ready to go at it again, Nokea placed her hands in between her legs, and slid them off my shoulders.

"Jaylin, when are we going to stop this?"

"Tomorrow. We're going to stop this tomorrow, so come on, let me finish," I said, trying to get her back into position.

"No we're not. We agreed to end this earlier, and that's what we're going to do. We can't keep doing this to ourselves. All this back-and-forth, wishy-washy stuff is driving me crazy. For once, let's just stick to the plan and see how it goes."

I let out a deep sigh and tried to move next to her in bed, but she got up and headed for the door.

"Goodnight," she said.

I huffed, "Goodnight, Nokea."

* * *

After lying in bed for hours, wishing I had something to get into, I finally dozed off. Around four o'clock in the morning, I crept into the kitchen to get a piece of cake. I could tell somebody had been there before me because there was a big chunk missing from it. I chuckled and hurried back upstairs before Nanny B saw me. Instead of going back to my room, though, I cracked the door to Mackenzie's room to check on her and LJ. I noticed he was gone, so I went to the guestroom where Nokea was to see if he was in bed with her. When I whispered her name, she sounded wide awake.

"What?" she said, softly.

"Is LJ in bed with you?"

"No." She pulled the covers back and got out of bed. "I thought he was in Mackenzie's room."

"He was earlier." We walked down the hallway together to Nanny B's room. She was sitting in a rocking chair reading LJ a story, while he slept in her arms. She placed her finger on her lips to keep us quiet. Then she motioned her hand for us to get out. We both smiled and closed the door. Nokea went back to the guestroom and got in bed. I leaned against the doorway, watching her lying in the dark.

"What? Why are you standing there looking crazy? If I didn't know any better, I'd think you were Freddy Krueger or somebody trying to come get me," she said.

"Ah, I want to come get you, but only in a good way."

"Jaylin, please let it go for the night. Stop trying to tempt me, all right?"

"You're the one who started it. You got your naked ass out of the tub teasing me and shit. Let me just come in and spank that ass one last time."

"Spank? Now, you know I don't get down like that."

I walked into the room and closed the door behind me. The room was pitch black and I got in bed with Nokea. "Well, show me how you get down. From previous experience, I know you're capable, but I'd like to feel it right now."

Nokea held me, and by mid-morning, we had seriously gotten down. Gotten down on some sleep because she wasn't giving in. She actually stood her ground, and even though I was disappointed, I was glad at least one of us was sticking to the plan.

Chapter 16

Scorpio

As hard as I tried to fight it, I was miserable without Jaylin. It had only been one week since I'd last seen him, and there I was, acting as if it had been a lifetime.

After he'd dissed me at his office that day, I had to get away. I'd called Shane later that night and apologized for my ignorance. He wasn't home, so I left a message on his voicemail. I wasn't trying to be his woman, but deep in my heart, I knew calling him because Jaylin wanted me to was tacky on my part. And for Jaylin to ask me to do something so immature was stupid on his.

I'd guessed their history together was more intense than I thought. And letting Shane go down on me was the worst thing I could have ever done. The last thing I wanted was to give them the opportunity to sit around and talk about me.

When I'd left Jaylin's office that day, I went to

my old boss, Jackson, and begged him to help me. He'd always been there for me, so he had no problem giving me the keys to his get-away house in Denver. I had very little money on me, so he wrote me a check for $5,000. I promised him that I'd pay him back. I'd borrowed money from him before, so he knew I was good for it. All I needed was a few months to get myself together. I thanked him for his help and jetted.

I knew there was no way I could stay in St. Louis to finish school, so I had to put my career on hold. I wasn't too happy about doing it, but Jaylin would be a setback for me if I hung around any longer. Being away from Mackenzie was the hardest thing I had to do, but the last thing I wanted was for her to see how unstable and miserable I was. I knew she would question me, and I wasn't prepared to tell her what a cruel person Jaylin had been to me, since she loved him so much. Realistically, I couldn't even offer her stability right now, and I knew she was in good hands with Leslie. Jaylin had everything in his control, including her. I had no one to blame but myself for thinking he'd have my back forever.

After I came back from a superstore I'd found in Denver, I put on a kettle of water to make some tea. The stove was one of those old-fashioned ones, white with black burners. Jackson's get-away house turned out to be a real hole in the wall. It had one small bedroom covered in dingy flowered wallpaper, with buckling hardwood floors. The bathroom had a white tub and sink with rust spots, looking as if they hadn't been cleaned in years. The tub itself slightly tilted to the side, and looked like it was about to fall through the floor. The kitchen wasn't too bad, but it wasn't cut out to be any woman's dream. There were foundation cracks in the walls and the appliances were seriously outdated. The cabinets had been refinished with a glossy cherry-oak wood, though, which gave some life to the room. The living room was nothing to brag about either, especially since it was empty and was painted light green. But, who was I to complain? For a person who didn't have anywhere else to go, I'd just have to cope with the spider webs I'd been brushing off the walls since I'd been here.

With some of the cleaning products I'd gotten at the store earlier, I tried to remove the stains in the tub, but eventually gave up. I'd been taking wash-ups since I'd gotten there, and it would've been so nice to relax in a tub. But so much for that. By late evening, I called Leslie to check on Mackenzie. Every time I called, Leslie had been beating around the bush. Either Mackenzie was asleep, or she was outside playing. I'd wondered if she'd gotten a chance to see Jaylin, and when Leslie finally told me Mackenzie had been with him since Friday, I was a bit upset with her. She explained how Mackenzie lit up when she saw Jaylin, and said that she didn't feel right taking her away from him. I knew how tight their bond was, so I didn't trip as much. I thanked Leslie and called Jaylin's house anonymously.

I was praying that Nanny B answered, but when Jaylin did, I hung up. I waited a few minutes before calling back, trying to get up enough courage to talk.

"Hello," he said, sharply.

"Jaylin, it's me. Where's Mackenzie?"

"Busy."

"Busy doing what?"

"Busy minding her own business."

"Kids her age don't have any business."

"Yeah, they do. She's got more business than you have, so what do you want?"

"I want to talk to my daughter, that's what I want."

"So, you didn't call to talk to me?"

"No."

"Okay, cool."

He gave the phone to Mackenzie.

She was so happy to hear my voice. I told her I had to go visit my sick cousin in Denver, and would be back soon. I asked how things were going at her new pre-school, and with Jaylin, and she seemed overjoyed. She told me about her new best friend, Megan, and told me LJ was walking. When I asked if she wanted to visit with Aunt Leslie, she said no. She begged me to let her stay with Jaylin and I told her she could.

We spoke for at least fifteen minutes and I told her I'd see her soon. I asked her to put Jaylin on the phone and he continued with his attitude.

"What?" he griped.

"I just wanted to say thanks for watching Mackenzie. You have no idea what it means—"

"Look, don't fool yourself. I'm not doing this for you, I'm doing this for me. Take all the time you need. Hell, take a year or two all I care, she'll be fine."

"I don't plan on being gone that long. I just need time to sort through these feelings I—"

"Scorpio, remember, you said you didn't call to talk to me. You talked to Mackenzie, so I'll holla at you later. Besides, I'm watching the football game right now."

"Okay, well I'll call to check on her in a few days. If you need me for anything, call Leslie. She knows how to get in touch with me."

There was silence, and then he hung up. I couldn't believe how cold he was. I put the receiver back down on its base, and poured a cup of tea. Feeling awfully lonely, I pulled a blanket off the bed and carried it into the kitchen. I stood by the old-time metal heater against the wall, banging on it to get the heat started. Wrapped myself in the blanket, I sat at the kitchen table.

Jaylin was on my mind; I'd never expected our relationship to turn out like this. I folded my legs against my chest and started to cry. I cried because being in Colorado was such a setback for me. I thought I was finally getting ahead by at least going back to school, but now even that seemed like a thing of the past. How was I ever going to manage without him? I'd been able to keep money in my pockets before I met him, but taking off my clothes for men was something I didn't want to start doing again. It was a last option for me, but it was still an option. Either way, I had to come up with a plan. This house was giving me the creeps, and I had to make a better life for myself if Mackenzie would ever want to be a part of it. If I never went back to St. Louis again, I didn't even know that she'd miss me. As long as she had Jaylin, she seemed to be just fine. And that hurt.

I decided to call it a night, and spread the blanket

on the living room floor to lie down. I turned on the tiny black-and-white TV that had a wire hanger for an antenna. I flipped through the fuzzy channels, and as I searched for something to watch, the phone rang. The only people who knew how to reach me were Leslie and Jackson, so when I heard Jaylin's voice, I was shocked.

"What did you say?" I asked.

"I said the football game is off. I'm ready to talk whenever you are."

"How did you get this number? I called your house anonymously. Did Leslie give it to you?"

"Scorpio, don't play yourself, all right? You know better than I do that I have ways of finding out things when I want to. And no, Leslie didn't give it to me."

"Well, how did you get it? Jackson, right?"

"Let's just say you don't cover your tracks very well. Is Denver as cold as St. Louis is? I'm sure it is, but if you want to stay cold, oh well."

"Okay, so you know where I'm at. Now what?"

"Nothing. Stay there. I'm just calling you back because you sounded like you wanted to talk."

"I did, but I don't feel like talking now. Besides, what I have to say doesn't matter anyway."

"You're right, it doesn't." He hung up.

I took a deep breath. The last thing I needed was Jaylin calling here with his mess. It puzzled me where he'd gotten his information, so I called Leslie to find out. She didn't answer, but when I called Jackson's place to ask him, he stuttered when he said he hadn't talked to Jaylin. I knew Jaylin must have gotten the information from him, and that money was probably involved. I yelled at him for snaking me, and told him I might as well have stayed in St. Louis if I had known he would tell my whereabouts. In an effort to avoid all bullshit, I took the phone off the hook for the rest of the night.

The loud buzz of the TV woke me, so I reached over to turn it off. Chilly, I lay on the floor swaddled up in the blanket. The floor seemed to had gotten colder, so I decided to take my chances with the mattress on the bed. The alarm clock showed three twenty-five in the morning, so I tried to get back to sleep.

As I dozed off, I heard a soft knock at the door. I looked at the clock again and it now showed five minutes after four. I slowly walked to the door, thinking somebody was at the wrong house. But when I turned on the porch light and saw Jaylin, I couldn't believe my eyes.

"Why are you here, Jaylin?" I asked, whispering through the door.

"Just open the door. It's cold out here."

I truly didn't want to be bothered. Just who in the hell from St. Louis was backstabbing me? I turned off the porch light and headed back to the bedroom. Time away from him was what I needed, and that was what I intended to get.

Jaylin banged harder and then he stopped. I closed my eyes and prayed for strength. But when I heard footsteps coming down the hallway, I sat up in bed. I could barely see because it was dark, so I reached over to the lamp and turned it on. Jaylin stood in the doorway swinging a set of keys in his hand.

"Now, I come all this way to see you and this is how you treat me, huh?"

I rolled my eyes and moved my messy hair away from my face. "Why are you doing this? Did Jackson give you a key too?"

"Baby, you know we brothas stick together. With some help of a little cash, he told me everything and offered me a key to get in. He said you would be difficult, and didn't want me to waste a trip down here."

I yanked the covers off me and got out of bed, bumping Jaylin's shoulder as I passed him. I ignored him and went to the kitchen so I could check on why the heater wasn't giving off any heat. As I banged on it, Jaylin leaned against the kitchen counter with his arms folded and stared at me. He had on a long tan cashmere coat and tan leather pants. His V-neck cotton cream-and-tan ribbed sweater matched his cashmere boppy hat that was tilted to the side, showing his curly black hair. The aroma he carried with him made me want to melt right into his arms. He looked spectacular, and I was doing my best to avoid him. I'm sure he wanted to make me clearly see what I was missing.

"Damn!" I said, continuing to bang on the heater. He unfolded his arms and came to me. I looked awful and didn't want him getting too close.

"You know you're going to break the damn thing if you keep hitting on it like that. You're probably better off buying a space heater." As soon as he said that, the heat kicked on. I walked away and sat at the kitchen table, laying my head on my arm to look up at him.

"Why can't you just leave me alone? Haven't you tortured me enough?" I asked.

He removed his coat and put it on the back of a chair. I couldn't help but notice his big bulge in his huggable leather pants, and my eyes dropped to the floor so I wouldn't stare. "Torture?" he said. He turned the chair around and straddled it. "Is that what you think I'm doing to you?"

"Yes. Yes, I really do. All I'm asking for is time to get myself together, and you won't even allow me that."

"I'm not here to torture you, Scorpio. I kind of missed you. Came all this way to see if you would come back with me. Christmas is coming soon and I don't want you here all by yourself."

"I'm okay. I think I'm going to stay here for a while. Maybe even see if Jackson will let me rent this place out if I agree to fix it up a bit. So, don't get too comfortable with Mackenzie being around. If things go according to my plan, I'll be sending for her soon. You'll just have to visit her here."

"Really," he said, looking around at the kitchen. "This place actually needs a lot of work. Are you sure you want to bring Mackenzie to this type of environment?"

"Jaylin, she hasn't always had the finer things in life and neither have I. For me, this ain't all that bad, especially if I fix it up like I want to. Mackenzie will just have to adjust, and this place has some potential. Like it or not, sorry, she's going to live wherever I live."

Jaylin took off his hat and put it on the table. He

picked up a toothpick and twirled it around in his mouth. "Scorpio, why don't you cut the bullshit and come home with me? This ain't no way to live. It's dirty, muggy, and colder than a motherfucker in here. It really doesn't suit you at all, and if you think I'm going to allow Mackenzie to come here with you and suffer, you're sadly mistaken. There's no potential in this, and if you want to fuck yourself, then do so. Don't make Mackenzie suffer, though, when she doesn't have to."

"What is so wrong with me wanting my child with me? I don't care how bad this place might look to you, but once I fix up everything, it's going to look nice. Like I said, it might not be what you're accustomed to, but Mackenzie and I will be just fine. Besides, it's about time I had something to call my own. That way I don't have to worry about anybody trying to run my life. You know what I mean?"

"So, this is about your independence, huh? Trying to prove to old Jaylin that you don't need any handouts from him. I'm cool with that, so let me not waste anymore of your time."

He stood and grabbed his coat from the chair. I stood too, and watched as he put it on. As soon as he picked up his hat from the table, a roach crawled across it. He shook it off and stroked his goatee.

"You sure this is what you want to do?" he asked.

My eyes filled with water. "This is not what I want to do, but this is something I have to do for me."

He pulled his coat back and reached for the

keys in his pocket. He tossed them on the table and caught me taking a glimpse at his goods.

"I'm not going to come back here again, so don't worry. And I'm not going to beg you to be with me, so don't worry about that either. I really thought you understood me better than anybody, but I guess I was wrong. And before I go, if you'd like to get your fuck on, just say so. Don't just stand there staring me down, being all fake and shit like you don't want me." I didn't respond, so he put his hands in his pockets and stepped up to me. His lips touched my ear, "Are we fucking or what?"

I shook my head, "No. Not this time. I need a life absent from you, and I insist on having it."

"You think so," he said, walking behind me. He reached his hands around the front of my silk robe and tried to untie it. I grabbed his hands and stopped him, but when he unzipped his pants, and pressed his hardness against me, I felt defeated. I bent my body over the kitchen table and let him hold my hips from behind. He flipped up my robe, and got a good look at my naked ass. I felt so ashamed. With tears in my eyes, I relaxed my body on the table and enjoyed the way he toyed with my insides. He held his dick in his hand, and circled my pussy with the thickness of his head, until he had the pleasure of soaking me. I reached back and helped him enter me, and when he did, he hit my insides from every angle that he could. It was just enough to make me think about what I was missing, and then he backed out. Continuing to torture me, he zipped his pants and used the tip of his tongue to lick his name tattooed across my ass.

He had no intention of finishing what he started, and as I remained on the table, he covered my butt with my robe. He leaned over me and whispered in my ear, "With a pussy that wet, you'll never get rid of me. I got more waiting for you at home, and as good as you are, a place like this doesn't excite me. Stop fooling yourself, Scorpio, and wake up before it's too late." He left the kitchen.

I fought hard trying not to go after him, but when I heard the front door open, I couldn't let him go.

"Jaylin!" I yelled from the kitchen. "Wait!"

"What's up?" he said, holding the door open. "Have you changed your mind about coming home with me?"

"I'll come back only if you're willing to make some changes. You have to stop taking advantage of me, and is it so hard for you to show me some respect? Did you come all this way just to walk in here for fifteen minutes, tease the hell out of me, and go back home? All I wanted was for you to tell me you love me, you miss me, and that you can't live without me. If not that, then share with me how much you've missed making love to me. Deep in my heart I know you're feeling something for me, but I need to hear you say it. I need assurance from you that all this bullshit is going to stop. So, yes, I'm miserable without you, but I refuse to go back to the way things are."

He slammed the door. "Look, I did tell you I missed you!" he yelled. "And as for living without you, trust me, I can. There's no need for me to go through all that other bullshit when you know how I feel. I'm not going to say what you want me to say, or feel how you want me to feel. That's stupid. If coming all this way wasn't enough for you, then fuck it! It was a waste of my time and yours too. Bottom line is I love everything about me. Why in the hell should I change because you want me to? If anything, you need to adjust to dealing with my ways, if we're going to be together. You've always said you would, but I guess since you got brothas out there sucking your pussy now, you want things to change. Fuck that, baby, I just can't do it."

I was in tears listening to him. "Regardless of what you say, Jaylin, sometimes we have to make changes for the ones we love. I've given up a lot for you and made plenty of sacrifices to make you happy. You haven't changed one damn thing for me. You know how much your cruel words have an impact on me, but you continue to ridicule me. You know how much you've hurt me. Can't you at least think about shit before you say it?"

"I'm not changing shit about me, and you need to woman up. You've always portrayed yourself to be a hard woman, so deal with it. My arrogant ways and attitude shouldn't bother you at all, and none of this is new to you. It's not like I just started acting this way—"

"But . . . but you are different. Ever since Nokea didn't accept your proposal you have treated every woman that steps to you like shit. That includes me. The only one who gets your respect is Nanny B, and that's because you ain't fucking her."

"Whatever, Scorpio." He opened the door and stepped onto the porch. "I got some business to take care of in St. Louis. Are you coming with me or not?"

I shook my head. "No. I'm not coming back until you—"

"Hey!" he yelled, loudly. "Suit yourself. I'm out of here. I'm not wasting anymore of my damn time!"

He walked off.

I closed the door and foolishly hoped that he would knock again. But when he didn't, I peeked out the window and watched a taxi drive down the street. I pretty much figured he wasn't coming back anytime soon, but I knew the longer he stayed away, the easier it was going to be for me to manage without him.

Chapter 17

Jaylin

My plane didn't touch down in the Lou until Monday afternoon at four-fifteen. And after being searched by security, I didn't get home until almost six o'clock that night. Nanny B said the phone had been ringing like crazy and told me which calls sounded important. When she mentioned Nokea, I knew I had to call her back first. She also mentioned Mr. Schmidt, but I decided to put him off until I got to work.

I couldn't wait to tell Mackenzie I'd seen Scorpio. I hated to pretend everything was cool, but to make her feel better I told her Scorpio would be coming home soon. I even stopped at a toy store to buy her a new Barbie doll, and told her it was from Scorpio so Mackenzie wouldn't think her mother had forgotten about her. I was somewhat disappointed that Scorpio hadn't come back with me, but I also knew what a pain in the ass she could be at times. I'd hated to see her living like that, but if she didn't want to come back with me, I wasn't going to make her.

When I'd called Jackson and asked where she was, he declined to tell me. I'd offered to pay back the $5,000 he mentioned that he'd loaned, and kicked out another grand for the phone number. That had bought all the info I needed. The key to his place in Denver had cost me another grand. I guess I'd been desperate to see her, and even though I pretended I wasn't missing her, her absence was killing me.

Before I sat down for dinner, I called Nokea. She sounded okay when she answered the phone, so I wasn't sure what the urgency was all about.

"Is everything all right?" I asked.

"Yes, Jaylin. Everything is fine. I was just calling to see if you would watch LJ on Friday night. I have an engagement that I don't want to miss."

"I thought you said it was important? You know I'll always watch my son, Nokea."

"I didn't tell Nanny B it was important. She just tells you it's important whenever I call so you'll call me back."

"Yeah, but that's cool. Stephon's card party ain't until eight o'clock Friday night, so I'll be here up until then. Once I leave, Nanny B will be here. And if you don't mind me asking, what kind of engagement do you have?"

She laughed. "I . . . I have dinner plans with someone."

"Who, Pat? Did you and her work things out?"

"No, we didn't. I called her several times and she refuses to talk to me."

"Damn, that's messed up. Sorry to hear that, but that's how y'all women are. Men, we can be friends forever. We might have our ups and downs, but we always stay boys. So, if you're not having dinner with Pat, then who are you having dinner with?"

"Jaylin, I'm having dinner with Buckethead."

"Who? Who in the hell is Buckethead?"

"You remember . . . The Denzel Washington look-alike at the Mobil gas station we stopped at on your birthday. Actually, his name is Collins but—"

"Whoa . . . whoa, wait a minute. I remember who you're talking about, but you said you wasn't interested in him. And how did you get in touch with him anyway? I tore up your number, and I know that fool wasn't desperate enough to piece it back together."

"Yeah, well, actually, I saw him somewhere else and I wasn't wearing that dress you hated so much, either. He gave me his phone number and I called him."

"That's foul and you know it, Nokea. You said that you didn't even find him attractive. Besides, he looked a lot older than you are. I'm not going to watch LJ while you're out kicking it with this motherfucker either."

"Fine, then I'll just ask my parents to watch him. Also, I never said that he wasn't attractive, you insisted that he wasn't. Truth be told, he's a very attractive man and he's only forty years old. That's only nine years older than me."

I was truly hurt, but we'd agreed to get on with our lives without each other. Thing was, I couldn't believe she wasn't wasting any time. "Okay, Nokea.

Sorry, but I don't want this new man of yours around my child. So, every time you and him get together, I want LJ here with me."

"Now, I won't promise you all that because I would like for him to see how handsome my baby is. When we make plans, sometimes I'll bring LJ over there and sometimes I won't."

"Whatever, Nokea. I'll see you on Friday, and bring LJ over early. I'm going to take a half day at work so I can spend time with him before I go to Stephon's place."

"How's Stephon doing? I haven't talked to him in a while. I think I'll call him when we get off the phone. Is he at home?"

"Nokea, don't play. I know we agreed to go our separate ways, but I don't want you getting all chummy with Stephon again."

She laughed. "Chummy, huh? We got a little bit more than chummy, didn't we?"

"By the way you're setting that thang out there now, I'm sure y'all did. But don't be trying to hurt my feelings, all right? Bad enough I'm allowing you to go on this date with Buckethead."

"It's Collins. And you're not allowing me to do anything. I still love you, but if it's time for anybody to move on, it's definitely me. So, on another note, you'll have to pick up LJ from here on Friday. I'll still be at work, but Mama will be here. I'll tell her to expect you."

"Cool. And if I don't get a chance to talk to you before Friday, don't go having sex with him yet. Allow yourself a little time to get to know him. I think you might be rushing things a bit."

"Sure, *Daddy*, but I'm not that type of woman.

And whenever I do decide to have sex with him, remember, that's my business, not yours."

"You're right. But, honestly, I'm not prepared to accept you sleeping with another man yet."

"Thanks for being honest, but get over it. If I can recall, I wasn't prepared for you sleeping with all the women that you'd slept with either. So, I'm not trying to sound harsh when I say this, but deal with it. You've made your choice."

"Good-bye, Nokea."

"Talk to you later, Jaylin."

She hung up.

This was some crazy shit. If Nokea's sleeping with this man wasn't enough to hurt me, the thought of him being a tiny part of my son's life truly was. If she was going to move on, fine. But LJ definitely wasn't going to be caught up in the mix.

I felt a slight bit down on myself because Scorpio and Nokea were both trying to make a move out of my life, so I changed clothes and took Mackenzie to the movies. She was always the one person who could pull me out of my misery, and by day's end, she did. We didn't get home until eleven o'clock, so I tucked her in bed and finally got some rest before going back to work. Before I dozed off, I called Jackson and thanked him for the information. I told him if Scorpio called in need of some money to give it to her and I would repay him double. I was sure he figured out how much money he could rack up on, and after he joyfully agreed, we ended our call.

*   *   *

Schmidt buzzed in for me to come see him as soon as I walked into my office. I asked Angela to pour me a cup of coffee, and went to see him. He was on the phone and whispered for me to have a seat. He seemed a little upset with the caller, and when he mentioned his wife's name, I knew exactly what he was going through. Women were created to be pains in the ass. Wives, girlfriends, whatever—they all have issues. A man just can't get a break.

Schmidt slammed down the phone and walked over to the door to close it. He took a seat and made quick conversation.

"Jaylin, how's everyone doing? You know, the kids, your nanny, your girlfriends?"

"Everyone's fine, Mr. Schmidt. Why do you ask, though? You never seemed to care before."

"Oh, Jaylin, I've always cared. That's why I asked you to come see me this morning. I want to make sure you're happy, and if you're not, then I'm not. Somehow, that ties in with us losing money."

"I'm fine, but why do you feel your business is losing money if I'm not happy?"

"Well, I got a phone call the other day. It was a call from one of my clients who makes me a very wealthy man. You might know him, Robert McDaniels. Robert simply told me if I didn't get rid of you, he would take his business elsewhere. When I asked why, he said something interesting to me. Do you know what it was?"

I shrugged. "Yeah, I guess. He told you I fucked his wife. So what?"

"Exactly," Schmidt said, walking over to the window to look out. "That was my point. I asked him how many men have slept with his wife, or how many times he has stepped out on her. When he couldn't answer, I made it perfectly clear to him that, no matter how much business he took away from me, it could never amount to as much money as you've made for this company over the years. So, trying to replace you was out of the question. He was angry, but I'm sure he'll get over it."

"I appreciate you having my back. But, uh, I don't want to be responsible for you losing that kind of money. I'm sure that one day it will come back to haunt me, you know what I mean?"

"No, it won't. As of yet, he hasn't done anything. I've known him for over twenty years, and I think his trust for me and our friendship means more to him than he realizes. I could be wrong because he's known for being a stubborn old bastard, but my intuition tells me he's not going to do a damn thing with his investments."

"All right, but off the record, Mr. Schmidt, he needs to back off me. I have some serious plans for him if he doesn't."

"Now, don't go talking like that, Jaylin. He'll back off. I'll give him a call later, and he and I will discuss this over a late dinner tonight. By the end of the day, this thing is going to be behind all of us. Personally, I don't think he's up to battling every man who has slept with his wife. She's a beauty, but she's a woman who knows how to get around. And let's keep that off the record. How did you get yourself involved with her, anyway? Your girlfriend is one fine young woman, and there's no way I would even give Heather McDaniels a second look with someone like her."

"Experience, Mr. Schmidt. It was all about experiencing something different. I like variety. Nothing wrong with exploring every once in a while, is there?"

He smiled and put his hands in his pockets. "Yeah, exploring has gotten me in trouble plenty of times. But I have a good wife. She's forgiving, and as long as I bring home my paycheck so she can spend it, she's fine with that."

I made my way over to Schmidt and shook his hand. "Thanks for believing in me and recognizing my hard work. Not too many bosses out there actually know what kind of good people they have working for them, especially black people. It means a lot to me and I owe you one."

"You just get back to work and don't be slacking on me like you've been doing lately. With you not being in the office on Mondays anymore, and taking half days, it's slightly hurting the business." He put his hand on my shoulder and gripped it. "Just between you and me, Roy cannot do what you can do. So, tell me, is it the money? Do I have to dish out more money to keep you around? Tell me, what do I need to do to keep my number-one producer excited?"

"I'm excited, Mr. Schmidt, and I have plenty of money. It's just my personal life has changed so drastically over the past few years. I have another daughter and a son now. Honestly, I've been thinking about retiring. Thinking about moving far, far away with my kids. And don't let me forget about my nanny. She'd definitely have to come too."

"Don't you go getting any ideas," he yelled and pointed his finger at me. "Retirement at thirty-three is out of the question. You have too much to offer this company, and I don't ever want to hear you talk like that again. Let's just talk about how much more I can offer you to stay."

"I don't know, Mr. Schmidt. Money is not the priority here. Besides, retirement is just a thought. I'll give you notice if I decide to do so, all right?"

"No, it's not all right. I will hear no such thing. Now, get out of my office, and get back to work before I fire you." We both laughed. I thanked Schmidt again and jetted.

Stephon, Shane, Ray Ray, and me kicked up a serious poker game in Stephon's basement and listened to the song that was made for me: "Pimp Juice," by Nelly.

"I don't care how old that song is, it's the motherfucking cut. Man, turn that shit up!" I said to Stephon. He picked up the remote and blasted it as we all sung the lyrics out loud. When Ray Ray started putting his own lyrics into it, Stephon turned it down and we all looked at Ray Ray like he was crazy.

"Now, that's ridiculous," I said. "If I can't sit here and enjoy listening to Nelly the right way, you gotta go."

Shane and Stephon gave me five.

"Screw you, man," Ray Ray said. "Hip-Hop wouldn't be nothing without me. I invented the shit."

I huffed, "Whatever, fool. Quit imagining shit and get back to the game so I can win some of my money back."

I was two grand in the hole and Ray Ray was taking everybody else's money too.

"I'm out," Shane yelled and slammed his cards on the table.

"Me too," Stephon said. "Motherfucker took all of my money."

"Well, I might have a little somethin' somethin' here," I said, flickering through a hand of three kings and two queens.

"Negro, whatever you got, ain't gon' touch what I got." Ray Ray put up five hundred dollars more. I met his bet and laid my cards on the table.

"Pow-dow, playa, what's up? Give me my damn money!" I stood and got ready to grab the money. Shane and Stephon laughed and patted my back.

"Hold up, Pimp Daddy. You brothas know I ain't going out like Thelma and Louise, Bonnie and Clyde, Mighty Joe Young, or Kunta Kinte. Put that shit back down and take a look at this." Ray Ray laid a hand with four aces on the table and slid all the money back his way.

"Bullshit," I yelled. "You be cheating, man. Ain't no way you got four aces." I looked at Shane and Stephon. "Y'all let's search this fool." They laughed and we picked up Ray Ray's two-hundred-sixty-pound body, shook him, and carried him over to the couch. No cards fell, so on the count of three, we tossed him.

"Now what?" he panted. "No cards anywhere, you sorry bunch of sore fucking losers." He picked up a plastic cup and threw it at me. I ducked and plopped down on the leather sofa next to him completely out of breath. Shane and Stephon sat down on the other side huffing and puffing as well.

"You robbed us, man. What are you gonna do with all that money?" I asked.

"Buy me some booty and pay some bills."

"So, you paying for your shit these days, huh?" Stephon said. "If that's the case, you should have stayed married and gotten it for free."

"I know you fellas ain't up in here talking shit like y'all don't pay for no booty. Ladies rolling around in Corvette's and shit . . . living up in Condo's and wearing Rolexes. Bitches ain't gotta work a day in their lives unless they want to. So, touchy subject, my brothas. Y'all fools paid up and paid out."

"That's Jay," Stephon said. "I ain't giving nobody shit but this fat, long piece of goodness hanging between my legs."

"Stephon, please," I said. "Now, you know better. I can recall several times you told me you spent money for . . . Let's see, a cruise, a Movado watch, some bikes for this chick's kids, and what about that treadmill you paid almost a grand for? Told me the woman needed to tone it up and you bought her a treadmill."

Shane and Ray Ray busted out laughing. They both fell on the floor laughing so hard.

"Ha-ha, silly motherfuckers," Stephon said, cutting his eyes at them. "Get y'all asses up! Shane, I know you ain't laughing. Felicia told me about all the shit you did for her, so get your ass off the floor before I start talking. And if I can recall, back in the day, you were breaking the bank for some sistas.

I remember you scraping up money to buy what's her name . . . uh, uh, Vizette, that's it . . . a dog. She had to have a cocker spaniel, or you weren't getting no booty."

"Yeah, I remember that shit," I said, giggling. "We talked about your ass bad."

"Fuck y'all," Shane said, getting off the floor. "Personally, I was in love with the woman and wanted to do something nice. I don't mind spending money on a woman, especially if she's worth it. If I had nearly as much money as Jay got, I probably would be spending money like that too. Who knows, I can't really say."

"Right . . . right." I shook my head and bumped knuckles with Shane. "Hey, if she's worth it then why not?"

"Question is, what do you consider worth it?" Stephon asked. "I guess my idea of being worthy might be different from y'alls because I'm straight up a tight-wad. Ain't too many women getting into my pockets. That's why I don't fuck with Felicia no more. First, because the bitch lied about the baby, but then she was trying to get into my pockets. The only thing in my pockets is a pair of Scorpio's panties that I have as evidence after I boned her."

When Stephon pulled Scorpio's panties from his pocket, I sat up. My heart raced when he gave them to me. "Nigga, don't play."

"Who in the hell's playing?" He gave me a serious look. "After her shaking a brotha down, I collected those just the other night."

Relieved, I knew Stephon was lying because Scorpio was in Denver. That still didn't explain how he'd gotten her panties, and I knew they were hers because I'd bought them. For the hell of it, I wanted to see how far he'd push me. "Yep, these are most certainly her panties. I bought them myself and I can even smell her scent. Question is, though, how did you get them?"

He looked at me, then turned his eyes to Shane. "This fool about to have a heart attack, man. Should I break it down for him before he pass out?"

"Go ahead," Shane said not cracking a smile. "You should tell him how much fun we both had tapping that ass and watching his name jiggle while we hit it."

"It's like that, huh? And both of y'all—damn. Why didn't nobody invite me to the party?"

"Cause we figured you was busy," Stephon said. "Busy shaking down that white gal you've been messing with."

"Ah, okay. But I'm never too busy to fuck Scorpio, though. Not only that," I said, standing up, "but I'd better be going before somebody gets hurt."

Stephon and Shane started laughing. "Man, sit down. You know we just playing with your ass."

"Playing? Naw, brothas," I said, jumping on Stephon and playfully choking him. "You don't play with no shit like that."

We all laughed, and after I choked him, he pretended like he was out of breath and gagged for air.

"Whew," he said. "I'm glad I was joking. You should have seen the look on your face when I told you I had sex with her. That picture could be worth a million dollars."

"Stephon, I knew you was lying, fool. Well, at first I didn't know, but after you said the other day, that's when you fucked up."

"Whenever or whatever," Ray Ray joked. "You straight up looked like you saw three ghosts when you thought he tapped that ass. That was some funny shit there. I'd pay a million to see that look again my damn self."

"Fuck y'all. So, he caught me off guard. And the only reason he did that was because Scorpio and me been having some problems lately." I looked down at her panties again and moved them around in my hands. "Without a doubt, these are the panties I bought. Now, how in the hell did you get them?"

Shane reached over and snatched them from me. "Thank you very much," he said. "But, uh, these belong to me. If memories are all I can have, I'd like to keep them."

I chuckled and shook my head. "You damn right that's all you're going to have. All these fine-ass women in St. Louis and you brothas all up on my shit. I've said it once and I'll say it again—she's mine and mine only. Find somebody else to fuck y'all broke-down asses."

"Broke-down?" Stephon looked offended and cleared his throat. "That's pretty bad, Jay. Not trying to go there but, uh, Felicia, Nokea, Sandra, Leslie, Gina, Angela, Chris, Stephanie . . . and all of the other women that we've shared didn't seem to think a brotha was so broke-down."

"It's obvious that you want everything that I had, or should I say, have. It's in your nature to go behind me, and I don't care to know or understand why. Now, can we please change the subject before I have to go off on your ass for trying to be like me."

"Negro, please. I just have to let you know that you ain't the only good brotha in St. Louis shaking the sistas down correctly."

"Never said I was, and sounds like your insecurities are messing with you. But as I was saying before we got off into this other bullshit, my idea of being worth it is if she takes care of me, I take care of her. That can only mean one thing because financially, no woman can assist me with that. If she can take care of my physical needs, meaning pop that thang how I like it, she can have just about anything she wants."

"See, my views are slightly different," Shane said. "First, I must be in love with a woman before I even start to invest my money. I'm not talking about spending money at the movies, or shit like that, I'm talking about serious money. If she's intelligent, beautiful both inside and out, and can make love to me for at least an hour, I'm hooked and eventually I will fall for her. Thing is, they must come in that order. Lately, I've been finding women who give me one or the other—never the full package. So, I'm chilling. The last time I had sex was roughly over, uh . . . maybe, five months ago."

"Shiiit," I said. "Feel that nigga head Stephon and make sure he all right. And even though his dick ain't been in action, we for damn sure know his mouth has."

Stephon laughed, reached over to Shane, and touched his head. "He seems to feel okay, but I would rather die than go without having sex for five months. Are you fucking gay or something?"

Shane laughed. "Man, please. Now, I love me some pussy. You brothas know that, but if it ain't right, I'd rather do without. It took me a long time to start seeing shit that way, and I got tired of throwing my dick on the table for any and every woman. Most of them be treating they shit like a piece of gold, and making a brotha go over and beyond, so what's wrong with me being particular?"

"Ain't nothing wrong with it at all. And by all means," I said, grabbing myself. "This motherfucker here worth more than fifty pots of gold. However, I got some serious fucking needs that have to be met. Need to be met quite often, I might say. So, I'm not depriving myself for nothing."

"I'm gonna have to side with Jay on that one," Ray Ray said. "You talk a good game, Shane, but ain't too many fellas looking at it like that these days. You're for damn sure a better man than me 'cause if she wants it, and I got a condom, she can have it."

Stephon reached over to Ray Ray and slapped his hand. "Now, that's my fucking motto. And since you brothas sitting around here talking about all this booty, I'd say it's time to shake some brothas down. Time to get some ladies in the house to entertain. Mona got some bootilicious-ass friends and they're at her house right now having a lingerie party."

"Well, what you waiting on?" I asked. "You didn't expect me to sit up here all night with no hard legs, did you?"

Stephon got up to call Mona. "Shane, are you cool with this? When I say bootilicious, I mean these ladies are *bootilicious*."

"Hey, don't let me ruin the party. Y'all brothas go ahead and knock yourselves out. I'm chilling," Shane said.

Before Stephon left the room to call Mona, he pulled me aside to make sure everything was cool. I let him know I wasn't tripping off his comments, and more than anything I realized how much he and I were alike. We both always spoke our minds and wanted to have the final word. When he came back he pumped up, "Right Thurr," by Chingy and said the ladies would be over in about an hour.

Shane and I went behind the bar and started making some drinks, while Ray Ray went to the bathroom.

"Jay," Shane said, handing me some glasses. "You mentioned things weren't going so well with you and Scorpio. What's up with that?"

I dropped a few ice cubes in the glasses and looked at him. "She jetted. She left me and said she needed time to sort through shit. So, I'm giving her all the time away she needs."

"I see. But, uh, I thought you might want to know that she called me the night we met up at Freddy's. She apologized for leading me on and for not telling me the truth about her feelings for you. She also told me you put her up to calling me."

"Yes, I did. I had to know who or what she really wanted."

"Now that you know, don't blow it, man," he said, reaching into his pocket and giving me her panties. "Stephon knew I had those from my previous encounter with her, and asked me to bring them tonight to play a joke on you. Don't take it personal, okay? If anything, I knew all along she loved you. I could see it in her eyes every time your name came up. She's a special type of woman, Jay, and you're lucky to still have her."

I tossed Scorpio's panties in the trashcan behind the bar, and told Shane how much I appreciated him for not interfering. We continued making drinks, and when I looked up, Ray Ray and Stephon were firing up a joint. I walked over by to the couch and set the tray of drinks on the table.

"What the fuck is up with this shit? Naw, fellas, we don't do drugs up in here." I snatched the bag of weed from Stephon's hand. He took a hit from his joint and blew the smoke in my face.

"Quit tripping, fool. Brotha need a little herb every once in a while to settle the mind," he said.

"Settle my ass. Don't disappoint me, cuz," I said, sternly. "We ain't going out like that. And you of all people should know better."

"Jay, why you tripping?" Ray Ray said. "It ain't nothing but a lil' weed. Cool out, all right?"

"Man, you cool out." I raised my voice. "Messing around with drugs has fucked up too many people in my family. I ain't about to sit around and watch nobody I care about do that shit. Smoking weed leads to other things, and you and Stephon need to put that shit out. *Now!*"

"I'm with Jay this time," Shane said. "We got too much going on for ourselves to be sitting here tripping like that. Drugs are drugs. I don't care what shape, form, or fashion they come in, they all can damage the mind."

"What a terrible thing to waste," Stephon said, putting out the fire on the joint. He fanned the smoke with his hand and Ray Ray helped. "Y'all fellas up in my house trying to tell me what to do. Luckily, I have respect for y'all."

Shane and me were sitting on the couch playing video games when the doorbell rang. He was kicking my butt at boxing and we were acting a bit silly from drinking so much. When the ladies came down the steps, I nudged Ray Ray because he had fallen asleep on the couch and was snoring loudly. He quickly straightened up and rubbed his waves back.

Mona and her lady friends came around the couch and stood next to us. Since Stephon's leather couch circled half the basement, there was plenty of room for everybody to sit down.

"Shane, Ray, Jaylin," Mona said. "These are my girlfriends Amber, Jeanette, Daisha, and Kennedy." They spoke to us and we spoke back. I leaned back on the couch and smiled. I looked at Shane, who gave me a devious grin.

"Five months without no ass, bro," I whispered. "Are you pushing for six after seeing what we just saw?"

He snickered and whispered back. "It's five of them and four of us. I at least need two since it's been such a long time. Which two is the question?"

We took another glance at the ladies on the couch. I already had scoped the sista I wanted. Daisha. In my eyes, she was bad and was the best looking of the bunch. Had on a gray leather jacket that was unbuttoned in the front and showed her hourglass figure. Her black sheer camisole underneath revealed the healthiness in her breasts and was just enough to arouse me. Most of all, I was excited by the way her leather pants hugged her hips, and showed a gap between her legs that was, without a doubt, waiting to be filled. I glimpsed over to get a second look, and dug the shit out of her short, neatly trimmed curly haircut. Kind of reminded me a little of Halle Berry, but not quite.

"So, what are you thinking, Jay?" Shane whispered.

"I think I'm about to celebrate Christmas a little early. How about you?"

"Right, but, uh, with which one?"

"Daisha, man. That's who."

"Damn, that's who I was feeling. If not her, then Jeanette." Just then, Amber laughed at Stephon's joke and crossed her leg. Her dress slid over and showed her dark coffee brown legs. Shane had confirmation. "Okay, Amber. Amber and Jeanette. You can have Daisha."

"What about Kennedy? She ain't short stopping," I said.

"No, she's not but her ass is just too damn big for me. I like ass, but that's too much ass for me. If I can sit a drink on top of that motherfucker while she's standing up, I don't want it." We softly giggled. "Besides, she's Ray Ray's type. He can work with that."

"What y'all brothas over there whispering and laughing about?" Ray Ray asked loudly.

"I know, Ray," Mona said. "I was thinking the

same thing. I brought my friends over here to mingle and the two of them being all anti-social."

"Sorry about that," Shane sat up straight and clinched his hands together. "We didn't mean to be rude. Jay and I were just talking about how lovely your friends look. How we'd actually like to get to know them better."

"Funny," Jeanette said. "We were just talking about the same thing before Stephon started telling his crazy jokes."

"All right, Jeanette," Stephon said. "Don't let me start talking about your buck-eyed mama."

"Stephon and Jeanette, please," Mona interrupted. "Don't start this today. The two of you get on my nerves with this joaning stuff."

Mona took Stephon's hand and escorted him upstairs. I offered to get the ladies some drinks, and when I got up, I just so happened to ask Daisha to help me. She followed me to the bar and rubbed her hands together.

"Tell me. What can I help you with?"

She really didn't want me to answer that question. "You can start by giving me a few of those glasses above your head." She reached up and grabbed the glasses. I looked over and Shane was sitting in between Amber and Jeanette, chatting with them. Ray Ray was talking to Kennedy, and I was pleased to see that things were going according to the plan.

"Now what . . . Jaylin, right?" she asked.

"Yes, Jaylin." I gazed at her breasts. "Now, you can take off your jacket so you don't waste any alcohol on it when we get down on making these tequilas and sour-apple martinis."

She removed her jacket and laid it on one of the barstools. Impressed by how well she mixed class with her sexiness, I couldn't wait to get into her tonight.

"Should I take off my pants," she joked. "I don't want to spill any drinks on them either, right?"

"Hey, do whatever you gotta do. I was just looking out for you when I asked you to take off your jacket. Your outfit looks kind of expensive and I'd hate to see you mess it up"

"I was just kidding, Jaylin. The jacket is off, but the pants are most certainly staying on."

What a disappointment to hear that, I thought. I reached for a towel on the rail behind me. "Let me wrap this around you. That way if anything spills, it won't get on your pants, okay?" She let me wrap the towel around her waist, and as usual, my mind was in the gutter.

"Thanks. Now, let's get to work."

Daisha and I fixed seven sour-apple martinis and ten tequilas. When we finished, she popped a cherry in my mouth and we carried the drinks over to the table. I ran upstairs to see if Stephon and Mona wanted one, but when I saw his bedroom door closed, I tiptoed back downstairs.

I sat next to Daisha, and picked up a glass along with everybody else to give a toast. "Let's drink to not letting good things go to waste," I said, somewhat thinking about Scorpio again. If not her, then Daisha.

Ray Ray put his two cents in. "I'll drink to if she want it, and she got a condom, then she can have it."

All of the women's mouths opened, and me and Shane looked at him in disbelief. "Damn, I was just playing," Ray said. "Can't you people take a joke?"

"Yeah, man, that's cool, but, uh, these ladies might not have wanted to hear that. Show some respect, all right?"

Ray Ray apologized and we got back to our drinks.

As the night went on, I realized that Daisha and I really weren't good company for each other. She was too quiet, and when I tried to kick up a conversation, her answers were quick and sharp like she didn't want to be bothered. Sensing her coldness, I eventually stopped talking and started playing video games again.

Shane, however, was running his game and running it well. After entertaining Jeanette and Amber for about an hour, he managed to continue his conversation in another room. Even Ray Ray and Kennedy seemed like they were enjoying each other's company. So, determined to give it another try with Daisha, I put the game down and asked if she wanted anything else to drink. She suggested a Smirnoff Ice, so I got up to get it. She followed me over to the bar and sat on a stool in front of it.

"Are you married or engaged—which one?" she asked.

I laughed. "Neither, but why do you ask? Do I *act* like I'm married?" I handed her a glass and a Smirnoff Ice from the refrigerator.

"Yes, you really do. Most married men are somewhat shy like you are. Kind of afraid to talk, you know what I mean?"

"Shy? No, I don't think so. I just backed off since I got a feeling that you didn't want to be bothered."

"Sorry, but it has nothing to do with you. I've been divorced for almost six months, and sometimes it's difficult trying to meet new people."

"Hmm . . ." I said. A divorced woman was nothing but trouble in my eyes.

"Yep. Things just didn't work out between us. He was headed in one direction, and I was headed in another. Really nice guy, but he just wasn't for me."

I leaned against the bar and watched Daisha's lips suck from the Smirnoff bottle. I was really feeling up to having sex, but didn't quite know how to break it to her just yet. When she saw Kennedy and Ray Ray on the couch kissing, she suggested we go into another room for privacy.

I led her to the room with a queen-sized bed and started to remove my shirt as we hit the door.

"Wait a minute, sweetie," she said in a proper tone. "I don't get down like some of my associates may, and I don't even know you like that."

I hit the lights, took the drink from her hand and started kissing her. She accepted my kiss and we worked our way back to the bed. I pulled her body on top of me, but she paused again.

"Hey, Jaylin, look . . . I'm serious. I'm not ready for this and what's the rush?"

I tried to undo her camisole, but she backed away from me and got off the bed. "Where are you going?" I asked, frustrated.

"Did you not understand anything I've said? I mean, I'm feeling you, but not enough to give myself to you like that. I barely know you, Jaylin, and I came in here so we could be alone and talk. If you came in here for something else, I'm sorry, I didn't mean to mislead you."

I sighed and got off the bed too, to turn on some music. I got back in bed. "Can I at least hold you while we talk?" I asked.

She laid down next to me resting her leg over mine, and her head on my shoulder.

"So, what is it that you want to talk about?" I asked.

"There's plenty for us to talk about. For starters, how old are you and what's your occupation? Do you have a degree, and if so, in what? When you're finished answering that, do you have any children? If so, how many? And what do you like to do in your spare time?"

I sucked my teeth. I was not up to answering a bunch of questions that really weren't any of her business. But after we lay in bed for a while, getting to know each other, I actually found out some interesting things about Daisha. She really seemed to have it going on for herself. She was a registered nurse at St. Luke's Hospital, had a house in Ballwin, no children, and spoke French very well. She made me laugh a few times, as I tried to figure out what she was saying in French. I had taken a French course in college, but couldn't remember shit.

When Mona knocked on the door and asked if she was ready to go, Daisha said no, so I offered to take her home. I figured Shane wasn't quite ready either because I could hear all the action in the room next to us. Daisha and I quietly laughed at all the panty-popping going on, and even though I straight-up wished it was me, I couldn't force Daisha to do anything she didn't feel comfortable doing.

I woke up at my usual time, four o'clock in the morning. I was finally coming down from all the alcohol I had been drinking. Daisha was knocked out on my chest, so I eased over and tried not to wake her. That was impossible.

"Are you ready to go?" she asked, in a sleepy voice while stretching.

"Yeah, I guess. I need to go to the bathroom first, though." I turned on the lights and she covered her face.

"Jaylin, that light is too bright, honey. Please turn it off."

"I wanted to see how beautiful you look in the morning."

She smiled and removed her hands. "You're a charmer. I bet you tell all the women that line, don't you?"

I laughed and headed to the bathroom. Daisha really was beautiful, and for the first time, it fucked me up that I laid in bed with a woman and didn't even fuck her. I kind of enjoyed her company too. And the best thing about her was that she didn't even snore.

Once I finished my business in the bathroom, I tapped on Shane's door to let him know I was out-tie. He yelled for me to open it.

"What did you say?" He laid back on his elbows and I checked out the two sleeping sistas by his side.

"I'm gone, Bro. Give me a holla tomorrow."

"Will do, my brotha. Until next time."

I waited by the bar for Daisha to put on her shoes. Ray Ray and Kennedy were lying on the couch knocked out, and since they still had their clothes on, I didn't suspect anything deep had gone down with them. Obviously, Shane was the lucky one. His charm and looks must have worked wonders.

Daisha grabbed her purse off the couch and we headed upstairs. As she walked in front of me, I grazed my hand on her ass just to touch it. She turned around and smiled.

"Jaylin, don't play."

"Sorry, but I couldn't help myself. You shouldn't have put all that in my face."

She moved over and I walked in front of her. As soon as I got to the top of the stairs, she squeezed my ass. I backed her against the wall and stood in front of her.

"I don't like women who play games, Daisha. If you want to, we can always finish what we started last night."

"Games? No, I don't play them. But when you put something like that in my face, there's no telling what I might do. As for finishing up . . . oh, I intend to. Today, however, is not the day."

She leaned in for a lengthy kiss, and as we got more into it, I grinded against her. She pushed me back.

"Wait until we're alone, okay?"

"Whatever you say, Daisha. You're the one running this show."

When we got upstairs, Mona and Stephon were in the kitchen playing around. She had a sheet wrapped around her and he was in his boxers dripping with water.

"Are you leaving?" he asked. Mona took a cup of water and splashed it on him. "Quit playing, Mona. I'm already drenched." He opened the refrigerator and pulled out a pitcher. I covered Daisha with my jacket and we ran through the kitchen. Stephon tossed the water on Mona and it splashed everywhere.

"Holla at me later, man. Bye Mona," I yelled as we jetted. Mona and Daisha waved good-bye to each other.

I drove Daisha to her house in Ballwin. From the outside I could tell it was a well-kept, two-story home. The lawn was manicured and the landscaping had to have been done by professionals. I was a little disappointed when she didn't invite me in, but I guessed that inviting me in wasn't her way of doing things. She gave me a peck on the cheek and said she'd call me soon.

Everything was cool on the home front. Mackenzie's best friend Megan had spent the night and LJ was fast asleep in Nanny B's room. I took off my clothes and lay naked in the bed. Feeling a bit lonely, I called Scorpio, but the number was busy so I hung up. I tried a few more times and realized she must have taken it off the hook. I was really starting to miss her. Didn't have enough guts to go see her again, so the best thing I could do was wait until she was ready to come around.

Chapter 18

Nokea

Life was so unpredictable. Who would have thought that a date with Collins would lead to one of the best times of my life? I knew how handsome he was, but his class showed even more when he picked me up for dinner. He was a true gentleman, and seemed to be the kind of man I'd dreamt of having in my life for years. Age was definitely only a number, and his tint of gray hair mixed in with his thinly trimmed beard truly turned me on. I couldn't help but admire the way his chocolate skin meshed with his dark brown slanted eyes. His height and slimness gave his black tailored suit all the help he needed to sway me in his direction.

During dinner, Collins kept me laughing and smiling the entire time. I finally got a chance to know more about him. He was part owner of Jefferson & Assoc., a computer technology company, and had offices in St. Louis and Detroit. Most of his time was spent running back and forth, making sure business was running smoothly. He had an eighteen-year-old son, who was a freshman in college, and an ex-wife of five years. I didn't ask why she was now an ex, but I was sure time would tell. Right about now, there was nothing he could say or do that would turn me off. He was perfect for me, and had come into my life at the right time. Had he come any sooner, I may not have been ready.

When he drove to his house in Ladue, my eyes lit up. He lived alone in a five-bedroom, four-bathroom house on acres and acres of land. I asked if he got lonely sometimes and he admitted that he did. Since his wife had moved out, and his son had moved away to college, he'd been thinking about putting the house up for sale and moving to his smaller house in Detroit. He said the house in Detroit had only four bedrooms, and lacked the extra living space of the one in Ladue.

Either way, the man had it going on. I was flattered to be in his presence and told him just that as we laid on two square velvet pillows by the fireplace, drinking wine. The off-white, clean carpet gave our bodies all the plush we needed.

"Thank you for being so kind," he said. "This evening has turned out wonderful, all because of you."

"Because of me? I haven't done anything special, but that doesn't mean I don't intend to."

"Just being here with me, Nokea, is truly enough. I've been skeptical about pursuing another relationship, but when I saw you that day, I couldn't get you out of my mind. It was so ironic that I saw you again at Cardwell's."

"I agree. And meeting you again couldn't have come at a better time."

We kissed, and as the night went on, we connected even more. One thing led to another, and before I knew it, our clothes were off and our bodies were sweating from the heat generated by the fireplace, and our passionate lovemaking.

Finally, I felt like there was a light at the end of the tunnel. Collins's timing couldn't be more right. I knew Jaylin was a man of the past, and I had no problem moving forward with Collins. My parents would be elated about him; Collins was the kind of stable man my father always wanted me to have.

Collins drove me home, and we sat in his car and smacked lips for a while. He invited LJ and me to spend a week with him in Detroit. He said that his entire family gathered there for Christmas every year and he wanted us to come along. Not really having any plans, other than to spend time with my parents, I told him we would love to. I was really looking forward to going, until I picked up LJ from Jaylin's house around three o'clock that afternoon and broke the news to him.

"You have got to be out of your rabbit-ass mind, Nokea," he yelled while sitting at the kitchen table, eating a sandwich.

"Jaylin, look, I could have lied to you, but I'm trying to be as open with you as possible about LJ. Allow me to be happy, please."

"You can be happy all you want. Run off with this joker you know nothing about, I don't care.

But, LJ is staying right here with me. He will not be caught up with you chasing around after some dick."

"It isn't like that and you know it. Don't you know and respect anything about me? I am not the type of woman to drag my son along with me if I don't feel comfortable with the situation. If you're that bothered by Collins, why don't you meet him for yourself?"

Jaylin put his plate in the dishwasher and I stood next to him. He glared at me and swallowed. "You are asking too much of me and you know it. I got a bad-ass feeling about this shit, and if you fuck me over again, Nokea, I swear—"

"I'm not trying to mess you over, Jaylin. All I would like to do is take my son with me to Detroit for one week, that's it. Please don't make me feel guilty about doing this. All I'm asking for is your support."

He turned away from me to look out the window. I could see the hurt on his face, and when he closed his eyes, I knew he was trying to calm himself. "You fucked him, didn't you? That's what this shit is about. And don't lie to me because I've known you long enough and can tell when you're lying."

"Believe me, this has nothing to do with—"

"*Did you fuck him!*" he yelled, searching my eyes for a response.

"Would you please calm yourself down? I don't want Nanny B and the kids hearing—"

"You did, didn't you? I can't believe you did it."

"Jaylin, I had to move on, but—"

"Get out, Nokea!"

"Please—"

He stood face-to-face with me and gritted his teeth. "I said, get the fuck out of my house!"

"I'm not leaving without my son."

"Fine, take him." He walked toward the kitchen door. "Make sure you're ready to hear from my attorney tomorrow."

"And you make sure you're ready to hear from Collins's attorney."

He quickly turned. "What did you just say?" He rushed over to me and put his finger in my face. "Did you just say what I think you said, Nokea?" A look I had never seen was on his face. Maybe I shouldn't have gone there.

"Look, Jaylin. I don't want this to escalate—"

He grabbed my collar and leaned against me. "Bitch, if you ever bring up another motherfucker—"

Before I knew it, I was smacking the living daylights out of him for calling me a bitch. He grabbed me tighter and lifted me up. He banged my head against the cabinet, and when he let go, I felt dizzy and fell to the floor. Afterward, he pulled me off the floor by my arm and shoved me into the living room. He was in a rage and tossed me into a living room chair. His arms straddled the chair and he leaned in front of me. "You're a silly-ass woman, Nokea. Every time a man puts his dick inside of you, you wanna drag my son into your mess. You'd better learn how to watch your mouth because it's liable to get you hurt. I'm so sick and tired of you putting me through this shit with LJ, and I promise you, this is the last time I'm going to let you do this to me." He stood up. "So, tell your new ancient-ass man to bring it on. You are not taking my damn son home with you today, nor will you take him to Detroit. Now, get the fuck out of here like I told you to." He started to walk away.

Nanny B stood on the Romeo and Juliet balcony with LJ and Mackenzie, looking down at us. "What is going on down there?" she yelled.

"Nanny B would you bring my son to me," I asked, standing shakily from the chair.

Jaylin turned and sucked in his lip. "You wanna fuck with me, Nokea?" he yelled. "I will kill you over my son!" He grabbed my neck and choked me. After tripping me to the floor, Nanny B ran down the steps and yelled for him to stop. I squirmed around, barely able to breathe with his tight grip and body weight on top of me.

"Jaylin!" Nanny B yelled. She tried to pull him off me, but he ignored her and squeezed tighter. The only thing that stopped him was when Mackenzie started crying and yelling, "Daddy, please stop!" He looked at her and LJ, as both of them stood watching us in tears. Taking deep breaths, he fell into the couch. Nanny B helped me off the floor, as I coughed and tried to catch my breath. She put her arms around me and asked for my car keys. When I reached in my pocket and gave them to her, she picked up LJ and looked at Jaylin.

"I'm taking them home. This is outrageous, Jaylin. You really need to get yourself together," she said, furiously.

He didn't say a word, just laid his head back on

the couch and looked up at the ceiling. Mackenzie was still crying, and she sat on his lap and put her arms tightly around his neck. Nanny B, LJ, and I left.

On the drive home, I told Nanny B what happened, and she kind of sided with Jaylin. She said he was wrong for putting his hands on me, but she didn't agree with me wanting to take LJ to Detroit for Christmas. Like Jaylin, Nanny B felt as if I didn't know much about Collins, and explained what a disappointment it would be for LJ not to be around on Christmas Day. I understood how they both felt, but he was my son too. And to get our lawyers involved would only make the situation more chaotic. I'd had the pleasure of seeing Mr. Frick, Jaylin's attorney, in action for him several times before. Frick was an asshole, but he definitely knew how to win a case for Jaylin. I had less than three weeks to work with before Christmas, and I hoped by then Jaylin would calm down and see things my way. If not, LJ and I were going to Detroit with or without Jaylin's consent.

Late Sunday afternoon, I spoke to Collins and told him what had happened. He insisted he wasn't trying to interfere, and expressed how much he wanted LJ and me to go with him. He even suggested getting to know Jaylin better, so Jaylin would feel comfortable with LJ being around him. He'd gone through the exact same situation with his son when his ex-wife had remarried. He told me how difficult it had been for him to cope with another man trying to step in. Before we hung up, he apologized for putting me in a tough position, and told me he was willing to do anything to make it better. We agreed to see Jaylin at work on Tuesday and talk the situation out with him.

When I called Jaylin's house the next day, Nanny B asked how I was doing and told me Jaylin and Mackenzie had been gone all day. He'd refused to talk to her about our dispute, and had stayed in his room until morning. She accused me of hurting him, and after I reminded her of everything he had done to me, I ended our conversation. I didn't want to be disrespectful to her because she had really been there for all of us, so I later called back and apologized. More than anything, I understood that she had a serious bond with Jaylin and was like the typical "mother" looking out for her son.

Collins picked me up around noon on Tuesday, looking dynamite in his tan Brooks Brothers suit. I had taken a couple days off work so I could get this issue between Jaylin and me resolved.

On our way up the elevator in the Berkshire Building, my stomach felt queasy. I was a nervous wreck. Collins kissed my hand and told me to relax, which was, of course, easy for him to say since he hadn't had the pleasure of seeing the full potential of Jaylin's ire. The other day was the first time he'd ever put his hands on me. I'd never thought things between us would go to that level. Pressing charges against him crossed my mind, but I decided against it. I knew we could work this out somehow.

Collins was relaxed, strutting with confidence

into the lobby. He asked Angela for Jaylin, and when she confirmed that he was in, my heart dropped. She asked Collins for his name, her eyes flirting with him. I stepped forward and told her to let Jaylin know I was there to see him. When she buzzed Jaylin's office, he said that he was eating lunch and asked for me to come on back. I took Collins's hand and led the way.

When we walked through the door, Jaylin was on the phone laughing with someone. He was eating a lunch tray of *Gourmet To Go,* and his smile vanished when he saw Collins's hand joined together with mine.

"Daisha, I'll call you back later, all right?" He hung up and looked me in the eye. "You just don't get enough, do you?"

"Please," I said. "I just thought it would be a good idea if you met Collins. So, Collins, this is Jaylin, and Jaylin, this is Collins." Collins offered his hand to Jaylin, but Jaylin just looked at it. Collins pulled his hand back.

"Jaylin, listen," he said. "Trust me when I say that I know how you feel. The only reason I'm here today is because I was faced with the same dilemma not too long ago. My ex-wife's husband tried to be a father to my son and I wasn't having it. So, I'd like to take just a little of your time so you can get to know me better and understand that I'm not trying to replace you. From what Nokea's told me, you're a good father and there's no need for me to step in when you're handling your business."

Jaylin got out of his chair and closed the door. I noticed that he and Collins checked out each other's attire. I was glad it wasn't a contest or anything because they were running neck-in-neck.

"Have a seat," Jaylin said, sitting back in his chair. We did, and when Collins folded his leg, Jaylin glanced at his expensive-looking leather shoes with tassels on the flap.

"First, I'll tell the both of you that I do not like taking care of personal matters in the workplace. Second, I do not like to be put on front-street by anyone. And third, Collins, I apologize for not shaking your hand when you came in here. This chaos between Nokea and me go way back, and I'm sorry you had to get caught up in the middle." Jaylin reached out and gave Collins a handshake, then looked at me and slightly rolled his eyes.

"I didn't like the idea of coming to your workplace either," Collins said, "but sometimes these kinds of places seem to work out better, instead of talking out matters at home. When my ex-wife's husband came to talk to me in my home, many months after the damage had been done, I was arrested for assault on the brotha. If he had come to me in the beginning, and given me the opportunity to know what kind of man he was, and let me know what his intentions were, the assault never would have happened. After all is said and done, we're pretty good friends now, however, I still have my moments when the situation bothers me. Especially when my son comes home from college and wants to stay with them instead of me. I have to man up about the situation and let him decide, because if I don't, it will drive him away."

Jaylin placed his hands behind his head and leaned back in his chair. "Collins, this is all very new to me. I have three beautiful children in this world, and it's like I'm fighting each and every day to keep them in my life. I haven't a clue where my oldest is. I've hired detectives to find her and somehow, thanks to her mother, she's just vanished. My other daughter is now living with me, but it's just a matter of time when her mother is going to come for her and take her away—I feel it." Jaylin spoke with pain in his eyes. "I . . . I'm not her biological father and I know I'd have a tough fight keeping her with me. So, really, LJ is all I got to hang on to. If you and Nokea run off with him, I have nothing."

"But, Jaylin, we're not trying to run off with him," I said. "All I would like to do is take him to Detroit for one week. That's it. You act like we're talking a lifetime."

"Nokea, you say that now, but my biggest fear will be the day you call and tell me you're moving to Detroit with Collins. Let's be realistic here, there's a possibility of that happening, so who knows. I'm letting you know now that occasionally visiting my son is not going to be enough for me. Whether you realize it or not, he needs me and I need him. So, question is, how do the both of you anticipate on working around this scenario, or have you even thought about it?"

"Jaylin," Collins said. "Honestly, my future plans do include living in Detroit. I mentioned that to Nokea last night. I could actually see myself with her because she's a beautiful person, and I've longed for a woman like her." Collins reached over and touched my hand. "But one day, she might have a serious choice to make. A choice that I probably will not support when it comes to LJ because this is a personal issue for me and I truly believe that a son needs to be with his father. But remember, we're talking five or ten years from now."

"Okay," Jaylin said, resting his elbows on his desk. "I have no problem with LJ going to Detroit with the both of you for Christmas. But I need something in writing from your attorney, Nokea, that says if you move to Detroit within the next five ... . up to ten years, you move alone and LJ stays with me. By then, he should be old enough to tell us what or who he wants. And at that time, if he wants to live with the both of you, so be it. I'm cool with that. This is the best I can offer right now. These days, I have to look out for what's in my best interest."

"I'm so glad the two of you are good at predicting my future," I said. "Who says I'm moving anywhere? I know that it's stretching things a bit, but, Jaylin, don't you think this is taking things too far? I've only known Collins for a short time, and you're already planning my future for me."

"Nokea, I like to prepare myself ahead of time for things. The unexpected is what hurts. Just a few months ago, I never thought I would be sitting here having this conversation with you and Collins. And vice versa, I would assume. So, if you want my consent, you need to work with me on this."

Collins and I looked at each other. "I'd probably be asking for the same thing, baby," Collins said. "I don't like the idea of getting your attorney involved, but sometimes it's for the best. Just know that I will never make you choose between your son and me. If this situation ever occurs we will work together to do what's right."

I seriously had a problem with giving Jaylin some papers that said if I ever left St. Louis he could have full custody of LJ. It wasn't like leaving St. Louis was in my plans, but you never know. However, I agreed to it, and after Jaylin seemed cool with the arrangements, we got ready to go.

Jaylin and Collins shook hands again, but before we left, I asked Collins if I could speak to Jaylin alone. He agreed. I closed the door behind him and stood in front of it.

"You have to know that I never wanted to hurt you," I said. "I'm sorry for the way all this has turned out, but I do have to move on."

He stood in front of me. "I know. And I'm going to try hard to accept that. Collins seems like a really decent man, Nokea. I'm a little jealous, but you deserve someone like him. And before I forget, I'm sorry for cursing you the other day, I'm sorry for putting my hands on you, and uh, I'm even sorry that it has to be this way."

"I am too." I opened my arms for him to hug me. He squeezed me tight, and after he let go, I kissed his left cheek. When I saw how much lipstick I put on it, I wiped it off.

"Jaylin?" I said.

"Yes."

"Who's Daisha?"

"What?" He grinned and held my hand.

"You heard me. Who's Daisha? The female you were talking to when we walked in."

"She's just a friend, Nokea."

"Really? What kind of friend?"

"Nokea . . ."

"Okay, I won't pry, but I just want to make sure you're happy."

"I am. Really, I am. If not, then one day I will be." He opened the door. "Hey, have you talked to Pat yet?"

"No," I said, walking out. "She won't talk to me. She got her number changed and everything. When I call her at work, she never comes to the phone, so I gave up."

"Well, don't. All friendships can be mended, no matter what, especially if you wasn't the one at fault."

I gave Jaylin another hug and he walked me to the lobby. Collins was admiring Jaylin's awards on the wall.

"Man, you got it going on, don't you?" he said.

"I'd like to think so. I got plenty more of those at home," Jaylin bragged.

"Well, why don't you give me a call?" Collins pulled out his business card and handed it to Jaylin. "I have my money invested elsewhere, but if I can switch everything successfully and keep it in the family, I will do so." He nudged Jaylin.

"Sounds like a plan. I'll make sure that I call you."

We waved good-bye and Jaylin stood by Angela's desk, talking to her. As Collins and I waited for the elevator, he leaned forward and kissed me, then gave me a hug and we rocked back and forth together. I couldn't stop thanking him for handling his business with Jaylin so maturely.

Before I stepped onto the elevator, I glanced at

Jaylin again and he smiled, then nodded his head. The last time I saw him do that was when I was walking down the aisle to marry Stephon. This time, I felt as if he was finally letting me go and giving me the go-ahead to move on with my life.

Chapter 19

Scorpio

I had really jazzed up the place since Jay-Baby had gone back to St. Louis. I called Jackson and cursed him out again for giving Jaylin the phone number and key. And when I finished chewing him out, he apologized. He said he'd make it up to me by sending me some more money so I could fix up the place like I wanted to. He advised me to do whatever I wanted to do to it, and sent me another check for $10,000 to get things started.

I tried to make the place feel like home, and went on a shopping spree. There was hella work to be done, and by the time I finished, it finally felt kind of livable. I bought a new sofa-bed for the living room, an entertainment center, two space heaters to warm up the place, white paint for the dingy walls, and even had a plumber come over to replace the old vanity, sink, and tub in the bathroom.

As for the bedroom, I covered the old wallpaper with light blue-and-yellow flower-print wallpaper. It looked much better. I finally had a feeling that I was here to stay.

I had even gotten myself a job at a small café around the corner. It was close by and I needed the money to pay Jackson back the fifteen grand he'd already given me.

I'd been away for almost a month, and talked to Mackenzie every day around three-thirty in the afternoon while Jaylin was at work. Once I got off the phone with her, I normally took it off the hook because I didn't want him calling me. I had a feeling he was trying to call because I knew he was missing me as much as I was missing him. But until he was willing to make some changes, I was staying right here.

Work was over, so I made my way home down the blistering cold streets of downtown Denver. I made some hot chocolate and called Jaylin's house to talk to Mackenzie. I was so glad when she picked up.

"Hi, sweetie," I said.

"Hi, Mommy. Are you still coming home?"

"Yes. Is everything okay?"

"Yes. Nanny B and me are in the kitchen making some cookies."

"You are? Will you save me some?"

"I guess. That's if Nanna doesn't eat them all up," she whispered.

"Well, put a few of them in your room for me, okay?"

"No. Daddy said food in the room causes bugs, so I'll keep them in my coat pocket."

"Thanks, honey. So, are you still coming to see me in a few weeks? Mommy can pick you up at the airport and we'll spend Christmas together."

She huffed. "I guess. Can Daddy come along too?"

"Not this time, Mackenzie. We need to have a little girl talk and Daddy can't hear it."

"Okay. But, Mommy, he's really been bad lately. He cried after he beat up his *wife* the other day. I was scared and I cried too." I heard Nanny B say something to Mackenzie in the background, and then Mackenzie gave the phone to her.

"Hello, Scorpio," she said.

"Hi, Nanny B. How's everything going?"

"Fine, just fine. I picked up Mackenzie from school and we're in the kitchen making cookies. Her friend Megan is spending the night tomorrow, so I'm trying to get things ready."

"Thank you so much Nanny B. You are an angel sent from heaven. I don't know what we would do without you."

"Well, I enjoy living here. Mackenzie and LJ have brought new joy to my life. I don't have much of a family anyway so I enjoy their company. Jaylin's too. Don't let me forget about him."

"Nanny B, what was Mackenzie saying about him and Nokea fighting? Is everything okay?"

"Yes, and there's nothing for you to worry about. They got into an argument over LJ and Jaylin got upset. You know how he can get at times, especially when it comes to these kids. And by the way, have you mentioned to him that Mackenzie is spending Christmas with you?"

"No, I haven't. I was going to ask my sister to fly

to Denver with Mackenzie. I'll call him the week before and tell him then."

"No, I think you should tell him today. Honestly, I don't like the way you or Nokea handle things. He's been a good father to these children, and you all have to learn how to compromise with him, instead of telling him what you're going to do. Now, this leaves both of us with no one to share Christmas with. I guess I'll just have to go to my sister's house and visit with her."

"I'm sorry, Nanny B, but I miss my child. We have never spent the holidays apart and we're not going to start now. Besides, Mackenzie wants to come see me. I know she misses me just as much as I'm missing her."

"I understand, but please let Jaylin know ahead of time. Don't throw this on him at the last minute and ruin his holiday. It just doesn't make sense to do that."

"Sure, I'll call him tonight. If you get a chance, tell him I'll call him later."

"Thank you," she said and gave the phone back to Mackenzie.

We talked for another ten minutes, and before we hung up, I told her how much I loved her and how anxious I was to see her. She seemed excited about seeing me too, but I wasn't sure how long it was going to last without Jaylin being around. The last thing I wanted was to invite him to stay with us because one thing would lead to another, and I would be right back where I started. So, him coming with her was not even an option.

I got off the phone with Mackenzie, and called the exterminator to come over again. The spray he'd used the first time didn't seem to be doing the job, so he was back in a flash. He sprayed the entire house again, and told me his time would only cost me a kiss. I laughed and hurried him out the door. As fine as he was, and as horny as I was, I thought about breaking the brotha down, but a new man was not on my agenda right now. The last mistake I made was with Shane, and I didn't intend to make any more.

Later that night, I got buck-naked and pulled out the sofa-bed in the living room. The heat was turned up and I was sweating like hell. I took Nanny B's advice and reached for the phone to call Jaylin. When he answered, he put me on hold because he was on the other line. He sounded perky, so I figured it was Stephon. But when he left me on hold for damn near five minutes, I realized it must have been a female.

"Yeah, what's up?" he asked.

"Nothing much. I just called to talk to you about Christmas."

"What about it?"

"I'd like Mackenzie to spend Christmas with me. I know you probably have plans, but Jaylin, I'm really missing her."

He sounded like he was smacking on something. "Well, come spend Christmas here with us. Why does she have to come to that rattrap with you?"

"Because I want to spend Christmas with her alone. And I'm fixing up this rattrap, just in case you want to know."

"Really?" he said, smacking harder. "Let me guess, Jackson gave you some money, didn't he?"

"Yes, but I intend to pay back every dime. I'm working at a café around the corner so I can do so."

"Um . . . interesting. But, uh, I talked to Mackenzie earlier, after Nanny B told me about your plans. I'll bring her to Denver myself. I promise you I won't stay, but I'll expect to have her back with me by New Year's."

"Did she say she wanted to come back by New Year's?"

"Yes, and she also said that she wanted me to stay with her. But knowing how you don't want me around, I told her it's best that she spends some time with you." He smacked again.

"What in the hell are you eating?"

"I wish it were your pussy, but these strawberries just have to do."

"Some things you say are just ridiculous, Jaylin." I closed my legs tight and wished for the same thing. There wasn't anything I wanted more than to feel him inside me.

"Ridiculous? What's ridiculous is you being in Denver depriving the both of us from being together. But go ahead, baby, and keep up with the bullshit. You're going to miss out on a good thing. And by the way, have you been taking your phone off the hook? I've tried calling a few times and couldn't get through."

"Yes, because I don't want you calling here persuading me to do something I don't want to do. I'm doing just fine and I'd like to keep it that way."

His phone clicked. "Hold on," he said, then clicked over. He clicked back. "Say, I'll see you the Sunday night before Christmas. I already called to make reservations, and because of the rush, I prefer to leave out on Sunday."

"That's fine, but why are you rushing me off the phone? You don't waste any time meeting people, do you?"

"And why are you assuming that it's a female on the other end?"

"Because I know you, Jaylin. When you're upset, you think with your dick and not with your brains."

He laughed. "You are getting really good at this, Scorpio. Besides, I'd hate to persuade you to do anything you don't want to do. So, ciao, gotta go." He hung up.

I flipped through the channels, trying to find something to watch. Unable to focus, I got frustrated thinking about Jaylin being with someone else. I was normally there to keep his mind preoccupied, but without me around, there wasn't no telling how much trouble he was getting into.

I fell asleep thinking about him, and woke up in a sweat after dreaming about him fucking me. Trying to calm myself, I got in my new tub and fantasized about him being in there with me. No matter how hard I tried, I couldn't shake the thought of him from my mind. I wanted him so badly that I rushed out of the tub and called his house. I let the phone ring two times, and as I was about to hang up, he answered in a sleepy voice.

"Jaylin?" I whispered.

"What?" he said. "Who is this?"

"It's me, Scorpio."

"Do you know what time it is?"

"Yes, but . . . I just needed to hear your voice."

"Okay, so now that you've heard it, good-bye."

He hung up.

I took a deep breath and closed my eyes. How stupid of me to call him. Like he really was going to come all this way and make love to me, and tell me he was going to change. I was out of my mind. But as I got ready to get back into the tub, the phone rang. I rushed to it knowing it was him.

"Hello," I said, softly.

"Say," he said.

"What?"

"I'm lonely."

"So am I. That's why I called you."

"Then come home."

"I will when you change your ways."

"No can do."

"Not even for me?"

"No, not even for you. I love who I am and I'm hoping that you figure out a way to accept me."

"As much as I want to, I can't."

"Then I can't put my life on hold for you any longer. Goodnight, Scorpio. Maybe next time."

"Yeah, maybe so." I hung up.

Chapter 20

Jaylin

I was up all night thinking about Scorpio. I called that punk-ass Jackson and told him not to get carried away with the money-giving bullshit. With him sending her $10,000 that meant I was already $20,000 in debt with him. And that didn't even include the money I'd already paid his slick ass. I also told him that he better not take any money from Scorpio, and if he did, the deal was off.

Since I couldn't get back to sleep, I got up and took an early morning drive to the Waffle House for breakfast. I knew Daisha was getting off work at six o'clock in the morning from the hospital, so I called her cell phone to see if she wanted some company. She told me to meet her at her place, and I was all smiles. I left Angela a message on her voicemail and told her I would not be in.

I was able to read females so well, but I really couldn't figure out what kind of game Daisha was playing. She seemed to be digging the shit out of me, but whenever I mentioned sex, she always changed the subject. We had been on the phone more than anything, and as much as I was enjoying our conversations, I was ready for her to shake a brotha down, especially since it had been awhile since I'd last had sex. It wasn't like I couldn't get any sex, but right about now I had to have a certain kind of pussy. Any woman just wasn't going to do, and the ones who could satisfy me were straight-up bullshitting. Nokea was off with her new man and probably wasn't even thinking about me. Scorpio was holding back, playing games, knowing that she damn well wanted some of this, and Daisha, I wasn't sure if she could please me or not, but I was dying to find out.

I pulled in front of Daisha's house just as she was getting out of the car. She was trying to pull a huge duffel bag from her trunk, and I rushed to help. I put it on my shoulder and she looked relieved.

"Thank you." She walked in front of me to the front door, and once again, I had the opportunity to check out her backside. Her ass was perfect. I couldn't wait for the opportunity to see how well that motherfucker could move.

We entered her house and she asked me to have a seat in the living room. I was thinking more like the bedroom, but I followed her directions.

I sat in a burgundy executive-style leather chair, and looked around the room. It was a bit old-fashioned for my taste, but was spotless. She had magazines neatly laid on a round glass table that sat on a green rug covering the shiny hardwood floors. Her wedding picture was displayed on the fireplace mantel, so I checked out the groom. He looked okay, but she seemed much too pretty to be with someone like him. When I heard her coming down the stairs, I eased back over to the chair. She leaned down on the steps and invited me upstairs to her bedroom.

"I was getting ready to take a shower, but I didn't want to leave you downstairs all alone," she said. We made our way up the steps together, but when we got to her room, I stood in the doorway as she sat on the bed.

"You can come in," she said, removing her shoes. "I promise you I won't bite."

I laughed, wishing that she would. "So, are you tired?" I asked as I sat next to her. "I know you probably had a long night at the hospital, and you sounded pretty tired when you called me last night."

"Exhausted more like it. I normally come in, take a shower, and I'm out until three or four o'clock in the afternoon."

"Well, if you want to get some rest, I can come back later."

"No, that's okay. I can rest with you here, can't I?" She went into the closet and came out with a few pieces of clothing in her hand.

"I can use some rest myself."

"Then we'll rest together."

After she closed the bathroom door, I removed my jacket, shoes, and hat, and scooted back on her sleep-number queen-sized bed. Her room was very feminine: dressed with light-purple, pink, and eggshell white. Purple pillows shaped like flowers were all over the bed, and two white wicker chairs sat in front of a bay window. What I admired about the whole damn house was the cleanliness about it and the smell of peaches. A clean house was a must for me, and Daisha was already presenting herself to be my kind of woman.

I lay my head on her pillow and waited for her to come out of the bathroom. When she did, she had a towel wrapped around her head with her pink cotton pajamas on. She removed the towel and teased her short hair around with her fingers. Extremely pretty, I thought, and could pass for my sister quite easily—if I'd had one.

She pulled the covers back and got in bed next to me. When she lay on her back and closed her eyes, I moved closer to her.

"Are you falling asleep already?" I asked.

"Shh . . . I'm praying."

"Oh." I moved back over and she opened her eyes.

"You didn't have to move. I just like to thank God for the wonderful day He's already planned for me, that's all."

"Nothing wrong with that. Did you thank Him for me, too?"

"I thanked Him for you yesterday, but if you're asking me if I thanked Him for allowing you another day, you need to do that."

"Okay, I will." I closed my eyes and thanked Him. "There, done deal."

She smiled, turned on her side, and looked at me. "You are an interesting man, Jaylin."

"And why do you say that?" I turned to face her.

"Because, I've heard some crazy things about

you. Mona and I were talking the other day, and the things she said about you, I'm having a hard time believing."

"Damn! What did she tell you?"

"Bottom line, she said that you were a serious ho."

"Really? Not just a ho, but a *serious* ho?"

"Yes. She also told me you have several lady friends and you treat them like crap."

"Keep going. This could get pretty ugly. Tell me more, please."

She laughed. "Anyway, I told her the same thing about Stephon. I also told her I saw more in you than just that and we squashed it. So, tell me, is she right, or am I wrong?"

"Depends."

"Depends on what?"

"Depends on what you see in me that she doesn't see."

"I see an arrogant, confident, classy, put-together, educated, aggressive, controlling, wealthy, handsome, persuasive man who loves to have sex with women."

"Now, *that* was a mouthful."

"So, now, am I wrong, or am I right?"

"Depends."

"Depends on what, Jaylin?"

"Depends on if this arrogant, confident, classy, put-together, educated, aggressive, controlling, wealthy, fine-ass man is going to persuade you to make love to him this morning."

"No."

"Well, then, you're wrong and she's right."

"No, she's not," Daisha said, playfully pushing my shoulder.

"Yes, she is. Because that's how women perceive a man like me to be. Forget all the wonderful things about me, nobody ever looks at that. It's always the bottom line and that's I'm a *serious* ho. Truth of the matter is, I love myself and I do what makes me happy. If that means being with more than one woman, why is it looked upon with so much negativity? Eventually, most people settle down, but I just haven't found the right person to settle down with."

"Are you looking for someone to settle down with?"

"No. I'm never looking. See, men are different. Most of the time, love for us comes totally unexpected. We don't actually go around looking for a woman to marry. A woman has to catch us off guard, kind of slip into our hearts for us to settle down. Sometimes we don't even know the feeling is there until she's gone, and that's when we have to learn from our mistakes and move on."

"Sounds like you've been there and done that before. Question is, are you learning from your mistakes?"

"Nope. Can't honestly say I have. That's because I don't mind making mistakes. I believe everything happens for a reason, and if I make a hundred mistakes in my lifetime, I won't sweat it. When God connects me with the woman He made for me, I'm sure everything will fall in place."

"Jaylin, I agree, but you have to draw the line somewhere, especially when you keep hurting women in the process. One day, those mistakes are going to cost you big time, if they haven't already. The days of finding good sistas are just about over because we are getting tired of the, excuse my French, but the bullshit. Men are losing out right now and don't even know it. So, anytime a good woman comes your way you'd better hold on to her and I mean tight. If you don't wake up, you're going to find yourself being without."

"You're a smart woman, Daisha. And I honestly appreciate your opinion, but I'll never be without."

"Well, you're going to be without this conversation because I am getting tired. Come over here and hold me so we can get some sleep."

Daisha turned her back to me and I eased behind her and held her. She placed her hand on top of mine and turned up her cheek for me to kiss it. I kissed it and breathed in the scent of her fresh body. As I continued kissing down her neck, she slightly turned and lifted my chin.

"Jaylin, I recently ended a marriage that I wanted so desperately to work. And even though I come off being hard on you, I have needs just like everyone else does. Don't hurt me, please. I've been hurt enough, and don't make me regret making love to you this morning, okay?"

She pulled my shirt over my head and I leaned forward to kiss her. Immediately thinking about my unfinished business with Scorpio, I turned my focus on fucking Daisha. I unbuttoned her pajama top, looked at her succulent breasts, and cleared my mind. She took off her pajama pants and there was no turning back for me. Her ass was just as I had imagined it, smooth and plump enough for me to work it how I wanted to. She placed her head on the pillow, and I stood to remove my pants. I gazed at her naked body and tried to figure out where to adventure first. When she gave me a hint and widened her legs, I moved in between them. She was moist and warm, and I was so ready to dive into it.

"Uh, where's your condom?" she whispered.

"Sorry, I didn't bring one inside. I didn't think we'd get this far, but, uh, do you have one?"

She moved her head from side to side. "I haven't had sex since my husband moved out. I didn't anticipate you and me going here either."

"Would you like for me to go outside and get it?"

She sighed and felt my nine waiting to crack her wide open. "No. Just don't forget it next time, okay?"

I nodded. My dick didn't waste no time going inside. Being sexually deprived for weeks, I felt myself wanting to come, just to get one nut out of the way. Daisha seemed so into it, so I held back to make it last.

She felt good and it was better than I'd imagined. The way she softly moaned and touched my ass, as we rocked our bodies together, seriously turned me on. And when she came, she was calm about it. She took my head and placed it between her breasts, squeezing her legs tightly around my waist. When her moment was finished, no questions asked, she rolled on her stomach and let me shake up things from behind. I remained gentle with my strokes, until she rose up on her knees. I had the pleasure of watching her ass in motion and had to let go.

"You know better," I said, tightly holding her hips and expressing my desire to come.

"Jaylin," she said, softly. "Don't you dare, especially when I'm so into you right now."

I definitely couldn't disappoint her, so I took a deep breath, and regrouped. She was still on her stomach, so I circled her hole with the tip of my head, teasing her. She aggressively forced me in. I wanted to feel her for at least another hour.

"Are you okay now?" I whispered, as I expanded inside of her.

"Uhm . . . more than okay," she mumbled. I went in deeper. "Okay," she moaned, "Better, oh, so much better."

I rolled her over backward on top of me, spreading her legs, massaging her clitoris with one hand and her breast with the other.

"Oh, no, Jaylin." She trembled. "Never in my entire lifetime better than this."

I kept stroking Daisha at a slow pace just so neither one of us would come. She was grinding down on me and wasn't cutting a brotha no slack. When I heard her pussy talk to me, that was my cue to pick up the pace.

"Daisha?" I whispered in her ear.

"Yessss," she whispered back.

"I'm getting ready to make you come. This time, I want to feel it. Don't hold back and I want to hear you say how much you enjoyed this, okay?"

"Stop talking so damn much and just do it!"

I slammed myself further in, and rubbed my head against her clit on my exits. Feeling every bit of me, she tried to get up, but I held her hips tightly with my hands and didn't let her move.

She took deep breaths. "Okay . . . now I see," she cried out while rocking faster with me. "I see what the big fuss—" she screamed my name and laid beside me.

"Yes?" I said, leaning slightly over her.

"That's a shame."

"What . . . what did I do?" I smiled.

"*That* was not supposed to be that good."

"And neither were you. So, I'm sorry, and I'll take it back."

"No, you can't have it back."

"So, it's yours for keeps."

"Yes, it is. Only if you'll let me keep it."

"Whenever." I gave her a peck on the lips. "However." I circled my tongue around her nipple. "And wherever" I scooted down and licked her between the legs.

"Come here," she said, laughing. "I have to be honest with you about something."

"What?" I said, lying next to her again.

"I didn't intend on having sex with you so soon. I hope I didn't come off too easy, but there was just something about you that I liked. Normally, I don't give myself to every man I meet."

"Daisha, I truly believe that. I just hope you don't have any regrets, especially after how we just got down."

"No regrets, Jaylin. You have no idea how much I needed, or should I say, wanted to feel like that."

"Tell me about it. It's been a long time for me too."

"Really? Well, it's been almost one year for me. I stopped sleeping with my husband months before the marriage was over, but on the day he left, we did do a little somethin' somethin'. He never took me to that level, though, and your hard work was appreciated. Anyway, come over here and hold me so we can get that rest we talked about earlier."

"Rest my ass. I'd say lets make up for some of this lost time you and I seem to have had."

"Where do you get all of your energy from? Are you serious?"

"As a heart attack." I opened her legs with my foot and eased in between them.

"You are going to find yourself in trouble messing with a woman like me—you handsome devil."

"I love trouble, baby, bring it on."

Daisha didn't lie. After messing around with her for hours, my ass was in trouble. I felt drained and she was still going full force. She talked bad about me, but still told me how much she enjoyed herself. I enjoyed myself as well. Every time I thought you couldn't teach an old dog new tricks, a different woman would come along and show me something new. On a good day, Daisha could actually outlast me. Thing was, I was going to enjoy every moment of competing with her.

When I woke up and looked for Daisha, she wasn't there. I glanced at my watch and it showed almost six o'clock P.M.. *Damn, where did the time go?* I thought. I pulled the covers back and slid into my Calvin Klein jockey shorts.

I heard Daisha downstairs on the phone, so I went down there to see why she let me sleep so long. As I was coming down the steps, I could see her sitting in the living room with her legs folded. She was gazing at the burning fire in the fireplace.

When she heard me step down onto the hardwood floors, she turned her head.

"Mona, I'll call you back later, okay?" she whispered, then looked at me. "Hey, sleepy head."

I sat on the floor in front of her and she put her legs on the floor so I could lay my head against them. As she rubbed her hands in my hair like Scorpio used to, I started to think about her. And when Daisha noticed how quiet I was, she snapped me out of it.

"A penny for your thoughts," she asked.

"Naw, a nickel for your kiss," I said. She leaned down and kissed me. "I'm just thinking about what a wonderful day I had with you, Daisha. Usually, I'm anxious to leave, but for some reason I feel a sense of peace when I'm with you."

"Good. And I hope you continue to feel that way. I wish I could stay here with you all night, but I have to be at work by nine. If you want to, you can stay the night. I won't be back until at least six or seven o'clock in the morning."

"That won't be necessary. I'm getting ready to go home. I, uh, need to spend some time with my son before he goes to Detroit and with my daughter before she goes to Denver. The next few weeks are going to be tough for me, so please don't be offended if you don't hear from me. By all means, don't take it personal. When I'm upset, sometimes I prefer to be alone."

"Well, you shouldn't be alone on Christmas. I have plans to go to Florida where my parents live, but I was just there on Thanksgiving. If you'd like, I can cook dinner for us and we can celebrate Christmas and New Year's together."

"That's nice, but we'll see. I'll let you know next week."

Daisha headed for work and I headed home. There was something different about her, but I just couldn't quite put my finger on it. Maybe it was how good the sex was between us, but that might have been because I haven't had any for a while.

Either way, she could be a real setback for me, especially when I thought I was feeling something special for Scorpio. Trying not to think about her so much, I focused my mind elsewhere and sped up to get home.

Mackenzie's best friend Megan was staying a few days with us while her parents were out of town on vacation. Nanny B had cleared it with me the week before, and I'd said it would be fine as long as it was cool with her.

I walked through the door to find Mackenzie and Megan running around the house like they were outside on a playground, making all kinds of noise. Having a slight headache, I asked them to be quiet. Mackenzie yelled back, "Shut up."

My eyebrows rose. "What did you say?"

She put her hands on her hips. "I said don't raise your voice at me!" she screamed.

Nanny B came out of the kitchen. "Mackenzie, I heard you all the way—"

"Naw, that's all right, Nanny B, I got this one here." I took my belt off my pants. "Get your butt upstairs right now, Mackenzie! Go to your room!"

She gave Megan her doll and stomped upstairs to her room. Nanny B took Megan into the kitchen and came back out before I started up the steps.

"Jaylin, don't you hit her and I mean it. I know she can get out of hand sometimes, but she's just a kid. Don't blame her for learning all that bossy stuff from those kids she go to school with."

"Nanny B, stop making excuses for her. I don't care where she's learning that stuff from. First me, and now the school. Bottom line is she will not disrespect me and I mean it." I ignored Nanny B and went upstairs to Mackenzie's room. She was lying across the bed, crying like somebody was killing her.

"Get up!" I said angrily. She ignored me and continued to cry. "Mackenzie, did you hear what I said?" I yelled.

She stood with tears pouring down her face, and was barely able to catch her breath. He beautiful eyes went straight to my heart as she stared at me and rubbed them. "I want my mommy," she burst out. She ran up and hugged me around the waist. "Daddy, please, don't hit me. I want my mommy."

I closed my eyes and hugged her back. "I want her too, sweetheart. In due time, though, all right? I promise you, in due time."

We sat on her bed and I wiped her tears as she sat on my lap. "Mackenzie, I'm not going to hit you, but you are not allowed to speak to me like that. Do you understand?" She nodded. "I don't care how your other friends talk to their parents, we don't talk like that in this house, okay?" She nodded again. "Why would you talk to me like that anyway? I thought you loved me."

"I do love you Daddy, but . . . I'm afraid of you."

"What? Since when did you become afraid of me?"

"Since you tried to kill your wife downstairs. I told my friends about you choking her and they said you're a murderer."

Damn stupid kids, I thought. "Mackenzie, you can't be telling your friends what happens in our home. And you tell them your daddy is not a murderer. I would never do anything to hurt anyone— it was all a big mistake, baby. My *wife* knows I wouldn't do anything to purposely hurt her."

"But she was crying."

"And so was I. But that's because we don't enjoy hurting each other like that. Please don't be afraid of me. I love you and I will never hurt you."

She hopped down off my lap and wiped her eyes. "Can I go downstairs now to play with Megan?"

"Yes, Mackenzie. But let's go call Mommy before you do and tell her we're coming to see her."

"But I thought we were going to see her on Christmas."

"I know, but let's surprise her and go see her earlier."

We called Scorpio but the number was busy. I made arrangements for us to leave Thursday night instead of the Sunday before Christmas. Even though I lost my money for the tickets, Mackenzie needed to see Scorpio and so did I. It was time for me to change my game plan, because Mackenzie was watching my every move. I truly believed her bad behavior was from her missing Scorpio.

* * *

Our plane touched down in Denver around ten o'clock Thursday night. Mackenzie was all bundled up in her new pink-and-white coat that I bought. Her long fluffy hair was hanging out of her hat, and she looked adorable. I knew Scorpio was going to be glad to see her, but there was no doubt that I would miss her. I had already bought Mackenzie a puppy for Christmas, but I wasn't going to pick him up until she came back home.

When the rental car assistant pulled up with our car, we were on our way. Before I'd left St. Louis, I stopped by Jackson's place and paid him his money. He showed me another check that he sent her for $5,000, so I knocked that one out too. He claimed the only reason he sent the money was because she made it clear to him that she was never coming back to St. Louis. I guess by the way she was spending money to fix up the place, maybe, just maybe, she was there to stay. I made him promise to never tell Scorpio about the money because she would be furious with me if she knew I was taking care of her expenses in Denver as well.

We pulled in front of Jackson's house, and Mackenzie rushed to open the car door. I reached in my pocket for the second key Jackson gave me before I left. I put the key in the door and whispered for Mackenzie to be very quiet. When we walked in, the TV was blasting. Scorpio was lying naked on her stomach across the sofa bed. She was asleep and held a body pillow close, with her legs wrapped around it. I guessed she thought it was me.

I directed Mackenzie to go back into the bedroom,

so she could surprise Scorpio when I woke her. Mackenzie quietly tiptoed down the hallway.

I moved in closer to Scorpio and smiled at how pretty she was. Her long hair was spread out over the pillow and her skin looked silky smooth. She actually had on a white silk thong and my imagination took me to where the string was lying. I couldn't see her breasts because she held them closely to the body pillow. I swore that if it weren't for Mackenzie being with me, I would have torn into her right then and there.

Instead, I spit on my hands, rubbed them together until they felt nice and warm, then I smacked her ass as hard as I could. She jumped from her sleep and grabbed for her robe.

"What are you doing?" she yelled. "That shit is not funny." She put on her robe and cut her eyes at me. "Why are you here, Jaylin?"

"Damn! Happy to see you, too, Scorpio."

She pulled her hair back and abruptly walked to the kitchen. I followed her. "Where's my child?" she asked, standing against the refrigerator.

"Where's my hug?"

"You don't get one after scaring the shit out of me and hitting me on my ass like that."

"Couldn't resist."

"Well, it's not made for smacking. Just in case you can't remember."

"I know, it's made for me, right?" I walked up to her and put my arms around her. "Can I at least have a kiss?" I rubbed my hands on the cheek of her ass to cool it off. "Sorry about that and I promise I'll make it up to your ass later."

She pecked me on the lips and removed my

arms from around her. "No, thanks. Where's my child, Jaylin? Did you come here without her?"

I took Scorpio's hand and walked her back into the bedroom where Mackenzie was. Mackenzie had even hid by the side of the bed. After we walked in, she jumped up and yelled for Scorpio. They kissed and hugged each other. Even though I was happy to see them together, I couldn't believe that a small part of me was actually kind of jealous.

Trying to allow them some time together, I went back into the kitchen. I thought about LJ and pulled out my cell phone to call Nokea. I knew they were heading out on Monday, so I called to make sure she was bringing him over to spend the weekend with me before they left.

"I'll drop him off before I go to my hair appointment early Saturday morning. Is that okay?" she asked.

"Yeah, that's fine. Anyway, how are things going? Every time you bring LJ by I hardly get a chance to talk to you anymore."

"Everything is fine, Jaylin. Actually, couldn't be better. You don't sound too good, though. Is everything okay with you?"

"Yeah, I'm cool. I'm dreading being alone without my children on Christmas, but I'm cool."

"What about Mackenzie? Is she going somewhere too?"

"Yeah, I'm in Denver now, bringing her to see Scorpio."

"Oh . . . I didn't know, I'm sorry. You're welcome to come to Detroit with us. Collins wanted me to ask you the other day, but I knew you would probably say no."

"Thanks, but you know that is out of the question. I'm not that comfortable with the situation yet."

"Well, what about Stephon and Ray Ray?"

"Nokea, they have their own lives. Don't worry, I'll be fine. I'll do something to keep myself occupied."

"Darn, Jaylin, I feel so bad. Look, if you want LJ to stay with you, that's fine. I'll take him some other time with Collins and me."

"I will consider no such thing. I told you that I'm cool. Take him with you and Collins. You'd better take me up on my offer because it might be your last chance."

"Are you sure?"

"Yes, Nokea. Look, I'll see you soon. I gotta go, okay?"

"All right . . . I love you."

"Love you too."

I hung up.

Nobody knew my true pain but me. All my life I had a serious fear of being alone. My fear came from spending those years in an orphanage and having no one to come see me but Nokea and her mother, on occasion. I guess when my grandfather passed away he must have felt guilty, and that's why he left me so much money from his real estate business. It was probably his way of making up for lost time, and for betraying his deceased daughter, my mother.

After sitting in the kitchen for about thirty minutes, thinking, I got up to check on Scorpio and Mackenzie. When I walked back into the bedroom, Mackenzie was cuddled up in Scorpio's arms sound asleep. Scorpio kissed Mackenzie and whispered for me to be quiet as she slid out of bed. She walked down the hallway, and I followed her into the living room. She sat on the sofa bed, placed her hands over her face, and cried.

"Thank you so much, Jaylin. You have no idea how much I've missed her. And for you to ask me to let her come back with you, I can't. There is no way, I'm sorry."

I sat next to her. "Look, don't stress yourself out about it. I'm not going to fight you over this anymore. She's your child and I know more than anything how much she means to you. I'm just sorry you won't come back and work this out with me."

"Not right now, I can't." She wiped her eyes. "Did you see what I've done to this place?"

"Yeah, I have. It doesn't look too bad either. I kind of like it."

"Like it enough to live here yourself?"

I laughed. "No . . . I don't like it that much."

"I'm sure you don't. I guess you wouldn't trade in your mansion for a place like this anyway."

"No, I wouldn't. But it says a lot about a woman's character who would, especially for the sake of her own happiness." I stood and went into the kitchen to get my coat. There was no need to stay and prolong my misery.

"Are you leaving already?" Scorpio asked, trailing behind me.

"Yes, I think its best, especially while Mackenzie's still asleep."

"Okay. When she wakes up I'll tell her you said

good-bye." Scorpio reached over and hugged me. I held her tight and didn't want to let go. I did, and made my way to the door.

"Can I have my key?" she asked.

"No, no way. This key is worth a lot of money to me. Trust me, you don't want to know."

"If you paid Jackson more than ten dollars for it, you're a fool. He's a serious money hustler and will do anything to make a dime."

"I'm sure he would, but whatever, my loss . . . I guess."

"So, if you're keeping the key, that must mean you're coming back, right?"

"One day, maybe I will. Who knows?" I winked and opened the door. Scorpio stopped me.

"I love you, Jaylin. And thanks again for bringing Mackenzie."

"Ditto. And anything to make you happy."

I got to the car and looked back to see Mackenzie standing on the porch. When I waved, she started crying hysterically. I got out of the car and pulled her back into the house to get her out of the freezing night air.

"Why are you crying, Mackenzie? I'll be back to get you." Seeing her cry was really starting to work my nerves. I kneeled down to calm her, but she hugged me and wouldn't let go. I looked up at Scorpio. "Why don't you just come home? This is just downright ridiculous for us to be apart like this."

Mackenzie kept her arms wrapped around me. "Oooo, Daddy, don't go. Please don't leave me. I'll be good, I promise. I don't want to stay if you don't stay."

"Mackenzie, I can't stay. You said you wanted to spend time with your mommy, so please, I'll be back." My eyes watered.

Scorpio leaned down next to Mackenzie and me. She swallowed, and I could see the anguish in her eyes. "Mackenzie, if you don't want to stay with me, you don't have to. You can go home with your daddy."

Mackenzie hugged Scorpio's neck too. "I want to stay with you, Mommy, but I want Daddy to stay with us too. Why can't he stay? Please let him stay," she begged.

"I can't stay, Mackenzie. I promise you I'll be back." I kissed her cheek and stood up. This was too much for me, so I tightened my coat and quickly opened the door. Without looking back, I listened to Mackenzie yell and scream my name, but I kept on walking to the car.

I couldn't take the pressure. It was killing me not knowing if Scorpio was going to be a part of my life anymore. When I reached the end of the street, I pulled the car over and broke down. My throat ached and pain rushed all through my body. *Why did life have to be so damn difficult?* I thought. First Jasmine, then LJ, and now Mackenzie. *How much more of this can a brotha take?*

After sitting in the car soaking for a while, I tried to get myself together. I wanted to go back for Mackenzie, but I couldn't. Instead, I drove back to the airport and waited for my plane back to St. Louis.

On the trip home, a very attractive stewardess tried to entertain me, but I wasn't interested. She gave me her phone number. When I got to Lambert Airport, I threw it in the trash.

Nanny B had hired some fellows to put up a twelve-foot Christmas tree, which was up by the time I got home. They had decorated it with off-white and gold trimmings. When she told me they were coming, I'd had no idea it was going to look so magnificent. She had left some cookies on the table, with a note saying she was going to her sister's house and wouldn't be back until the day after Christmas. There was a number where I could reach her, and a present for me on the table with a card on top.

I lay back on the chaise, looking at the white lights on the tree as they flashed on me in the dark. Then I opened Nanny B's card and started to read:

> *Merry Christmas, my dear. I wanted to give this to you personally, but I wasn't sure when you would be back. Save me a slice of the pineapple upside-down cake, and I'll see you when I return, Love You, Bertha. P.S. Christmas dinner is in the refrigerator and the house is spotless just how you like it.*

I smiled because I'd thought her name was Brenda. When I asked her, she would always tell me to call her Nanny B, so I just assumed the B was for Brenda. Maybe because it was the name of an old girlfriend of mine.

I opened the box to find a silver-and-gold photo album laced with black velvet cloth. An old black-

and-white picture of Mama and me, from when I was a baby, was on the front. Inside were pictures of my grandfather, Stephon when he was a baby, my Aunt Betty, my cousins. Even a picture of my father was in the far back. After a picture of LJ and Mackenzie, there were some blank pages, then the last page, which was a photo of Nanny B and my grandfather. I pulled it out and looked at the back, which read:

Anthony Jerome Rogers & Bertha Marie White
married June 1953.

Well, I'll be damned, I thought. *She was my grandmother?* I didn't remember much about my grandmother, but she didn't look anything like Nanny B. I knew very little about my family's history, but there was no way in hell she could be my grandmother.

Curious, I got up and ran downstairs to look through an old cedar chest I kept in a closet. When I opened it, I could tell someone had been rummaging through it because the pictures weren't as neat as I'd had them. I looked through them one by one until I found a wedding picture of my grandparents. The picture was of the grandmother I'd remembered. The back read:

married May 1971.

I was too little then to remember. Nanny B was married to him before he married my grandmother. Question was, which one of them was my mother's mother. Had to be Nanny B because my mother was already twenty-one when my grandfather remarried in 1971.

I put the pictures next to each other; Nanny B didn't look like my mother, the other woman did. Still confused, I grabbed all the pictures and ran back upstairs. I thought I was losing my damn mind, but when I thought about who introduced me to Nanny B to begin with, it started to all make sense. Stephon's mother, my Aunt Betty, did. She told me about a nanny who did a superb job cleaning, and told me how much I could trust her.

I wanted to call Nanny B at her sister's house first, but instead, I called Stephon to see how much of this he knew about. It was early in the morning, but I desperately wanted some answers.

"Yeah," he said, sounding asleep.

"Man, wake up."

"Negro, I'm tired. What's up?"

"Do you know who my nanny is?"

"Jay, you ain't sleeping with your nanny, are you?"

"Naw, fool. I mean, have you ever seen her besides her being over here?"

"Uh-uh, why?"

"Because I think she's our grandmother."

"Fool, what you over there smoking? Our grandparents were killed in a car accident, remember? Jay, I hope you ain't smoking that shit, man."

"Naw, listen, I'm serious. Nanny B gave me a picture of her and Grandpa for my Christmas present. Well, the picture was in a photo album she gave me. Anyway, on the back, it said they were married in June, 1953. But then, there's another picture of him with our grandmother that says they were married in 1971."

"Sounds like the apple doesn't fall far from the tree. Sounds to me like Grandpa had his mack on."

"Could be . . . Definitely could be. But, uh, you've never seen Nanny B before? Especially since your mother hooked me up with her."

"Man, I really can't say that I have. Let me think about it for a while, and if something comes up, I'll call you back. Anyway, why is this so important to you?"

"Please, Stephon. How can you ask me that? If she's our grandmother, then that explains everything."

"Everything like what?"

"Her attachment to me. To Mackenzie, to LJ . . . Everything."

"My love for you. My understanding you," said a voice from behind me.

I whirled around and saw Nanny B. My heart dropped and I jumped up from the couch. "Turn the fucking lights on! Now! Jesus Christ!" Nanny B turned on the lights.

"Jay!" Stephon yelled. "You all right, man?"

"I'll call you back," I said, and hung up on Stephon. My eyebrows rose and I looked at Nanny B. "Tell me . . . what in the fuck is going on? Who in the hell are you?"

"Sit down, Jaylin," she asked and sat on the couch.

"I ain't sitting nowhere until I find out what the fuck is going on."

"Please, sit down. I'll tell you everything, just

have a seat." My heart was racing as I sat next to her on the couch. She put her hand on my leg. "I was close to my sister's place, and I turned the car around thinking about how important it was for me to come back here and tell you my story."

"What story, Nanny B, damn it what story?"

"I'm not your blood grandmother, but I was married to your grandfather in 1953. When I met him, he had two beautiful daughters, and a son, like you. He was much older than I was, but I loved him and his children more than life itself. Your grandmother had run off with some other man and left your grandfather and her kids behind. So, when he met me, I gave them all the love I could muster and someone they could look up to, even though I was only eighteen years old at the time. Your mother was my favorite. She was the oldest and was twelve years old when I met your grandfather. She was by far the prettiest child I'd ever seen."

"Was she as pretty as me?" I smiled

"Yes, a lot prettier. Anyway, when your real grandmother decided to come back, your grandfather asked me for a divorce to marry her. I was devastated. I had given up everything for him, and I do mean everything. But there wasn't nothing I could do. He was still in love with her and I was out. When your mother and Aunt Betty had you and Stephon they would bring y'all by my house so I could see y'all, but even that soon stopped. Your grandfather threw a fit about me keeping in touch, and cut off all ties."

"Was he that mean, Nanny B?"

"Stubborn," she looked at me and smiled. "Just

like you. So, anyway, when I found out your mother had been killed, I cried for months. Lord knows I was hurt. Since I couldn't have any children, she was like my child. All three of them were. But when I showed up at her funeral, your grandfather turned me away. He said I needed to stop interfering and move on with my life. So, that's what I did. I kept in touch with your Aunt Betty for a while, but mostly by phone. When she got herself on drugs, and I found out she lied to me about getting you out of that orphanage, I really didn't want anything to do with her. Then, one day she called and told me you were looking for a nanny. She made me promise to never tell you the truth, and begged me to look out for you like I'd looked out for them."

"No, not Aunt Betty, Nanny B. She hated me. The things she used to do and say to me I never understood."

"Baby, she didn't mean to hurt you. Those drugs made her a totally different person. But she was very jealous of your mother. Like Stephon is of you. They loved each other, though. Nothing could keep them apart. Your mother's death is actually what sent her over the edge."

"But why didn't you just tell me all this before? Why tell me all of this now?"

"Because I was afraid to tell you. If I had told you a long time ago, you would have turned me away, Jaylin. You would have found no purpose for me. Now, you know what my purpose is. It's to love you, to take care of you, and to make sure you do the right things when it comes to your children."

Thinking about how much Nanny B knew about

me, I shamefully stood and walked over by the tree. "Have I disappointed you? Do you think my mother is proud of me?"

"Yes and no. You and Stephon are the spitting image of your grandfather. I watch the two of you with all these women and how disrespectful y'all can be . . . I just shake my head. But the love that you have for your children is what I'm proud of. I know your mother is proud of that too. Being in that orphanage might have hurt you, but it helped you in some ways, too. It helped you open up to children in a way you probably never would have been able to."

"You're right. I never want any child to have to suffer like I did." Nanny B walked up to me and took my hand. "Nanny B, why did Grandpa leave me his money, though? Why not Stephon, or my other cousins? More so, why not his own son?"

"Jonathan, that's your uncle, moved away years ago. He married some white woman in Kentucky and nobody's heard from him since. When your grandfather died, he left eleven-and-a-half million dollars to me in his will. I was shocked and didn't know what to do with the money. I truly didn't want one dime after what he put me through. So, I got a lawyer, decided which one of his grandchildren I wanted to give the money to, and since I loved your mother so much, I didn't have a difficult choice to make."

I chuckled. "But I only got nine-and-a-half million. Where's the other two?"

"Well, the lawyer suggested that I take a little something for my pain and suffering, so I did." She laughed. "But, Jaylin, I never wanted a dime.

That money is growing in a mutual fund right now, untouched. I'd like for you to put it up for your children. All I ever wanted was to be a part of this family, and if my being a nanny got me here, so be it."

Nanny B and I hugged each other tightly, and she talked some more to me about my family. She'd really loved my grandfather, and it seemed to be his loss to let go of a woman so special.

"I got one more question for you," I said. "How old are you? You told me you were fifty-seven, but if my calculations are correct, you're actually a bit older than that."

She laughed. "How old do I look? Can't I pass for fifty-seven or even forty-seven?"

"You really could, but I'm worried about all the things you do around here. All the driving and everything you do for the kids. And the cigarettes, those can't be good for you."

"I'm a blessed healthy young woman, Jaylin, that's all you need to know. But how did you know about my cigarettes? I only smoke them every once in a while, and when I do, I go outside."

"Mackenzie told me. I didn't believe her, but when I checked your pockets, I saw them."

We laughed. The doorbell rang just then, and we looked at each other, not knowing who in the hell could be at the door so early in the morning. When Nanny B opened the door, Stephon came rushing in.

"What's going on, man? Why did you hang up on me?"

I looked at my watch; More than an hour had passed since I'd talked to him. "You can't move no faster than that? I could have been over here dying or something," I said.

He plopped down on the couch. "I had to get dressed. Damn. But what's all this crazy talk about Nanny B?"

I opened my mouth to tell him, but Nanny B stood behind him and shook her head, her lips forming the word, "No." "Nothing, dog," I said. "It was a joke. She was messing around with me because she knew how upset I was about Christmas."

"But since the both of you are here, why don't I whip y'all up some breakfast? Besides, I'm hungry myself." Nanny B said.

"Sounds like a plan to me," Stephon said. Nanny B went into the kitchen and started breakfast. "Man, you straight-up lucked out on a good-ass nanny. You just can't find them like that these days."

"I know, man. Deep in my heart I truly know."

Nanny B cooked a scrumptious breakfast for us: cheese eggs, grits, bacon, sausage, toast and jelly, and some buttermilk pancakes. Shit was off the hook. After Stephon left she told me not to tell him the truth because she didn't want him to feel hurt by her decision to give the money to me.

I talked to her about my situation with Mackenzie and she advised me to back down. She told me to allow Scorpio and Mackenzie time together and assured me Mackenzie would be coming back soon.

Nokea dropped LJ off early Saturday morning before heading to her hair appointment, as planned. I was feeling a slight bit better, which she could tell when she finally came in to talk to me this time. Her whole attitude and outlook on life had changed. I was seeing a different side of her, one that I admired and respected more than anything. I was sure Collins was the reason, but I was kind of disappointed in myself for being with her all those years and not bringing out the best in her like Collins did.

I spent the entire weekend alone with my son. Nanny B had even left for her sister's house on Friday, after spending most of the day with LJ and me. We really couldn't do much, but I showed him how to play cards, how to use the remote control, and even how to make investment transactions on my laptop. He loved being in the water, so I let him splash around in the tub after I filled it with bubbles.

Late Sunday night, we bundled up and went outside to hoop. Of course, he won but I considered it cheating since I had to lift him to make the ball go in the hoop.

Nokea called around ten o'clock that night to say she was tied up at her parents' house and would send Collins over to pick up LJ. When I accused her of having a shitty excuse, she laughed and said she wanted me to be comfortable with Collins. She claimed the more time we spent getting to know each other, the better off I'd be. Slightly pissed about being forced into this situation, I still went with the flow.

Collins was there by ten-thirty to pick up LJ. When the doorbell rang, I was in the bonus room playing pool. LJ sat in the middle of the table knocking the balls in the holes when I missed the shot. I picked him up and ran downstairs to get the door. When I opened it, Collins smiled and came inside. He stood in the foyer and looked around with his hands inside the pockets of his long black trench coat.

"Wow, this is nice, man. You must hook me up with your interior decorator."

I smiled. "Naw, can't do that. She's my ancient Chinese secret."

"In other words, you don't want nobody's house resembling yours."

"Exactly."

He pointed to LJ. "You have everything ready for him to go?"

"Yeah, just about. I was upstairs playing pool, so there are just a few other things I have to get."

"Pool, huh. You wanna shoot a game? I'm actually pretty good at it."

"I'm better."

Collins grabbed my shoulder. "We'll just have to see about that. Before we get down to business, though, would you mind showing me around? I'd like to get at least some ideas for my house."

I carried LJ and toured Collins through the lower level of my house. I bragged about my large kitchen, my workout room, the theatre room I was having remodeled, my Olympic-sized swimming pool, and basketball court. I was sure Collins's house wasn't short-stopping in Ladue, but he seemed amazed. He stood in the doorway to my office and looked up at the Cathedral ceiling. I had a chandelier hanging from the ceiling that gave the room a dim, settled lighting.

"Now, this is an office. I would never leave my house if I had an office like this. My office has papers piled up everywhere."

"Yeah, it is one of my favorite places to be. Kind of relaxing, if anything."

We walked up the steps and went into my bedroom, since it was the closest to the staircase. Collins looked at the glass entryway and smiled.

"Now, how do you ever get down in your bedroom if people can see straight through here?"

"Easily. That glass is the last thing on my mind when I'm in here with a woman."

Collins laughed and I continued the tour. He stood in my bedroom gazing at the vaulted ceiling, the flat-screen TV on the wall, the white furry chaise, and the fireplace in the far corner of the room. He shook his head and sat on my California king-sized bed, covered with white-and-gold silk Gucci sheets. "Jaylin, how old did you say you were?"

"I didn't. But I'm thirty-three years young."

"You are blessed, my brotha. Truly, truly, blessed. I'm forty," he cleared his throat, "years old and good fortune didn't come my way until three years ago. Just recently I was able to start my computer business in Detroit, as well as in St. Louis. I had to partner up with a few brothas just for that to happen. If you got it going on like this at thirty-three, and don't have to count on anyone for anything, my hat goes off to you."

"Yeah, it feels kind of nice to stand alone." We walked out of my bedroom. "Now, Collins, your compliments will not stop me from giving you this ass whuppin' I'm about to give you on this pool table."

He laughed and I continued the upstairs tour. I showed him the other bedrooms, a wine cellar, and the bonus room where the pool table was. He looked over the Romeo and Juliet balcony that viewed into my great room down below.

"I'm afraid of heights, but I would really love something like this in my house. Whoever hooked this up for you, they did a damn good job."

I nodded and we got down to business with our game. At first, LJ wouldn't let me put him down, but once he had fallen asleep, I laid him on the couch.

When all was said and done, Collins had lost four out of the five games we played. He leaned against the pool table and puffed on a cigar.

"You're pretty good, Jaylin."

I bent over and shot the eight ball in to win the last game. It went into the hole. "Good at everything I do, Collins."

His cell phone rang. When he looked at it, he said it was Nokea and answered. "Yeah, baby." He paused. "I know. I'll be there in a few." He paused again. "Okay, I'm sure he won't mind." He held the phone out to me.

"Hello," I said.

"Do you mind if I come get my son now?"

"Collins is here to pick him up. I know you ain't tripping?"

"I sent Collins over there almost two hours ago. I've been calling your house, thinking the two of you got into it or something. Why haven't you answered your phone?"

"Because we've been playing pool. Come on over anyway, I want to tell you something in person."

Nokea hung up and we played one more game of pool. When she got there, Collins and I were sitting in the living room drinking cognac and talking. I opened the door and Nokea immediately inhaled the alcohol on my breath.

"I just know the two of you haven't been in here drinking with my baby around." She walked over to Collins and gave him a kiss.

"Naw, baby. He's been asleep for a while," he said, tipsy.

Nokea walked to the bottom of the stairs. "Is he in his room, or your room, Jaylin?"

"Neither. He's in the bonus room on the couch."

She looked at us and rolled her eyes. "That's dangerous. He could fall on the floor and bust his head. Careless men, I tell you." She walked up the steps.

I shrugged. "Good luck, man. She's a tough cookie."

"Isn't she? But, she's the boss." He smiled and winked. "I like to let her think that, anyway."

We laughed, and Nokea came down the steps with LJ. Collins met her at the bottom stair and took LJ's diaper bag off her shoulder. I took LJ out of her hands and kissed him. When Nokea reached out to take him back, I gave him to Collins.

"Take care of my son, Collins. I want him to come home safely."

Collins put LJ on his shoulder and grabbed my hand. "You bet'cha, I will. And have a Merry Christmas, Jaylin." He walked out the door with LJ, but Nokea stayed behind and gave me a hug.

"So, what did you want to tell me in person?" she asked.

"Call Pat, she's ready to talk."

"And how do you know this?"

"Because I just do," I said, giving her Pat's new telephone number.

Nokea walked out toward the car, then turned and looked at me as I stood in the doorway.

"I love you," she mouthed.

I placed my hand on my heart and nodded.

After they pulled off, I went upstairs to take a shower. I laid across my bed and checked my voice-mail that said I had thirty-five messages waiting. After I spent fifteen minutes listening to the calls, I jotted down the important ones and deleted the rest. Daisha, Shane, Stephon, Brashaney, Felicia, Ray Ray, Higgins, and Schmidt had called several times, Mackenzie and Scorpio had called once, Nanny B had called to check on me, and Pat had called to thank me for bringing LJ over to see her. I wasn't sure if my visit would be deemed a success or not; the rest was up to her and Nokea.

Chapter 21

Nokea

Collins' house in Detroit was awesome. He played it down like it wasn't as spectacular as the house in St. Louis, but this one was the best. And he'd had the audacity to brag on Jaylin's house. With decorating, yes, Jaylin had him beat, but since I was infatuated with the size of the house, rather than the look, Collins had it going on. I found myself comparing the two of them a lot. Sometimes I had to catch myself when talking to Collins, but he always understood once I apologized. After so many years of being with Jaylin, it was hard not to compare them.

Anxious to get in touch with Pat, I told Collins I had to make an important phone call, and went into his study. It looked like a library, which had books lined up on a built-in bookshelf spanning an entire wall. I sat in the chair behind his desk and dialed Pat's number. When Chad answered, I almost hung up, but I was too anxious to talk to let him spoil things.

"Hi, Chad. Is Pat there?"

"Yeah, Nokea, hold on."

Pat took a minute to pick up, and when she did, she was laughing. "Hi, Nokea. Hold on while I go shut the door." She put the phone down, then came back. "Okay. Where are you? I tried calling you today and your machine said you were gone for the holidays."

"I'm in Detroit with Collins. Didn't Jaylin tell you when he spoke to you?"

"Yeah, he mentioned it, but we mainly talked about what happened between you and me. Listen, don't think I haven't thought about what you said. I just needed time to figure out what was really going on with Chad. Now that I know, I want to tell you how sorry I am for saying those things to you. I was just so angry with you about the Jaylin and Stephon situation that when you told me about Chad, I really thought you had lost your mind."

"Pat, you know me better than anybody. Even though I was going through hell at the time, I never would have wanted you to suffer with me. I was weak and Chad saw an opportunity."

"Yes, he did. I actually just got up enough nerve to talk to him about the ordeal last month. He admitted it and explained everything to me. He claimed I had an attitude like it was all about me. He wanted children, and I didn't. He didn't want me to work, and I did. He wanted a new house, and I didn't. The list goes on and on. And the bottom line is when I didn't compromise, he felt like he needed something else. You weren't the only woman he approached. But the question is, do I agree with his reasoning? No, I don't. But we've been married for twelve years, Nokea, and to me, my marriage is worth saving."

"But why haven't you called me to say that? I've been miserable without our friendship. You were the only true friend I had and you have no idea what it did to me when I lost that."

"Again, I'm sorry. Please understand how hard it was for me to swallow. Thing is, I just didn't have the nerve to call and tell you I was wrong. You know how stubborn I can be. Not only that, I was embarrassed and ashamed about the situation. My husband wasn't supposed to be that way. He wasn't supposed to do those kinds of things. I put him so high up on a pedestal, and didn't realize he was capable of doing what any other person might do. Note that I said person, and not just men, because women are capable of doing the same thing too, trust me. I'm speaking from experience."

"Well, I'm glad everything is going to work out between the two of you."

"I'm glad too, but we have a long road ahead of us. One thing I learned from this was to never judge a woman in her situation again. I thought about all the times I came down hard on you because of Jaylin, only to find myself fighting through the same mess. I always talked about how I would never put up with this, or put up with that, but honey, you never know what you'll do until it becomes a reality for you."

"You're right. You're definitely right about that. Anyway, did you get a chance to see my handsome baby?"

"Girrrrl . . . he is adorable. Jaylin and I were fighting over him. I begged him to let LJ stay but he wouldn't let him. I cried as I held him in my arms, and after he left, I made up my mind."

"You're going to try and have a baby, or adopt one now?"

"Nooo, ah, ah. I'm going to creep into your house and take yours. If not, I must get me a dog." We laughed. "By the way, next time you talk to Jaylin, thank him. He really cares about you Nokea. All these years I thought he was full of shit, but I saw a side of him I never knew existed."

"I told you. He's not all that bad."

"No, he's not. But, he's still a ho, let's not forget that." We laughed again. "So, last question, then I'm going to let you get back to your new man. I want to meet him as soon as you get back. Anyway, Jaylin told me how much you've changed since you've met Collins, and I can hear the happiness in your voice. Question is . . . are you still in love with Jaylin?"

I looked down at the desk and made squiggly lines on it with my finger. I took a deep breath and answered Pat's question as best as I could. "Pat, my love for Jaylin will always be buried deep in my heart. Collins or any other man will never be able to replace what I shared with him. So, do I love him? Yes. Am I in love with him? Yes, I am. But it's a love that I have no desire to go back to."

"Well, I'm happy for you. But honestly, I think— and please don't take this the wrong way. You know how I always have to voice my opinion. But I think the two of you still love each other and want to be together. Now, again, that's just my opinion."

"You're wrong Pat, but I respect your opinion. Anyway, tell Chad I said hello and I'll see you when I get back. I'll bring Collins over to meet you and then you'll see for yourself how happy I am."

"I don't doubt your happiness, however, I do doubt your heart. Bye, girl. Have a Merry Christmas and kiss my baby for me. I love you."

"Love you too."

We hung up.

After talking to Pat, I called my parents to let them know we'd made it to Detroit. As usual, Daddy was upset with me for not being home for Christmas, but he really needed to let go and let me live my life. Mama told me to have a good time and said that she'd see us when we got back.

When I hung up, I sat in the study for a while and thought about what Pat had said. Honestly, I really wasn't sure how I felt. Only time would tell. I at least knew that for right now I was happy, and that's all that mattered.

Collins was standing in the doorway holding LJ, who had a fudge cookie in his hand and chocolate all over his face. He looked so cute, and after seeing them together, I hoped more than anything this would all work out for the best.

Since Collins' family was coming in the following day, we had one night to spend together alone. Around eleven o'clock, I laid LJ down for the night so we could spend some quiet time together. When I came downstairs, he was leaning over the fireplace and poking at the fire, trying to get it to flame up. I sipped some hot chocolate he'd made us, covered up with a thick blanket, and watched him.

When the flames kicked up, Collins lifted me up from the chair and sat me on his lap.

"Are you cold?" he asked.

"No, I'm fine. This blanket is just so warm I couldn't let it go."

He took the cup of hot chocolate from my hand and kissed it. "How did Jaylin ever let you get away, Nokea?"

"Don't know. But I'm so glad that I found you."

"How glad?"

"Really glad."

"How glad is really glad?"

I stood up and dropped the blanket to the floor. He smiled and looked at my naked body. "So glad," I said. "And I would love nothing more than for you to make love to me right now."

Collins and I went to his bedroom and made love. We were so into each other that we didn't wrap up things until almost three o'clock in the morning.

We were awakened the next morning by a knock on Collins's bedroom door. When his mother and father came in and saw us in bed, naked, I was humiliated. That was not how I thought I'd meet them. His mother announced that they'd be downstairs, and closed the door.

I buried my face in my hands. "Now, that was embarrassing. I thought you said they wouldn't be here until noon."

Collins kissed my forehead and laid back in the bed. "It's okay, baby. Trust me, it's okay."

"For me it's not. You can't tell me it's okay that your mother just saw me naked in bed with her son. It might be okay for your father, but moms, I don't think so."

"Nokea, calm down. It's not like they just walked in on some teenagers, or a one-night stand. I've talked to my parents about you. They know how I feel. And I'm sure they know you and I make love. After all, they're the ones who taught me sex is a beautiful thing when it's shared with the right person."

Collins put me somewhat at ease, but I was still a bit uncomfortable about the whole thing. We got up, showered, and got dressed. I went into the other room to check on LJ while Collins headed downstairs. LJ was still asleep, so I headed downstairs without him.

Collins's mother was in the kitchen putting some groceries in the refrigerator, and Collins and his father sat talking at the kitchen table. When he saw me in the entryway, Collins stood next to me and introduced me properly. His father shook my hand and introduced himself as James, but his mother just smiled and waved. Completely ignoring me, she went back to the groceries. I tried to break the ice by asking if she needed help. When she shook her head "no," I looked at Collins and whispered, "I told you she was upset."

Collins, James, and I sat at the kitchen table. Knowing that his mother had an attitude, Collins looked at her while biting into an apple. "Mama," he said. "Are you mad about something?"

"No, honey, what makes you think I'm mad about something?"

"Because you're not saying much and you won't

look at me when I'm speaking to you. It's not like you to be so quiet."

She looked up and smiled. "Let the truth be told, Collins, nothing excites a mother about seeing her baby in bed with a naked woman, especially one he's not married to." I gave Collins another look and didn't say a word.

"But Mama, your baby is forty," he cleared his throat, "years old. Can I at least make love to a woman, in my own house, if I want to?"

By this time I felt like crawling under the table. His mother wiped her hands on a towel and came over to us, putting her hands on the back of my chair. She looked back and forth at us. "Can a mother feel the way she wants to, when she wants to? I don't care how old you are, you're still my baby." She bent over and kissed him, then she kissed me on the cheek. "Nokea, you have a son, don't you?"

"Yes, ma'am, I do."

"Stella, call me Stella. But would you, or could you ever imagine yourself walking in on your son in bed with a naked woman and being excited about it?"

"No, I wouldn't. Even if she were his wife, I would be a slight bit bothered."

She looked over at Collins. "I love you, baby, but mamas are always going to be mamas." She kissed him again. He smiled and finished his apple.

I excused myself from the table when I heard LJ upstairs yakking. When I came back into the kitchen with him, Stella had a fit.

"Chile, look at here, look at here." She took him

from my hands. "He is one handsome baby." She kissed LJ's cheeks and he reached for her long gray hair. When he placed his lips on her cheek and slobbered on it, she thought it was so adorable. They went back and forth playing the kissing game, and when I reached for him, she snatched him away. "No way, honey," she said. "Go get your own. This here is my baby."

I laughed and sat back at the table.

"Mama," Collins said. "I'm getting a little jealous, you know?"

"Well, too bad. Your mama done found herself a new baby, since the old one won't do right."

Feeling more at ease, I started helping Stella with breakfast. I did most of the cooking because she couldn't find it in her heart to part with LJ. When we were just about finished, Collins wrapped his arms around me and kissed me. Stella playfully rolled her eyes, then took LJ into the other room.

As Collins smooched with me, he walked me outside on the deck. It was cold, but he kept me warm as he stood behind me and squeezed my waist.

"I'm falling in love, Nokea."

I turned around and placed my arms on his shoulders. "So am I. But, I'm scared, Collins. This seems too good to be true. I keep thinking this is going to end up like Jay—"

He interrupted my words with a kiss. "I promise you it won't. All you have to do is open your heart and free him. Once you do that, this will all work itself out."

"But I have freed him."

"No, you haven't. I feel his presence in you right now. I feel it when I make love to you, and I see it in your eyes when you mention his name."

"That's because there's so much history between us. My time with you is going to hopefully wash those memories away. Now, if you're asking me to forget about him, I can't. But what I can do is move on with the man I do love and that's you."

Collins nodded, and before we went back into the house, he gave me a long and juicy kiss.

After his four sisters and their families showed up, the house was jammed packed. Everyone couldn't wait to tell me all the crazy stories about how overprotective their older brother was. Some of the things they told me I couldn't believe. He tried to deny it when his sister, Charlotte, said he beat up several of her boyfriends because he didn't like them, and threw eggs at them when they came to the house. When Stella came out with the truth, he admitted to it and said that at least he'd apologized.

On Christmas Eve, mostly everyone had gone to sleep by midnight. LJ was knocked out in the bedroom with Stella and James. I went into the study to call Jaylin, to let him know LJ was fine, but he didn't answer. I left a message on his voicemail and told him how well everything was going. Before I hung up, Collins stood in the doorway and heard me tell Jaylin that I loved him.

I tried to explain. "That's just something we say to—"

Collins walked over to me and placed two fingers lightly on my lips. "Shh . . . don't. Don't explain. Let's just go to bed."

He turned down the lights in his study, and I followed him into the bedroom. I sat on the bed as he went into the bathroom for a shower. I couldn't even imagine how he felt, but I truly hadn't meant any harm.

Trying to see what was taking him so long, I took my clothes off and went to join him in the shower. His hands were pressed against the tile and he didn't turn around to face me. Steamy water dripped on his face. I couldn't tell if he'd been crying, but I could tell from his expression that he was upset. When he felt me brush against him, he looked me over, then turned back around. I wrapped my arms around his body and touched his chest.

"I'm sorry," I said, lying my head against his back.

"Don't be. Saying you're sorry all the time only means trouble in a relationship. Please, don't be sorry for something you truly feel. I know you love me, but I also know you love him too. Trust me, though, the better man will prevail, and I know that I will."

We finished our shower, and after he dried me, we cuddled in bed. Collins placed his head between my breasts and fell asleep. I stared at the ceiling for a while, thinking about how God had blessed me with such a wonderful man. Shortly after, I dozed off.

Chapter 22

Scorpio

Mackenzie and I were having a pretty good time together. After Jaylin had left, she really didn't say much to me, and cried herself back to sleep. I truly felt her pain and held her in my arms as we cried together. Thing was, we weren't sure if he was coming back this way or not.

By the next day, though, things started to get better for us. I took Mackenzie to work with me and everyone loved her. My boss even let her take orders from a few tables. She got a kick out of all the attention. When he paid her twenty dollars for working, she was all smiles and said that she wanted to use the money to buy Jaylin a Christmas present. I promised her we would go to the mall and get something nice for him.

We bundled up and walked home together. And since it was snowing outside, Mackenzie couldn't wait to play. We made snowballs and blasted each other with them. As soon as we got home, she rushed into the house to call Jaylin to tell him about her amazing day. He wasn't there, though, so I told Mackenzie to leave a message.

I was disappointed when we still hadn't heard from him the next day. It wasn't like him not to call back, but I knew how upset he had been when he'd left. Knowing him, he probably needed time to deal with the situation, so I left him at peace.

Right before Christmas Eve, Mackenzie and I took a bus ride to the mall. We browsed the shops looking for something for Jaylin, but when Mackenzie insisted nothing was good enough for him, I found him something myself. It didn't cost much, but it was a gold pen set, and I asked the woman who sold them if she would engrave his initials on the side for me. She said that she could for a small fee.

As we stood and waited for her to finish, I saw a man making ornaments with peoples' photos on them. I hurried the lady with the pens so that Mackenzie and I could have our picture taken. The man put our picture on a colorful Christmas ornament and scripted the words 'we love you' beneath. It was so cute, and I knew Jaylin would love it when he got it in the mail.

Mackenzie drove Santa Claus crazy, telling him a list of things she wanted. And after I pulled her off his lap, we rushed to the post office to overnight our package so Jaylin would get it on time.

At the end of the day, we were so exhausted that we took a taxi home and ordered a pizza when we got there. I flopped down on the couch and Mackenzie turned on the TV. When the phone rang she ran to the kitchen and answered it. I sat up and listened. I could tell by the excitement in her voice it was Jaylin.

"Yes, Daddy. I know. We bought you a present today." She smiled as I walked into the kitchen. "I'm not going to tell you." She paused. "You did? Okay, but when are you coming to get me?" She frowned and listened to him. "I know, but here's Mommy. I love you too."

Mackenzie gave me the phone.

"Hello," I said.

"Hey. I just wanted to tell you that I mailed Mackenzie a little something for Christmas. I also bought her a puppy, but I'm not going to pick him up until she comes back, or whenever she comes back."

"I'm sure she'll be excited about that. And you know she'll come back to see you soon. So, don't even sound like that."

"Are you coming with her?"

"Jaylin, we already talked about this. I'd really like to stay here for a while. Mackenzie can go to school here. I already checked into it."

"So, I see you're making some serious plans, huh?"

"If that's what you want to call them, then yes, they're serious. I still love you, but I am not coming back under the same conditions."

"Suit yourself, Scorpio. It's been over two months and I'm not going to wait on you much longer."

"Don't. If you feel as if you need to move on, please do. Maybe you'll change for someone else. For me, it seems to be such a difficult thing for you to do."

"You can't change a man who don't want to change, baby. But you for damn sure can accept him for who he is. Adios Amigos, I'll talk to you soon."

"Jaylin! Don't hang up. Why is it that every time I talk to you, our conversation has to end like this? Listen, I don't want you to move on with anybody else. You have all that you need right here. But I do want things to be a lot better between us. Just think about it, okay?"

"I've been thinking about it for months now. How much thinking do you want a brotha to do? How do you plan to work this out with me, if you're in Denver and I'm in St. Louis? You're putting up a hell of an effort trying to work things out with me. I've been there twice and that's it for me. The only time I'm coming back is to get Mackenzie. After that, you're on your own and I mean it. So, keep playing around if you want to, you're going to miss me when I'm gone."

He hung up.

I put the phone down. Mackenzie wanted to call him back, but I told her no. I told her he was leaving the house, because I wasn't about to call back and kiss his ass.

When the doorbell rang I thought it was our pizza being delivered, but it was the United States Postal Service with Mackenzie's present. Jaylin had said it was just a little something, but it was two huge boxes wrapped in green shiny paper, and a big red bow was on top. I signed for the packages and closed the door.

Mackenzie couldn't wait to see what was in the boxes, so I let her open one. She tore off the paper, and when she opened the box, she pulled out a white fur coat with a fur hat to match. Her eyes widened. When she put it on, she looked darling. Inside that box was another small box with a card taped to it. I opened the card and found $1,000. I read the card to her:

> *I'm sure you're going to need your coat living in Denver, and the money should take care of all the Barbies you want until I get there to see you. As for the necklace, keep it close to your heart and think of me always. I love you, Daddy.*

I laid the card down and we opened the small box. In it was a silver heart-shaped locket with a pink three-carat diamond centered in the middle. A picture of him and Mackenzie was inside and on the back were her initials, MJR, engraved along with "Daddy LUVS U."

I closed my eyes, and held back my tears so Mackenzie wouldn't see me cry. I didn't want her to think I was a basket case with all the crying I'd been doing, so I quickly got myself together.

Anxious to see what was in the second box, I let Mackenzie open it, too. And just when I thought he had already done enough, she pulled out another white fur coat and hat, but this time, it was for me. Another necklace and card followed. The only things my card said were for me to come home, and how much he missed me. My necklace had a white diamond with only his picture inside, and on the back were the initials SAR, for Scorpio Antoinette Rogers. I smiled and held it close to my chest. No doubt about it, it was time to go home and claim my man. I had put it off for as long as I could.

I rushed to call and tell Jaylin my decision, but he didn't answer. Instead of hanging up, I left a voicemail thanking him for the gifts, and telling him how much I loved him.

On Christmas Day, Mackenzie and I didn't get up until noon. We stayed up late watching the *How the Grinch Stole Christmas!* and *Rudolph, the Red-Nosed Reindeer*. I tried Jaylin at his house again, but still got no answer. Desperate to talk to him, I even called Stephon's house to see if he'd heard from him. When he didn't answer, I figured they were probably somewhere together, so I chilled and waited to hear from him.

It was just the two of us, so there wasn't much to cook, but I wanted it to be a special day for Mackenzie. She stood on a chair and whipped up the chocolate cake mix as I checked on the baked chicken in the oven, then put the boxed macaroni-and-cheese on the stove and waited for the string beans to cook.

The phone rang and we both rushed to it. I was truly disappointed to hear Jackson's voice and not Jaylin's. He wished us a Merry Christmas, and since I didn't have call-waiting, I rushed him off the phone just in case Jaylin was trying to call.

At six o'clock, we set the table and blessed the little food we had. All Mackenzie ate were a few spoonfuls of the macaroni and cheese, and she picked over some of the chicken. When I asked why she wasn't eating, she insisted she wasn't hungry.

I pressed because I could tell something else was bothering her.

"Mackenzie, you can tell me, what's wrong?"

She kicked her feet underneath the table. "Nothing. I just don't like the chicken. It tastes kind of funny."

"What's wrong with it? I thought you liked chicken."

"I do. But I like Nanna's chicken. Even Daddy's chicken tastes a lot better than yours."

"Well, thanks, honey. It really makes Mommy feel good when you don't like my chicken."

She frowned, looked at the chicken, then tooted her lips. "Can I throw it away? It's spoiling my appetite."

"Yes, Mackenzie. Go throw it away. And don't ask for anything else to eat today, okay?" She got off the chair and dumped her whole plate in the trash, including her macaroni and cheese. "I thought you liked the macaroni and cheese." I said.

She shook her head. "That taste funny too. Can I have a piece of cake now?"

"No, you may not. If you didn't eat your food, then you can't have any dessert."

"That's not fair," she yelled. "I can't help it if you can't cook!" She stormed out of the kitchen, and as she went down the hallway, I heard her say she wanted her Daddy. Hurt by her words, I went after her and grabbed her arm.

"Listen, Mackenzie, I have no idea what is wrong with you, but watch your mouth. Do you understand?"

She nodded and pouted, then she folded her arms and sat on the bed. Frustrated with her attitude, I turned her over and spanked her good. I wasn't going to put up with her mess like Jaylin does. Just because she got away with clowning on him, she wasn't going to get away with clowning on me. The last thing I'd intended was for our Christmas to turn out like this. I had done everything I could do to make it a special day for her, but nothing I did was good enough.

I hit her a few more times on her behind, and afterwards she climbed into bed with her dolls. Being too hard on myself, I went into the bathroom and closed the door. That was the first time I'd ever spanked Mackenzie. I looked in the mirror, feeling terrible. The thought occurred to me that maybe I'd done it because I was disappointed that Jaylin hadn't called. That idea made me feel even worse.

I stayed in the bathroom for a while, splashed water on my face and dried it with a towel. I went back into the bedroom, where Mackenzie had fallen asleep while cuddled with her dolls and fur coat. I kissed her forehead and grabbed a book on my dresser to read.

I read several chapters, and while munching on some popcorn, I glanced at the clock. It was almost seven. I wondered why Jaylin still hadn't called. I'd thought he would call at least to speak with Mackenzie, but the night was still young. I got back to my book and anxiously waited to hear from him.

Chapter 23

Jaylin

I didn't get an ounce of sleep Christmas Eve thinking about LJ and Mackenzie. I wondered how their night was going, and wondered if they were missing me as much as I was missing them.

I laid in bed for countless hours looking up at the ceiling and listening to my phone ring off the hook. In no mood to talk to anyone, I picked up the caller ID to see who it was each time, and put it right back down. But when Daisha called for the fourth time since six o'clock in the morning, I finally answered. She insisted that I shouldn't be alone on Christmas and wanted me to go to church with her. When I declined, she begged me to go and said it would truly brighten my day if I did. She was being very persistent, so I told her I'd be ready in an hour.

I showered and changed into my dark gray suit, then put a white dress shirt underneath. I chose a tie Nokea had bought me to match the suit, and slid into my shoes.

As I was combing my hair, Daisha rang the doorbell. As usual, she looked classy in her dark gray silk suit, with a white scarf gathered around her neckline. Her short curly hair was neatly cut, not one strand was out of place. We laughed and talked about how well we matched each other without even having planned it.

By the time we arrived at church, it was packed. Daisha introduced me to everyone as a long-time friend, and smiled when some people talked about what a cute couple we made. During the short service, I glanced at Daisha a few times and she was all into it. When the choir sang, she squeezed my hand, and laid her head on my shoulder. I saw a few tears roll down her face and I reached over to wipe them.

Afterward, she introduced me to a few more people, then we jetted. On the drive home, she asked me if I enjoyed myself. I told her that I did. I kissed her and thanked her for the invite. I really had enjoyed myself. Pastor Davis's message was quite interesting and the choir's singing had brought tears to my eyes. I couldn't help it, because the thought of LJ and Mackenzie being without me kept coming to mind.

Before we headed back to my place, we stopped off at the cemetery where her brother was buried and laid flowers on his grave. Daisha said he was her twin brother, and had been killed in a car accident almost five years before. She said she always visited his grave because she never wanted him to think he'd been forgotten.

I felt bad, because Mama had been gone since I was nine years old and I never went to the cemetery to visit her. I guess I was so upset about her leaving me, that I never thought much about it. When I talked to Daisha about my feelings, she told me it wasn't like Mama left me by choice. I agreed, but I still had a hard time understanding why Mama wasn't a part of my life when I wanted her to be so badly. Now, though, I had Nanny B, and for me, that was good enough. I could feel Mama's presence in her, and actually, when I thought about it even more, I had been feeling Mama's presence all along.

Instead of going to my house, Daisha wanted to stop by Stephon's place to give Mona her present. I hadn't gotten anything for Daisha, and felt kind of bad. When I apologized, she told me not to worry about it. She said it wasn't a big deal, since she hadn't gotten me anything, either.

Stephon and Mona knew we were coming, so the door was already open for us. No sooner than we walked in, Mona rushed to the door and twirled her fingers in Daisha's face, displaying an engagement ring. I congratulated her and politely asked her where the groom was. She pointed to the kitchen and said that he was in there with Shane. I pushed through the kitchen doors.

"Oh, no, you didn't!" I yelled.

"Oh, yes, he did!" Shane said, sitting at the table next to Stephon. "And did it straight up behind our backs."

"Y'all brothas know how I feel about Mona. So, don't pretend that y'all didn't see the shit happening," Stephon said.

"Honestly, I didn't. You've only known her for a few months." I peeked out of the kitchen door to make sure Mona couldn't hear me. She and Daisha were talking, and opening up their gifts from each other. "Man, you just told me you were with Rachelle the other night," I whispered. "Come on, dog, what's up with that?"

"I know," Shane said. "Brotha just told me he went and knocked out Felicia for one last time. Man, you seriously should have thought about this, before making such a commitment."

"Shane! Jay! Get out my business. I know what I'm doing. Mona is the kind of woman who understands me. She knows what I want, and she knows what I need. Most of all, she ain't tripping off no other females. So, prepare yourselves, she's going to be my wife whether you fellas like it or not."

Shane and I looked at each other and shrugged our shoulders. "Stephon," Shane said. "I'm happy for you, but—"

"Shane, please don't start with all that theoretical bullshit." Stephon walked over to the kitchen counter and leaned against it. "Life ain't about that all the time. Y'all brothas both know that the chances of anyone having a monogamous relationship these days are slim. If the woman ain't cheating, the man for damn sure is. All I'm saying is enjoy what you have for as long as you can have it."

I held my hands open and gave Stephon a hug. "This time, I hope it's right. I support you because I love ya. However, I do not agree with any of that bullshit you just said. Marriage is supposed to be a sacred thing between two people and two people only. I can't seem to get to that point yet, but if you insist that maybe one day you will, congrats, and I wish you well."

"Get your ass over here and give me a hug, fool," Stephon yelled at Shane. Shane stood up and gave his congrats too.

We all stood around talking. "You know what's funny?" Shane said. "Why every time a man announces he's getting married it feels like he's planning a funeral, looking at it from his boys' point of view. It's just so hard for us to be happy no matter how hard we try. I can recall all the fellas who stepped to me and said they're getting married. I was hesitant to simply say congratulations."

"I know man, it's scary," I said. "Things are just not what they used to be."

"But you can't let statistics scare you out of it," Stephon said. "See, Mona understands that you have your Good Dogs and your Bad Dogs. A Good Dog will take care of his woman, take care of the kids, and take care of the finances. However, he will stray every once in a while, truly meaning no harm, and wouldn't give up his wife for nothing in the world. But a Bad Dog, he's dissing his woman, not taking care of the kids, barely hanging onto a job, and fucking everything in sight. He will trample from one woman to the next and get married about three, fo', five times, just to uplift he's ego. Problem is, too many women be liking these Bad Dogs. Why? I haven't a clue."

"So," Shane said. "Do you really consider yourself a Good Dog?"

"Mona thinks I am, or if not, she thinks I can be. Honestly, though, I'm just a Good Dog who loves a woman with some bad-ass pussy, that's all."

We all laughed and gave each other five.

"Mr. Shane?" I said. "Whatever happened with you and Jeanette? Daisha told me you decided to kick it with Amber. What's up with that?"

"Well, if you would answer your damn phone, or call a brotha back sometimes, you would know. I just felt a better connection with Amber. And yes, I did get down with both of them that night, but I talked it out with Amber, asked her if we could still kick it and she's cool. It's nothing serious, we just hang out every once in a while. What about you? I see you're hanging pretty tight with Daisha. Does that mean Scorpio's history? If so, let a brotha know so he can make his move, please."

Stephon had the nerve to give Shane five. I looked at both of them and smiled. "Never, ever, *ever* will I let her go. You brothas need to hang it up. Daisha's cool, digging her like a motherfucker, so who knows. But Scorpio's right here." I placed my hand on my heart and winked. "And Nokea's right there too."

"Fuck you, man," Stephon said. "I'm giving up on your ass. You don't know what the hell you want."

"Uh, I know what I want. Thing is, though, I don't have to choose. You're the one getting married, remember, not me."

"Jay, let me put it to you this way," Shane said, getting ready with some more of his theoretical bullshit. "If the world were ending and God said you can choose one woman to live the rest of your life with in heaven, and Scorpio, Nokea, and Daisha were standing right in front of you, who would you take with you?"

Stephon moved in closer so he could hear. "You brothas all up in my bit-ness, ain't y'all? But, uh, to answer your question, I'd quickly take Scorpio's beauty, her sexy-ass body, and good-ass pussy, then I'd take Nokea's charming, loving, and so thoughtful and caring ways, then Daisha's sexy, intelligent, smart, creative, spiritual mind and wrap them all up in one. After that, I'd make my way on up the elevator."

"You are so full of shit," Shane said. "But if it ever comes down to it, and you have to decide which one of them you want to be with, what you just said about them might help you find your answer. What is the most important thing to you? Scorpio's good-ass loving, Nokea's thoughtful caring ways, or Daisha's spirituality?"

"It's called variety, Negro," I said. "I like variety, so I'll never choose. The truth is, if I did choose, I believe I'd eventually get whatever additional things I needed from just one of them. That's just the type of women all three of them are."

Our conversation was getting pretty deep, so Daisha and Mona came into the kitchen to shut us up. We sat around until five o'clock, and then Daisha said she was ready to go. Shane left and said he was going to spend some time with his ex-girlfriend's family, and Mona and Stephon were anxious to spend their first night together as an engaged couple.

On the drive to my house, Daisha talked about how happy she was for Mona and prayed that Stephon would treat her right. I didn't say a word because I knew deep down he wouldn't be right. He just didn't have it in him, but I was starting to wonder if I did. I enjoyed being with Daisha, but I was missing Scorpio more and more each day. I couldn't help how I felt. Maybe this was a time for me to consider making some changes. I had messed up with Nokea, and I couldn't figure out if I was going about this thing with Scorpio the wrong way or not. Some days I felt so much love for her, but there were other days that I felt as if my love could be considered lust. I often struggled with this love business, and my past issues with how I felt about women in general made this extremely difficult for me. I was determined not to lose out again, but for now, my day belonged to Daisha.

There was a small package in the doorway and I picked it up. When we entered the house the phone was ringing, so I set down the package on the bottom step.

I rushed to the phone, but when I saw Scorpio's number on the caller ID, I let it go into voicemail. I had listened to her message last night, and she'd thanked me for the gifts, but I wasn't in the mood to talk to her.

Ready to get our grub on, Daisha and I took from the fridge the turkey, dressing, ham, scalloped potatoes, greens, yams, and cornbread that Nanny B had cooked, and warmed it up. We piled our plates high, and went upstairs to my bedroom to get comfortable. I lit the fireplace and turned on the TV. Before we sat down in bed to eat, Daisha reached for my hand and blessed our food. Our shoes hit the floor and we rested our backs against the headboard.

"This is really delicious," Daisha said with her mouth full. "Did you say your nanny cooked this for you?"

"Yes. She is an awesome cook. That's why I have to faithfully work out, because if I don't, my ass will be in trouble."

"You do have a nice body, Jaylin. How often do you work out anyway?"

"I used to work out every day. I've been kind of getting lazy, so now, I'm down to about three or four times a week."

"And how often do you get a work out from having sex?" She batted her eyelids and bit down on her fork.

"Are you asking me if I've had sex since I was last with you?"

"Yes."

"No, I haven't. But I do like to *work* it out at least—"

"Be honest, Jaylin."

"Okay, honestly, I like to work it out about seven days a week. Five days would suffice, but seven days would be perfect." I reached over and fed Daisha some potatoes, since she didn't have any on her plate. "So, what about you?" I asked. "How often do you like to 'work out'?"

She swallowed the potatoes. "Those are delicious, I should have taken some myself. I could probably work out seven days a week too, depending on who I'm with. However, with my busy schedule, I'd say I could probably get around to it . . . maybe, once or twice a week." She reached over and put some collard greens in my mouth. "Now, did I just blow my chances with you?"

I smiled and chewed. "No, you didn't. The key words you said were 'depending on who you're with.' And depending on who you're with, your busy schedule isn't going to stop you from making love to a brotha if he's good." I reached over and put another spoonful of potatoes in her mouth. "Wouldn't you agree?"

She chewed. "I guess, but he has to be awfully darn good."

I took her plate and put it on top of mine. Then I laid both plates on my nightstand. I scooted over and Daisha raised her skirt and straddled me. She removed her scarf from around her neck and wrapped it around mine. I started to undo her blouse. "Damn good, huh? What if he was extremely damn good?" I asked.

She leaned forward and whispered in my ear. "Then I'd sex his sexy-ass up seven days a week, or until he had enough of me."

The phone rang. Daisha rose up, and when I looked at the caller ID, I saw it was Stephon. I picked it up.

"What, fool, what is it?" I yelled.

"Damn! That's how I get treated?"

"I'm in the middle of something, man."

"I'm sure you are, but I was just calling to tell you that you left your Rolex over here. Now, if you want me to take this motherfucker to Lee's Pawn & Jewelry and pretend that I didn't see it, I will."

"I'll pick it up tomorrow. So good-bye." I hung up on him and the phone rang again. I quickly answered. "Now what, Nigga?"

"Hello, Jaylin." It was Scorpio.

Daisha quickly grabbed the phone. "Look,

Stephon, you and Mona really—" she paused and I snatched the phone from her.

I placed it against my forehead for a second, took a deep breath, then put it against my ear. "Yeah," I said.

She hesitated. I could imagine her pain on the other end. "Uh . . . do you have company?"

"Yes."

She hung up.

I put the phone down and looked up at Daisha still straddling me.

"That wasn't Stephon, was it?" she asked.

I shook my head. "No, but don't worry—"

"I'm sorry. Had I known I never would have grabbed the phone."

"I know, and as I was getting ready to say, don't worry about it." I started to undo her blouse again. "Anyway, where were we?"

"You were just about ready to show me how extremely damn good you are."

"That's right, I was, wasn't I?"

I sexed up Daisha and showed her just that. She whispered to me several times during sex that it couldn't get any better than this, and I agreed.

Daisha had fallen asleep, so I took our plates downstairs to the kitchen and washed them. On my way back upstairs, I noticed the package that I had earlier laid on the steps. Curious to find out what it was, I sat on the couch and opened it. Enclosed was a pen set with my initials engraved on them, and an ornament with a picture of Scorpio and Mackenzie cheek to cheek, smiling. The words

'we love you' were underneath. I placed the ornament on my lips and kissed it, then put it back into
the box.

In deep thought about Scorpio, I leaned back
on the couch and looked at the blinking lights on
the Christmas tree. It was time to leave the past in
the past. How I was ever going to be able to move
on, I wasn't sure. But one thing I knew, and that
was I couldn't stand to hurt Scorpio any more than
I had already.

I closed my eyes, and suddenly Aliayah's "I Care
For You" played loudly throughout the house. I
smiled as Daisha sang and slowly came down the
steps, heading toward me. She straddled my lap
and continued to sing along with the music. When
she finished, I clapped my hands and held her
hips.

"You're trying to seduce me, aren't you?"

"No, I just want you to forget about where
you've been and think about where you're going."

"Is that with you?"

"I hope so. But you tell me, is it?" Daisha leaned
forward and kissed me.

"Wait a minute." I backed up and looked at her.
"I thought church women are supposed to be
nice."

"We are nice, very nice I might say, but we also
know how to get down when we have to."

"Ain't nothing wrong with that."

I kissed Daisha and laid her naked body back on
the couch. Sex was being served again, and al-
though I tried hard not to think about Scorpio, I
couldn't shake her from my mind for shit. Nearly
ten minutes into it, my rhythm got faster and

faster. I was sweating and breathing hard, trying to catch my breath. Daisha held me tightly around my neck, and we both looked down and watched me slide in and out of her. Excited about how wet my thang was, and at the peak of us coming together, she yelled my name and I yelled out, "Scorpio!" *Damn!* I thought. *I fucked up!* I dropped my sweaty forehead onto Daisha's chest.

She lifted my head and gave me a blank stare. "What did you just call me? Did you just say what I think you said?"

I was embarrassed, and shamefully lowered my head. "Daisha, I'm sorry. I just—"

"You just need to get up off me."

"Look, I understand how you feel, but I just got caught up in the moment."

"With her or with me? So, please, get up," she said, calmly.

There wasn't anything else I could say to Daisha to make this uncomfortable situation any better, so I got up. She didn't waste any time going upstairs, putting her clothes on, and leaving. Since I stayed downstairs on the couch the whole time, all I heard was the front door slam behind her.

Feeling so badly about what had happened, I rushed to the door to catch her, but her car had already gone down the street. I slammed the front door and sat on the steps. What hurt me the most was that I knew I had just blown it with a very special woman. I had never in my entire life called a woman by another woman's name, especially during sex.

I went into my office, called Daisha's voicemail, and left her a lengthy apology. I then called Scorpio and tried to clear up my situation with her. When she picked up on the first ring, I could tell she was wide awake. There was no doubt that she had been waiting on my call.

"Say, are you busy?" I asked.

"Yes," she said in a shaky voice. I could tell she'd been crying.

"I just . . . I just called to apologize for earlier. A friend of mine—"

"Jaylin, please don't. There's no need to explain. I'm tired, baby, and I can't do this anymore," she cried. "Mackenzie's unhappy, and I'm unhappy because I can't make it without you. All I ever wanted was for you to love me, but your way of loving me has hurt me more than anything in my entire life has. After tonight this will all be over with. You will never have to worry about me again."

"Wait a minute. You're not thinking about killing yourself, are you?"

"I don't know what I'm thinking, but just know whatever I decide to do it's for the best."

"Scorpio, don't be talking like—" She hung up.

I called back, but the line was busy. I called back again, and again, but still couldn't get anything except a busy signal. I started to panic. I feared for the worst, and ran upstairs to get dressed. I called the airport to see when the next non-stop flight was to Denver, but there was nothing until four-thirty the next afternoon. I called Enterprise and had them bring me a car.

If Scorpio killed herself, I would never be able to live with myself. And Mackenzie, I thought, what about my baby Mackenzie? Thinking about her, I started rushing even more. I could be in

Denver in about ten or eleven hours. Either way, nothing was going to stop me from going.

I reached downtown Denver at twelve-fifteen that afternoon. When I pulled in front of Jackson's house, I hopped out and left the car door open. No one was inside. I looked around and didn't see anything unusual at first, but in the bathroom was an empty Tylenol bottle by the sink. I stood for a minute, then I remembered Scorpio telling me about her working at a café not too far from there. I rushed back outside and got into the car.

I hated myself for putting her through so much. As I sped down the street the car slid on the ice, so I finally slowed down. I drove down street after street, and that's when I saw her walking with her hands in her pockets. Her face was turned away from the gusty cold wind. I pulled over to the opposite side of the street in front of her. She looked up, shocked as hell to see me.

"Get in the car," I demanded. She rolled her eyes and kept on walking. I ran up behind her and grabbed her arm. "It's too damn cold out here to be bullshitting, Scorpio, so get in the fucking car!"

She snatched her arm away. "Fuck you, bastard, let go of my arm!" She tried to pull it away, but my grip was tight. I pulled her to the car, opened the door and shoved her inside. I rushed to the driver's side, but she managed to open the door, and started to get out. I ran back over to the passenger's side and stood in front of her, the door between us.

"Get back in the car so we can go talk about this, please," I said.

"No," she shouted. "Why can't you just leave me alone? There's nothing else for us to talk about, okay?"

"No, it's not okay. Let's just go back to the house and talk. If you want me to leave after that, I promise you I will leave."

She hesitated, but finally got back in.

I drove to Jackson's place in silence, and when we got there, she rushed inside. I popped the trunk and pulled out two black suitcases, then followed her into the bedroom. I tossed the suitcases on the bed and opened one.

"Get your shit and let's go. Where's Mackenzie?" I asked. Scorpio didn't say a word. She headed toward the door, but I pushed her back on the bed. "Don't fuck around with me, woman! Where's Mackenzie?"

She sat up on her elbows. "She's next door playing with the neighbor's daughter, and we're not going anywhere with you, Jaylin."

"Like hell. This damn game you're playing is over! It ends today, baby, and I mean that shit!"

I went to the closet and started removing her clothes. As I slammed them into the suitcase, she took them back out. We went back and forth for a few minutes, until I got seriously tired of her resisting. I grabbed her wrist and twisted it back.

"Leave the damn clothes in the suitcase!" I yelled.

"No," she yelled back, then balled up her fist and punched me on the face.

I bit down on my bottom lip and grabbed her hair. My leg went behind hers and I tripped her. She fell hard to the floor and started with the tears. I didn't give a fuck because my head was banging from her punch.

I grabbed her collar and pulled her up on the bed. I wanted to fuck her up for punching me, but instead I shoved her backward and continued to fill the suitcase. I opened the dresser drawers and cleared them out, too. She scooted back on the bed, covering her face with her hands. I ignored her cursing at me, and filled the other suitcase with some of Mackenzie's belongings and shoes. Once everything was inside, I locked both suitcases and put one of them on the floor. I held the other one in my hand, then reached out my other hand for Scorpio to take it.

"Come on, let's go," I said. She wouldn't take my hand, so I dropped the suitcase on the floor. I plopped down next to her, moved her hair away from her face and put my hand on her cheek to wipe her tears. "What do you want from me, baby? I've begged you to come back with me. I've come here three times and you still tripping. Tell me, what more can a brotha do?"

She touched my hand and looked me in the eyes. "Change. All I want you to do is change the way you are. Not only for me, but for yourself. You can't be happy with the way you are. With how you treat people and how you talk to them. There's no way you're happy with yourself. There are so many good things about you, but what's really important is how you treat me."

"What do you mean by how I treat you? I've

done more for you than anybody. I've bent over backward for you, just to make you happy. But if my changing is going to get you out of this . . . this hellhole today, then I'll change." I stood up. "So, come on. Let's go." She still didn't move.

"You know you don't mean it. You're just saying that to get me to come back with you. I guarantee you the same ol' stuff is going to happen over and over again—"

"No, it won't." I took her by the hand and pulled her off the bed. I wrapped my arms around her and pecked her lips. "I promise you this bullshit between us ends today." She dropped her head and I lifted her chin. "I'll change. It doesn't matter if it's for you, or for me. I'll do it because I love you and I don't want to live another day without you. I lost one good woman, baby, and I'm not about to do it again. I'm sorry it had to take this for me to realize you're the woman I want to be with, but believe me when I say that I've had an emptiness in my life since you've been gone."

She touched the side of my face. "Please don't say this to me if you don't mean it. I can't—"

I put emphasis on my words by giving her a lengthy kiss. Our lips smacked hard as we floated our tongues in each other's mouths. We stood for a moment in a tight embrace, not wanting to let go.

"Let's go get Mackenzie and tell her Daddy's taking her home," I said.

"No, not yet. I just need to hold you for a little while longer. I've missed you so much and I can't go another second without making love to you first."

She started to unzip my pants, but there was no way I could get down with her before taking a shower. Daisha and I had just done our thang several hours ago, and it didn't even dawn on me to hit up a shower before I left. As for taking a shower here, that was out of the question.

I moved back and grabbed her hand. "Baby, wait. I got something special waiting for you at home. Let's wait until then, okay?"

"This won't take long, Jaylin. I've been without you for months, and this will be a quick one, I promise you."

My dick hung from my pants, but I sat Scorpio on the bed. I lifted her waitress uniform, and kneeled on the floor in front of her. She leaned back and I rested her thighs on my shoulders. I removed her wet silk blue panties and gazed at what I had so long hoped for. I used my fingers to separate her slit and lightly rubbed her neatly-shaven soft hairs. My dick remained at full attention, but I dipped my tongue deep inside of her. I licked against her walls, and plucked my tight lips over her hard clitoris. She held my head as tight as she could so I wouldn't venture elsewhere.

"Jaylin, I miss this sooo much, I swear I do." She moaned and combed her fingers through the curls in my hair. "If you ever, ever make me do without you again, I swear I—" Her body jerked and I slid out my tongue.

"You'll what?" I smiled and looked up at her.

"Damn you!" she yelled and squeezed her legs tightly together. "Don't fuck with me, please, not right now!"

I parted her legs again and sucked in all of her

juices. She was dying to have sex, but I couldn't play her like that and give her Daisha's leftovers. Again, I promised to make it up to her later.

I didn't know who was the most excited, Mackenzie or me. She ran into my arms and held me so tight that I could hardly breathe. We sat in the living room and talked, while Scorpio ran around the house packing everything she needed. I told her she'd have to probably come back for some things because there was no way everything would fit into the car.

Mackenzie was jumping up and down on the sofa next to me. "Mackenzie, stop that before you fall," I said, holding her so she wouldn't.

"I'm sorry. But Daddy, is Nanna at home?"

"No, but she'll be there later. Why?"

"Because I'm hungry. Mommy made a yucky dinner for Christmas and I didn't want to eat it. She got mad at me and cried when I said it was nasty. Then she spanked me really hard for not eating it."

"Well, Mackenzie, you probably hurt her feelings. You have to be careful what you say to people because words can be hurtful. As for the spanking, I'm sure she didn't mean it."

"Yes, she did. But what kind of words, Daddy? Do you mean words like bitch and slut—words like that?"

"Where do you get all this stuff from, Mackenzie? And yes, I do mean words like that, but you shouldn't be saying them. If you've heard me say them, I was wrong and I don't ever want you to say them to anyone, okay?"

She nodded, laid her head on me and wrapped

her arms around my neck. After a few minutes she stood on the sofa again and whispered in my ear.

"Daddy, I got a secret."

"Oh yeah, what kind of secret?"

"It's about Mommy."

"Really? And what might that be?"

"She kissed another man the other day."

My brows went up. "Say she did. Who was it?"

"The extermer—I mean, the bug spray man."

"Really?" I looked to see if Scorpio was listening to us. "How many times did she kiss him?"

Mackenzie tilted her head like she was in deep thought, then smiled. She held up three fingers, then five. "Uh, I think about five times."

"Did he ever spend the night?" I asked. Mackenzie shrugged. "Did you ever see him in bed with her?" Mackenzie nodded, then moved her head from side to side. "Did you ever see them—"

"No, no, no," Scorpio said, standing in the doorway to the living room. "You know you need to stop asking her all those questions. If you want to know, ask me and not her." Scorpio looked at Mackenzie. "Besides, she shouldn't be running her mouth anyway."

Mackenzie looked at Scorpio. "Sorry, Mommy, but Daddy told me to tell him if you were cheating."

I took a deep breath. "Come on, are you ready?" I said. "This child is too damn smart for her age. I told her to keep an eye on you, that's it. Where all this cheating stuff comes from, I have no idea."

"I agree. And yes, I'm ready."

Scorpio grabbed a few more bags, and I took everything else out to the car. As she locked the door to the house, I gave Mackenzie a high-five and thanked her for telling me the truth. Even if Scorpio was in Denver getting down with the exterminator, I couldn't be mad because I for damn sure was in St. Louis doing my thang.

While I drove, Scorpio reached over and rubbed the back of my head.

"I miss these ol' nappy curls. Straight-up missed running my fingers through them."

"If they were nappy, you wouldn't be able to run your fingers through them. My curls are naturally beautiful and soft curly-curls. If anything, you must be thinking about the exterminator, right?"

She laughed. "I knew you were going to go there. You just couldn't leave it alone, could you?"

"You're damn right I couldn't, especially when you pretended to be so alone, and so lonely. Those nights I called and you had the phone off the hook, you were getting your fuck on, weren't you?"

"Ooo, Jaylin. Now, you know better. I'm nothing like you. He was just someone to help pass my time away. The only thing we ever did was kiss a few times and that's it."

"That's it?"

"Yeah, that's it. As fast as my orgasm came today, you have the nerve to ask."

I looked back at Mackenzie, playing with one of her dolls. "You'd better watch what you say. You-know-who back there will be at school telling the teacher how quickly you had an orgasm."

We laughed.

"Since we're on the subject, who was that who took the phone from you?" she asked.

"Daisha."

"Daisha Voo."

"No, Daisha McMillan. She's a really nice woman I met while you were away playing games."

"So where's Daisha at now? I know you don't still plan on seeing her."

"Nope."

"Why not? All your other women seem to always keep hanging around."

"Well, she's different. Besides, she's upset with me for calling her by your name."

"That's understandable. It's a good thing you're still alive." Scorpio moved her hand from behind my head. "It wasn't during sex, was it?"

"Naw, it was during one of our conversations." I lied because I didn't want to hurt her feelings.

"Whew . . . I was getting ready to say. If it was during sex, and you didn't die, she's definitely a better sista than me."

I looked over at Scorpio and smiled.

I was worn out from driving and glad to be home. We got everything out of the car and went inside to chill. Mackenzie was asleep, so Scorpio carried her up to her room and laid her down. Then she came into my room, fell back on my bed, and stretched out her arms. I took off my clothes in the closet.

"Home at last," she shouted. "Thank God I'm finally home at last!"

"What do you mean by home?" I asked. "The key to your condo is on the nightstand." I walked over and held out the key to her.

"You can throw that key away, or give it to someone else. Since you forced me out of Denver, I'm staying right here with you."

I tossed it back on the nightstand. "You're lucky I'm renting the place. If I wasn't, you'd be up in there right now."

"Is somebody already living there? And what about my car? Where's that at?"

"Shit, I sold that car to one of my neighbors. If you look out of the window, you'll see it right in their driveway. Their daughter turned sixteen less than a month ago and they bought it for her."

"Now, you know you ain't right. You act like I was gone for years or something."

"I didn't know if you were coming back. I was just trying to get some of my money. Besides, I had something else to do with the money anyway."

"In the meantime, what am I supposed to drive?"

"I don't know. The junkyard might still have your get-out-and-push Cadillac you came over here in. I'm sure nobody else wanted it."

"For your information that Cadillac got me from point A to point B. It sure as hell got me over here to fuck your brains out that night."

"I agree, so let's not talk about the Cadillac. If you need a car, you can drive mine. I'm kind of getting tired of the 'Cedes anyway. It's time for something new. Besides, I still have the Porsche."

"I see how you are. Give me the old car, huh? You can let me drive the Porsche, can't you?"

"Naw, that's my baby. And are you out of your mind? What sista wouldn't like to drive around in a black 500 SL Roadster Convertible Mercedes Benz?"

"Not too many. So, make sure I get a key tomorrow."

I changed the sheets on my bed, and started my bath water. Scorpio was busy hanging her clothes in the closet, so I got in the tub and checked my messages. LJ's "Da-Da" calls put a serious smile on my face, and Nokea said they'd call me as soon as they got in. Nanny B said she'd be back by Saturday, and Felicia called again. I didn't know what the hell she wanted, and personally, didn't care. There was no message from Daisha, not that I expected there to be, but I at least wanted to know if she'd accepted my apology.

I sunk my body deep in the tub filled with hot steamy water and bubbles. I realized what a lucky man I was and was happy that my woman was home. All I had to do was change some of my ways, and even though I knew it would be a challenge, all I could do was try.

My bubbles started to dissolve, so I turned down the lights and added more water and bubbles. Scorpio came in with a lit scented candle and laid it on top of the Jack and Jill sinks. She was already naked, and I watched her ease between my legs with her back facing me. I must have seen her naked body a million times before, but each time felt like the first. She pulled her hair to the side and laid the back of her head against my chest.

"Must your thang be poking me in the back like that?" she asked. "You can't be that hard already." She put her hands in the water and touched me. "Oops, sorry, I forgot how—"

"How big it is? And it is starting to rise, right

now. You can't expect to put all that in my face and for it not to respond."

I rubbed up and down her arms, then held my hands in hers.

"I'm so glad to be back home with you," she whispered. "I've dreamed of this moment for many nights."

"Shh . . . listen," I said, as Natalie Cole was singing "Inseparable" over the intercom. I reached up for the volume knob to turn it up. I kissed Scorpio on the back of her head, and we listened to the song together. When it was over, I lowered the volume and Scorpio turned her face to the side to kiss me. I avoided her.

"Quit playing with me," she puckered. I turned my head again, but she grabbed it and forced her tongue inside my mouth. She backed up when she felt something inside and took it out. "What's this in your mouth?"

Her eyes widened as she set them on an eight-carat princess cut platinum diamond ring with flowing diamond baguettes on each side.

"You never did answer my question." I said, feeling her body tremble.

"Wha . . . what question?" she asked, still gazing at the ring.

"The necklace. When I mailed it to you, on the back were the initials SAR. You still haven't responded."

She looked at me. "I haven't responded because you've never asked."

"Well, I'm asking now. Would you, Scorpio Antoinette Valentino, have me Jaylin Jerome bad-ass

Rogers, for better or worse, rich or for richer, in sickness and in health, and nothing will keep us apart?"

She grinned, as I could see tears rolling down her face. She wiped them. "Only if you get on your knees and ask. You know, I'm just not feeling the effect of your proposal with you still sitting in this tub."

I laughed and kneeled beside the tub. I placed the ring on her finger and kissed it. "I love you, Pretty Lady, but I am not going to repeat myself again. So, are we going to do this or not?"

She grabbed me around my neck and pulled me back into the tub. Water splashed everywhere, as I wrapped her legs around me and looked her in the eyes. "Yes," she said. "I would love more than anything in the world to be your wife."

"Are you sure that's what you want more than anything in the world? I thought you might want this . . . this thing I got between my legs laying into you right now."

"The wife and the dick thing are a tie. But right now, if I have to choose, please give me what you got and give it to me good."

I grinned. All she had to do was ask. We got our dripping wet bodies out of the tub, and I carried her into the bedroom. I laid her on the bed. Knowing exactly how I like it, she positioned herself and bent over. I moved her close to the edge of the bed and stood behind her. Before inserting myself, I held her pussy in my hand, just to get a good feel of it. Her insides moistened fast as I rotated my fingers deep within her. She lowered her head and started to moan. Instead of letting me do all of the work, she sat in front of me and swallowed my goods in her mouth. I closed my eyes, my legs weak from her tightening her jaws. Before I could even think about coming, she straddled me on the floor and slammed my thang inside her. I sat up to suck her breasts, while she took deep, fast strokes on top of me. She seemed to be having her way with me, so I laid back on the floor and enjoyed the ride.

Scorpio and I exchanged juices for at least an hour, and since she was somewhat wearing me down, she stopped my last come, deciding it was time to clean up. She brought her pussy up to my mouth and rolled it over my lips. I opened my mouth wide, and sucked in until she couldn't stand anymore. She tried to move away, but I tightened my arms around her thighs and gave her what she wanted.

"Jaylin, stop baby, please," she cried out.

I licked my lips and shook my head. "Naw, baby, I can't stop. Not after fucking me the way you just did. This ain't over until I say it's over. Besides," I said, changing positions and putting one of her legs high on my shoulder, "you asked me to give it to you good, didn't you?" I went inside again.

"Yessssss, I did. But never in my wildest dream did I imagine you would give it to me this damn good. You must have missed me more than you're willing to admit."

"I did, baby. I missed you and this good-ass pussy you be dishing out. If I had to go another day without it, I would have lost my mind."

Scorpio smiled and continued to let me have my way with her. She had even tightened up a bit, but the warmth inside of her that I always felt was still there.

We finished our business on the inside, and grabbed some blankets to go outside on the balcony. She leaned over it and I fucked her like fucking was going out of style. I'm sure the neighbors got sick of hearing my name being yelled, but it was the perfect time for them to take notes.

By morning, we had fallen asleep on the chaise while cuddled in the blankets. I woke up before Scorpio, and put on some clothes to go downstairs to my office.

Having everything already planned, I typed my resignation to Schmidt and thanked him for my thirteen years at his brokerage firm. I drew up the Amendments to my will, making Nanny B my sole beneficiary, and LJ and Mackenzie my contingents. I wasn't sure what to do about Jasmine yet, but I recently put another detective on the case to find her, since the one I'd hired before had given up so easily. And as much as I loved Scorpio, a prenuptial had to be prepared. She wasn't going to be happy about it, but I was sure that she'd understand.

After I finished my paperwork, as I'd always done in the past, I wrote a healthy check to the orphanage I'd been in. Then I called my attorney, Frick, and made an appointment with him on Monday. He had other suggestions about my assets and said he'd talk to me about them further.

The rest of my day went down as one of the most peaceful days of my life. We picked up Mackenzie's poodle, and the smile on her face made me want to cry. She, of course, named the poodle Barbie, but as long as Mackenzie was happy, I really didn't care. We spent the remainder of our day catering to the dog, watching movies, and eating up everything in the house.

Everything was relaxing and going smooth. When Nanny B came home on Saturday, we told her about the engagement. She was thrilled and cooked a huge dinner to celebrate. I had no plans on telling anyone who she really was, because it was our secret. However, she did ask me to tell Mackenzie and LJ the truth when they were old enough to understand.

New Year's came and we didn't do much at all. Scorpio and I took Stephon and Mona a bottle of wine, but we weren't ready to make our engagement known until a definite date was set. Stephon questioned me about the ring on Scorpio's finger, but I told him it was a well-overdue Christmas present. I could tell Mona was jealous because every time she looked at Scorpio, she couldn't keep her eyes off the ring.

During our visit, though, I pulled Mona aside and asked her how Daisha was doing. She kind of ignored me at first, but then said that Daisha was doing fine. I still thought about Daisha occasionally, so I asked Mona to tell her hello. After she said that she would, Scorpio and I left to enjoy our New Year and new life together.

Nokea and Collins finally made it back from Detroit with LJ. I asked Nokea to bring him over, but she explained how exhausted they were from the ride. I wanted to see him so badly, though, that Scorpio and I drove to Nokea's house to get him.

Nokea opened the door with LJ in her arms and invited us in. I reached for him and he damn near jumped out of her arms to get to me. I sat on the couch with him and gave him plenty of kisses. Scorpio and Nokea stood by the kitchen's doorway and talked.

When Collins came into the room he spoke to me, and Nokea introduced him to Scorpio. I noticed how he lustfully checked her out like every man does when she crosses his path, but I wasn't the least bit bothered. I went right back to playing with LJ, and Collins came over and sat in the chair beside me.

"Did you all have a good time?" I asked.

"Yes, we had a wonderful time," he said. "How about you?"

"Best time of my life."

"Good. Glad to hear that, but you almost didn't get your son back. My mother fell in love with him and we had to literally fight with her to get him out of her arms."

"Yeah, he is quite charming, isn't he?"

"Yes, he is. But I didn't mention that once we got him away from her, we had to get him away from my sisters. Nokea barely got a chance to hold him the whole time we were there."

"I sure didn't," Nokea said. "And I was mad too. But they really showed both of us a lot of love, Jaylin." She sat on Collins' lap, and Scorpio sat next to me, reaching for LJ. I gave him to her, but Nokea had a look like it still bothered her.

We all kept the conversation flowing, and Nokea asked if we wanted anything to eat or drink. I said yes, and she asked me to come into the kitchen. As soon as I walked in, she drilled me.

"So, what's up with the ring on Scorpio's finger? Are the two of you engaged or something? I don't mean to pry, but I couldn't help but notice."

"Nokea, you know I've always been up-front with you, so yes, we are."

"When is the wedding?" she snapped with a noticeable attitude.

"Don't know. We haven't set a date yet."

"Soon? A year or two from now . . . when?"

"Nokea, when we decide, I'll tell you, okay? Are you upset with me?"

"No, I'm happy for you."

"Well, why do you sound so harsh?"

"I'm not."

I moved closer and stood in front of her. "Yes, you are."

"Okay, I am. I guess I'm a tiny bit jealous, but that's to be expected."

"You're right. But don't waste too much time on it. You have yourself a decent brotha. Don't blow it."

She reached up and touched my eyebrows to straighten them, "If it doesn't work out, you know I'm always here, don't you?"

"I'll keep that in mind." I embraced her, then kissed her cheek. "I love you Shor-tay," I mocked.

She smiled. "Don't be calling me that. That name is only for Stephon to call me. And I love you too, Mr. Soon To Be Married Man."

Nokea told me that she and Pat had mended

their friendship. And when I broke the news about Stephon's engagement, she damn near threw me out of the house, saying we were both out of our minds.

Scorpio and I left with LJ and stopped at KFC to get some chicken so Nanny B didn't have to cook again. I was worried about her doing so much at her age, but she was claiming to be young in body, mind, and spirit. One of my main reasons for retiring was so I could help her out with Mackenzie and LJ. And since Scorpio was already planning on returning to school, I would be there to help Nanny B when Scorpio wasn't around. This was such a huge change for me, and only for the woman that I loved, I promised to take it one day at a time.

Chapter 24

Jaylin

After several months of being a changed man, things couldn't have been better between Scorpio and me. We still hadn't decided on a wedding date, and the engagement was still on the down-low. I was ready to do the marriage thing and get it over with, but she wanted everything to be right. She said that she wanted to make sure my playing days were over before she gave me a date. I was cool with that and went with the flow of things.

Scorpio was already back in school and I was at home being the nanny for the kids. Instead of Nokea's mother watching LJ while Nokea was at work, she brought him over every day. If Nokea was too tired to pick him up, or wanted to spend time with Collins, she let him stay the night. I didn't care, and if I had it my way, LJ would be living with me on a regular basis like Mackenzie was.

As for Mackenzie, she was quite a character.

Scorpio and I knew we had our hands full, and no matter how much we pretended that it wasn't happening, she was way out of control. Every time I'd try to spank her, Nanny B would save her behind. If not that, she'd cry and make me feel sorry for her. I couldn't find it in my heart to hit her, but Scorpio could. She feared Scorpio more than she did me. And every time she did something wrong, all I had to do was say Scorpio's name and she'd straighten up. But it only lasted for a day or two, then she'd go right back to getting in trouble.

Every Saturday was Family Day, so we went to Plaza Frontenac to find a graduation present for Scorpio's cousin. As Scorpio pushed LJ around in his stroller, and I held Mackenzie's hand while looking through the store windows, I noticed Mona and Daisha going up the escalator. Scorpio had stopped to look at some shoes, so I watched them from behind the dark shades I wore. Daisha looked different somehow. When Mona stepped out from in front of her, I realized Daisha looked like she was pregnant. I hadn't talked to or heard from her, but I remembered how funny Mona had seemed on New Year's.

Anxious to find out what was up, I told Scorpio I'd seen an old friend of mine from college, and I was going to go catch up with him. She went into the shoe store and told me to meet her there when I was finished.

I rushed up the escalator and looked around. When I saw Mona and Daisha heading for the parking garage, I hurried to catch up with them. They got on the elevator and it closed before I could catch them. I watched the numbers to see if the elevator was going up or down, and when it showed down, I ran down the stairs. By the time I got to the first floor, they were walking to the car. Mona opened the door to Stephon's BMW, and when Daisha opened the passenger's door, I ran up to the car. I gasped to catch my breath, reaching for the door before she closed it.

My eyes dropped to her stomach. "Are you pregnant?" I asked. "Please don't lie to me because it's pretty obvious."

She glanced at Mona, then looked back at me. "Yes, I am."

"Is it my baby?"

"Jaylin, look, I'll call you later, all right?"

"No, Daisha, just tell me. I need to know, please."

She fidgeted, and then lowered her head. "No, it's not your baby."

I moved Daisha away from the car door and closed it. "You're lying. I know you're lying because I can tell by how nervous you are. Please, Daisha, tell me the truth. The truth is so important to me."

"Yes. Yes, Jaylin, this is your baby. Our first time together I conceived a child. I didn't want to tell you because I didn't want to interfere with your life. I heard about how happy you were and I didn't want to interfere."

"I am happy, Daisha, but you couldn't possibly think I wouldn't want anything to do with my child."

"I just didn't want you trying to talk me into having an abortion. This is my first child and I want to have it. An abortion is not an option for me."

"Who said anything about an abortion? We

could have talked through this. I don't want you going through this alone."

Mona cleared her throat. "Look, Jaylin, we gotta get Stephon his car back so he can get to the shop. Why don't you just call her later?"

"Is that okay? Can I call you later?" I asked.

"Yeah, I guess." She opened the car door and got in.

I squatted beside her and placed my hand on her stomach. "We can work this out, okay?"

"That's what got us in trouble to begin with. Remember, all that *working out?*" she smiled.

"Having a child is never trouble, Daisha. It's all about how you handle the situation. I'll call you later."

I stood and watched as Mona and Daisha pulled off.

Why now? I thought. When everything in my life was going so perfect. I rushed back inside to find Scorpio. When I saw her and the kids standing in line for cookies, I slowly walked toward them, thinking how another woman being pregnant could crumble my relationship with Scorpio.

She saw me and waved for me to come in her direction. For the past several months, she had been on cloud nine. All the trouble we went through just to be together and now this. I really wasn't sure how I was going to tell her, but I knew I couldn't keep it a secret for long. If I did, that would be like denying my own child, and I had no intention of doing that.

Mackenzie ran up to me and took my hand. We walked up to Scorpio and LJ, and Scorpio opened a bag to show me the shoes she bought.

"Baby, did you see them?" she asked.

"Yeah, they're nice." I was dazed and barely looked at them.

"Are you okay? Did you catch up with your friend?"

"Yeah, I did. That's what took so long."

"Well, you don't look too good." She felt my forehead. "You're not warm, but maybe we need to get you home into a nice comfortable bed and place a beautiful woman beside you."

"Uh-huh."

"Jaylin!" she yelled. "What is wrong with you?"

I snapped out of it and kissed her cheek. "Nothing, baby, I'm just tired. Listen, can we go? I need to lie down for a while."

After we got the kids some cookies, we headed home. I didn't say much in the car and I could tell Scorpio knew something was wrong. I went from being perky to being a complete slug.

At home, I asked Nanny B to take the kids because I needed some quiet time alone with Scorpio. I thought about what to say to her, and knew the faster I came out with it the better.

Scorpio was putting her bags in the closet, and I sat on the bed staring at her. Noticing my mood, she stopped in her tracks. "Jaylin, why don't you get some rest? You haven't been getting enough sleep, and I'm sure all this ripping and running you've been doing with me and the kids is taking a toll on you."

"Yeah, it might be, but, uh, come here for a minute." I scooted back on the bed and patted my hand on the spot in front of me. "Sit right here for me."

She had a look of concern on her face and sat in front of me. "Jaylin, you're scaring me. I don't like it when you have that look. Are you sick or something? Please don't tell me . . ." Her eyes watered. I promised myself that I would never hurt her again, and placed my fingers on her lips.

"Don't say anything. I have something I need to ask you, okay?" I said, softly. She nodded. "How do you feel about having another baby around?"

Lines appeared on her forehead and she touched my hand. "You know about the baby? How did you find out about the baby?"

"What do you mean by how did I find out? I just found out today."

"But I . . . I haven't told anyone about the baby yet. I wanted to surprise you and tell you over a nice quiet dinner tomorrow. So, how did you find out I was pregnant when I just found out a few days ago?"

My mouth hung wide open. I couldn't believe what she said. "Are you . . . Did you just tell me you're pregnant?"

"Jaylin, you just out of the clear blue sky asked me how I felt about having another baby. I assumed that you knew. But since you've blown my surprise, yes, I'm a little over four months pregnant. Can't you tell by how fat I'm getting? And not only that, sweetheart, I have a date for our wedding in mind."

There was a blank expression on my face. "So, you're pregnant?"

"Would you snap out of it? Yes, you're going to be a daddy, again."

"You're sure you're pregnant?"

"Yes! And I have the ultrasound picture to prove it." She went to the closet and pulled a card from the top. She opened the card and took the picture out of it. "I was going to give this card to you tomorrow, along with the picture." She gave the picture to me and I looked down at it.

"But, this is just a black-and-white sketchy picture."

"And this is the baby," she pointed to a figure on the picture. "Right there."

"Right where?"

"There!" she pointed to it again.

"Are you sure?"

She snatched the picture. "Jaylin! If you're not happy about the baby, then don't be. I'm sorry, I thought you truly would be." She rolled her eyes and looked away. I pulled her close to me and laid her head on my chest.

"Baby, I'm sorry. I am very happy about the baby, but stunned more than anything. You . . . you caught me completely off guard. I didn't think you wanted any more children."

"Excuse me, but all this fucking we be doing and you never thought about me getting pregnant? Especially lately. We've been having sex every single day, two and three times, and you didn't see this coming? Besides," she said, twirling her fingers in my hair. "I always thought about having a blood child with you. And since you're such a wonderful father, and we're going to get married, I've thought about it even more. When the doctor confirmed it, I was shocked, but I immediately thought about that day we were in the kitchen making love and you asked me where I saw us five years from now. Do you remember?"

"Yep. I remember it like it was yesterday. I asked you that question, thinking it was over because I was in love with Nokea. In my mind, I was planning a future with her, but you still had hopes for us."

"You're right, I did. And I knew how much you loved her. But at that moment, I said I saw us with some more children. I visualized what he or she would look like. And you know what else?" she smiled.

"What?"

"You'd better be careful because twins do run in my family."

I shook my head. "No, not twins. Twins would send me over the edge."

Scorpio laughed and asked me if it would be okay if she broke the news to Nanny B and Mackenzie. I told her it was fine and she ran downstairs to share the news with them.

Not being able to swallow the news about having two babies on the way, I took off my shirt and lay flat on my back. What in the hell was I thinking? Thirty-three, five children, and by four different women. I for damn sure was headed for a life full of chaos. I should have used condoms on every occasion, and if I had, there's no way I'd be in this situation right now. There was no way in hell Scorpio would marry me knowing that I had another baby on the way. And Daisha, she was too much of a good woman to be played off by anyone, especially at a time like this when she needed me the most. What in the fuck was I going to do? This was one time I had no solution.

Nanny B and Mackenzie were hyped about the news, and everyone had finally shut down for the night. Scorpio and I made love for hours, celebrating our new baby and our wedding date, which was scheduled one year from today. A whole lot of things could happen in a year's time, but one thing I was certain of, and that was I intended to do everything in my power not to hurt Scorpio again.

Unable to sleep, I stayed in the tub for a while then slipped into my khakis and put on my soft, baby blue polo shirt and cap. I quietly slid on my loafers, and, needing some fresh air, drove to AJ's liquor store on Union Boulevard to buy a bottle of Hpnotiq and a six-pack of Bud Light.

I drove to Forest Park, parked my car near the Art Museum, then climbed all the way to the top to sit. I took a few swigs of the Hpnotiq and popped open several cans of beer. Feeling the way I did, I dared anyone to come fuck with me right about now, including the police. I looked at the stars, and tried to find Mama so we could talk. I didn't hear her voice so I guessed she was busy. I felt sick to my stomach from drinking, and poured a little alcohol on the ground for my relatives who weren't there. If anything, I figured since I was pop'em out like crazy, I'd have this family back to its entirety in no time.

I got fucked up and stumbled back to my car. Missing Nokea's comfort at a time like this, I headed on my way to see her, but then I thought about Collins being there. So, instead, I found myself driving to Daisha's house.

I parked in her driveway for a while and tried to sober up. When I thought I had, I went to the door and rang the shit out of her doorbell. Barely being able to stand, I leaned against the screen door and waited for her to open it. When she finally did, she looked at me like I was out of my mind. She moved aside for me to come in and didn't say a word. My eyes watered and I fell to my knees. I wrapped my arms around her waist and pressed my head against her stomach. Still in silence, she rubbed her fingers through my hair, and I knew she understood my pain.

I looked up and spoke softly. "Just hold me. Please, baby, just hold me."

She kneeled to my level and looked me in the eyes. A tear rolled down her face. "I love you, Jaylin. From the first day I met you, I knew that I was going to fall in love with you."

I released my arms from Daisha, and crawled to her living room. I didn't even deserve to have a woman like her love me. I turned onto my back and laid there, thinking about where in the hell I truly wanted to be.

The idea occurred to me that maybe Scorpio had gotten pregnant by the exterminator. But then I realized that maybe that was my way of trying to walk away from our commitment, and I dropped the thought. Then there was Nokea. Damn, was I deep down missing her. I just threw her to a brotha like Collins who was for damn sure waiting for the catch. It was times like this she could make me smile, and make me feel as if I didn't have a worry in the world.

I soaked in my pain, and my head started spinning. Moments later, a blurred vision of Daisha's naked body stood before me. I felt her hands touching my body, but I didn't have the strength or the courage to stop her. I felt a draft as she unzipped my pants, and tried to force my eyes to stay open. She straddled herself on top of me, and leaned forward to whisper in my ear. All it sounded like was mumbo jumbo to me, but whatever she said, I definitely knew where this night was headed. I snickered as she placed my hands on her thick breasts, and when I felt her juicy insides working me over, I closed my eyes again.

The sunlight beaming through the window awakened me. My head was banging, and I rolled over on the floor, trying to figure out where in the hell I was. I looked down at my slack dick and realized I was naked. I tried to get up, but the pounding in my head wouldn't let me.

I laid on the floor for a few more minutes, then managed to maneuver myself over to the couch. Having a vague memory about last night, I rolled my temples around with my fingers. I glanced at my watch. Nine-fifteen in the morning. I figured Scorpio was going to kill me, and as I looked around for my clothes, my headache caused me to sit back down.

I continued to look around the room for Daisha

and my clothes, then noticed an envelope on the table with my name written across it. I reached for it, leaned back on the couch and read it.

Good morning, handsome. Your son and I had a few errands to run this morning, but I'll be back soon. Last night was magnificent, and I'm so glad you finally found your way back to me. I prayed many of nights for your return, and now after you confirmed your love for me last night, I truly understand your purpose for being a part of my life. Breakfast is on the kitchen table and I'll understand if you're not here when I get back. Take all the time you need to break the news about your change in plans to Scorpio, and call me if you need a shoulder to lean on. Love Ya, Daisha.

I tore up the letter. What the fuck Daisha was talking about? *My son? Love and change in plans?* I thought. What in the hell did we talk about last night? By the looks of things it was obvious we had sex, but damn, other than that I couldn't remember shit.

I sat on the couch, and thought about what I could have said to Daisha. I saw my clothes neatly folded on the dining room chair, so I went to get them. I took my cell phone from my pocket and called home to talk to Scorpio. I wasn't sure what I was going to say, and when she answered, I was at a loss for words. "Hello," she said.

"Baby, it's me."

"Jaylin, where are you? I rolled over in the middle of the night and you were gone," she said, hurtfully.

"I'm, uh, on my way home now."

"Okay, but, where have you been?"

"I went for a drive to clear my head."

"All night? You know, I thought these days were over between us. There's no way in hell you've been just riding around in your car all damn night, Jaylin."

"You're right, I haven't. But I'll tell you what happened when I get home."

Scorpio hung up.

Feeling down on myself because I was on my way home to tell the biggest lie of my life to keep my woman, I went into Daisha's kitchen and sat at the table. There wasn't no need for me to rush home because it was obvious the damage had already been done.

On the table, Daisha had four buttermilk pancakes stacked on a plate with some cheese eggs, hash browns, and grits on the side. In the center of the table were some yellow daisies in a vase with a note that said:

pulled from the garden especially for you.

I smiled as I cut into the pancakes, then I thought about my requirements from the beginning that I'd always wanted my woman to have. I'd often said that she must be African American, bodacious, have a degree, be able to cook, have a good job, drive a nice car, no kids, and be willing to cater to my needs. Daisha was all that and then some. The total package and there I was with Scorpio, the woman I love, who had only met a few. It wasn't that I was disappointed. It just reminded me that sometimes what I ask for, I sure in the hell won't get.

I finished breakfast and washed my hands. I took a deep breath, dreading home. I wanted to make things right with Scorpio, but I knew she'd put up a fuss.

I hadn't put on one piece of clothing yet, and stood in the hallway looking in the mirror. I brushed my hair and heard a car door slam. Feeling terrible about telling Daisha I made a big mistake last night, I waited for her to come in. It took a moment, so I laid the hairbrush on the table and walked to the front door. I pulled it open and almost lost my balance. Scorpio stood on one side of the door, and Daisha was on the other side. My heart raced, but I grinned to play it off like everything was cool. Scorpio gazed over my naked body, and stared at me with a devilish look in her eyes. Her fist went up and she punched me hard in my right eye. I could almost feel it swell, but dropping my head in shame seemed like the most appropriate thing to do. Maybe, for me, that change she wanted so badly just wasn't going to come.